MW01256507

THE FALLEN & THE KISS OF DUSK

Crowns of Nyaxia Novels

Book 1: *The Serpent & the Wings of Night*

Book 2: *The Ashes & the Star-Cursed King*

Book 3: *The Songbird & the Heart of Stone*

Standalone Crowns of Nyaxia Novels

Six Scorched Roses (novella)

Slaying the Vampire Conqueror

THE FALLEN & THE KISS OF DUSK

A CROWNS OF NYAXIA NOVEL

The Shadowborn Duet
BOOK TWO

CARISSA BROADBENT

TOR PUBLISHING GROUP · NEW YORK

This is a work of fiction. All of the characters, organizations, and events portrayed in this novel are either products of the author's imagination or are used fictitiously.

THE FALLEN & THE KISS OF DUSK

Map illustration and chapter ornaments by Rhys Davies

A Bramble Book
Published by Tom Doherty Associates / Tor Publishing Group
120 Broadway
New York, NY 10271

www.torpublishinggroup.com

EU Representative: Macmillan Publishers Ireland Ltd, 1st Floor,
The Liffey Trust Centre, 117–126 Sheriff Street Upper, Dublin 1, DO1 YC43

The Library of Congress Cataloging-in-Publication Data is available upon request.

ISBN 978-1-250-36781-5 (hardcover)
ISBN 978-1-250-40676-7 (signed)

First Edition: 2025

Printed in the United States of America

10 9 8 7 6 5 4 3 2 1

For every mortal heart trying to find their way home

Note

Please note that this book contains content that may be sensitive for some readers, including graphic violence, discussion of grooming and sexual assault, discussion of religious trauma, off-page torture, animal death, and sexual activity.

HOUSE of BLOOD
SIVRINAJ
RYVENHAAL
MORTHRYN
SHADOWBOR
CASTLE
HOUSE of NIGHT
HOUSE of SHADOW

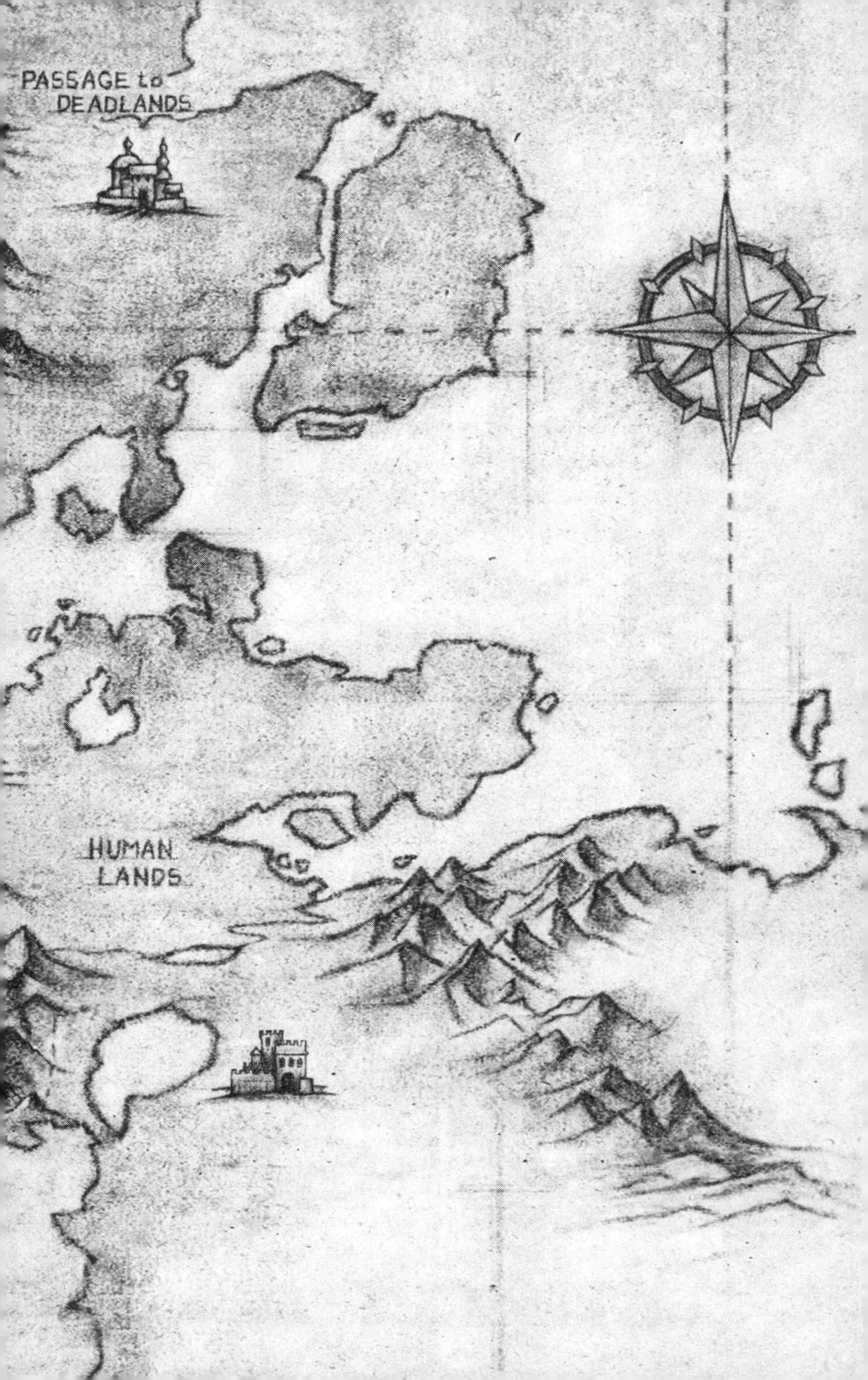

PASSAGE to
DEADLANDS
HUMAN
LANDS

The Fallen & the Kiss of Dusk

PROLOGUE

This is the tale of how a fallen one ascends.

Long ago, I told you a tale of a chosen girl who fell to the darkness. Now I will tell you the tale of a boy who was born within it.

His very existence was the product of generations of mistakes. He was born on a desolate island off the coasts of the vampire kingdom he could one day come to rule. The boy learned young how to survive on the blood of squirrels and fish, or the rare, ill-fated human travelers who would stumble by. He was small, but he had a way with death.

He could have spent his whole life there, had it not been for the small fact that he was a prince.

The man came when the boy was eight years old. When he arrived at the shore, he had slipped his hands into the pockets of his fine but simple black suit and surveyed the scene before him—marshy forest, waterlogged soil, stone ruins covered in ivy.

The boy watched him from his hiding place in the reeds. Instantly, he knew this man was unlike anyone he had ever met, even if then he could not explain why. He crept closer, closer, careful to remain hidden.

But the man didn't even move as a tendril of shadow wrapped about the boy's leg, dragging him into the open.

The boy's back hit the mud. The man casually stared down at him, spindly fingers of darkness winding around his shoulders, his arms, his hands.

The boy had played with magic before. He knew how to lure in the young fishermen who occasionally came to these shores, how to ease their fear just enough to coax them to his grip. He knew how to whisper comforts to the foxes he tamed in the woods, the ones he treated much kinder than the humans. He always knew when someone was watching him, and somehow, the shadows always seemed to end up exactly where he needed them.

But he had never seen magic like this before. Magic that tasted like power.

"Get up," the man said.

Get up. Get up. Get up.

The boy was standing before he knew what was happening.

The man looked the boy up and down with icy fair eyes.

"The king has come for you," he said.

The boy was silent, wary. His mother often spoke of crowns and kingdoms. *You are a king,* she would slur. *And it is my blood that makes you so.*

The man lowered himself, perching gracefully at the edge of a stone so that he was at eye level with the child. He heard the boy's unspoken thoughts.

"Your father's blood is nothing to scoff at, either," the man said, amused. "And he has sent me to retrieve you."

The boy had been warned countless times of the danger of his lineage. His mother used to read him bedtime stories of slain princes, bastard-born royalty just like him who died for the crime of being too strong or too weak, too hungry for power or too avoidant of it. *You are a king,* she would say. *Survive long enough to take your crown.*

He should run, he thought to himself. This was exactly what she had warned him of.

He stepped backward. He expected the man to move after him, but he did not.

"You can go," the man said calmly. "I will wait."

"You'll kill me."

The boy's voice was small, weak with disuse. He did not speak often.

"I will not kill you."

The boy didn't believe him.

"I speak the truth," the man said. "But you're wise not to trust me."

The boy didn't know how to word his objections.

"You're thinking that there are many worse things than death," the man said, answering what remained unspoken. "Very wise of you. Yes, boy. I am truthful when I say I won't kill you. But if you want the difficult truths alongside the easy one, I will give you those, too. If you come with me willingly, I will evaluate you. Your father believes that you could be a useful asset as a potential heir. If you prove yourself to be so, you will never go hungry again. You will sleep in a bed. You will drink the richest human blood. You will wear fine clothes. And you will serve the crown until the day it no longer needs you."

The boy asked, "What happens when it no longer needs me?"

"Then we will take whatever parts of you are useful and discard the rest."

This was no threat. Just straightforward fact. The boy appreciated that, even as fear prickled at the back of his neck.

"Is that what you'll do now, if I run?" he asked.

"Not this night. Maybe another, if your father gives the order. But I don't know these lands as well as you do. Maybe you run far enough, fast enough, that I let you be. Maybe your father loses interest and calls me back to go kill someone else before then." The man smiled. His eyes were very old, though his face was young. "But I know you will not run."

He was right. The boy would not run.

The child said, "What makes you so certain?"

"Because you look at this the way a starving vampire looks at blood."

The man opened his palm, shadow unfurling within it. The boy's heart stuttered at the sight of it.

"I am not offering you an easy life," the man said. "It will be a life judged by the value of the blood you spill upon it. Your father told me to come here and tell you that you could be king one day. Perhaps you will be, but more likely your father will kill you if you get too powerful, or your siblings will if he decides not to. You will sacrifice beyond what your mind could ever conceive today, and there is only a chance of a chance of a chance that there will ever be a crown on your head in exchange. But I am offering you something far more valuable than a crown."

The boy hesitated before he asked, "What?"

"When dawn comes, you hide behind the curtains and you peer out into the world when it's drenched red under the sunrise," he said. "And sometimes you feel it, don't you? All those secrets hiding in the haze between the light and the darkness. The books are nothing, boy. Nothing. The things you will see if you learn to walk this path will devastate and delight you."

"Magic," the boy said, and the man scoffed, sudden and violent.

"Magic," he spat. "Any vampire can do *magic*. I am not talking about the common gifts. You smell like death, boy. Carve out your heart for it and it will give you the world in return. Do you know what it means to conquer every unknown? It means a life free from fear. Think of that. *Freedom*."

The boy was silent.

The man spoke to all his secret dreams. He knew that he could survive on this soggy patch of land forever. But for what? For the next fisherman's carcass? The next swallow of rancid fish blood?

The boy did not want glory. He did not want a crown.

He wanted freedom.

The man's eyes glinted like stars in the dusk.

"So tell me, young prince," he said. "What is the next step in our dance?"

Some moments remain permanently engrained into one's memory, even over the centuries of a vampire lifespan. The boy would remember everything about this one. And yet, oh, how the shadows shift upon the past depending on the light of the present. For years, the boy—the man, the prince, the king—would look at this as the night he was saved.

Only centuries later would he understand the truth.

He had thought the sacrifice came in the form of blood and guts and the pleas that he would never be able to scrub from the inside of his skull. He had thought the sacrifice came in the form of the permanent marks on his body and the invisible ones on his soul.

He had been wrong.

He realized it many years later, when he felt the power of the gods course through his veins, and finally, finally, he received the very thing that his mentor had promised him that night—illumination into every dark corner of the world, power beyond anything he ever could have imagined.

And he cared about none of it, because he was losing the love of his life.

Carve out your heart for it.

In that moment, he would hear his instructor's words. He would think of that little boy. *Turn away,* he'd beg his past self.

But the boy takes the man's hand every time. Death, after all, is inevitable.

This is the tale of how a fallen one ascends.

He does it in countless cascading decisions, over years, over centuries.

He does it with the desperation of a starving soul willing to sacrifice anything, everything, for a single chance at redemption.

But in the end, he loses her every time.

PART ONE

DEATH

CHAPTER ONE

Mische

What does it feel like to die?

Everyone has asked that question, but perhaps acolytes more than any other. Acolytes are obsessed with death—maybe because it is both the ultimate sacrifice and the ultimate reward, the greatest thing we can offer our gods and the greatest thing they can offer us. No acolyte was spoken of in greater admiration than those who left this life ablaze with their love for Atroxus. None wanted to die in their beds.

I did not die in mine.

I died at the doorstep to the underworld, a traitor's weapon in my hand, drenched in the blood of the god who had given me everything. I died covered in the ashes of his remains and the burns of his punishment.

I died alone, listening to the screams of the love of my life.

What does it feel like to die?

Would I remember how to answer that question?

I'd comforted countless grieving souls in my time as a missionary. We were taught that death was a peaceful end to a grand fight.

When I died, I realized that we had been wrong.

What does it feel like to die?

When I died, it was with my god's blood on my hands, my lover's pleas in my ears, and the oblivion of eternal darkness—not eternal dawn—seared into my eyes.

When I died, it did not feel like the peaceful end to a grand fight.

It felt like the beginning of one.

I LAY ON the ground and stared at my hand, which I held in front of my face. Beyond it, colors danced in the eternity of the sky. My skin was smooth and brown and glistening with the faint translucent dust of death.

I just kept staring at that hand. It looked so alive, and so, so dead.

Blink. I closed my eyes and saw palm trees, a blue sky, white sand. Vostis, the place that had once been my home. The place I had once given my very soul to.

Open.

The underworld hung over me. Unmistakable.

"Get up," the voice said.

I tore my eyes away from the sky, away from my hand, to the angular face of the man who leaned over me. He swept a strand of long, fair hair behind his ear and gave me an appraising stare.

We had never met—not directly. But of course I recognized him. I'd seen him in countless paintings. I'd seen his visage illuminated over the skyline of Sivrinaj, the capital of the House of Night. And I'd seen his likeness torn down by Rishan soldiers, after Raihn had killed him.

Vincent—dead vampire king of the House of Night—held out a hand to me.

"Get up," he said. "I hear we have some work to do."

I stared at him blankly. Beyond him, a split of lightning arced across the sky. Except—no, not lightning. They just kept growing, splitting, bursting open to reveal waves of warring light and darkness—purple, black, blue, green, the essence of galaxies. They reminded me viscerally of something so familiar, something that made my heart ache, but I couldn't place it.

My lashes fluttered.

Once, as a child in Vostis, I had been caught in a riptide. I had fought and fought, but every time my head bobbed beneath the surface of the water, I was a little farther from shore. What had shocked me then was just how quiet it was. Almost peaceful.

That was what this felt like.

Deceptive, dangerous peace.

"Mische Iliae." Vincent clutched my arm, yanking me from the riptide. "You cannot go. Not yet."

I stared at him, confused. Behind him, the cracks shivered across the sky.

Cracks like the sun shattering, as I thrust an arrow into the throat of the god I had once loved.

Cracks like the beautiful scars across Asar's face.

Asar.

The name flooded over me. With it came the memory of an agonized voice and the final words I had heard.

Stop! I need her!

It was this memory, more than Vincent's grip, that jerked me awake. A harsh, disorienting reality struck me.

I had died.

Gods help me. *I had died.*

A powerful force shook the ground. In the sky, the streaks split open, gushing light like blood through torn stitches. Silhouetted, winged bodies slithered through them.

Souleaters, I thought dimly. They were souleaters.

But this realization snagged something sharp in my overwhelmed, blurry mind.

Souleaters shouldn't be in the underworld.

A wave of darkness passed over me. I felt oblivion beckoning—true death, offering me a welcome embrace. The sun called to me. The scent of the sea. The peace of an easier past.

And oh, I was tired.

But Vincent pulled me closer. "If you go, I cannot find you again. Whatever you are feeling now, it is false. *It is a lie.* You have *work* to do."

A memory of my sister flitted past.

My sister kneeling beside me in the church. *Death is the ultimate offering. Death is the ultimate peace. The grand end to our destined battle.*

My sister in the last memory I had of her—a wraith, kneeling before Atroxus, drowning in admiration as I killed him.

As I betrayed her.

As I listened to the man I loved being dragged away.

As I watched the sun shatter in the sky forever.

A burst of fury tore through me. The answer was suddenly clear.

What kind of a choice was it, anyway? I was already damned.

With a grunt of exertion, I grabbed Vincent's other hand. A gushing current of light roared past me, but he held firm. I glimpsed his smirk of satisfaction.

"Correct choice," he said.

He didn't understand. It wasn't a choice at all.

But I didn't have time to say that as we both fell beneath the darkness.

MY EYES OPENED. Above me, the souleaters wound through the sky. Slow cracks spread across the heavens.

My surroundings shifted and changed. Blink, and the scent of sulfur was replaced by that of the ocean, the lush, sweet aroma of the forest, the elegant whisper of jasmine incense.

I sat upright, the world twisting with the sharpness of the movement. Before me was an altar adorned with a gilded depiction of the sun, rays spilling across the marble floor. Atroxus rose over it, stone hands outstretched, empty eyes spearing me. Somehow, they were every bit as enraged as they had been in his final moments.

This, somehow, managed to elicit a real reaction.

Panic.

I pressed my hand to my chest. I felt as if my heart should have been pounding against my ribs, my lungs gasping for air, but instead, all that panic manifested as . . . silence. As if nothing existed beneath my skin at all.

"Odd, isn't it?" a low voice said.

I turned to see Vincent leaning against a pillar, arms crossed, gazing out to the soupy mists through the windows.

"The sensation fades quickly," he said. "Soon you won't remember what it felt like at all."

"It?" I croaked.

"Living."

Gods, I was going to throw up.

I *wished* I could throw up.

I tried to stand, and nearly toppled over. Not because my muscles offered resistance, but because they didn't—the movement was too easy, too unburdened by flesh or gravity or the weight of my body.

Because I was dead.

I was dead.

This thought hit me, more surreal than ever, as I stared at the Citadel tapestries.

Vincent cast me a disinterested glance.

"The visions will fade. The things you see here change. More pleasant for some than others, I hear. Punishment or reward, depending on how your immortal soul was judged. Which is it for you?"

I dragged my gaze up to Atroxus's face, exactly as I remembered it in life—powerful, all-seeing, absolute. It all felt so real, just as I had begged to see it for decades.

Yet the answer was so clear:

Punishment.

I pressed my hands to my eye sockets, hard—hard enough that it should have hurt, but didn't—and when I removed them, the mists before me had cleared. I no longer was looking at the Citadel.

I stared, silent.

Vincent's voice came from behind me. "We need to start moving. Best not to stay in one place too long here."

His words faded off into the background like sand worn down by the sea.

Distant, ghostly silhouettes wandered across the landscape—a landscape that constantly changed, revealing glimpses of grand cities and desolate plains, of oceans and mountains and ravines, of blood-soaked battlefields and bustling metropolises. A million fragments of a million different lives. Maybe they might've been beautiful in a sad kind of way, had it not been all so terribly overshadowed by the destruction.

Cracks ran through the ground, the sky. No, cracks wasn't the right word for them—they were more vicious than that, more organic. Wounds, gushing black and red. Massive beasts lumbered across the horizon, their eyes perfectly round, gaping windows through their silhouetted forms. They plucked souls from the ground, shoving them fistful by fistful into their mouths in too-slow, too-smooth movements.

It was horrifying.

"Is this—am I—"

I didn't know how to ask the question. My voice sounded far away and hollow.

Again I pressed my palms to my eyes and rubbed, hard. But when I pulled them away, the scene before me was the same.

"What is this?" I demanded.

Vincent stared at me like I was stupid. "This is the underworld."

"I know. I mean, what is *that*?" I stabbed a finger out to the view. "All of that? Is that—some kind of vision? Or is that *real*?"

For a moment I could hope—hope that maybe this was my own personal divine punishment, the mist and the monsters and the cracks and the lightning.

But the faintest ghost of a wince passed over Vincent's face.

"Unfortunately," he said, "it is real."

No. This wasn't right. The Descent had looked something like this, falling prey to the decay of two thousand years of neglect. Sure, in the Descent there were souleaters and monsters and ravines that swallowed souls. But the underworld was supposed to be safe. The underworld was supposed to be shielded from all of that. And this—gods, this wasn't decay. This wasn't neglect. This was—

It was hell. No soul, not even the most deserving, would find peace in a place like this.

I shook my head dumbly. "You're wrong. It's not supposed to—"

At those words—*you're wrong*—Vincent straightened sharply, the anger of a challenged Obitraen king flashing in his eyes. But before he could speak, a grinding roar wailed through the air.

I whirled around. "What was that?"

"We need to leave," Vincent said, grabbing my wrist as if he intended to haul me around like a sack of flour. But I remained rooted in place, frozen by dread. In the distance, through desolate puffs of mist, fresh cracks of bright red slithered across the landscape. A distant, crooked tower, silhouetted against the white, collapsed. Souls scattered like frantic ants.

A second tower started to fall, painfully slowly.

I stared, horrified.

"Are those *people*?" I choked out.

"They were," Vincent said coldly. "Soon, they will be nothing."

I couldn't look away as the structure fell in slow motion, crushing countless dead beneath it. The hunched-over monsters had turned their attention to the wreckage, closing in to scoop up the fleeing souls. One swept up an entire handful of them and raised them slowly to a wide, gaping mouth of white nothingness.

Another boom. The ground quaked.

"We—we have to help them," I managed, because it was the only thing I could think to say—but even as the words left my lips, I knew how ridiculous they were. The only thing I could do was stand there and watch as dozens more dead fell.

Vincent gave my wrist an unceremonious tug.

"Move," he barked. "We need to leave before—"

I pulled my hand away and whirled to him.

"You don't get to drag me around without telling me what's going on."

Anger flashed in Vincent's silver eyes, reminding me that in life, he had been one of the most ruthless vampire kings. Once, that disrespect would've been enough to send me to my death.

But I was already dead. So what the hell could he do to me now?

"You have some nerve speaking that way to *me*," he hissed, "when *you* are the reason this happened."

Me?

My mouth opened, but no words came out.

"Do you think I'm eager to be doing this with *you,*" Vincent went on, "who helped push my daughter to the man who killed me? In life, I would have—"

"What do you mean, *I'm the reason this happened*?"

Vincent was silent. His silver eyes took me in, feet to head, in an assessment that I clearly was failing.

"What do you remember of your death?"

My death.

Pain skewered me—burning straight through the center of my chest. My hand flew to it.

A sword through my heart. A god tossing me aside. And fire—

I died. I died. I died.

The truth twisted inside me. And with it came a sudden grief so intense it made me want to curl up on the ground.

I felt something wet on my cheeks, falling like rain.

I blinked and saw my final moments. Asar's face over mine. And gods, the pain in those eyes.

Not rain.

How could my chest hurt so much if my heart was no longer beating? I pressed my hand to it like a tourniquet, a futile attempt to quell the bleeding.

But I could feel a little solid thread somewhere in that ache. A little sharp stab of pain that reminded me of the spell Asar had drawn between us, once—the spell that had allowed me to pull him from the ritual circle.

I clung to that thread of familiarity. Pain that felt so *alive*.

"I killed Atroxus," I managed. "And the sky—and Asar—and the gods—and—"

Asar's tears. Shiket's blade. Fire everywhere.

And darkness. So much darkness.

"You killed Atroxus," Vincent confirmed, though his tone seemed almost insulted he had to admit I'd done such a thing. "The sun fell as he did. Ushering in an endless night."

He sounded practically lustful. Like he was lost imagining all the things he might've done with such a gift in life—all while he gave me a critical once-over, as if he couldn't imagine how I, of all people, had been responsible for it.

That made two of us. The words still echoed in the back of my head, reverberating with my disbelief.

"You attempted to resurrect Alarus," he went on. "But instead—"

"I saved Asar."

I remembered pulling him from the ritual circle, clinging to that tether to him that I refused to sever.

And yet, with the memory of my choice, I saw another face, too. Saescha's, tilted to Atroxus's light, bright with adoration.

"You saved him in a sense," Vincent said. "You refused to sacrifice his soul to the resurrection spell. But the spell was already in motion. You ended it before you completed it, but the incomplete resurrection, along with the destruction of the relics Alarus used to construct the underworld, put stress upon the underworld that it couldn't bear. Thus."

He gestured to the wreckage around us. I stared out into the mists, dread rising in my chest. Far in the distance, another mountain collapsed in slow motion. Silently, mundanely, hundreds of souls fell beneath it.

I shook my head.

"No. That can't be—I can't have—"

"It is. You did. And this is only the beginning. It will collapse if your lover doesn't take action."

I whirled back to Vincent. Somehow, for some reason, I expected this was some kind of joke. But he was stone serious.

"You mean Asar," I said.

I remembered the gods dragging him away. Dragging him away as he screamed for me.

"Where is he? Is he—" I almost couldn't bring myself to ask. "Is he alive?"

"From what I hear, he's better than alive. He holds the power of a god." Again, that hint of envy. "And only with that can he repair the underworld before it disintegrates altogether."

"He will." The words slipped out easily. The memories hit me with such piercing intensity—Asar leaning over countless broken doors, repairing countless shattered glyphs, leading countless lost souls back home. With them came a flood of affection.

"If the underworld needs to be repaired," I said, "Asar will do it. There's nothing he loves more."

And yet, as I said the words, I thought of his tears on my face, and I wondered if perhaps they were untrue.

"He is imprisoned by the White Pantheon," Vincent said. "He isn't doing anything as long as that remains true. And, I'm told, if he is to do this, he needs you."

"Me?"

"You conducted the spell that gave him his power. I'm told he will need your help to gain enough of it to do what must be done."

Strange that the dead still got headaches. I rubbed my temple. "But . . . why?"

He looked irritated by this question. "I'm a messenger. Don't expect me to understand the intricacies of your Shadowborn tricks."

A wrinkle formed between my brows at a new thought and a new cascade of questions.

"A messenger," I repeated. "So a god sent you."

Vincent said nothing in a way that I knew was a confirmation.

"Nyaxia?" I said.

It would have to be Nyaxia, wouldn't it? Vincent had worshipped her for a lifetime of centuries. Her favor, after he won the Kejari, had put the crown on his head.

After a moment, he said, "No. Not Nyaxia."

"Then who?"

"It isn't your concern."

"It *is* my concern. And why *you*? I don't even know you."

He looked offended. But even at the best of times, I wasn't known for my tact, and these were not the best of times.

Vincent was a vampire king. And what would any vampire king do to regain their throne after it was snatched away from them so brutally? What would any vampire king do for *revenge*?

I hated being so cynical. And yet.

He let out an annoyed breath. "Look."

He pointed to the sky, where the upside-down mirror of the underworld hung over us. I wasn't sure at first what he was gesturing to, until I noticed that he was tracing a shape with his fingertip. When I looked carefully, I saw that the wisps of light and darkness were not, in fact, random. They collected around the cracks and then extended in a shape that reminded me of veins splitting through a body. I'd seen such patterns in the Descent, too.

"Every structure has weak points," he said. "All planes are connected to each other—the land of the gods, the land of the mortals, and the land of the dead. What happens here will soon affect the mortal world, if it hasn't already."

A chill ran up my spine. I didn't need Vincent to tell me what that might look like. I'd spent months witnessing the terrible consequences of the Descent's slow crumbling. The thought of those nightmares spilling into the land of the living was horrifying.

"The boundaries between planes are thinner in some places than others," he went on. "And some vampire kingdoms were built around these pressure points, precisely because of the power they offered."

Now I understood. "Like the House of Night."

"I spent centuries building my kingdom. Dead or no, I refuse to let it fall."

Of course, it was all about a kingdom. But the sheer enormity of this responsibility settled on my shoulders. Dizzy, I leaned back on my heels, head in my hands.

"Your lover will be looking for you," Vincent said. "I have been told to bring you toward the veil."

Asar.

I will find you.

An oath that I felt down to my soul, even now. But my heart ached. With grief, and with the ghost of our connection.

I had lied to him. I had planned to betray him. And even in saving him—in saving all of vampire life—I had still managed to lead the world to the doorstep of so much death.

Saescha's face flitted through my mind.

But then I thought of the way Asar had looked at my skin, marred by my greatest shames, as if it was still worthy of worship.

I was no stranger to divine missions. I had committed my life to my faith. Had given it every part of my body and soul, in every literal and figurative way. But in the end, the god I had given my soul to had been ready to slaughter my entire race without a second thought.

A small part of me was devastated by this, even now, after everything.

But a bigger part of me was angry.

I turned to the underworld. A sea of suffering.

I heard a million invisible souls crying out, Asar had told me once. *They needed someone.*

And now, they needed me.

He needed me.

I looked at Vincent.

Going on a mission to save the world with my friend's dead father was not at all what I expected to be doing in death.

I said, "Tell me what we need to do."

CHAPTER TWO

Asar

It is a myth that vampires can see in true darkness.

Like cats, vampires can see in nearly all real-world circumstances. But we need just a little sliver of light—no matter how slight. The reflection of the moon or the shimmer of the stars. The near-invisible glow of the atmosphere over the horizon, indistinguishable to inferior human sight. One little wisp is enough to illuminate an entire world.

True darkness was very rare. Most vampires had never and would never experience it.

I was not one of them.

My mentor, Gideon, had believed it was important to learn how to function without your senses. One could find, he said, far more powerful skills without the lazy payoff of sight or sound or smell. When I was a child, he would often lock me in a dark windowless box for days. Funny that now, when I was less mortal than ever, I would feel so close to that fragile younger version of myself.

The cell where the gods imprisoned me was the first time in centuries that I had experienced that kind of unending darkness.

Gideon had taught me that every weakness could become a strength if you embraced it enough. That the most resourceful minds would find the tools to sharpen nothingness to a blade if offered nothing else.

He had been right. And here, between mortality and divinity, I reached into the darkness and honed myself against the whetstone of a single memory.

Mische's death.

In life, her skin had smelled of cinnamon. But when I held her at the end, I breathed only the scent of ash. She had been nearly unrecognizable, her skin charred, her freckles hidden beneath the blood. Her eyes, though—her eyes had been the same, honey brown and gold and amber.

She had slain a god. The kind of act that would cement her in legends.

But the woman I'd held had not felt like a legend.

She felt mortal. Fragile and fading like a smothered flame.

In the darkness, I experienced that final embrace over and over again. And then after it, I felt the gods tear me away from her. I watched Shiket, the goddess of justice, drive her sword through Mische's chest so thoughtlessly. Like she had been nothing more than a pest to be swatted away.

I wasn't sure how long I had been here. Weeks, maybe, or months. I could feel the strange, unfamiliar stirring of divinity in my chest. Mische had pulled me out of the resurrection circle, in an infuriating act of selflessness that I had never deserved.

But she had pulled something else out with me, too. Some part of Alarus, the ancestor buried generations back in my bloodline. A seed of divinity, germinating in my soul.

None of it mattered as much as that memory of her body falling beneath Shiket's blade. I lived it again, again, again.

My arms ached against my restraints. The chains around my wrists, ankles, and throat burned with every pulse of divine light. They shortened them every time I misbehaved, and now, I couldn't move at all. A single strand of greasy hair dangled down against the tip of my nose, itching miserably.

My head lifted, muscles screaming in protest, as a door formed before me. The light was disorienting, and it made me unpleasantly aware of my physical form.

Two figures in long white robes stood before me. Sentinels.

The powerful build of their physiques was clear even beneath the obfuscation of their clothing, which hid whether they were male or female. Their hair was covered by hoods and their faces by masks of polished gold, free of features, decoration, or imperfection.

As they approached, I saw my distorted reflection in the gleaming surface of those masks—dirty, thin, limbs forced out against this slab of marble. I looked like a corpse at the center of one of my rituals. The thought almost made me laugh, even though I couldn't quite figure out the joke.

They sent two this time. That was, I had to admit, a little satisfying.

In the beginning, I had been tended to by the winged creatures that acted as the gods' footmen here in Ysria. But they were servants, not warriors. I'd killed four of them by the time the gods decided I required more security. That was when they started sending the Sentinels. They were divine soldiers of Shiket. Once, they had been human. But they had been chosen in their death to ascend to immortality and serve her as guardians of the just—or whatever Shiket deemed "justice" to be. They were shells of their former selves, subject to greater decay than even the worst wraiths I had encountered in the Descent. It was an honor Shiket offered to only a select few of the greatest warriors that followed her.

Supposedly. To me, it seemed like a terrible deal. Give up your soul in exchange for endless almost-but-not-quite life. Spend eternity doing the dirty work of the gods instead of finding peace in death. Sentinels may have looked more civilized than wraiths, but they were just as lost.

But then again, some people never did find peace in death. Some were not equipped to face the truth of themselves within it, and others still refused to believe that death was its own kind of eternal life. I had no pity left to spare for the ignorant. Especially not ones that served *her*.

The goddess who had skewered Mische and tossed her aside like garbage, and still had the gall to claim she represented *justice*.

I wasn't angry. Anger was a fool's emotion. It made you slow and stupid.

What I felt was hatred. Cold, sharp, precise.

The Sentinels began working at the restraints around my wrists. They wore gold gauntlets, more refined than any that could have been crafted by mortals. My shoulder wailed in protest as they released one of my chains, my hand dropping like dead weight. It had been a long time since I'd supported my own body. My other wrist followed, and before I could move, the Sentinels linked my shackles together in front of me.

One lifted its faceless head and touched the chains. Pain shot up my wrists as light doused my face. My teeth ground against a hiss of pain.

"Godlight," the smaller of the two Sentinels said. Their voice was sibilant, as if distilled from an echo of an echo, hiding all marks of who they had once been in life. "Perhaps you hold a drop of a god's essence in your lineage, but your flesh is still mostly that of an accursed. Remember that you remain vulnerable to the light of the Just, vampire."

I didn't much like being so condescended to. But I said nothing. They were afraid of me. I could smell it like sweat. We both knew I knew it, and we both knew it meant I'd already won.

I looked down at my hands, flesh bubbling beneath glowing metal.

The other times they had sent Sentinels after me, it was to interrogate me or to retrieve pieces of me for the gods' experimentations—a lock of hair, a sliver of skin, a vial of blood. But this was the first time I'd been taken from my cell. Interesting.

"Taking me on a walk?" My voice was rough with disuse.

One of the Sentinels pushed me toward the door. "Perhaps they have at last decided to execute you, god slayer."

"I'm not a god slayer."

The taller of the two laughed. It was an unpleasant sound, a rasping death rattle. "Only a coward pleads his innocence to the executioner."

I stopped walking abruptly.

"I am not *pleading my innocence,*" I hissed. "I'm giving credit to its rightful owner. I did not kill Atroxus. Mische Iliae did, and she deserves to have her name painted in the stars for it."

The Sentinel scoffed. "The stars have already forgotten your whore, fallen one."

Perhaps it was the fact that I was in the land of the gods, or perhaps it was whatever Mische did to me when she pulled me out of that ceremony. But my body felt different than it had before, like the layers of resistance between my mind and my muscles had been thinned.

I moved fast.

One moment, the Sentinels were leading me to the door of my cell, and the next, I was across the room, my fingers digging into one Sentinel's shoulders, pushing them against a pillar. A spiderweb of cracks surrounded their body. The chains around my wrists and ankles flared searingly bright. But the pain was an afterthought.

"By the light of the Just," the other Sentinel was bellowing, "the White Pantheon commands you to stand down!"

The Sentinel's golden mask reflected my face back at me, distorted by the curve of metal. My eyes were hollow, my skin wan, my scars brutally stark. My left eye was ink black, shadows pouring from it.

I jammed one hand beneath the collar of the Sentinel's armor, right around their throat. I felt no skin there, only metal. Their mortal past was so far away. They had done all they could to forcibly shed it.

"You have the nerve to claim you know what the stars remember?" I snarled. "*You?* A creature that sold your soul to forget what you once were?"

"Get off me!" they snarled, as their partner yanked at my restraints. "You cannot kill a Sentinel of the White Pantheon!"

And yet, still, that spark of fear, so much brighter now.

No, a mortal could not kill a Sentinel. But was I mortal?

I didn't know. And they didn't, either. Beneath that metal mask, they were weighing their luck.

"Kill you," I repeated, scoffing. "Ignorant, to think death is the worst I can offer you."

The free Sentinel looped the glowing chain around my neck and pulled, and the surge of pain was too much even for me. I dropped the Sentinel and stepped back.

The Sentinel touched their throat as they steadied themselves against the pillar.

"It is so easy to provoke your kind. You fall prey to such simple taunts. *Move.*"

They gave me an abrupt shove, and I resumed walking.

Whore, they had called her. It was such a dull, unsophisticated insult. They thought *that* was what had provoked me?

Whore was one thing. But to claim that the woman who had literally changed the course of the divine world, who had saved countless lives and touched countless souls, would ever be *forgotten* . . .

Never. Mische Iliae would be remembered by the bones of time itself, and I knew it because I would write her story there with my blood if I had to.

She was not done with this world. Only the ignorant believed that death was an end. It certainly would not be for her.

But I shut my mouth and kept walking.

CHAPTER THREE

Asar

The land of the gods was sprawling. It was said even divine beings could not see it all in an endless lifetime. But when mortals thought of the land of the gods, they thought of Ysria, the home of the White Pantheon. History was written by victors, and when the gods established their rule and built their grand paradise, they slathered its depiction over their followers' tapestries and paintings and holy books. In the mortal world, it varied depending on the context. In drought-plagued deserts, Ysria was a lush oasis. In hostile tundra, it was a sun-drenched meadow. In the barren mountains, it was rolling golden fields ripe with deer to be slain and fruit to be plucked. Heat-scorched islanders dreamed of it as a fleet of ships bearing every terrain—ponds, forests, plains.

In Obitraes—where the gods of the White Pantheon were not saviors, but oppressors—it was often depicted as a beautiful prison.

So far, this seemed the most accurate interpretation.

It was a land of gold, with rolling fields of glimmering grass, diamond-bright flowers, grand temples of jeweled glass rising from light-drenched fields. The sky was blinding, empty white. Shadows across the landscape revealed hints of the mortal world. I watched a glimpse of a bustling human city in the darkness cast by a cliff as the Sentinels dragged me down a set of marble steps.

It was pristine, flawless beauty. And yet, it was all so artificial. There were no bugs in the soil, no mice in the stone, no clouds in the blinding sky. Every flower we passed was perfectly straight, facing up, with the same number of petals arranged in the same orientation in the same shade of blue, to eerie effect. As if the gods had seen some beauty in mortality but failed to realize that the imperfection of it was what made it remarkable.

I was brought to a large, circular outdoor patio in the shadow of the palace of the White Pantheon. It still bore the sigil of the sun at its peak, though even that was marred by jagged cracks reaching across it like desperate, broken fingers.

I tilted my head up, lifting my chin to the bright sky. It was rare I saw anything with this much light. But this was not sunlight. I knew it because it felt nothing like what Mische had described.

It feels warm and comforting. A fresh dawn makes you believe that the future can be better than the present.

With the memory of Mische's voice came the image of her smile, bright as a second chance.

No. This felt like false pleasures and a knife poised between your shoulder blades. Beautiful denial.

At the center of the stage was a pit of pure blackness, discordant against the too-bright beauty of everything around it. The shadows within sputtered and leaped like liquid boiling over. Stray droplets sizzled against the marble, leaving scorch marks. Its sheer *wrong*-ness radiated from it like poison fumes.

Standing around the pit were the gods of the White Pantheon.

When Nyaxia had first appeared to me, the sight of her had snatched the breath from my lungs. My entire body had reached for her, like she was calling to my blood itself. She was astounding and terrifying and though I resisted it, every animal instinct still longed to cut myself open to offer her my guts.

That was the presence of merely a single god.

Now, I stood before eleven.

Closest to me was Vitarus, god of the harvest, with his golden hair that seemed a little dimmer than the last time I'd seen him. Ix, goddess of sex and fertility, who still wept silent tears over Atroxus's death. Srana, the clockwork goddess of machinery, copper flesh gleaming. Ijakai, goddess of animals, with her long foxlike ears and her menagerie of creatures at her heels.

All of them turned to stare at me as I was led down spiraling steps. The conversation withered. I felt their wary curiosity pick me apart like carrion birds to a corpse.

None of them were at peace. The air and wind and soil roiled with their anxiety and anticipation. The sky shuddered with gleaming multicolored lightning cracks. The plains below undulated with choppy gusts of winds in dissonant directions. Waves of heat and cold pulsed through the air.

Once, before my exile, I had been commanded to destroy one of the island states off the coast of the House of Shadow—retribution for a slight against my father. I burned the ships and then spelled a series of delayed fires around the circumference of the island. While the army was distracted by the very prominent attack on their port, I poisoned the animals that would provide the last blood sources to the island. Most of the vampires succumbed to their hunger before the last of the flames, which took weeks to fully destroy the city.

I felt no guilt about what I did to those men—if the roles were reversed, they wouldn't have hesitated to do worse to me, and they'd have enjoyed it more. But I had been haunted by the final wails of the wolves. They knew much sooner than the vampires did that they were doomed. I still smelled their rancid panic long after I'd washed away the stink of smoke.

I tasted it now, as I was led down to the pit. That same trapped, desperate panic.

The Sentinels pushed me roughly down to my knees at the lip of the pool. I gazed down into the depths. It wasn't just darkness, I realized—up close, I could make out the shape of buildings and mountains and shorelines, all drifting by in endless blackness. Shards of gold floated atop the cloud-dipped surface.

This was a window to the mortal world.

It was already nearly unrecognizable, bathed in its eternal darkness and dotted with the broken pieces of what had once been the sun. I saw withered crops and darkened skies. Frost falling over fields, ice coating rivers. In a million meadows in a million lands, dead foliage skittered lifelessly across the dry ground.

A bitter pang of pride twisted in my heart.

You changed the world, Iliae, I thought. *You've terrified even the gods.*

Vitarus shot me a disdainful stare. Up close, I noticed that his left hand, the one that represented life, was withered and browning. The dry leaves adorning his arm crinkled to dust as he gestured to me.

"We do not need the help of vermin. I can raise the sun on my own. If you allow me to try again, to wear the crown—"

"If anyone can do it, it will be me," a deep voice boomed. A tall man with dripping long hair and fog clustering around his hands rose—Zarux, god of sea and sky. "The heavens are my domain."

Vitarus scoffed. "Perhaps if we wish for the sky to be covered in sea fog."

Flecks of lightning pulsed in Zarux's mists. "Your ability to grow flowers has proved useless."

"I am the one keeping your precious acolytes alive," Vitarus snapped. "Do not underestimate the strength it takes for me to grow crops beneath a sunless sky. Shall I let them perish? By all means, try yet again, and we shall all watch as your fifteenth attempt is miraculously successful."

"Yes, just as yours will be once we hand you a crown," Zarux replied, voice dripping with sarcasm.

"Hush," Ix whispered. Her stare, blue and doe-like, fell to me. She had the appearance of a beautiful mortal woman—lush curves swathed in ethereal white chiffon floating in a directionless wind, a round face with rosy cheeks dusted with the sheen of mortality, wide eyes that held the holy glow of new life. But her lips and hands were rusted red—centuries of dried blood from centuries of childbirth pains. "You forget yourselves, brothers."

"Indeed."

Shiket's voice fell over me like a wave of vengeful cold.

I turned to see her stepping through the mists at the opposite end of the basin. Her golden armor gleamed through the gray. It was strikingly beautiful—crafted by Srana, long ago. Tableaus of victory ran along the shape of her muscles encased in metal. The embossed figures moved in constant battle, depicting victories of the past, present, and future. A smooth, eyeless half helmet—a bisected version of the full mask her Sentinels wore—covered her forehead and eyes, ending just high enough to reveal a strong jaw, a stern mouth, the tip of an aquiline nose.

Yet all of these things, grand as they were, paled against Shiket's greatest pride. That honor was reserved for the six swords that extended from her back like wings of death. They were all magnificent. Each represented a different form of justice. Legends said that occasionally, Shiket had been known to gift one of these blades to a mortal follower, with the considerable caveat that the weapon would be destined to one day end them.

My gaze fell immediately to the top left one, just above her shoulder. A massive white broadsword, glowing with ethereal light.

The Blade of Retribution. The sword that represented a rightful death granted in a rightful punishment.

And, in a repulsive irony, the sword she had used to kill Mische.

"Our infighting accomplishes nothing, my siblings," Shiket said. "We must focus on what lies ahead."

Despite her heavy armor, her footfalls were silent as she crossed the platform and stood over me.

"Rise," she commanded.

I did. My gaze did not break from hers. I felt the shadows of my left eye flare without my permission, though I carefully controlled my expression.

Still, she saw that surge of smoke.

She laughed softly. "You need not hide your feelings, prisoner. It is no surprise to me that a child of Nyaxia, a fallen one, would so resent the justice of the light."

Some gods had come to visit me during my time in captivity—Vitarus, Ix, Srana. Several of the gods who'd had the biggest hand in Alarus's betrayal and death. They were afraid of me—or, more accurately, afraid of *him,* and whatever of him might be left in me.

Shiket had not visited me, and she was not afraid.

That was fine. Better when they underestimate you.

"Press your hands to the circle," she said.

I didn't move.

A flicker of indignation. "Do as you are commanded, prisoner!"

Her voice boomed with divine might. All my mortal muscles begged to obey. Still, I did not move.

Vitarus laughed. "Stupid vampire."

Srana's clockwork eyes *tick, tick, tick*ed. "Not stupid. Stubborn as his ancestor."

Srana, above all the others, was interested in me, and she never bothered to hide it. Perhaps because she was the goddess of science, and whatever I was defied all logic.

"And how well such defiance had gone for Alarus." Shiket grabbed the back of my neck and forced me down. "*Kneel.*"

My hands flew out before me, pressing to the half wall just before my forehead bashed to the stone.

It took every ounce of my self-control to keep from reacting as the flood ripped through my veins.

I had devoted my life to mastering the darker, less honorable arts of magic. I'd learned how to wield death itself. And yet, that was a candle—this was a wildfire.

I felt myself connected to the sea and sky and earth. Felt my awareness reach all the way to the boundaries between the mortal and immortal worlds, the underworld, the human world, vampire world. I felt the deaths of countless mortals at once, stretching out to the oblivion of time. I felt the musty familiarity of Morthryn, the halls of the Descent, the tormented pain of the ailing guardians, the weight of countless lost souls.

And for a split second, I felt her.

Her.

Far away, buried beneath the onslaught of sensations.

But I'd know her anywhere. I'd memorized her soul. I'd pressed her final moments into my heart like preserved rose petals.

It distracted me, disoriented me. I sagged against the stone wall.

The liquid within the reservoir churned and spattered, the flecks of it burning my cheeks.

Dimly, I was aware of the other gods kneeling before the pit. The flood of power grew stronger as each of them pressed their hands to the circle as I did—like spokes of a wheel clicking into place as it turned, faster and faster. The shards of gold shuddered and quivered with the force of it.

My power was being leveraged without my permission, reaching out to the shards that remained of the sun. My mortal vampire flesh screamed against it. The pain was unbearable, but I couldn't pull away. Before me, the pieces of the sun slowly dragged toward each other. Searing gold light scorched the surface of the pit, opening burns on my nose, my cheeks.

But magic quickly spiraled out of control.

"Do not let go!" someone cried through the chaos. But it was too late. The surface of the water exploded in foamy waves. A barrage of boiling droplets and razored shards fell over me.

When I opened my eyes again, I was staring at that white empty sky, my back against a freshly cracked stone wall.

"Useless!" a deep voice boomed. "He is useless!" Kajmar, god of illusion and performance, jabbed a finger at me. "Let us slaughter him and return to the ether whatever drops of our power he stole. Perhaps then we can—"

"We cannot raise the sun, Kajmar."

Even among gods, the voice, ageless and eternal, stopped the sands of time itself. Acaeja, goddess of fate and spellcasting. Her large, white eyes settled on me. Six majestic wings spread out behind her, each offering glimpses of different fates. Now, each of them depicted glimpses of a world bathed in darkness.

"I have told you this time and time again," she said. "We must accept what fate has given us."

A muscle feathered in Shiket's jaw. An oddly mortal tic. I might've found some satisfaction in that, if I hadn't still been clinging to that ghost of Mische's presence.

"Look at what is happening while you fight among yourselves.

Humans suffer. Justice goes undone." Shiket violently gestured to the pool. With a wave, the ripples took a new shape, though the images within were blurry and dim. It took a moment for me to recognize it: Obitraes. The blade-sharp peaks of the House of Shadow, the rolling dunes of the House of Night, the frozen mountains of the House of Blood. The view was distant and dark. Gods of the White Pantheon couldn't see much of Nyaxia's territory.

"Nyaxia prepares to take advantage of her new eternal night," Shiket snarled. "This is not the time to fall into infighting. Especially not when we have one of her own here among us." Her gaze locked on me. "Let us start with the most deserved punishment."

"He shall not be killed, Shiket," Acaeja said.

A sneer flitted over Shiket's face.

"Why? What use is he? Even Nyaxia did not want him."

"Nyaxia is ruled by her emotions. If she had been thinking strategically, she would have taken him. And she may still change her mind yet."

"All the more reason to eliminate him. If there is ever a time to stand for what is right, is it not now?"

Right, she said.

A smirk brushed the corner of my mouth. Barely a twitch, and yet, Shiket still saw it.

"Justice is funny to you. Typical of a fallen one."

"I think it's amusing," I said, "that creatures as powerful as you are so stupid."

Shiket drew herself up to her full formidable height. Her helmet gleamed. Her six blades glowed. And even I, through my hatred, had to admit that she looked every bit the legend.

I almost regretted speaking.

Almost.

Shiket's revulsion radiated from her like smoke from a funeral pyre. She hated me, and she did not bother to hide it.

But she had not looked at Mische that way. I, with my drop of immortal blood and my crown and my confusing origins, was at least worthy of Shiket's revulsion. Mische had simply been inconsequential.

That earned my hatred, too. Hot enough to match that of a goddess.

"No mortal speaks to a god that way," Shiket hissed. "Not without punishment."

But I was already lunging for her.

There were no shadows up here, and yet, my magic was stronger than ever. I could feel the darkness speaking to me, as if through roots driving all the way down to the underworld.

Shiket, of course, was ready for me, the Blade of Retribution drawn. We collided in an explosion of gold and darkness. She was not trying to kill me. If she were, I would already be dead. Still, I held my own against her. I poured all my newfound power into my strike. When I countered, my fist closed around a jagged rock, and when she drew back to strike me, I reached for her mind and twisted. The rock made contact with the side of her face.

I sensed her surprise—so satisfying—for only a split second before she recovered, hitting me with the flat of her blade so hard that I flew back against the edge of the basin. I barely caught myself before I toppled into the pit, my fingertips brushing the surface of the water with a wave of searing pain.

I lifted my head with great effort and gave her a bitter smile. I tasted blood at the corner of my mouth. The rest of the gods watched with vague amusement. Even in the ashes of their king, these fights were little more than petty entertainment. To a god, after all, nothing really mattered.

I leaned back against the wall to hide that I wasn't sure if I could stand.

"Why stop there?" I sneered.

Half a taunt. But half a genuine plea: *Send me to the underworld. Send me home. Send me to her.*

Shiket looked all too ready to oblige.

"He has the blood of Alarus in his veins," Acaeja's voice said from behind me.

She spoke quietly. But the words made Shiket halt mid-movement. And though she hid it well, I felt it anyway:

Uncertainty.

I was no major god. I should—*should*—fall outside of the pact that prevented the killing of major gods by each other.

But they didn't know what I was any more than I did.

Shiket's lip curled. "And it makes him so very arrogant, just like his ancestor."

One arm extended to her nearest Sentinel, and before my eyes could even track the movement, the guard's head was off in her hands with a wet tear and a brief, garbled shriek.

Silver blood spattered me, pouring from the Sentinel's now-severed head.

Sentinels were not quite alive, but they still held some vestiges of their former mortality. Their blood was like molten steel. Beneath the crystallized rot, it still held the unmistakable scent of humanity.

I hadn't felt hunger in captivity. But at the sight of the blood, a sudden, excruciating wave of starvation struck me. I jerked forward, stopping just short of lapping up the puddle from the ground.

Shiket's laugh slithered around my throat.

"Look at him. A slave to his desires, like all Nyaxia's fallen ones." She kicked the broken body aside. My eyes tracked every smeared streak across the floor. "He is no god. Take him away."

The Sentinels—seemingly unmoved by the unceremonious death of their comrade—seized my arms and hauled me to my feet. I snarled and spat, fighting against their hold with every step.

And I waited until I was back in my cell, alone in the dark, before I let my attention turn to *it*: the key to my freedom, stolen beneath the distraction of my performance. A performance so good because it was exactly what they expected me to be. Just an animal.

I smiled a little at the steady throb of it, tucked beneath my shirt, right against my heart.

That little broken shard of the sun, burning like a grudge.

IT DIDN'T TAKE long for the gods to decide to kill me.

At least, it wasn't long by a god's estimation. In mine, I felt every passing second. The shard against my skin held the distilled power of the sun itself—the very antithesis of my being. I felt it chew through skin layer by layer, then set in on muscle.

But I knew I was being watched. So I didn't twitch, didn't make a sound. I'd just shown them—gods and Sentinels alike—how easy I was to defeat. Reminded them I was nothing but a tainted mortal.

Good. Let them keep believing it.

At last, they came for me. They sent three Sentinels this time, but they were less wary than the last time. My show had worked.

I wasn't sure where they were taking me, and I didn't care. When they reached for my restraints, I moved.

I went for the smaller one first. Magic filled my lungs like the euphoric smoke of a Pythoraseed addict's inhale. Magic had always felt easy when nothing else was. Something that I understood far better than court politics or vampire viciousness. But now, it took on an intensity that might have been terrifying if it didn't feel so damned good.

I used a wave of darkness to fling the first Sentinel across the room, sending its metal body crumpling against the columns. Behind me, I felt the nagging intention of its companion's strike before they moved, seizing the fallen Sentinel's sword as I whirled.

A crash rang out as I slipped past their blade, sending them stumbling against the wall, then smothering them out with a wave of darkness. They huffed a curse in a human language I didn't understand, which almost made me laugh. Perhaps Shiket had done all she could to separate these warriors from who they had been in life, but put them in an unexpected situation, and it would still be the profanities of a life a thousand years past that came flying from their lips.

I didn't wait for them to recover. I raced through the door into pristine marble hallways, only to nearly fling myself directly into a large, armored body.

A final Sentinel stood in the doorway, golden sword drawn. "Your rebellion ends here," they said.

Their blade pulsed with the glow of divine light. Even from this distance, its presence burned my exposed skin. Behind me, I heard the two fallen Sentinels recovering. Seconds, and they would be here, and my one chance at escape would be gone.

I let out a long breath through gritted teeth. I pressed my hand to my chest, then raised it in surrender.

"You can't blame a man for trying," I muttered.

I felt the Sentinel's ripple of satisfaction as I extended my wrists to be cuffed again.

And as soon as they were close enough, I drove the shard of the sun, hidden until this perfect moment, into the Sentinel's throat.

The Sentinel let out a hollow scream as the sun melted through metal and whatever lay beneath it. Silver blood spattered my face. The Sentinel fell to their knees.

I yanked the shard from their not-flesh, pushed them down the opposite hall, then wound a cloak of darkness around myself and fled.

I'd done what I could to make sense of the layout of my prison, though that wasn't saying much. This place was even more convoluted than Morthryn. I was convinced that it had changed since my last walk through these halls. When I dove through the gates the Sentinels had left open, I was presented with three hallways. I didn't remember there being three the last time I was brought out of my cell, but I didn't have time to second-guess myself. I picked the left branch and ran—right next, then center, then winding around a circular hallway that I could've sworn was just taking me right back to where I started. I could hear distant commotion. Above me, the white sky cracked with sudden lightning. The mess I'd left behind had been discovered—faster than I'd hoped. If I was lucky, they would take the location of that final body at face value and go hunting for me in the wrong direction.

Would it be enough to fool a god, though?

I'd thought long and hard about what I'd do once I got free, but the truth was, I didn't know enough about Ysria to have anything resembling a "plan." There would be a path to the underworld somewhere in the land of the gods, even if long abandoned. Perhaps if I made it beyond the gates of the prison, I could figure out how to follow the tether in my heart that I'd felt at the pool. I could—

"Asar!"

I stopped short and nearly slammed into a corner.

That voice.

Mische's voice.

Unmistakable.

All thoughts dissolved.

I whirled around. A long, empty white hallway stood before me, silent.

"Asar! Where are you?" The note of fear in her voice had my heart leaping.

A trick. A trap.

It was what I would have done.

But Mische had killed a god. The White Pantheon had dismissed her, but perhaps they'd thought better of it and somehow dragged her back here for further punishment. I touched my chest—the echo of the anchor that had once connected us, which I swore still, sometimes, pulsed with her distant presence.

It could be her. A sliver of a chance. A sliver of a sliver of a chance.

Foolish. Naive. I knew it, but that was never going to stop me.

I looped around the corner, and then another, following her voice. And then at last I came to an open gate leading to a narrow staircase.

At the bottom of the stairs, gold liquid lapped at a shore of ivory sand. And kneeling in it, battered and burned, was Mische.

She looked exactly as I remembered she had when they dragged me away. Her skin was covered in ash, the darkness of it obscuring the seeping burns that Atroxus's light had left over her skin. Her hair, caramel curls, hung limp, heavy with blood, over her face. But those eyes. Those eyes.

Even as she had died, they'd looked just like I had imagined the sun.

Now, they glistened with tears. Her mouth curled into a shaky smile. "Why are you crying?"

A million unspoken words—of adoration, of apology, of love—drew tight in my chest. None of them made it to the surface.

We didn't have time.

I threw myself down the stairs. The moment my bare feet hit the gold water, Mische began to fall, as if the sand beneath us had simply opened up.

"Asar," she begged, reaching for me. I tried to catch her. But it was no use.

I was falling, too.

CHAPTER FOUR

Asar

"He's dead. You killed him."

"I didn't kill him. He's a god."

"He's not a god. He's a mortal who stole some magic off a corpse. Basically a grave robber."

"I hear his kind enjoy that kind of thing."

The voices blended around me. A woman's, soft and curious. An older man's, rough but oddly melodic, and then a younger one, bitter with sarcasm.

"Hush," the woman said. "He's waking up."

I was restrained again, though this time, I could tell immediately, not with god-forged chains. When I lifted my head, I was rewarded with a cacophony of pains. My left ankle throbbed fiercely, and when I moved, my shoulder made a cracking noise that didn't sound altogether pleasant.

If the fall had injured me, it could have done far worse to Mische, who had already looked close to death.

I was in a small room that looked nothing like my Ysrian prison. It seemed more suited to be the home of some human farmer. Stone walls, dirt floor, modest wooden furniture, a fire in the hearth. A few sparse windows revealed only gray, hazy clouds. No doors.

Three people stood before me, gawking like I was a museum curiosity. A young woman with enormous dark eyes, fair freckled skin, and copper hair. Curiously, she had a plate of bronze metal bolted across one side of her jaw—some kind of prosthetic, perhaps? Beside her was an older man with slicked-back salt-and-pepper hair. Then a younger one, with a tall, svelte frame, bronze skin, and sharp features. His eyes were completely black—no iris, no pupil. A white wolf sat beside him.

We were alone in this room. No Mische.

"Where is she?"

My voice sounded pathetically weak.

The woman shot the older man a questioning look.

"Asar," Mische said. I blinked, and there she was—kneeling on the ground, burnt and bloody. "Why are you crying?"

Blink, and she was whole again, dressed in worn clothes from our travels through the Descent, giving me a broad smile. *"What's your favorite hobby?"*

Blink, and she was wearing a gold slip and silk robe, extending her hand to me as she bit the lush curve of her lower lip in a way, I was certain, she had no idea had haunted me ever since. *"Dance with me."*

Memories. They were memories.

I slammed my mental doors closed, cursing myself.

Gideon would've been ashamed of me for failing to recognize this for what it was. I hadn't even felt the invasion—maybe because I'd been desperate to believe what I was seeing. I knew the strength of that firsthand. Countless times, I'd been the one plucking memories to use against my target. Still, this was skillfully executed, and very different from Shadowborn magic. Even now that I was looking for it, I only barely felt the touch upon my mind.

"Sorry," the old man said, not sounding very sorry at all. "Can't blame you, though. She's a pretty one."

I caught my possessive remark between my teeth.

The man looked human—he held the signs of age that evaded vampires, lines around his eyes, gray in his beard and hair. Still, there was something odd about him that I couldn't place. He was tall, with a strong face and an elegant way of carrying himself. Oddly elegant, actually, in ways that seemed to defy his appearance. His eyes, bright blue, stared through me.

My gaze shifted to the other two. The woman fidgeted nervously with a plait of hair over her shoulder, and I noticed that her hand was constructed of metal, too—copper and bronze and countless gears, ticking with her every movement. The younger man stared at me with his black eyes narrowed, stepping possessively closer to her.

I reached out for their minds, ready to rifle through their memories. But then my brow furrowed.

Instantly, I knew that despite their appearance, they were not human. Not vampire, either. I couldn't quite push my way into their thoughts.

"Let me go," I said.

"I'm sorry." The woman sounded genuinely apologetic. "We cannot."

"You couldn't go anywhere, anyway." The black-eyed man gestured to the mist-covered windows. "There is no path to Ysria here."

"I have no interest in going back to Ysria. *Let me go.*"

I imbued my voice with the syrup of compulsion—*Let me go. Let me go. Let me go.*

Compulsion was easy to use once you realized that it wasn't about force—the key was to sweeten your desires until your target lapped them up like sugar water. Still, my hold on their minds was slippery, and the movement of my own magic clumsy.

The woman stepped forward, eyes glazed, but the younger man stopped her.

"Careful." Then, to me, "Rude way to treat your hosts, vampire."

"There is no need to be rude to our guest, either, child."

The voice came before her form did. Ageless, transcending mortality.

Acaeja emerged from the shadows.

All other thoughts and senses fell away but for her. The urge to fall to my knees consumed me like a wave of nausea. Her wings unfolded behind her, nearly stretching the width of the tiny room. Right now, four of them depicted fiery damnation. Two depicted pitch-black nothingness.

Aceaja's large white eyes surveyed me.

"Forgive our accommodations, Asar Voldari, King of the House of Shadow, Warden of the Descent, and descendant of Alarus." Her voice plucked through my titles with detached curiosity, as if rummaging for something useful. "Understand that we must work with what we have. I could not intervene in freeing you from your cell. You needed to come here of your own accord."

She turned to the three figures before me. "Well done, my soldiers."

The older man's eyes roved over me. I felt his fear and his curiosity, both equally powerful. "Is he one of us?"

"Let me go," I said again.

The compulsion was stronger this time. All three of them started toward me.

Let me go. Let me go. Let me—

Acaeja lifted a hand. "There is no need for that. You are no prisoner. Release him, Kayeh."

The woman hesitated before bowing her head. "Yes, Weaver."

The vines around my arms and legs slithered away like banished snakes. I fought a wince as my weight pressed down upon my injuries, bone scraping against bone. It would heal fast enough. I touched my wrist and the marks on my skin where the vines had touched me—burns. The touch of divinity, albeit not as strong as those of the chains in my cell.

I watched the woman—Kayeh—whose eyes were aglow with fading light.

The magic of Vitarus, I realized. But not just that of an acolyte, I was sure. Not even a very skilled one. It felt different than that.

"You're demigods," I said.

That was why my compulsion didn't work well on them. Why their magic defied the boundaries I'd set up against it. Why their presence felt beyond mortal.

"He's clever enough," the older man said to the younger. Then, to me, he said, "Guess whose?"

I took him in for a moment—the confusing, ethereal grace about him, even at odds with everything else about his appearance.

"Kajmar," I said. The god of art and performance, and alongside it, illusion and deception.

Then, to the younger man, I said, "And you are Ijakai's."

That one was easy. His black eyes. His pointed ears. The wolf that now wound around his legs. The sight of the creature, and the man's hand rubbing its head absentmindedly, hit me with a stab of longing. Luce was not dead. I felt that, just as I felt it for Mische.

How convenient your instincts are, a familiar, cruel voice whispered in the back of my mind. *Your woman is still out there. Your dog is still out there. Is that really what you sense, or is it just denial?*

But those harsh words were met with softer ones—Mische, saying, *We all need faith, Asar.*

I blinked away the past, even though it pulled at me with open arms.

I had lots of questions, now.

If vampires were cruel when it came to succession, gods were downright vicious. Vampires would at least *carefully* cultivate heirs to ensure their line lived on, but gods were true immortals. Offspring were nothing but liabilities. This, of course, did not stop them from fucking their way across the mortal worlds—countless nubile, devoted acolytes were far too tempting to pass up. But they swiftly dealt with the consequences of those trysts. Some more mercifully than others.

It was a miracle that these demigods had not only been allowed to be born, but allowed to live. I had to imagine that someone had gone through great lengths to make sure they did. Perhaps that was true of me, too. All of us, rare artifacts.

I was reminded of the collection I'd so carefully cultivated in my office in Morthryn. I could practically imagine us on a shelf on that wall now, neatly labeled: "Seed of Kajmar, demigod. Seed of Ijakai, demigod. Seed of Vitarus, demigod. Seed of Alarus, vampire and ???"

I looked to Acaeja. "Am I to be added to your museum, now?"

But perhaps museum wasn't the right word.

Perhaps a better one was *armory*.

Because demigods weren't just rare curiosities. They were the deadliest weapons that existed against the White Pantheon. A piece of the power of a major god, without the restrictions that prevented them from killing each other.

Acaeja's face was still. "I am a protector."

What a joke. This was no sanctuary. But I couldn't bring myself to care about Acaeja's machinations. The longer Mische remained in the underworld, the harder it would be to bring her back, and the more of her I'd leave behind when I did.

I needed to go. Now.

My eyes moved past the row of demigods before me, past Acaeja. I now noticed that a single closed door stood behind her. Had it been there before? Did it matter?

I calculated what it would take to get to it. I could kill the demigods if necessary. Kayeh, the girl, would be the easiest. And judging by the way the younger man looked at her, attacking her would bait him into doing something stupid, and I could take care of him too. The illusionist was no warrior. He could sing a damned song about it all.

But getting through Acaeja—that would be difficult.

Still, Mische had managed to kill Atroxus with nothing but an enchanted arrow. What could I do with the magic her sacrifice had given me?

Acaeja's mouth twitched in cold amusement.

"Mine is not the head you long for."

How arrogant of her. No, Acaeja did not kill Mische. But she had allowed it to happen, and to me, that was just as worthy of punishment.

"I'm leaving," I said.

I started walking past her.

"Your kingdom has no king," Acaeja said. "Your sister has taken control."

"I don't care."

I cared so little that it made me want to laugh out loud, tell her, *What, you think I give a fuck about the House of Shadow right now?*

But then, she said, "Or perhaps you wish to retrieve Mische Iliae from the underworld."

At this, I stopped short.

"I weave fates, Asar Voldari," Acaeja said. "I see yours. And I see hers."

It was such blatant manipulation. I'd conducted enough myself to recognize it immediately.

And yet. I did not move.

"Leave us," Acaeja said to the demigods. "I wish to speak to him privately."

"Weaver . . ." Kayeh protested warily.

"I am in no danger. Go."

I remained still, back turned, as I listened to them file from the room—perhaps through yet another mysterious appearing door—leaving Acaeja and me alone. Only then, into the yawning silence, did I answer her.

"There's no *wishing,*" I said. "I *will* retrieve her."

"You would go back to death for another lover, even as the last one despised you for it?"

It was not the same. I knew this in my soul. I'd dragged Ophelia back from a death that already had taken her. Mische still had time. I was so sure of it, even if I couldn't identify how or why.

At last, I turned around. Acaeja's wings were spread. Each one depicted Mische's face—a close-up of her amber-gold eye, a blood-spattered curve of her cheek, a rouge-painted lip, a corpse-gray mouth. Glimpses of six different fates. She could be a queen. She could be a corpse. Perhaps in some futures, both.

"What is your offer?" I said.

Acaeja's face was eternally still. Yet her voice lilted with amusement. "Offer?"

"Gods make deals. That's what you're doing, yes? So let's make a deal."

She cocked her head slightly. The images in her wings shifted, but still, they showed me only Mische—Mische upon the throne of the House of Shadow, Mische standing over a wreckage of shattered marble, Mische on her knees in the ocean, head in her hands.

"She intrigues me," Acaeja said. "A soul of such simple beginnings. Mische Iliae is no chosen one. Her blood is plain as it comes. And yet, she sits at the apex of so many different fates."

Utopias and apocalypses danced across Acaeja's wings. A swell of pride tightened in my chest. With it, a pang of sadness.

I wanted to tell her, *Of course she could make or unmake the world. Have you met her? Anyone who had wouldn't be surprised.*

Instead, I said again, "Your offer."

A low chuckle. "So impatient you are to end the world."

She lifted her hands, each bearing ten long, elegant fingers tattooed with the twenty symbols of fate. Translucent threads of light pulled between them.

"What Mische Iliae did," Acaeja said, "stretched the bounds of possibility. I am not too arrogant to admit that even I did not think such a thing would come to pass. Luck was on your side that night."

"Strange to hear the goddess of fate speaking of luck."

"Fate and luck are twin sides to the same coin." The threads rearranged with the dance of her fingertips. "You and Mische Iliae conducted very advanced magic to create the resurrection spell. It was a small miracle that she was able to complete it without you, or that she was able to bring you back without killing you. Countless fates ended with your deaths that night, just as countless fates ended with the deaths of millions more."

Her wings showed me those alternate realities—my own mangled body in Mische's arms, a great shadowy figure rising from the water only to fall again moments later, an eternal sun rising over the vampire world. Just like that, millions gone. The fate that Mische averted that night.

"But in doing so," Acaeja went on, "she did not fully complete her spell. A passage to the threads of fate was opened and never fully closed. She entangled herself with you to pull you free, but never severed that thread."

As Acaeja's hands moved, the threads rearranged. Two shone brighter than the others, intertwined in a knot.

"The two of you are now bound inextricably," Acaeja said. "Yet, the threads fray under the pressure of this tension. As she did not successfully complete the ceremony, she still holds a piece of Alarus's power—power that belongs to you and could distill your role as god. The underworld crumbles beneath the pressure of this tension."

I pieced together what she was saying. "But it gives Mische a path back to life."

"It gives Mische a line of immortality to cling to. Yes. Thus, Asar Voldari, I offer you a choice. I can sever this connection. You will retain a bit of divine power—not as much as your potential holds, no, but some. Perhaps enough to make you a legendary king among your people. Enough to let you strike down your sister and challengers for your throne. Enough that perhaps you could even convince my siblings in the White Pantheon to let you live, should you pledge to use that power in a way that is advantageous to them. The stress placed upon the underworld will be released, and though it will continue to decay—perhaps faster than it once did—it will stand for another millennia or so, if we are fortunate. And Mische Iliae will fall away to the death she had once so longed for."

Acaeja's wings showed me myself upon the throne of the House of Shadow. The begrudging loyalty of my sister, my stepmother, the countless nobles who had once dismissed me. An army of thousands at my direction. Everything a vampire prince should want. Everything I had once wanted.

But those wings also showed me Mische. Charred and crumpled, in the ashes of the god she had slain.

I did not hesitate. "And the other option?"

"I can draw the knot tighter. It will offer you a path back to her. But it will place undeniable stress upon the underworld, and upon her soul. You must finish what you began and fully seize your power as the god of death. You cannot do so without her, as she holds part of the key to your power, and similarly, she cannot regain life without that power, either. But you will have a matter of weeks to claim the rest of your power before the underworld collapses, taking millions of souls with it in worlds above and below."

"And Mische." I could not bring myself to be ashamed that Acaeja was speaking of the damnation of millions of souls and yet I thought only of one.

"Yes."

It took me another moment to fully process what she was saying.

"You are telling me," I said, "that I will need to ascend to divinity."

A faint smile twitched at her mouth. "Yes, Asar Voldari. You will need to become a god."

At the sound of those words, I nearly sank to my knees.

She was offering me a choice. A choice between some power and a comfortable path to wielding it, to putting off the inevitable destruction of the underworld for just long enough that I could pretend it wasn't happening at all, to letting Mische's bones lie where they fell.

Or limitless power, accelerating the stakes to the point where none of it could be ignored. Power that would allow me to save Mische.

"And what would I have to do," I said, "to seize the rest of Alarus's power? Another resurrection spell?"

"Nothing so mundane, I am afraid. You and Mische Iliae would need to obtain and wield the three cores of Alarus's power." She opened her palm, and images unfurled in smoky silver from it. "His mask, which acted as the crown to his kingdom of Vathysia."

Vathysia—the heart of Alarus's territory, before it became Obitraes when Nyaxia created vampires. Most of it lay within the borders of what now was the House of Shadow. The image of the mask unfurled in her palm. It was bronze, reminiscent of a simplified skull, canine teeth pointed. It was a familiar image to me. A version of it adorned the Shadowborn crest.

"His eye, which granted him the power to see beyond the borders of mortality," she continued.

An eye joined the mask, gazing out into the perpetual distance. It was red, and all-seeing. This, too, was a familiar image. It was central to many depictions of Alarus, usually on his hands or forehead. It stared down from the grand window of Morthryn's facade.

"And at last," Acaeja said, "his heart, which contained the basest essence of his soul."

A third image joined the others—a black, beating heart, rivulets of gold throbbing through it.

"I will not disguise their dangers," she said. "Simply touching them would kill a mortal. Even I cannot say what wielding them will do to you, so I warn you, do not use them until you have all three. I am forbidden from helping you retrieve them. Shiket will try to stop you, once she learns of your task. Perhaps Nyaxia will, too, though I cannot predict her actions."

"I'm accustomed to finding five relics," I said drily. "Three should be easy."

"There is nothing easy about this decision, exiled prince. This choice demands great sacrifices from you. If you follow this path, you will never be king of the House of Shadow. Your lover will never be redeemed for her crimes against the White Pantheon. You will spend the next decades enmeshed in war the likes of which you never could have imagined. And the relics themselves will take things from you that you will never get back. If you believe this path leads you to a happy end, you must shed your naivete."

"But these are the only threads that lead to Mische's survival."

Again, that amused almost-smirk. "Very few of them. Yes. But I cannot say if they will lead to yours."

"And what do you want in return?"

Acaeja cocked her head. The empty white of her enormous eyes devoured me.

"What makes you believe that I ask for anything at all? My fellow gods prepare for a war that could destroy all. Perhaps now I only serve what is Right."

Right—she spoke not of moral goodness, but what was *Right* by fate itself.

"Then *fate,* I'm sure, will be getting plenty from these events," I said, sweet with sarcasm. If I accepted Acaeja's help, I would be giving her my fealty in return, even if it remained unspoken. No god was selfless. Especially not if I was being told to ascend to true divinity—an act that most gods would do anything to prevent. Acaeja must have much to gain if she was taking such a risk.

She leaned closer, blinking slowly. She smelled of the smoke of fallen empires and the flames that stoked new ones, birthing beds and deathbeds, sunrises and sunsets.

"We have little time, Asar Voldari," she said. "Soon, my kin will realize their mistake. I can offer you a path to the danger of the underworld or to the safety of your home, if you only tell me where you wish to go."

Between her fingers, the threads hovered—mine the black of

vampire blood, Mische's the gold of sunset, tangled in mid-air. Her six wings spread, the three on the left showing me myself upon the throne of the House of Shadow, ruling over the Shadowborn army, building an empire from eternal night. The three on the right, showing me death, destruction, and Mische.

It wasn't even a choice.

"Take me to her," I said.

Acaeja smiled as she straightened. Her wings went dark as fate shifted.

"Billions of threads," she murmured, "and not a single one where you say no."

And then she drew the threads tight, and the world rearranged.

CHAPTER FIVE

Mische

I didn't expect death to be so exhausting.

A body tracked time differently when there were no breaths to draw, no heartbeat to thrum, no steady tick of a pulse in your veins. Everything was too fast and too slow, as if I were trying to cling to consciousness with oil-slick hands. I did not sleep, but every so often, I would find myself staring into the darkness and seeing my past life. Traveling with my sister through the forest. Sailing with Eomin across the sea. Sitting with a mysterious vampire stranger in a garden, the knife of my decision hanging over my throat.

It was as if every passing second drew me closer to my deaths. My first death, with Malach's mouth on my throat and blood on my lips. My second one, with Atroxus's ashes on my hands, Shiket's blade through my chest, and Asar's screams echoing in my ears. Twin drains sucking my soul back, minute by minute. And I would've just let them sweep me away, if Vincent hadn't been there to grab my shoulders and give me a good shake, jerking me back to him with a cold, clipped, *No time for that. Move.*

Vincent was not good company. He made it very clear that he was not interested in conversation.

Not that I'd ever let that stop me before.

"They're persistent things, aren't they?" I chirped. "How many have we seen now? A dozen? Fifteen? I think I've lost track."

Vincent grunted a nonresponse as he yanked his sword from another mutated souleater, which wailed a protest as it slithered back off into the dark. The sound echoed, bouncing from direction to direction, sad and pained in a way that I tried not to hear. It was a small one, at least. Vincent was impressively efficient at handling them, but the biggest of them left us no choice but to hide and hope they'd pass without any trouble.

Though, hiding and waiting was mostly my role, anyway. I had no weapon, which made me useless—and Vincent made it clear he was uninterested in sharing how he'd gotten his all the way down here. At the same time, I couldn't help but be a little selfishly grateful that I didn't have to look too closely at the souleaters, which more and more resembled the beings they had once been.

"You'd think that maybe they'd find somewhere more interesting to hunt," I babbled on. "Can't imagine that we're all that appealing compared to the legions of souls back down there. Do you think it's because of competition? Maybe they've been chased out by—"

Vincent sheathed his sword and whirled to me.

"Dark Mother help me, girl, you *never* stop."

I blinked. "That's not true. I'm just—"

"It is relentless." He yanked his jacket back on. The spatters of souleater blood were slowly fading—it never lasted long—though he scowled at the stain in disgust, like he could still feel its existence. "Goddess help me understand why anyone would go through such lengths of breaking divine laws just to be subjected to *this* for the rest of their goddess-damned lives."

This was, perhaps, the most words that Vincent had said to me since he first found me. He didn't raise his voice—a vampire king rarely had to. Yet, the insult dug deeper into my heart than I would've expected it to, eliciting a brief whisper in the back of my mind: *Good question. Why* would *Asar go through so much for someone who had betrayed him?*

I blinked away the image of Saescha kneeling beneath her eternal sun and chased after Vincent with a few quickened steps.

"You don't have to do this at all," I snapped. "I'm sure I can figure it out on my own."

He scoffed, like this was a ridiculous idea unworthy of a response.

"I *can,*" I insisted. "Just tell me what to look for and I'll do it by myself. Then you can go . . ."

What *would* Vincent be doing now if he wasn't wandering around with me, making the intensity of his displeasure constantly clear?

I landed on, ". . . do whatever it is you want to spend your afterlife doing. And I'll be on my way. We'll probably all be happier, right?"

"You cannot make the journey on your own."

"I already survived one journey through the underworld, Vincent."

He stopped short and turned, his icy gaze spearing me. "You did not survive. That's why we're here. And *never* address a king by their first name."

I caught my laugh in my teeth when I realized he was not joking. "What do you expect me to call you? *Highness?*"

He stared at me.

Oh, gods. He actually did. Sun fucking take me.

In that brief lull in conversation, the silence fell over us both, smothering as the black, sunless sky. I shut my eyes hard, pushing away the sudden memory of my death. *Deaths.*

Malach's teeth. Atroxus's fire. Shiket's sword.

Asar's agonized pleas.

I shook my head and lifted my gaze just in time to see Vincent blinking, too, a shadow over his silver eyes. It was an expression I innately recognized. The twin to the one I was wiping off my face right now, too.

And this hit me with a knot of unease. None of this conversation seemed funny anymore.

"Do you feel it, too?" I said. "When it's quiet?"

"I don't know what you're referring to."

"Yes, you do."

Because *I* felt it, as he did. When I looked at Vincent, let myself reach toward his mind, I could sense the edge of his last moments. Raihn's bloodstained face. The certainty it would be the last thing he saw. Until Oraya. Oraya, crouching in the colosseum sands, weeping over him.

All of that, in less than a second. I could never push further into his mind—it was too intangible beyond layers and layers of death. He was, after all, no longer among the living. Even the strongest Shadowborn mind magic couldn't reach that far.

The look on Vincent's face sent a shiver up my spine.

"Are you asking if I feel my death?" he said, voice lethal cold. "If I feel the moment that Rishan trash murdered me in front of—my kingdom?"

The catch in his voice was so subtle I almost didn't notice it. Almost.

Rishan trash. I couldn't count how many times I'd heard those insults levied at Raihn during our travels in the Hiaj territory. Before I could stop myself, I said, "Don't call him that."

In a blink, Vincent was in front of me, his form bigger, eyes brighter, teeth bared. He was terrifying. The final monstrous image before, I was certain, thousands of deaths.

"He deserves worse," he snarled.

How much, I wondered, did Vincent know of what had happened in the mortal world since his death? I could see very little of it from down here—glances in my dreams, reflections in the sky, always of places I knew well in life. The Citadel, dark and uneasy beneath a sunless sky, the plants of the jungle slowly withering. Sometimes, I saw Raihn and Oraya, rifling through papers in the office my room in the Nightborn palace had become, but every time I reached for them, they were gone.

I swallowed the sudden, terrible fear that I was making a mistake. "I need to know the real reason why you're doing this."

Vincent hissed a laugh. "Are you afraid I'm out for vengeance, girl? Good. You should be. If I had lived—"

"*Oraya* rules the House of Night," I said. "*Oraya.* She rules 'your' kingdom now."

The name hit Vincent like a bucket of cold water. We had been traveling all this time, and never once did he mention her. Her name was like poison. Too toxic to touch, and even the fleeting mention of her sent him withdrawing.

Instantly, his demeanor changed. Blink, and he was once again several strides ahead, back turned. "I don't have time for—"

But I matched his pace. "I need an answer. Because mark my

words, Vincent, I will not help you hurt them. I don't know how much you have seen of these last few years. But Oraya suffered for everything she has. She's the one you're hurting if you—"

Vincent stopped short and whirled around.

"How *dare* you speak to me about her suffering," he spat. "How *dare* you question my intentions. Look at yourself, girl. You betrayed the man who is about to end the world for you. And yet I am being asked to put *her* fate in *your* hands. Why do you deserve that?"

I opened my mouth—

And I doubled over as the world went white.

The pain was unimaginable. It was as if my entire soul was being unraveled at the seams. If I'd had a stomach to empty, I would have been on my hands and knees in a pool of my own vomit. Instead, I just felt the ground, heaving.

"Mische. *Mische.*"

I barely heard Vincent's voice, or felt his hand when it grabbed my shoulder. I lifted my head with great effort and looked to the shattered mountains in the distance, to the bleeding rivers and the broken sky. The souls of the dead were moving faster than they usually were. Frantic, even. Like they were running to something, or away from it.

The hum grew louder.

"What is wrong with you?" Vincent demanded.

I watched the souleaters scatter like ants in the shadow of a boot.

"Something isn't—" I started.

The sky burst open like a rotting cyst.

Hell rained down over us.

CHAPTER SIX

Asar

The pain was unbearable. When I managed to open my eyes, I was on my hands and knees. A dull roar echoed in my ears, buried beneath a strangled sound that I realized came from me. My hand was clamped over my burning heart.

What had been so faint before that I wasn't sure if it was a figment of my own desperation now was unmistakable. I *felt* her.

"Rise." Acaeja's voice seemed louder now, reverberating through the fabric of fate. "The others will sense the change. Shiket will know you escaped, and she will send her Sentinels after your lost lover."

It seemed like something Acaeja could have mentioned before. Not that it would have changed anything. I got to my feet. The room was, indeed, shaking.

"Why is that happening?" I asked.

Acaeja's smile gleamed in the trembling firelight. Strange, I thought, that none of the paintings or tapestries had ever depicted that her teeth were sharp as those of vampires.

"It is not painless when fate changes. I should think you of all souls would know this. Now go. You do not have much time. I can offer you a door to the ether between worlds. It is up to you to follow the path back to her before Shiket's soldiers find her."

I did not just swear away my mortality for Shiket to sweep in and grab Mische before I could get to her myself. The door on the opposite side of the room no longer was closed. Now, white smoke rolled across the wooden floor, fragments of lightning flashing within it.

A distant crash rang out. Acaeja did not flinch.

"That will be her," she said. "Go, Asar Voldari. You agreed to play a game with high stakes. You do not get to waste your time as the cards are drawn."

I begrudgingly had to admit that she was right about that.

I went to the door. Beyond it, ominous shadows danced, barely visible, in the mist. They painted the ghostly outlines of drifting landscapes—cities, mountains, the endless black of the sea, all rushing by like fish in a current. And if I stared hard enough, I could almost see it, smell it. The underworld. Morthryn's broken peaks. The Descent's rivers of blood.

"What is this?" I asked.

"Have you ever wondered how gods travel? This is the spira. The web that connects our world. Gods scale it as spiders do, independent of the physical rules of the mortal world."

Whatever was beyond the door definitely felt divine. So divine that I found it hard to imagine it would not rip me apart.

As if she heard my thoughts, Acaeja laughed softly. "You are no god. But you are no mortal, either. I can grant you the protection to traverse the spira now. The door will remain open only temporarily, but long enough for you to reenter once you retrieve your lover. If fate is on your side, you will survive it."

I placed my hand over my heart—right over the dull throb that felt like Mische. *Sounded* like her, whispering, *Faith is all we have.*

Perhaps she'd been right about that all along.

And then I jumped.

CHAPTER SEVEN

Mische

My heart hurt.

It was a strange pain, hard and tangible, unlike any I'd experienced in death. It felt like a more acute version of the anchor spell Asar had cast when we first embarked on our journey. It felt like a fragment of *life*.

I was lying in the dirt, stomach down. I sat up, then frowned down at myself, confused.

A line of bright red light speared straight through my chest. Confused, I tried to touch it, only to be rewarded by a shock and an onslaught of images—a gold reflection of a silhouetted face, a set of six wings, a goddess's bloody smile.

What the—?

"Move, girl, *move*!" Vincent's voice bellowed. I could barely see him through the cloudy mist as he rose unsteadily to his feet.

I opened my mouth to respond.

But then a blunt, metallic force hit me across the back of my head, sending me back to the dirt.

There was nothing pleasant about this pain. This felt like it had felt when Atroxus had set me on fire.

It took me a moment to realize the scream of agony was mine. I tried to scramble to my feet, but a harsh grip yanked me backward.

I struck the ground. Above me, the sky tore to ribbons.

A figure leaned over me. I saw my own terrified face distorted in gold.

And then nothing.

I DREAMED OF a dead firefinch, rot consuming its open chest.

"It's dirty," Saescha said.

I looked up at her. Blood covered her chest, too. She looked at me like I was cursed.

"Not worth saving," she said.

I turned back to the bird. She was wrong. It was a phoenix. It still had so much to do. But the maggots squirmed and writhed in its chest, and even though I poked it, it didn't move.

"See?" Saescha said. "What did I tell you?"

I WAS STANDING, my back to a wall, my arms splayed and wrists bound. Gods, they *burned*.

I opened my eyes, fighting heavy eyelids. My chin was lowered, head sagging. The first thing I saw was my own body, translucent and ghostly. It never got less unnerving to see it that way—but that wasn't what made me jolt with shock. No, that was the bright red thread going straight through my sternum, shimmering and not quite solid.

I'd thought that I had imagined it. But this was very real.

The only words my mind could conjure were, *What the fuck?*

I was chained up in ruins, atop a crooked stone tower, half collapsed. Perhaps one of the crumbling buildings that I had seen in the distance as I'd traveled with Vincent. A spiraling staircase of uneven stone rose up, up, up into the bloody mist, disappearing into the noxious smoke. If I stared hard enough into it, I could see the veil above and the two massive forms lording over it—a serpent and a lioness, bearing golden skulls upon shadowy bodies, trying and failing to herd a glut of wayward souls.

I recognized this place, where the Descent met the mortal realm.

I'd crossed this passage with Asar, Chandra, and Elias when we began our journey to the underworld. Even then, it had been clear that the veil was weak and the guardians overwhelmed.

Now?

It was heartbreaking. Half the lioness's skull face was missing, creating the illusion of a mouth open in perpetual wail. Their desperation was palpable as they attempted to herd the souls back to their rightful path, but they were overwhelmed. Countless lost souls spilled through gaping tears in the veil, falling to the underworld like drops of rain.

The grief was overwhelming. Death should be a refuge. But there was no peace in this.

It made my heart ache to think of Asar, the man who had lorded over Morthryn and the Descent with such empathetic care, witnessing this. Together, we had *tsk*ed over broken gates and cracked stone. Flesh wounds, all while a cancer consumed what was beneath.

At this thought, the thread pulsed again.

"I wonder," a voice said, "what it must feel like to be so important to someone."

The sound had more in common with the tinny scrape of metal than it did with a voice—as if age and gender and melodic cadence had been all stripped away, leaving behind only the barest echoes of humanity.

I turned my head to see a figure silhouetted against the shifting light of the tears in the sky. Their back was turned, and their body obscured by long, white robes.

I tried to jerk forward, only to be rewarded by terrible burning where my restraints met my flesh.

"Godlight. Even in death, you are still a fallen one. There is no resisting it." The figure lifted their hand—as if examining it. "The power of the White Pantheon is all-consuming," they said, with a thoughtfulness that seemed strangely mortal.

"What happened? Up there?" I jerked my chin to the broken sky and the guardians fighting their fruitless battle in the distance. Something, I knew, was so deeply wrong.

The figure paused. Still, they didn't turn. Their head cocked, too slowly and too smoothly. "You seem concerned."

I choked a laugh. "Concerned? *Look* at that! Of course I'm—"

Another spear of pain bolted through my chest, leaving me gasping. An onslaught of images, too quick to decipher, flashed by. But I didn't need to see them to *feel* it. *Hear* it. Notes of a song that sounded like him. The next words of a sentence we hadn't yet finished.

"Asar." The name was a sudden exhale. I didn't mean to say it out loud.

But at this, the figure swiftly turned.

"So this is what earns your compassion," they hissed. "Alarus's guardians of the dead. Wayward wraiths. Your fallen lover. *Fitting.*"

With a flash of billowing robes and gleaming light, they were right in front of me. I found myself staring at my own reflection, face distorted in smooth curved gold.

I almost didn't recognize myself. I looked like—like a wraith. But that shock faded quickly compared to the shock of what I was witnessing.

"You're a—a Sentinel."

My voice trembled slightly.

I'd never met one in person—most, of course, never did. But like anyone else, I'd seen them rendered in paintings and tapestries and church carvings. I had spent lots of time in temples of Shiket. Shiket and Atroxus had strong overlap in their followers. The Order of the Destined Dawn frequently dealt with nearby cults of Shiket in our missions spreading the light. But I had never liked Shiket's temples. They felt like monuments to violence, every wall painted with depictions of glorified battles and lined with stone visages of Sentinels, staring down in eternal judgment from beneath those smooth masks.

They paled in comparison to the real thing.

As I stared at this twisted version of myself in the warrior's mask, I felt as if I were seeing every ugly mark upon my soul, burning my skin like the sun.

"You can't be here," I blurted out. "A Sentinel can't be in the underworld."

Sentinels were creations and servants of the White Pantheon. The underworld was territory of Alarus, and by extension, Nyaxia. Gods of the White Pantheon could barely see into this territory, let alone send their soldiers into it.

A low ting rang out beneath the Sentinel's mask—a laugh that sounded like the toll of funeral bells. "What shall stop me?" They lifted a gauntlet-clad hand to the sky. "You hide behind rules that you yourself have so callously destroyed. Even now, your lover shreds the veil to reach you."

Their head canted slightly, and somehow, I could sense their stare at my chest—at the thread of light, running straight through their body and continuing on the other side. It now rose into the sky, disappearing into the morass of lost souls.

He was coming for me.

That stupid, reckless, foolish man was coming for me.

But of course he was. Asar was a man of his word. And for a terrible, selfish moment, a giddy elation bubbled up in my heart.

Just as quickly, it shattered, as the reality of my situation hit me.

I was *bait*. That's why I was here.

"Tell me, fallen one. What made you believe that you could outrun justice?" The Sentinel's tone was genuine, like they wanted a real answer. "You have murdered a god of the White Pantheon. You have shattered the sun in the sky, damning millions to the darkness." They tipped my chin up, and I bit back a yelp of pain. Their gold-clad fingertips were razor-sharp. "Most disgusting of all, you swallowed the innocence of the human girl who had committed herself so fully to the god you one day murdered. And yet, you believed you would escape punishment."

Their fingers tightened.

"This is the vilest thing about Nyaxia's fallen children," they said. "Your indulgent, lustful *egos*."

Tightened.

The pain became excruciating.

My eyes fell over the Sentinel's shoulder. To the pile of glowing chains on the cracked stone floor. Godlight blessed, clearly intended for Asar.

I had to get out of here. *Now*.

But I didn't know where Vincent was. I had no weapon. And

while I could hold my own well enough in a fight, I certainly wasn't about to win in hand-to-hand combat against a blessed warrior of the divine—least of all when I wasn't sure if my ghost body was even capable of hand-to-hand *anything*.

You are a Shadowborn, Iliae. You are surrounded by your greatest weapon. I could hear Asar's voice in my ear, could practically feel his breath. *Use it!*

I had a lot of logical qualms with this advice.

But hell, how many times had I said that all we had was faith?

"Release me."

I did my best impression of Asar's voice of compulsion. It was comically low, distorted slightly by the Sentinel's crushing grip on my cheeks, and I had to admit, not very intimidating.

The Sentinel stared at me.

"Release me," I said again, in an attempt that was louder, more gravelly, and no more effective.

The Sentinel laughed.

"As I said, that ego is—"

A streak of darkness collided with us.

My body went flying with the force of the impact. One of my restraints snapped. The other screamed against my skin as it took the whole of my weight.

I looked up to see a tangle of white robes and gold armor and smoke and a bronze skull in the shape of a—

My heart leapt.

"Luce!"

Locked in her battle with the Sentinel, she let out a sound between a yelp and a snarl. The Sentinel moved as only a divine entity could—too smooth, too fast, not obeying the laws of physics. Quickly, they rolled on top of Luce and pinned her, divine sword rising—

This time, I didn't think. I just acted.

I inhaled, flooding myself with the darkness of the underworld. The song was so innate. It reminded me of a piano's rhapsodic notes beneath perfect, scarred fingers.

And then I expelled it.

Darkness whipped from the corners of the room, surging in

serpentine tendrils. They slithered around the Sentinel's body, ripping them away from Luce, who seized upon this momentary opportunity to wriggle free.

While the Sentinel fought to get their bearings, Luce dove for me. She pushed something metal across the floor toward me.

A sword. *Asar's* sword—the one he had given me to defend myself in the Descent. An intricate bronze hilt of vines and thorns, with a blade that was broken at the tip, smooth elegance giving way to jagged brutality.

I had lost it somewhere in the Sanctum of Soul. How had she found this? How had she found *me*? I didn't have time to care. I just knew she was the best girl ever for doing it.

I grabbed the blade and swung it wildly at my remaining restraint as Luce once again threw herself at the Sentinel.

One strike had the golden chain cracking.

A blast of light. Luce let out a yelp of pain.

I hit the chain again—

—and fell to the stone ground as it gave way.

Immediately, I scrambled back to my feet. The shadows listened to me easily now. I spoke to them like it was my mother tongue. They clung to my blade as I struck, just as the Sentinel was about to bring their sword down upon Luce.

But the Sentinel was quick. Their counter hit me across the face before I could even see it coming.

I tumbled back against a pile of stone, nearly falling over the edge. A few loose bricks toppled into the mists as the Sentinel cornered me.

"They were right," they hissed. "You cannot be saved—"

The souleater barreled through them in a smear of teeth and shadow.

The Sentinel staggered backward, clutching one arm, as the wailing beast took off into the bleeding sky. Apparently even the divine were susceptible to the teeth of creatures of the dead, just as the dead were susceptible to the touch of the divine.

"Move!" a familiar voice bellowed. And I stepped out of the way just in time for a figure to lunge at the unsuspecting Sentinel, sending them plunging into the mists.

The sudden silence was deafening.

Vincent watched the Sentinel fall, long blond hair whipping out behind him. I slowly straightened. Gods, fear made you feel a whole lot more alive. I could've sworn a heartbeat pounded against my ribs.

Luce bounded to me, and—no, I wasn't imagining it, because this thing aching in my chest was *definitely* a heart.

I dropped to my knees and wrapped her in a fierce hug. A million questions warred for dominance—*how did you get here, where did you go, how did you know where to find me?*

But the only words that managed to make it to the surface were, "Luce, you are the *best best best* girl."

It hit me that the last time I had hugged her, it had been with Asar beside me. The three of us against the world. And here, with Luce in my arms, the reality of all that had happened sank in.

I had died.

No, *I had been killed.*

Atroxus, my god, my husband, the being I had once trusted more than anything on this plane or the next, had sent me to my death.

I had not grieved myself. Not until now, when it struck me just how much death would have taken from me. Luce. Asar. All other embraces like this one.

"I missed you so much," I whispered. I pulled away and looked into her skull-socket eyes. "Where did you come from? Are you looking for him?"

Somehow, amongst all this sadness, the thought of Asar being without Luce and Luce without Asar seemed saddest of all.

But Luce just nuzzled my cheek. As if to say: *You. I came for you.*

The tears threatened to start all over again.

"Enough theatrics." Vincent pulled me to my feet, earning a protective growl from Luce. He cast her a brief, confused glance, before deciding it wasn't worth wasting his time on questions and instead jabbing a finger to the sky.

"You don't have much time," he said. "You could have done this the easy way, but apparently you and your lover are insistent upon stumbling into the most difficult possible course. Somehow I'm not surprised."

To think I had been considering thanking him.

I followed his gesture. If I'd had blood, it definitely would have drained from my face at the sight.

The veil was in a truly pitiful state—the tears opening wider across it, red and black dripping through like rancid honey. The glut of souls had already thickened, and the guardians struggled to contain them. The serpent hissed steam as it wove frantically between the wraiths, while the lioness lifted great, razored paws. Souleaters flocked to the broken veil, drawn by the frenzy of waiting, fresh souls. Some slipped through the open holes.

Of course—because it could never be easy—the single winding staircase before us rose right through it all.

Droplets of red pitter-pattered across the stone before us, like rain picking up before a monsoon.

"You're not telling me I have to go through *that,* are you?" I said.

"You certainly are going through it. And you're doing it quickly, before your lover destroys what's left of the veil trying to get to you."

Again, that bittersweet pang in my chest.

I didn't deserve it. Deserve him.

"What about when I get there?" I said.

"If you make it to the veil, hopefully this determined beau of yours will pull you through to the mortal world, if he's half as competent as I pray he is."

"But after that. What do I do after that? What do I do if I make it back to the land of the living?"

"If? Girl, there is no *if.* You *will* make it back to the land of the living. You *will* finish what you began. You *will* help your lover ascend, and you *will* fix the underworld before it collapses and takes my kingdom with it. *There is no if.*"

The enormity of these tasks, listed off like they were nothing, left me swaying beneath the weight of insurmountable fear.

"But I don't know how," I managed.

It was not lost upon me just how pathetic this sounded.

"There is no map for the path we must walk in times like this," Vincent said. "But we must seize the chances that are given to us. I'll follow you to help, where I can, though there is only so much I can see up there."

"How?"

"You are one of us. Your connection to the dead remains, even if you walk in the mortal lands."

A low thunder shook the earth. Luce barked up at the sky. A fresh stab of pain struck my chest. He was right. The time to go was right now.

But gods help me, I was so afraid.

Afraid to take on another mission that I could so easily fail. Afraid to go to a world where I could see the consequences of what I had done. Afraid to look Asar in the eyes and see his pain.

Did I truly deserve life, or whatever shade of it I was about to reclaim, when so many more innocent souls now languished forever in this broken underworld?

Vincent grabbed my chin and wrenched my face toward him.

"You chose this battle. You chose it when you took your first steps into Morthryn, and you choose it again now. You set out to change the world. You set out to create a god. So do it. This is the time for conquering, Mische Iliae. *Go.*"

There was no way out but through.

I pressed my hand to my chest, to the burning thread of connection.

And then, with Luce at my heels, I began to climb.

CHAPTER EIGHT

Asar

I'd walked the boundaries between worlds. I traversed the Sanctums of the underworld itself. But traveling as gods did nearly ripped my soul to shreds. Three-dimensional space flattened to a single all-encompassing sensation. Hills, forests, seas. The grandest of human cities, the grimiest of slums, the towering curves of the House of Night and spires of the House of Shadow. The algae clinging to rocks at the bottomless depths of the sea and the frost blooming on petrified trees upon the desolate peaks of the highest mountains. A beat of a butterfly's wings and the movement of the greatest armies in the world. All of it, experienced in equal measure, all at once.

At first, I was certain that I wouldn't survive it—or worse, that I wouldn't be able to navigate it. But I clung to that thread of fate that Acaeja had drawn to Mische.

I centered myself around that moment, where life had met death.

That moment, when Shiket's sword had skewered Mische's heart. When she had slipped away from me.

The rest of the word no longer mattered. The layout of the spira became—not *logical,* not quite, but something close enough, like blood through veins. In my world, every heartbeat pushed me to her. I only had to let it take me there.

Ahead, among the misty clouds, a familiar place took shape—

spindly hallways like roots, a sea of translucent red, distant glowing dots so far away they looked like specks of dust floating in the dusky light. The Descent.

A door appeared before me, nearly whipping right by, and I threw myself at it.

I had come to love the underworld. Even in the imperfection of the decay I couldn't fight, I admired the beauty of its construction. A path to usher souls from one existence to the next, empathetic and kind in its orderly efficiency. I'd spent years leaning over broken gates and decaying spells, and every one of those imperfections had hurt a little to witness.

What met me now was a travesty.

The veil, once smooth as the frozen surface of a pond, now churned—a membrane barely holding back the clawing hands from beneath. Jagged tears ripped through the silvery surface in both directions, sending puffs of red spilling like blood into the sea. In some tears, souleaters—more twisted than I'd ever seen them—tried to push through. In others, disoriented souls of the recent dead tumbled to the abyss below.

The lioness and the serpent, steadfast in their missions, attempted to rule over the chaos. But it was too much even for these great, ancient beasts to control.

When my weight hit the stone, the steps collapsed beneath me. I fell, skidding across the veil, cold and fragile as ice.

With the impact, I felt her.

A brown eye threaded with gold. A smattering of freckles. The scent of burnt spice.

Close.

So close.

I pressed my hand to the thread at my heart, the dripping line of red flickering through the smooth glass of the veil. My gaze followed it up, through the smoke, to—

A gate. A closed gate, intended for the recent dead, kept by the guardians. But a gate nonetheless. My path via Morthryn's steps had been destroyed. This was my next best option.

I lunged for it.

But then a cold shadow fell over me.

I looked up to see a golden lion skull staring me down. The guardian's face had broken more since I'd last seen her. Now her jaw and much of her snout was missing. The ethereal outlines of her form were uneven and trembling, like smoke beneath an unforgiving winter breeze. Her chipped fangs were stained with the gruesome remnants of her losing battle.

Not long ago, even I had feared the guardians who stood at the veil. The most powerful of the creatures Alarus had created to lord over his kingdom.

Now, I felt nothing but frustration. "Let me pass."

The veil barely holds. The lioness's voice sounded like the groan of collapsing stone. *Another door cannot be opened, lest the rest of it fall.*

"It is already falling. I am Alarus's heir. I command you to let me pass."

The lioness cocked her head. *You smell like him. But you are not him.*

Another bolt of pain. Another puff of mist. I felt Mische closer, as if her breath was pressed up against the other side of the veil.

I'd shatter it to get to her. I didn't even care anymore.

"I am doing this to gain the power to repair what has been broken," I snapped. *"Let me pass."*

Let me pass. Let me pass.

My voice boomed with compulsion. But the guardian didn't move, ancient eyes seeing more than I willingly revealed.

You love the underworld, heir of death, she said. *But there is something else you love more, and I have already sacrificed my home to this tale once before.*

An ugly, humorless laugh bubbled up in my throat. I could feel Acaeja's gift, access to the spira to make our escape, fading second by second. Could feel my connection to Mische, painfully fragile, pulling tighter.

Threatening to snap.

I looked down at my hand against the veil. My scars consumed the left one, gleaming blue and purple and black—brighter than I'd ever seen them—drowning out the flickering ink of my Heir Mark. All those conflicting strokes, staining me a king and a sinner in equal measure.

I'd already given up the kingdom. Might as well embrace the sin.

I was Alarus's heir. I held his power in my veins. No one, not even a guardian, could stop me from using it.

"I'm sorry, guardian," I said. "I swear to you, it will be worth it."

I lifted my hands. Wielding Shadowborn power had always come to me so easily, like breathing. A limb to be manipulated, a sense to be drawn on. This was many times stronger. This was my kingdom. My magic.

The guardian let loose a roar of defiance as I tore the door open by force, and I did not care what went with it.

CHAPTER NINE

Mische

The stairs floated in the ether, slightly askew, threatening to break as I climbed—first with unsteady steps, and then, as they grew steeper, on my hands and knees as if scaling a ladder. Droplets of red now poured from above, stinging my cheeks. When I craned my neck to look up, I realized that they were fragments of the veil, cascading down like summer rain.

The higher I rose, the less the underworld adhered to the logic of mortal physics. Wraiths fell from above in slow motion, tumbling to the underworld. In the distance, I saw pieces of the Descent I now knew so well suspended as if in layers of gelatin—the mushrooms of Body, the rivers of Psyche, the poppy fields of Soul.

With every step, my body grew heavier. Supposedly, I had no muscles, no bones—but I had to fight for every movement, like I was pulling against a quickening tide. Somehow Luce, of course, managed to traverse the stairs like they were nothing, occasionally nudging me as if to say, *Keep up!*

A sudden blast of force from above nearly threw me from the path. I caught the edge of a cracked stone step just in time to dangle from the edge.

With Luce's help, I dragged myself back onto the steps. My orientation seemed to have shifted. The veil was closer, somehow, standing before me in smoky, shimmering mist. Beautiful. Terrifying.

And through it, a figure against the fog. I couldn't see his features, nothing but the faintest smear of a human-shaped silhouette, but I knew. I'd know him anywhere.

Asar looked, felt, just as he had in that ritual circle. Mortal, god, vampire, prince, exile. In some realities, all at once.

Jagged cracks reverberated through the veil where his hands met it. With every strike, the thread to my heart lurched.

Before he rips apart the veil to get to you, Vincent had said.

Gods help me, that was exactly what he was doing. Tearing apart the fragile integrity of what still stood.

My selfish longing, for him, for life, bloomed hot in my chest, nearly—*nearly*—as powerful as a heartbeat.

Luce yipped in excitement. *Hurry,* she seemed to say. *Quickly, quickly.*

"I'm trying," I managed to grunt out. With a hiss of exertion, I pulled myself up the final steps. The veil was so close, I could *smell* mortality.

But before I could reach it, a great, serpentine form slithered in front of me.

You cannot leave.

The guardian—the viper—circled me, silver scales over silver scales. Her gold skull face stared into mine. Her voice sounded impossibly immortal, more akin to the shifting of the natural world than any human words. Yet, I still felt the desperation in it.

I gave her the only answer I had. "I have to."

If you leave, it will not make you alive. And it will not be the last time you are here.

CRACK, as another flash of lightning spasmed across the veil. The serpent lurched, as if she felt it through her own bones. Wails echoed in the dark as more dead fell to nothingness.

Luce snarled, and out of the corner of my eye, I saw a flash of white and gold. The Sentinel I'd evaded streaked across the sky, searching through the glut of wraiths.

"I'm sorry," I said to the serpent. "I have to go *right now.*"

Go! Luce insisted.

On the other side of the veil, Asar's silhouette again lifted his hands.

I didn't have time to think.

I raised my blade, and I brought it down, and the veil shattered.

Death swallowed me in a wave.

I am lying in the dirt in the Sanctum of Soul—

Then let me burn—

Fire everywhere.

My hands reached out blindly. I managed to grab something solid, but I wasn't sure what. Luce? The thread?

Keep moving, a voice urged.

Saescha kneels at the edge of the water, her face doused in sun—

Shattering gold in the sky—

Rain. There was rain on my face.

Not rain.

Why are you crying, Asar?

I felt my last breath cave in my chest, leaving cold, still emptiness behind.

Another step. Another.

Shiket's blade opens my ribs, pierces my heart.

And at last, those final echoing words:

I will find you.

I will find you.

I will—

A hand folded around mine—long fingers, raised scars, strong and steadfast as a vow fulfilled.

And all I could do was cling to that grip, a single lifeline of faith, as I flung myself into the open arms of the abyss.

PART TWO

A Crown

INTERLUDE

The boy was, at first, a miserable student.

He was brought to a castle on an island, yet another addition to a king's collection of valuable, dangerous secrets. It was a dark place where dark things happened. Still, the boy did not think of his mentor as cruel. He was calm, even pleasant. He never raised voice nor hand. All his cruelties were doled out not with anger, but straightforward explanation. It made it easy to consider them lessons. Nothing less than deserved.

At first, the boy failed, and failed, and failed.

Weeks passed, months, a year. The boy underwent a rigorous curriculum of deprivation. He was deprived of blood, of air, of space, of freedom from pain or work or exhaustion—keys jammed into a lock to see which one clicked. The boy's only window to a world beyond were the books that he threw himself into in constant study. His mentor had been right, that very first night. The boy craved that knowledge, that power—that freedom—more than he had ever craved blood.

He was a passable, even talented, pupil. But still, his mentor frowned, disinterested, at every new skill.

"You are capable of more," he would say.

"Perhaps you would be better off in a common boarding school," he would tsk.

And sometimes, he would simply say nothing, and that was the worst of all.

When the conditions grew harder, the deprivation more intense, the boy welcomed it. He was happy to try more torturous keys if it meant finding the one that would unlock his potential.

In his rare moments of freedom, he would walk out into the marshy darkness.

The island reminded him, in some ways, of his old home. He could sit in the quiet, feel the souls of the living creatures around him, and find comfort in his own insignificance.

One night, he saw a starving stray dog stalk through the reeds. She was black, and long-legged, her body thin and bony. He could feel her hunger so acutely. It reminded him of his own.

That night, the boy offered the dog some food. The dog refused to take it until he had left, but the next night, he excitedly checked to see that it was gone. He came to visit the creature the next night, and the next. She was skittish and wary. For weeks, she refused his offering until he was gone. It took months before she would eat in front of him, and months more before she would take meat from his hand.

But the boy, even at his age, was patient. He built his friendship with the dog slowly, night by night. A year later, and she bounded up happily to see him when he came to visit. She knew his movements; he could have sworn she even knew his thoughts. It was the deepest friendship he had ever known. He feared that he would be disciplined for his pet. But though his mentor watched this bond grow, he never intervened.

It was the boy's older brother—a jealous heir to the throne—who did that.

The prince came to visit, as he occasionally did. As the years had passed, he had grown more antagonistic. The boy was, at first, a mild curiosity, but when he remained alive year after year, he became a threat.

One night, the boy found his pet dead at his brother's feet, her body mangled. She had not been given a clean death. And when the boy had wept, tears smudging blood, his brother had laughed.

Laughed.

It was the laughter—the indifference—that had enraged the boy most. He held his dead friend for a long time. And then, at last, something within him snapped.

He dragged the dog's mutilated corpse back up to his bedchamber, and he did not come out for days. He crafted a pile of ancient books. Carved glyphs into the floor, onto his skin, onto what remained of his friend. He followed a map constructed from countless tomes and filled in the missing pieces with instincts that came, unspoken, from his soul.

The first time the boy successfully stepped through the veil, he would barely remember it. Asking him to describe it would be like asking one to describe how to breathe. The muscles worked, the magic bowed, and the underworld opened for him.

And from it, his friend stepped through, bounding back into his arms.

The creature no longer resembled a dog. Her slender black face was now a bronze skull; her lithe body was now crafted from soft, translucent shadow. But he knew, in his heart, that it was her.

He had been so exhausted that when she leapt back into his arms, the two of them collapsed in the middle of his ritual circle.

When he awoke, his mentor stood over him.

The boy sat up. The dog wound around him protectively. The mentor took in the sight—the blood-spattered, ruined floor, the piled books, the glyphs, the ritual circle.

"Well," he said. "I suppose your father will be pleased."

The boy held his breath in the ensuing silence. It was not the approval of his father that he sought.

At last, his mentor spoke. "Remember that feeling, boy," he told him. "Remember the anger. This is what makes you great."

The boy's dog—no longer quite a dog—nuzzled his cheek. He wrapped his arms around her.

His mentor watched and smiled to himself in satisfaction. He had, at last, found a key.

A shame, he thought to himself, that it would be such a painful one.

CHAPTER TEN

Asar

Welcome home, Warden.

The words were hollow in the quiet. A breeze rustled my hair, and the way it caressed the stone reminded me of notes I'd etched into my fingertips. I drew in a breath, and with it the comforting, crisp shock of cold.

Then warmth—burnt spice and fresh flowers.

I forced my eyes open.

And there she was.

I was lying on a tile floor. Frosted moss crawled across it, settling into the cracks in the stone. Morthryn—my soul recognized it, even without looking. Because I couldn't look at anything but her.

Mische.

We lay facing each other, not touching, but nearly nose to nose. Her face was so close to mine that I could see every detail of its perfect shape. Her eyes were closed, dark lashes half-moons against her freckle-dusted cheeks. Her mouth, full and lush, was slightly parted. Her caramel curls quivered in the breeze, one wayward strand clinging to the tip of her nose.

She never knew how often I had watched her sleep during our travels in the Descent. How I had committed her features to memory. The slightly asymmetrical shape of her upper lip, thanks to a nearly invisible pockmark to the right of her bow. The pitch of her eyebrows, dark and expressive even in rest. The precise arrangement of her freckles, rich brown across her nose and cheeks. I now remembered, far too clearly, the first time I'd gotten the insatiable urge to lick them from her skin—wondering if they'd taste like cinnamon-tinted blood.

I didn't move. My chest ached, perhaps because I was holding my breath, lest it disrupt this precious gift.

When I was a child and I'd first come to Ryvenhaal, I would leave my glasses of blood untouched for days at a time. I was used to starvation. I'd never experienced such abundance, and I was convinced that it had to be some kind of illusion. If I never accepted it to be real, it would hurt less when it was taken away.

I felt like that child all over again now. The woman before me was every bit as integral to survival.

Her eyes opened.

Sun take me, those eyes. Rich and deep, complex, brown threaded with gold.

Welcome home, the breeze whispered again, and I was certain that it wasn't talking about Morthryn, it was talking about *her.*

Her gaze took me in, traveling over my face, seeing more than I ever had intended to show her.

"Hello, Warden," she whispered.

"Hello, Dawndrinker."

Still, neither of us moved.

"You came for me," she murmured.

"I told you that I would."

She blinked slowly. Her eyes gleamed now.

"I'm so sorry, Asar. About Atroxus, and—"

It seemed outrageous—laughable, even—that she was thinking about any of that right now.

"It doesn't matter."

"But you don't understand, I—"

"I do understand. It does not matter."

She'd told me that once, in our travels through the Descent. That my past didn't matter. She'd said it so simply. I didn't think she understood that it had changed my entire world to hear that.

Right now, it was truer than ever. Gods and missions and eternal nights. All of it, meaningless bullshit.

"All that matters," I said softly, "is this."

She blinked, and a tear struck a path of gleaming silver across the curve of her cheek.

"I couldn't let you go," she whispered.

And it was this, after everything, that tear that begged to be wiped away, that snapped the final straining threads of my self-control.

"Mische Iliae, Dawndrinker or Shadowborn, living or dead, I will *never* let you go."

Before I could stop myself, I pushed myself up and swept her into an embrace. My mouth found hers immediately, like a compass seeking north. She threw herself against me, and my arms fell around her, and for a blissful moment, I was complete in a way I had been seeking for my entire life.

For just a moment.

Because we quickly realized that something was very wrong.

I'd memorized the way Mische's body had felt against mine, and it had not been like this. She didn't feel quite as solid as she should, as if beneath her skin was only air instead of muscle and bone. And when my arms folded around her, they just kept going.

Right after this realization came the wave of pain—*burning,* like I was sticking my bare flesh into the harsh rays of the sun, and with it came an intense wave of exhaustion. Mische let out a small, wordless groan and sagged against me.

Despite the pain, I couldn't bring myself to let her go.

Not until a sharp bark rang out from behind me, and a barrage of familiar footfalls.

Luce.

The intensity of my gratefulness to see her was smothered beneath my dizzy fog. Luce grabbed my arm and jerked me back, sharply but in a way that also seemed oddly apologetic.

Mische slumped to the floor, lashes heavy.

The dream shattered, and reality poured in like cold water.

All the things I had not noticed in my haze of drunken gratefulness to be in Mische's presence hit me at once.

Our surroundings. The spira had brought us back to Morthryn, yes—halls I'd know anywhere, blind or deaf. But the state of them now shocked me. The floor was shattered, mirrored glass broken into jagged lightning cracks. The walls were coated in dusty gray, as if doused in ash. The bronze rafters were broken and reaching to the sky with twisted, desperate fingers. The ceiling sagged and swelled around bulging gouges.

Once, I would have been appalled by this. Morthryn had been my child.

Now, I dismissed it all in favor of Mische, who had slumped back down to the floor, limbs splayed.

I had brought Mische back into the mortal realm. But as Acaeja had warned me, I had not yet brought her back from death. Not truly.

She was a wraith.

Her form was transparent, bleeding out into the air around her as if the brilliant, beautiful colors of her soul were leaching into water. Her eyes were closed. She was not moving. I knew the dead well enough to recognize a withering soul when I saw one, but now, a process that normally took many years was happening right before my eyes, second by second.

"Asar . . ." Mische mumbled weakly.

Luce paced around us in tightening, anxious circles as I reached for Mische. When I touched her, I let out another involuntary hiss of pain. The smell of burning flesh permeated the air. I yanked my hands away to see smears of rotten purple on my skin.

The living could not touch a wraith.

This conclusion floated by, inconsequential, because Mische was fading.

Luce let out a high whine. *Help her, help her!*

"I'm trying," I snapped.

I had dragged Mische back to the mortal realm not through painstaking research and ritual and sorcery, but by sheer force. That had been an easy decision. I was willing to sacrifice what remained of the veil if it meant giving Mische a chance at life.

Only now did doubt fall over me. Maybe I had been too rough.

Maybe the shock of what I'd done was too much for her already weakening soul, and it would perish in the harshness of the mortal world.

For a moment, it was Ophelia lying on the floor before me, body ripped apart, caught between death and life.

I pushed away this fear violently.

Mische was not Ophelia. Mische was not fully dead. I could still feel my connection to her burning between us, spider-silk thin, but strong.

Luce's bony snout gave me a firm nudge between my shoulder blades, so rough it pushed me to the floor. My skin brushed Mische's as I caught myself. Even that brief touch came with a wave of blinding pain.

But Mische stirred slightly.

I froze. My eyes darted from Mische's rapidly disintegrating form to my own exposed forearm. My scars were brighter now. They'd always held hints of luminescent blue and purple, barely visible. Now, they glowed like my blood had been set aflame.

The blood of an almost-god.

Blood that was a bridge between the living and the dead.

I grabbed Mische's sword and opened a messy gash in my forearm. Blood gushed free. Mische's nostrils flared, eyelids fighting to open.

Wraiths were creatures that were neither living nor fully dead. They starved for life.

And I could give her that. No matter the expense.

I offered her my bleeding wrist. "Drink."

Even nearly unconscious, Mische—infuriating, stubborn Mische—shook her head.

"Hush," I hissed. "Let me help you."

I pushed my wound against her mouth.

Agony. My vision went white. I'd been touched by wraiths before—sometimes enough that it nearly killed me. This was far worse. Mische was no ordinary wraith. I'd yanked her up from the belly of the underworld itself.

But I forced myself to keep my arm there, and I let out a breath of relief as her teeth—still solid enough to bite—dug deep.

Luce tensed, as if already preparing to drag us apart.

I watched the muscles of Mische's throat flex as she swallowed mouthful after mouthful. She had such a beautiful throat. I had noticed it for the first time the night we had ended up in the bath together, and she'd held her hair back to wring it out. I could smell the blood right under the surface of her skin, and all I had wanted to do was press my mouth to it and taste.

"Drink," I murmured again, though the word was now slurred.

I watched my blood trickle down those elegant arcs of her throat, watched it drag her just a little closer to life, until I no longer saw anything at all.

CHAPTER ELEVEN

Mische

Asar's blood tasted like—gods, what word could describe it? He tasted like life.

No. This was darker, richer, deeper.

He tasted like death.

The world narrowed to my mouth on his skin, his blood on my tongue, and the next swallow.

It was so intrinsically *him*. And every gulp made me hungrier, made me want to crawl over him and press my skin to his, wrap around him until we were a single form. Made me want to—

Something tugged at my arm. I instinctively batted it away. But the grip didn't let up.

Stop.

I became aware of frantic barking.

Stop!

I dragged myself away, letting Asar's blood-slicked wrist fall limp to the floor.

I was briefly so disoriented that I couldn't make sense of where I was, or what I was, or whether any of this was real. Surely, anything that exquisite was a dream.

The hand I'd used to hold Asar's arm was covered with his blood. My skin was bare, and faintly translucent. I felt . . . not quite alive.

But I didn't feel dead, either.

What was I just—?

Then the events that brought me here crashed over me. I whirled to Asar. He slumped against the wall. Purple impressions of my fingertips, barely visible beneath the dark smear of his blood and the red ink of his Heir Mark, bloomed up his arm.

Dread clenched my heart.

I was a wraith. And Asar had not only let me touch him, but drink from him. *Idiot.*

"Bathtub," I choked out. "The magical bathtub. Where?"

Asar was teetering so far over the edge of consciousness that he didn't even have a snippy retort for that terminology, which terrified me.

Luce jabbed her snout toward the staircase.

I reached out to grab him, but Luce snapped at me, then bolted to the other side of the room, where she retrieved a tattered curtain.

Right.

"Smart girl." I wrapped the curtain around Asar's exposed skin, hoisted him against my shoulder, and with Luce's help, we started up the stairs.

MY BODY FELT lighter than it had, though not quite in a pleasant way, like I met too little resistance with every movement. Apparently, though, I was stronger now—or maybe that was just a side effect of the warmth of Asar's blood suffusing my body. Asar was barely conscious, and by the time we reached the top of the staircase, Luce and I were dragging limp weight.

We were on the main floor of Morthryn. The first time I'd walked this hall, the eerie beauty of it had stunned me. Now, it was nearly unrecognizable. The floor had once been smooth as the surface of an untouched pond, but now it was tinted with cloudy dark green, cracks running across it like spiderwebs. The bone-like rafters, once elegant and bronze, were rusted over and cracked, some broken at half their towering height. The ivy and roses that had covered the wall had long withered.

Luce led me to a door at the end of the hall, past countless darkened arches. My heart clenched when we nudged the door open and dragged Asar inside. Despite all the decay, Asar's room was still so painfully familiar. Yes, deep cracks ran through the walls, faded brocade paper curling from them like old bandages. But the furniture, homey and well-worn, had clearly been selected by someone who had decided long ago exactly what he liked and had no desire to change anything about it since. A bed perfectly square to the wall, a faded green woven carpet, a small upright piano with ivory keys that, I knew, were worn with use.

I wanted to curl up in the imprint of his body on the bed. Press my fingertips to the scuffed piano keys. Roll myself in all these mundane marks of a life lived.

We dragged Asar through the bedchamber into the adjoining washroom. It was a near-identical twin to the one I'd brought him to the last time I had to save Asar's life with a magical bathtub. The claw-footed tub was already waiting, full of shimmering silver liquid.

At this sight, a powerful wave of love overtook me. Morthryn. Bless her.

I managed to free one hand to caress the doorframe. "Thank you, old girl," I murmured, and I was certain that Morthryn creaked in response.

With Luce's help, I hoisted Asar over the rim. Flecks of the not-water splashed over me. I gasped and lurched back. The sensation reminded me of the burns from Atroxus's flames.

But that made sense. It was a potion that washed away death.

Still, I couldn't bring myself to pull too far away from Asar. I drew my knees up and pressed my back against a dry section of the tub. Asar was not moving at all, his face pressed to the copper edge, a furrow between his brows. The urge to crawl in with him as I had that night, wrap myself in his arms, was so acute it actually hurt.

He groaned, fighting to open his eyes. His right hand, the unscarred one, hung over the rim, fingers twitching toward mine.

I so desperately wanted to close that space. Instead, I pressed my own fingertips to the tub, just beneath his dangling hand. Not quite touching, but creating the illusion of it.

It wasn't enough.

LUCE CURLED UP beside me, and I kept my hand there, as near to Asar's as I could get, as minutes, then hours, passed. I rested my other hand on Luce's ears, grateful that I could, at least, touch her—she was just as dead as me.

"Mische."

Asar's voice was so weak that my name was little more than a groan. I jerked upright to see his profile against the rim as he slowly rearranged himself. A sliver of dark brown through his heavy-lidded right eye, and a sliver of glowing silver from his left.

I forced a smile. "This seem familiar?"

"This is nothing like that." His voice was low and raspy. "I recall that you were in here with me that time. It was the most memorable part."

My grin wavered. Something about the weak, barely there tilt at the corner of Asar's mouth made my heart—or whatever was in my chest now—ache.

I scooted away from a cascade of liquid as Asar stood up. Luce whined an apprehensive warning, and Asar shot her an affectionate, reassuring glance.

He stepped out of the tub, then lowered in front of me.

For a moment, he stared.

We just stared at each other.

He looked . . . different. His left eye shone brighter now, pouring streaks of silver out into the shadows. His scars seemed deeper, too, and their shade had changed a little, luminescent purple and blue and silver shifting within them as if to reveal glimpses of his divinity. His Heir Marks flickered as they had in the Descent, the threads of red and white ink trembling like light through the trees—but I wasn't sure if I imagined that they were bigger than they had been, now extending up past his elbows and disappearing beneath rolled-up sleeves.

His clothes were simple and dirty, and not the same ones he'd been wearing in the Descent. His shirt was white, and so thin that the wet cling revealed the full expanse of his scars glowing beneath it. It revealed, too, fresh wounds—three long, jagged burns clawing across his right shoulder and over his chest, a scabbing wound on his throat over his chin, a smattering of bruises, and countless others in various stages of healing. He was thinner, and his eyes were hollower in a way that hinted at all the nauseating things he had endured at the hands of the gods.

Yet, despite all these marks of weakness, a strange power hummed its ethereal melody under the surface of his flesh. An undeniable reminder of his almost-divinity.

But the way he looked at me was the way my friend, my lover, had. His eyes were not those of a god or a king. They were Asar's. *My* Asar's.

My eyes burned. It felt a bit unfair that I didn't breathe, but I still gods damn cried. All I wanted to do, actually, was cry. Happy tears. Sad tears. I wasn't even sure anymore.

I wiped my eyes and held out my fingertips.

"Explain this! I'm dead and I still have to deal with this?"

He gave me a soft smile. "Fitting, isn't it, that the messy parts of mortality are the last to go." He unrolled his sleeve and carefully wiped my tears away with the fabric. "Let them come. And then we'll talk."

"We have so much to do," I said, even as I kept crying and crying.

But Asar dabbed my tears one by one. "Let them come."

CHAPTER TWELVE

Asar

Mische's tears came for a long time. I was so grateful for those tears, paint strokes of mortality all over the constellation of her freckles. Yes, she was still slightly transparent, though if you looked quickly you might not notice it. And yes, I could smell the death on her—the true nature of what she was. But those tears, and the way she scrunched up her entire perfect face around them, were all life.

Eventually, we decided that we'd had enough of crouching on the washroom floor. When I stood, I was so dizzy that I almost ended up right back on the ground, had Luce not steadied me.

Mische frowned. "You should stay in there longer."

I waved this idea away, even though I was secretly unnerved by just how much her touch had taken from me.

I turned back to look at her and couldn't help but pause.

Mische's clothes, apparently, had not made it through the veil with her. The exceptional details of her form that had been hidden when we were curled up on the floor now were on full display—the curve of her waist, the full swell of her breasts, the shadow of soft hair where her thighs met. Over her shoulder, the open door to my bed-chamber taunted me with just how easy it could be in another world to carry her to that bed, slide her thighs open, and worship there for the next few hours, days, or weeks. Show her just how grateful I was to have her back in the way my words failed to.

Even now, through the haze of my splitting headache and the residual burn of her touch, I still thought:

Hell, might be worth it.

When I put my less honorable thoughts aside, I noted the slight ghostly sheen to her skin. She looked much more solid now than she had before I gave her my blood, but I could still make out the outlines of the opposite wall through her form, and there was a shimmering gray pallor to the way light fell—or rather, didn't fall—across her flesh.

Still, there was something comfortingly mortal about the faint flush across Mische's cheeks.

"I should probably find some clothes," she said.

Should wasn't the word I would personally use, but I nodded as I turned to the bedchamber. The stain of death on Mische's skin was a visceral reminder. I had no time to waste.

"Clothes," I said, "and then I believe we have a lot to discuss."

MORTHRYN, EVEN IN its pitiful state, still kept its liking to Mische. We found clothing in my dresser that perfectly fit her—a shirt, trousers, jacket, and pair of boots that I was certain I had never put there. As Mische dressed and I changed into dry clothes, we talked.

Mische told stories the way a painter flung colors across the canvas—with grand, artistic gusto, expressions bright, hands flying, voice rising and falling like a piano's melody. She told me of her time in the underworld, of her help from the Nightborn king—that, even I couldn't make sense of—and her escape. I couldn't help but press my palm to Morthryn's swollen, crooked floorboards as she described the degree of the underworld's disrepair, like a parent soothing a sick child.

My storytelling was far duller, direct and factual. Still, Mische's eyes grew wider and wider as I spoke. I barely made it through a sentence without her peppering me with questions, some of which I found myself evading.

I told her the details of the mission Acaeja had given me, and the task we would have to accomplish. But I couldn't bring myself to share the specifics of what I had given up to make that deal. I could already feel her guilt, even though she left it unspoken. She didn't need to carry this, too.

When we were done, even Mische was quiet. The full weight of what we were about to do settled over us both. Saying it aloud made it feel more real. And more ridiculous.

I watched Mische's thoughtful brow lower over her eyes, then rise as her gaze slipped to me. A chill ran up my spine at the way she looked at me. Like she was taking me apart piece by piece, with a shadow of concern in the things she saw between them.

"Do you feel different?" she murmured.

Yes, was the simple answer. But I wasn't sure how. Whatever power my divinity gave me loomed just at the corner of my eye, and I couldn't capture the shape of it. And here, next to Mische, I felt more mortal than I ever had and, at the same time, more acutely aware of all that had changed.

"I feel more myself now that I'm here," I said. True in all the ways that counted.

A smile tugged at her cheeks. As she perched on the edge of the bed, I watched the way the blankets shifted beneath her weight. The indentation wasn't as defined as it should have been, like her form didn't quite obey the laws of the physical world.

"And you, Iliae? How do you feel?"

Her expression dimmed. It took a moment before the smile, soft and lovely as the sunrise, returned.

"I feel more myself now that I'm here," she said.

Of course, we understood each other's half lies.

One more item lay in the bottom of the open dresser drawer that had provided Mische's clothes. I reached in and closed my hand around leather.

"For you, I assume," I said, and handed it to her.

Black gloves, extending all the way to the elbow, in just Mische's size.

"It's probably for the best," I said. "To hide your . . . state."

She sighed—a wonderfully alive affectation—and put them on. I watched the beautiful expanse of her last visible skin disappear beneath worn leather.

"I used to wear gloves just like these," she said. "To hide the burns. But now . . ."

Her voice trailed off. But I knew what she meant: *I wish I didn't have to.*

I stood and extended my hand to her. After a brief hesitation, her fingers folded around mine, now safely concealed in fabric.

A poor substitute for skin. But it was something.

"One benefit," I said.

Mische's mouth curled. "I *guess* that counts."

Mische, Luce, and I walked the halls of Morthryn. Mische protested when she saw how slowly I was moving—the effects of her touch still lingered, frustratingly—but we didn't have time to sit around.

Morthryn's pitiful state twisted like a blade in my gut. My old apartment was exactly as I had left it so long ago, and yet, so different, bowing under the weight of Morthryn's accelerated decay. It was nothing special by the measure of the Shadowborn castle. It had been, after all, my exile. But it had also been my home. It was *still* my home.

I had met Esme for the first time in this hall, a wraith who had refused to move on to the Descent. She had been so transparent she'd been barely visible in the shadows, but still had delighted in showing me all Morthryn's secrets.

Back then, I'd been hanging on to life by a single fraying thread of will. The thought of clinging to it for centuries longer seemed so exhausting that I was on the cusp of severing it myself.

But Esme would have no sulking.

"They may tell you this place is a prison," she had told me, "but they only call it a cage because their minds are too small to see what it truly is."

"And what is that?" I'd replied, unconvinced.

She had spread out her arms. "It is a bridge to endless possibilities. It is the gate to the kingdom of the dead. It is a refuge for those who have nothing else. And perhaps, my disgraced prince, it can be a refuge for you, too, if you allow it to be."

I hadn't believed her then. But her words had given me enough purpose to get through the next night, and the next. I began to hear the whispers in the walls. And then the next thing I knew, centuries had passed and Morthryn had become not just my ward, but my companion.

It dawned on me only now that there had been many reasons why that had been true, even if I didn't know it at the time. Alarus's blood ran in my veins. No wonder that his home became mine, too.

Now, the hallways were silent.

"How did it get so . . . bad? So quickly?" Mische was whispering, even though we were the only ones here.

"Morthryn is a gate to the underworld. Whatever decay is accelerating down there would be felt here, too." I paused at one of the arches. The glyphs along its metal were dull, no longer glowing, and the eye at its apex covered in dust. No more inmates.

Morthryn never should have been a prison—it had been built thousands of years ago as a temple to Alarus and a bridge to the underworld. It was grotesque to use it as a place to dump criminals when it should have been treated with reverence. But the House of Shadow took great pride in the infamy of their torturous jail. If Morthryn had been emptied, that meant that they'd swiftly had to turn their focus elsewhere.

We reached my office doors. A deep gouge ran through the mahogany, slicing straight through the eye of Alarus at their center. I pushed them open.

"Holy fucking gods," Mische gasped.

My study had been ransacked. The shelves had been picked over, labels ripped and glass cases smashed, discarded artifacts scattered across the tile floor. Precious pieces of magical history had been stripped like they were common jewels. When I stepped forward, I heard a *clink* beneath my boot and looked down to see a broken frame. A piece of scripture that was more than four thousand years old, from the priests of Alarus back before Nyaxia had even been born.

It was downright desecration.

"Asar. Look."

The note of fear in Mische's voice made me turn. She stood in front of the windows. An ocean breeze swept her hair back. The glass had shattered, revealing a star-dotted night sky framed by jagged glistening shards. The moon was a dark circle against the velvet night.

I'd memorized this view over thousands of nights sitting in this office. The bay, peaceful under silver moonlight. The pointed spires of the capital skyline in the distance, lit up with the bustling glow of the city. The lush rolling hills and flourishing foliage of the gardens below.

At first, through my pounding headache, I couldn't make out what I was looking at. It looked as if the hills that I knew so well had become deserts, dusty sand rippling across them.

And then I realized: it was leaves.

Dry, crumpled leaves that had died of starvation waiting for a sun that never rose, leaving knotted, bare branches reaching toward the empty sky. All while the city was brighter than I'd ever witnessed it, glowing crimson as if every single distant stained-glass window was alight. And the bay—

The bay was full of warships.

Black ships bearing the deep green flags of the House of Shadow. And then, less familiar, white sails upon long, elegant boats, each bearing the red visage of a weeping lady.

The armada of the House of Blood.

"Shit," Mische whispered.

The consequences of an eternal night. Withering plants. An endless black sky. And a vampire empire ready to seize the opportunity they'd been given.

The gods had spoken of it. But seeing it made it real.

My mind bounced from question to question, building a web of unnerving potential answers. If the House of Blood was here, that meant that things were dire enough that Egrette was willing to put aside centuries of bad blood—but why, then, was there no House of Night? Was this Nyaxia's order? And if so, what did that mean for us?

"At least this will mean Nyaxia will, hopefully, be too distracted to pay too much attention to us," I said.

But Mische just stared into the sky. There was nothing, I had learned, that could silence her quite like when she felt that she had too much to say.

"You had better not be regretting it, Mische," I said.

Still, she said nothing.

"I saw it, when everything else had faded," I said. "You, driving that arrow into Atroxus's throat. It was more beautiful than any part of death or life I'd ever witnessed. The way you looked seizing fate with your bare hands. You saved the lives of millions that night. Atroxus deserved his end, god or not. Never regret giving it to him. *Never.*" I couldn't stop the hint of cold hatred from seeping into my voice. Because I wasn't thinking of Atroxus's attempted massacre of the vampire race. I was thinking about an eight-year-old Mische on her knees before him.

Seemed like proper punishment to me. Even if I would have preferred it to be a bit slower.

Mische gave me a weak, unconvinced smile. Then she turned to the ransacked office.

"You think that Nyaxia will be looking for us, too? I can't imagine that she's exactly going to be happy once she realizes that you're attempting to ascend."

I thought back to my last encounter with Nyaxia, with Mische's charred body in my arms. "No, I'd imagine not."

"At least being in Nyaxia's territory means the White Pantheon won't be coming for us anytime soon."

The gods of the White Pantheon had limited visibility into Nyaxia's territory, and never crossed into it. Still, this seemed only a small comfort. We had once thought that about the underworld, too, and Mische had still been attacked by a divine soldier there. Rules couldn't protect us if they were now being rewritten.

I peered out the window again, into the night sky. A faint red cast glowed from behind the moon, like the ring of an eclipse. My brow furrowed. At first I thought I had imagined it. Even now, it was so faint that it could be a trick of the eye.

But if it wasn't . . . we had just gotten very, very lucky.

"What?" Mische said, craning her neck to follow my gaze. "You're making that face."

I was going to regret asking. "That face?"

"The *decoding magical complexities* face. Like this." She lowered her brows over narrowed eyes and stroked her chin.

I had been right. I did regret asking. Still, I tried very hard to look offended and not amused. "I don't—never mind." I peered out at the moon and the pink cast behind it. "The mask is in the House of Shadow, and if I'm right about what I'm looking at, we have our opportunity to get it soon. If we can avoid attracting Nyaxia's attention until then."

"It's in the House of Shadow?"

"It's—"

A wave of dizziness passed over me, and I found myself leaning back against a desk not entirely of my own accord. One of the rotten wooden legs gave out, and I almost stumbled.

Mische caught my shoulder as I readjusted my weight.

"You need to rest here until you've recovered."

"No. I need to find my notes." I nudged a pile of tattered parchment with my boot. Heartbreaking. "Or what's left of them. I can explain as we work. We have no time to waste."

"I mean this in a nice way, but I don't think you're very useful like this."

"There's no nice way to call me useless, Dawndrinker."

"Only *temporarily* useless, Warden."

I let out a sigh of frustration.

Luce trotted up to Mische, holding a sword—the sword Mische had been carrying when I pulled her through the veil, which must have been abandoned downstairs.

"I never thought I'd see this again." I took the blade from Luce, turning it around in my hands. The weapon seemed to vibrate against my skin, familiar and unfamiliar all at once. It looked the same as it had when I had wielded it, and yet, something now seemed undeniably different. As if its magic now sang in a different key.

"It went to the underworld and back with you," I murmured. "Interesting."

I held it out to Mische, who shook her head. "It's yours."

"I think it stopped being mine a long time ago."

"I don't need a sword anyway. I can use my—" She held out her hands and wiggled her fingers in what I could only imagine was a comically exaggerated pantomime of either a hunting wolf or a very handsy drunk.

"Pray tell, what is that supposed to be?"

"My death touch," she said, as if it were obvious.

It was a genuine struggle not to laugh.

"You absolutely will not. We cannot let anyone see what you are. Especially not in the House of Shadow." I knew too well what happened to those deemed *useful and unusual* in the House of Shadow. The thought of Mische, in a tiny dark room, strung up along with all of Gideon's other—

I slammed the door against that image. I reached for the hood on Mische's jacket and raised it, careful not to touch her skin. Beneath the hood, she looked relatively normal. The sheen of death was easy to miss unless one looked very, very closely. But just in case, I also grabbed a pen from the desk and scratched a series of small glyphs into the edge of the fabric.

An illusion, to make her look more . . . alive. Gideon had specialized in the art of illusions, and though it had never been my strong suit, he had taught me well. It wasn't perfect, but it would suffice for casual glances.

"An additional precaution," I said. "And take the sword. Not a debate."

I handed it to her, and she reluctantly took it.

"There's a drawer at the bottom of the farthest bookcase in the other study." I gestured to the door. "Second to the ground. Gather everything in it and bring it back here."

Mische nodded, then disappeared through the door. I sagged into a chair, which groaned under my weight.

"Sun take me," I muttered. "Divinity isn't all it's said to be."

Luce wound around my legs. My hand fell to the top of her head, relishing the familiar comfort of the shape of it. She made a sound that resembled a purr.

I suppressed a smile. "Well, aren't you sentimental."

She gave me an accusatory glance.

"Me?" I said. "Never. I knew you'd turn up when it pleased you."

She let out a sniff that seemed to say, *You missed me, and I know it.*

My chest tightened. I stroked her shadowy body, scratching at the back of her neck. "Perhaps a little. Thank you, Luce." I cast a glance to the door. "And thank you for watching over her."

I rubbed her ears, and she let out a groan of pleasure. Then she sniffed me again.

"Do I seem different to you?" I asked.

She seemed to consider this. As it so often was, her answer was somehow obvious:

I smell new you. But I smell old you, too, and I prefer it.

My eyes narrowed. "Judgmental coming from—"

But then a sudden awareness made me jolt upright. I sensed a presence here, in Morthryn's halls. No, worse, multiple. Wraiths? Not wraiths. They were—

A crash rang out down the hall. A strangled half cry.

Mische.

Luce felt it too. She bolted through the door. I followed—half stumbling—through the study. Out in the hall, I saw—

Mische.

And a sword through her shoulder.

Everything froze. I took in the scene before me.

A Shadowborn soldier stood before Mische, knuckles white around his weapon, clearly caught off guard. More footsteps echoed from down the halls, both in front of us and behind, now rapidly approaching.

But all I saw was that blade.

"Get off of her."

The words shook with compulsion. But though I could feel my magic so close, the well deeper than it had ever been, in my weakness I couldn't break through to access it.

Mische let out a yelp as the soldier spun around to face me, pulling the blade free. There was no blood. The steel had simply passed right through her. She was, after all, a wraith.

But this logic meant nothing to me now.

The soldier's eyes landed on me and widened. He had not recognized Mische, but he certainly recognized me.

He gasped, "You're supposed to be—"

But he didn't get the rest out before I lunged for him. The shadows at the corners of the room quivered. The soldier's mind stood before me, as easy to snap as delicate, frost-brittle branches.

And yet, I couldn't quite—

Mische shouted in warning, "Asar!"

Luce lunged for the soldier.

But now a whole slew of them poured into the room, alerted by the commotion. All bore the green uniforms of the Shadowborn guard.

I reached again for my magic, that tantalizingly deep well, as Mische's blade was knocked from her grasp and Luce was smothered beneath three soldiers.

As a familiar presence rose up behind me.

As tendrils of darkness looped around, and around, and around my throat, and yanked.

My back hit the ground, and a familiar face looked down at me.

"What the *fuck* are you doing here?" Elias said.

Mische leapt at him with a grunt of exertion.

Mische, don't—! I shouted into her mind.

Too late.

Because Elias whipped around with his sword raised—his sword that I myself had enchanted for our journey through the Descent, to make it more effective against wraiths.

And his strike sent Mische to the ground.

I fought toward her. I was so, *so* close. Any other night, and I could have taken them all down with me. But the residual weakness of Mische's touch still drained me. The power was there, and it was strong enough, and I just couldn't reach it.

More footfalls. More soldiers. Someone shouted a command I didn't hear. I watched Mische roll over, eyes closed, hands over her stomach.

And it was the last thing I saw when I plunged into darkness.

CHAPTER THIRTEEN

Mische

Vincent looked disappointed in me. The expression made me even more sympathetic to Oraya's complexes. It really dug right into your chest.

"I didn't expect you to come this close to death again this quickly," he said.

I tried to rub my eyes, but I had no body. It was as if we were suspended in intangible darkness.

"How are you—"

"I told you I would follow you. And you've drifted closer to death now." He cocked his head, peering into the haze. "I cannot see everything, but what I do see already looks . . . suboptimal."

He made the word *suboptimal* feel like a grave personal insult.

"We're just getting started," I said defensively.

But he raised a hand, unmoved by excuses.

"You cannot let the Shadowborn queen end your journey here. And she will, if you make the wrong move. Or, you can use her to secure a path directly to what you need most."

"Asar is the rightful king of the House of Shadow," I said. "He has a Mark. Everyone can see it."

"All the more reason for her to execute him. But you're alive now because she would prefer to do it before the subjects she's failing to control. She is a woman, after all, and the Shadowborn have never been fond of that quality in a ruler. You will need access to the House of Shadow to complete your task. Use the scant tools you have at your disposal."

"Tools?" I repeated. I was finding it hard to think.

Vincent looked frustrated. "You carry a piece of the god of death in you. And your lover has more power than he has even begun to understand. Use it." He leaned closer. "Stop thinking like an acolyte and start thinking like a vampire."

MY EYES OPENED.

A pack of predators stared at me.

More than I could count—Shadowborn and Bloodborn. Some of the Shadowborn were dressed in court finery, bosoms heaving over velvet corsets and muscles highlighted in tailored brocade. Others donned the formal uniforms of the Shadowborn military—long green leather jackets, the Shadowborn crest staring from their lapels. The Bloodborn lingered together at the edges of the room, their eyes hungrier, their forms leaner, clad in their sharply tailored uniforms of white and red. Elias stood in front of me, flanked by guards.

I was in the ballroom of the Shadowborn castle, my hands bound. A sea of vicious finery spread out before me. Columns of black metal and gleaming bronze framed the room, painstakingly crafted in the likeness of thorny vines. Windows of intricate stained glass depicted the most brutal legends from Shadowborn history. A blade-sharp breeze tugged at my jacket, and I noticed that the windows along the far wall had all been removed and the velvet curtains ripped out—a triumphant victory over the sun that would never rise.

Twists of darkness writhed at the edges of my vision, and at first, I thought they were an aftereffect of my unconsciousness. But when I scanned the crowd, I saw the shadows intermingled with the guests, too. They seemed . . . oddly humanoid.

But that was low on my list of concerns right now.

My hood was still, thankfully, secure—though I didn't know how easy it would be to tell what I was, if someone looked closely enough.

I tilted my head and breathed a too-quick sigh of relief to see Asar beside me.

His wrists were bound too, and a writhing blindfold of shadow wrapped around the top half of his face, leaving only the strong profile of his nose and chin uncovered. Advanced Shadowborn magic—a level of security that I, apparently, didn't warrant. He stood, but his posture was slightly slumped. He wasn't conscious, not truly.

Under Asar's tutelage in the Descent, I'd learned how to wield my Shadowborn power. But I'd never mastered the art of mind speak. Still, now, I had no choice but to try.

Asar! I prodded. But I got no response.

"What an intriguing surprise," a woman purred.

Oh gods, I knew that voice. I slowly faced forward.

I'd been in this room once before, presented as a gift to Raoul on his birthnight, only for Asar to save me just before execution. Now, I was being presented to his daughter—Asar's half sister, and my former would-be executioner, Egrette.

She sat upon the Shadowborn throne, a chair of black steel and bronze roses. The back of it extended up against the windows, all the way to the House of Shadow crest rendered in stained glass. She wore a gown of green and gold. Emerald fabric wrapped around her waist and draped over her bust. Her long chestnut hair cascaded in smooth waves over her shoulders, the Shadowborn crown perched atop it.

Several figures were seated at a table beside the dais—clearly, an honored position. A beautiful dark-haired woman I recognized as Egrette's mother, several Shadowborn nobles in unmistakably fine clothing, and—

At this, I blinked hard in confusion.

A fair-haired man wearing a white suit, a black cigarillo between his fingers, giving me a curious smirk. Septimus, prince of the House of Blood. The very same man who had once attempted to help Raihn and Oraya's rivals overthrow the House of Night.

He looked just as surprised to see me as I was to see him, though he seemed much more amused about it. He leaned back in his chair with lazy curiosity as Egrette smiled at us and descended the dais steps.

"Excellent work, General," she said. "You have returned my long-lost brother to us for his final justice."

Behind me, incessant barking rose to a pitch. Luce. "Will someone shut that thing up?" a guard snapped. I tried to turn around, only for a blunt impact to force my head forward again. I ducked my chin, shying away from it—not because of the pain, which I barely felt, but because one wayward touch would expose what I was.

My mind worked quickly.

Egrette stood before Asar, who was still motionless. I recognized a performance when I saw one, even one this good. Every movement, from the delicate step down the dais to the predatory twitches of her expression, was designed to exude authority. But her lingering stare at Asar's hands was all genuine—at the lines of ink over them, tangling with his scars. His Heir Mark. Though the Shadowborn style of dress usually commanded long sleeves, Egrette's had been shortened, revealing red ink on her hands and forearms, too.

Shit. So it was as we had feared, when in the Descent—Egrette had an Heir Mark too, just as Asar did. But how? We had theorized that if she did have one, it would be because Asar was closer to death than life. But he was in the land of the living now. How could the House of Shadow end up with two simultaneous Heirs?

Even more perplexing, up close, the difference between the two Marks was stark. Both adorned their hands and forearms in red ink—and some white, in Asar's case—but the styles contrasted wildly. Egrette's Mark was delicate, swirls and curves that evoked the painterly strokes of shadow magic or the elegance of Shadowborn architecture. Meanwhile, Asar's was harsher, more organic, like roots or lightning—a complement to his scars—and while Egrette's ended in whorls around her long fingers, Asar's bore the eye of Alarus on the backs of both his hands.

Egrette's, I also noticed, didn't flicker as Asar's did.

Still, she did not seem to find this much of a comfort. I felt her uneasiness like ripples upon the surface of a pond. Just as Vincent said, Asar's reappearance was both a threat and an opportunity to show off her power to her new, bloodthirsty court.

She spread her arms. "The Wraith Warden," she boomed. "Exiled necromancer, traitor, and deserter of Nyaxia herself. We have been searching for him for months, and now, he is here." She turned to her spectators, bearing bloody fangs. "Perfect timing, as we all gather at the call of our Dark Mother. She has given us a mission to spread her vengeance to all that have defied her. How appropriate, to start that mission by punishing a traitor. Shall we show him what happens to those who defy the crown?"

Hisses of approval rose from the blood-drunk nobles. I had no doubts that Egrette had used Asar's absence to paint him a traitor.

Elias held out a jeweled dagger, and Egrette took it with all the grace of a debutante accepting the hand of a suitor, before whirling back to Asar.

Oh no, this was not good.

Blood still soaked through Asar's jacket where Elias had stabbed him—still beaded at the mark my teeth had left in his wrist. If Egrette wanted to kill Asar now, when he was still suffering from the weakness of my feeding, she probably could—it was probably the *only* time she could. Perhaps even she sensed that.

I needed Asar to be the most terrifying version of himself. I needed him to be the version of himself that I had seen through the veil. More god than mortal.

I needed him to use the power that even he didn't understand.

And I needed him to do it *now*.

Think like a vampire, Vincent had said. But he didn't know me at all. This wasn't thinking like a vampire. This was thinking like an acolyte. Because I knew how to get Asar to do what I needed him to, and it meant leveraging the same tool I'd once wielded to force Raihn to seize his own potential, too: myself.

"Stop!" I screeched. "Don't hurt him!"

I let my voice crack with frantic fear. It was a performance uncomfortably close to the truth.

Hundreds of vampire stares shifted to me, and I tried not to shrink under them. I prayed that the hood and Asar's spell of illusion would hold up. But at least I was insignificant. No one here would be looking too closely at me, other than to laugh at the pawn in Asar's story.

Egrette paused. I felt her magic prodding at me like a carrion bird picking at a carcass, and I opened my mental doors just wide enough to show her what I felt for Asar. It didn't have to be a performance. That was real, and it offered Egrette something interesting: the opportunity for greater cruelty.

"Ah, I remember you," she said. "You were just a broken little bird when I last saw you. How surprising that you survived his journey."

Oh, if only she knew.

"Don't hurt him," I begged. "P-please, don't hurt him. I wanted to run away but h-h-he insisted on coming back—"

"Oh, my." She smirked at the crowd as if sharing an inside joke. "What is this? A love story?"

The nobles chuckled. Even the Bloodborn, who had seemed disinterested, glanced at each other in amusement. All but Septimus, who watched with an intrigued stare as he exhaled a plume of smoke.

Egrette reached for my face, and I jerked away from her touch in a way that hopefully passed as fear.

"To those of you who do not know," she said to her audience, "this is the murderer of my dear older brother, Malach, who was slaughtered in the House of Night. Slaughtered, no less, by one he had Turned himself." She laughed, glittering and deadly. "Should we be surprised by this? Asar has always been happy to take Malach's leftovers. His blade, his title, and now, his Turned whore."

I knew that her words were engineered for entertainment, and I was intentionally participating in the show. Still, they stung more than I expected.

"P-p-please," I wept. "You can take me—punish me. I deserve it more—I—I—"

Egrette's dark eyes glistened, seizing the idea that I offered to her on a gilded platter.

"What a thought," she said. "Perhaps you should go first. What do you think?"

The Shadowborn nobles, now invested, leaned forward in their seats. Egrette had them rapt. *The cruelty is always the game,* Raihn used to tell me. *You just have to know how to play into their rules.*

Well, look at me now. He'd be proud.

Egrette had now made up her mind. I was to be a part of Asar's punishment, a set piece in her display of dominance.

"Awaken him," she said to Elias, who shot me a more uncertain glance. But he obeyed, unraveling the shadows that clustered around Asar's eyes.

The rest happened so quickly. The Shadowborn guards seized my arms and forced my shoulders back, presenting my chest. Out of the corner of my eye, I saw Asar gasp and fall to his knees as the spell was stripped, still disoriented. Too slow.

Asar, get up! I urged silently, even though I wasn't sure if he could hear me at all.

Egrette smiled, dagger glinting in the moonlight. "At last, justice for Malach."

Would the knife kill me? Probably not—but it would reveal what I was, which didn't seem much better. And what if the blade was enchanted, as Elias's had been?

A tiny, tiny voice in the back of my head now whispered, *Maybe this wasn't such a great idea, Mische.*

Luce's distraught barks peaked. I tried one last time to reach for Asar's mind. *Asar, I think it's time to—*

Egrette raised the blade.

And just as she began to bring it down, the room plunged into an eerie, static silence. The candles snuffed out. The room fell to slow, ominous darkness, shadows painting across my vision like bandages winding around and around and around us all.

And a voice, quiet and booming at once, said, *"Get your hands off my wife."*

CHAPTER FOURTEEN

Asar

Get your hands off my wife.

The words were more reflex than a deliberate decision.

I saw Mische on her knees, surrounded by Shadowborn guards, Egrette preparing to drive a blade into her heart just as Shiket once had, and nothing else in any mortal or divine plane existed at all.

Elias's brows arched in surprise. Egrette's smile wavered.

Wife?

Mische's flood of relief was tempered with a note of confusion.

Wife?

The spectators whispered to each other, scandalized.

Wife?

Egrette cocked her head, attempting to keep up her cool facade. "My, what *were* you up to down there?"

But the things that had been holding me back now felt as inconsequential as spiderwebs. The dregs of my weakness from Mische's touch. The remnants of Elias's sedation spell. The enchanted chains that bound my hands. All of it, swept away with a single vicious stroke, revealing a pool of deep, rich power to be drawn upon.

I felt it all. Every sensation. Every thought. The bloodthirsty pleasure of each pitiful person in this room. The arrogant performance of Egrette, certain she was about to secure her throne. The grim resignation of the guards, ready to see to Mische's execution like it was just another mundane task.

It infuriated me. It *revolted* me.

The curtains flew back, the force of my magic stronger than the competing winds from the sea. Several stained-glass windows cracked. The roaring nightfire in the hearth sputtered, clawing for life. The dagger skidded across tile.

I didn't remember rising or moving. But then I was standing before Egrette. I almost laughed when I felt her understand her miscalculation. And what a miscalculation it had been.

"You underestimated me, Egrette." I spoke softly, and the words felt far away. Yet they vibrated in my bones. "Once I had thought you were the wiser one in the family. And yet, you drag me out here and you threaten what's mine. As if she's just an object to be used for your purposes."

Saying it aloud made my rage nearly unbearable. I was speaking to Malach, Raoul, Shiket, Nyaxia, Atroxus. So many unforgivable injustices.

Egrette, to her credit, kept her composure. But I saw the wheels turning in her head as she frantically considered her next move. Behind me, Elias drew his sword, and I snapped, "*Put that down,* or drive it through your own heart."

Put that down. Put that down. Put that down.

The blade clattered to the floor.

Egrette's face hardened, and I knew she'd made her choice. She was ready to fight. How sweet, that this threat to Elias was what pushed her to it.

If she did, she would lose.

She clung to power so tenuously. I could take it from her right now. I could end them all, and they would deserve it.

But a voice rang out in my head:

Asar, stop!

Mische, speaking into my mind. The realization struck me with a distant note of pride—that she had learned this skill.

I turned slightly. She was still on her knees, and the look on her face stopped me like a hand seizing a strike mid-swing.

Ever so slightly, she shook her head.

Don't do anything you can't take back, she said silently to me. *We need the House of Shadow. Remember?*

At first, I didn't even know what she was talking about.

Then the logical memories pieced back together.

Our mission. Alarus's relics. Ascension.

And Mische's fate. Her *eternal* fate.

This thought tempered my rage. Barely.

I turned back to Egrette. She was terrified, and we both knew I knew it. But she lifted her chin.

"Why did you come back, brother?" she hissed.

We can't start a war here, Mische said into my mind. *But now she's seen what you can do, and she knows that if she fought you, she would lose. Use the leverage. Give her something she wants.*

I hesitated, careful not to look at her.

The realization dawned on me. Mische had engineered this situation. It was so cold—so Shadowborn—that it genuinely surprised me. Still, the image of Mische on her knees thrummed in my heart, and it made it hard to stay my hand.

Perhaps Mische sensed that, because she said, *It's not about revenge, Asar. Sometimes mercy can get you further if you give it at just the right time.*

I could kill Egrette now—kill most of the people in this room. I knew that with inexplicable certainty, now that the hint of divinity in my blood was so close to the surface. But Mische was right. Doing that would spark a conflict that would spread far beyond this moment. And it would certainly attract the attention of Nyaxia faster than we were prepared to deal with it.

All the while, Acaeja's voice echoed in my head:

You will never be king of the House of Shadow.

The crown was so close I could reach out and snatch it from Egrette's head. But even if I did, I already knew that fate dictated it would never remain on mine. I had traded that future away. I would do it again a thousand times if I had to.

After a lifetime of craving its acceptance, I now looked at this room, this castle, these people, with nothing but disgust.

Let Egrette have it all. She deserved it.

And yet, I still had to force the words up my throat when I said, "I came here to offer you my alliance."

Egrette's perfectly arched brows shot up.

The shock rippled through the room, palpable. The nobles sat forward in their seats. Even Mische's surprise nipped at the back of my mind. *Mercy,* after all, was a far cry from *alliance.*

Egrette didn't know what to make of this, either. Her smile faltered before recovering. "So I may expose my back to you to be stabbed," she said sweetly. "How kind of you."

She won't believe you, Mische said to me. *None of them will. You have to be a little more persuasive.*

Persuasive. Ridiculous. Like I had to sit here and convince my sister to accept a gift she didn't even deserve.

Stop whining, Mische snapped. *Remind her that the nobles want you two to tear each other apart and that she should show them where to shove it.* A pause, then, *Maybe with nicer words than that.*

She was surprisingly good at this.

Aloud, to Egrette, I said, "I am genuine. I came here to support your throne. Not steal it."

Into her mind, I told her, *We have more in common than we ever acknowledged. Two spare Heirs fighting for Malach's scraps. Look around you. Surely you can see how eager they are to watch us destroy each other.* And then I added, because there was no improving upon perfection: *Wouldn't you enjoy showing them where to shove it?*

Egrette's eyes flicked to the crowd. Back to mine.

What do you have to offer me for the risk of keeping you alive?

As if she had a choice at this point. She could not kill me even if she wanted to. But I'd let her keep her pride by talking this way.

If I bow to you now, in front of all of them, it will make them respect you, I said. *Show them a united front and that's a wall that even they can't tear down.*

Her brow twitched.

And what do you want in exchange?

I want a role in building this kingdom beside you, I said. *I want safety and positions of respect for both myself and my wife.*

Wife. Even spoken in my mind, the word sent a shiver up my spine. It was a useful lie—calling Mische my wife linked her inextricably to me, so that no matter her past crimes, no one would dare touch her if I managed to secure my own position.

But the truth was, I hadn't been thinking logically when I'd blurted out the word. It had just felt like the correct one.

Appeal to her dreams, Mische said into my mind. From the outside, it must have looked like Egrette and I were silently staring each other down. *Not to her anger. People will do anything for hope.*

Typical missionary.

Still, I said silently to Egrette, *Think of what this kingdom could become in the hands of people like us. People who actually had to fight for what we have in life, instead of being handed it, like Malach was. Like our father was. We could do great things.*

But perhaps Mische, in all of her sentimentality, had been onto something. Because now I could sense Egrette's emotions warring—the distrust that I expected, and the genuine hope that I had not. I wasn't sure why it surprised me so much.

I had only one card left to play.

I lowered to my knees.

"Queen Egrette," I said, "I offer you my oath. The Shadowborn crown is yours. I will never attempt to take it from you. You are the rightful queen of the House of Shadow."

At this, another ripple of surprise. I felt Mische's most acutely of all.

Because I had just offered Egrette an oath—the same magic that bound Shadowborn soldiers to their service. True, I carefully worded mine now, and true, few magical oaths were all-encompassing, especially not when I wasn't even fully mortal anymore.

But ultimately, I had no interest in challenging it. I was more than happy to trade away something I no longer wanted.

Egrette stared at me, serious. I knew that she was pushing at my mind, searching for signs of dishonesty. I let her. She wouldn't find any.

Besides, we both knew I had backed her into a corner. I had shown them all my power. I had shown her that she could not defeat me by force. And I had offered her a single lifeline to save face in front of subjects who were just looking for a reason to reject her.

In the end, my oath worked out exactly as I hoped it would.

It made Egrette believe me, even if just for tonight.

"Very well, Asar Voldari," she said. "I accept your oath. I accept your service. And I offer you mercy for your crimes. Rise."

CHAPTER FIFTEEN

Mische

Asar and I did not speak, not even into each other's minds, until we were in private again. We were given a suite in one of the spires of the Shadowborn castle. It took up its own floor, and was staffed with a small army of servants whom Asar immediately dismissed. It was grandly beautiful, the walls covered in dark ivy and bright red rose petals, the floor polished marble, the windows framed with black metal in such intricate craftsmanship it must have taken months to create a single one. The bedchamber held an enormous, velvet-covered bed, which Luce immediately leapt on and wriggled all over until she rested belly-up.

I couldn't really admire any of it. I was too busy wondering why Asar was such a gods-damned idiot.

As soon as the last of the servants was gone, I started, "Why would you—"

But Asar shot me a sharp look and pressed his finger to his lips.

I haven't warded against listening spells yet, he said into my mind. *Never assume you aren't being watched in the Shadowborn castle.*

He took a small, retractable knife from his belt, knelt by the doorframe, and began etching glyphs into the wood. He was very calm, like he hadn't just sworn away his crown.

I watched his hands work. I was reminded of the way I'd seen him kneel before broken gates in the Descent, and how those hands, gentle and thorough, had so transfixed me. They transfixed me now, too. I watched those beautiful fingers, and the ink of his Heir Mark dance over them.

I said into his mind, *Why would you do that?*

Asar cast me a quick, impressed glance over his shoulder. *You've grasped mind speaking quickly, Dawndrinker. I am impressed.*

It was almost disappointing that I was too distracted to really appreciate that praise.

You offered her an oath.

His hands stopped mid-movement, like what I said confused him. Then he stood and moved to a window, continuing his work there.

Yes, he replied. *And?*

"What do you mean, *and*?" I blurted out, but Asar shot me another sharp glance and pressed his finger over his lips.

Almost done.

It was hard to speak silently. *And,* I said, as pointedly as I could manage through the clumsy whisper of mind speak, *you actually* meant *it.*

Of course I did.

But you *are the Heir to the House of Shadow.*

Asar frowned.

"I don't understand," he said aloud—apparently now satisfied with his soundproofing. "Are you actually upset that I didn't take the Shadowborn crown from Egrette? You were the one who told me to *draw upon her hopes.*"

It sounded unflatteringly manipulative when he worded it that way.

"I said you can't take it *now,*" I said. "Not *never.*"

"I have no interest in wearing the Shadowborn crown now *or* ever."

He said it simply, like he genuinely didn't understand why I objected.

"Look outside, Asar." I thrust my hand to the window, which revealed the ships in the bay. In the distance, Morthryn's dark, crumbling silhouette stood, as if shrouded in grief. "There's an eternal night. There are thousands of soldiers in the bay. Egrette said that Nyaxia has called upon her armies. For what? To go conquer the human lands? The House of Blood has already started doing that. You know how bloody that will get."

"Not as bloody as the collapse of the underworld. Not as bloody as a war between gods."

He was right, but I got the feeling he was deliberately misreading my point.

"I told you once that you'd be a good king. That you could make the world better. I still believe that."

"The crown of the House of Shadow is not my priority."

"Because the underworld is your priority."

Asar finished his last glyph. He stood, then turned to me.

"You are too intelligent for us to be having this conversation right now. You know what my priority is. You know it because you just used it against me."

His voice grew colder, like a blade barely drawn. *Thwip,* as he retracted the knife and slipped it back into his belt. It now seemed ridiculous that I hadn't realized that he was angry. No—furious. Asar's anger was the inevitable rise of ocean fog. Slow and quiet, but all-consuming.

He took several steps closer, his stare skewering me.

"You think I don't see through you, Dawndrinker? We have traveled to hell together."

Guilt twisted in my stomach.

"I needed you to show them everything you were capable of, and fast," I said.

"And you thought the best way to do it would be to make sure that the first thing I saw when they pulled that blindfold off of me would be you at the tip of a blade."

Another step. Another. I was suddenly very conscious of the wall behind me, which I leaned against.

"Unnecessary." His left eye flared, smoke unfurling from it in a fresh plume. "Because I already see that every time I close my eyes, and often when they're open. Every time I sleep. Every time I dream.

I see you, and—" His words caught. "And Shiket's sword piercing your heart, and the moment of your death. *Every time,* Mische."

His voice broke, ever so slightly, around my name, reshaping it to a plea. The faintest crack in his smooth composure, and yet, it revealed so much.

My empty chest ached. With the memory of that sword, yes. But also with Asar's grief.

And with that ache came the stark truth that never got any easier to bear:

I was dead.

I had already sacrificed my life for this. And no matter what Asar believed, I knew it was not easy to escape death.

"I can't be the only reason you're doing this, Asar. You're—you're trying to become a *god*." It still sounded so ridiculous to say it aloud. "That needs to be about more than just me. That needs to be about something bigger."

My back was pressed to the wall, his body aligned to mine, a breath short of touching. His head ducked, and my chin lifted. I swept my gaze over his face—the light pulsing in his scars, the ethereal silver of his scarred eye, the deep brown of the other.

The corner of his mouth tightened in a wry smile.

"Why?" he said.

I watched his lips curl around the word, a breath and a thousand miles away, and a fierce twist pushed against the inside of my chest—a sensation so painfully close to a heartbeat that I could almost taste life on my tongue.

I was certain that I'd taste it on his.

Why. Because I was right here and yet so far away. Because all I wanted to do was capture his next breath in mine, and I couldn't. Because I didn't know if death would ever let me go, no matter what Asar achieved.

"Because I've learned that you can't live on grief," I said. "It's poison. It festers into bitterness and hatred. If you have nothing else to offer a heart, grief will just hollow it out until that's all that you are. A dangerous thing for a god, no?"

A thought flitted through my mind—a thought of Nyaxia.

Asar's hand pressed to the wall behind me, enveloping me in his presence.

"I'm not grieving anything," he murmured.

Liar, I thought. My eyes, heavy lidded, fell to his mouth.

Because I was grieving, too.

I was grieving fiercely.

In a weak attempt to break the tension, I gave him a lopsided smile.

"So. *Wife,* huh? I like that you can always keep things interesting."

His expression flickered. "It's the best way to keep you safe. My protection will extend to you. And it will ensure no one gets too close."

"Was the wedding nice?"

A twitch at the corner of his mouth. "It was elegant and tasteful."

My nose wrinkled. "Sounds like a nice way of saying *boring*."

"Fine. It was gaudy chaos."

"Much better. Did I get to wear a nice dress, at least?"

The smile he'd been holding back now bloomed over his lips like a flower in melting frost. "Oh, you were breathtaking."

I smiled, too, but my chest hurt. The quickening beat that had hammered against it sputtered out. Now, in the fantasy of a future that I would likely never get to have, I felt very dead.

Asar's nose nearly brushed mine. My eyes lifted to his. His lips parted.

But then an abrupt *BANG* had us both snapping upright. Luce leapt off the bed, snarling at the window.

We looked outside to see glitter fading in the night sky as a smattering of distant cheers rose from below.

"Fireworks." Asar let out an exhale. "I wasn't sure if I was correct when I noticed the moon in Morthryn. We're a few decades off schedule. But the obnoxious fireworks, the parties, and . . ." He nodded up at the moon, gleaming behind the falling sparkles.

I frowned once I realized what he was gesturing to. It was, very faintly, orange. A red ring of light shone from behind it, subtle but unmistakable.

"Why does it look like that?"

"That is what the moon looks like within a few days of the Night of the Melume."

I couldn't help a gasp. "Really? I've always wanted to see it."

The Melume was a legendary event in the House of Shadow, much like the Kejari was in the House of Night—though far less bloody. The House of Shadow was the oldest of the vampire kingdoms, having been constructed from the remnants of Alarus's territory. This, many believed, gave the House of Shadow a unique link to the past. On the Night of the Melume, the boundary between the past and the present thinned. It created a natural phenomenon that even great poets struggled to describe, in which the ghosts of the past walked among the living.

"It's beautiful," Asar said. "But more importantly, if I'm correct, it will be our chance to get the mask."

The mask is in the House of Shadow. He had started to say as much when we were in Morthryn, before we had gotten distracted by our ambush.

"We need the Melume for that?" I asked.

"Are you familiar with Vathysia?"

I'd read the name in some ancient religious texts. Vathysia was said to be the heart of Alarus's kingdom, before his murder, before Nyaxia, and before the existence of Obitraes.

"The House of Death," I said. "I thought that was a myth."

"Not a myth. Just old, old history. Vathysia existed. It encompassed parts of the House of Shadow, as well as the underworld itself. It was the territory of Alarus's most devoted followers. The mask is here. But it belongs to Vathysia. Not the House of Shadow."

I stared blankly at Asar.

"It means that it belongs to the past," he clarified unhelpfully.

"So is it here? Or is it *not* here?"

"It is here, *and* not here. The Night of Melume is a rare inflection point when those in the House of Shadow can draw upon Alarus's ancient magic, which predates Obitraes."

I pressed my hands together. "Ooh! Death magic!"

He gave me an odd look. "I never would have guessed when I first met you that you would one day be so giddy at the prospect of death magic, Dawndrinker."

"I like magic, Asar. All magic. Also, I'd probably be great at wielding death magic, now. Considering. You know."

He didn't seem to find this as amusing as I did. He turned back to the window.

"Some say that all Shadowborn magic is a bastardization of Alarus's magic," he said. "The Melume gives us an opening to a deeper well of power. The castle will use it to fortify itself, high-ranking sorcerers will use it to conduct powerful spells more easily, and certain ancient relics will make themselves more visible." He gestured to the House of Shadow crest hanging above the door, and the face that stared back at us from it. "Like the mask. The Mask of Vathysia."

I slowly processed this. "So we have to steal it."

"Yes."

"During a fancy ghost-rite party."

"Yes."

"That's the best place to steal things."

Again, a flat look from Asar. I threw my hands up. "What? It *is*."

Luce yipped in agreement.

"Death magic and heists," he deadpanned. "What an acolyte you are."

I looked to the ships outside, a lump in my throat. My eyelids were growing heavy. I was tired—no, exhausted, the sensation seeping into my soul rather than my bones. It was a strange feeling.

"So tell us, Warden, how exactly do we steal the most valuable artifact in the House of Shadow?" I said.

Asar was silent.

"Oh," I said. "You don't know."

"I've never seen the mask myself," Asar admitted. "It's carefully protected. There's only one person in the House of Shadow who likely knows how we could . . ."

His voice trailed off, like he'd ventured so deep into his own thoughts that words couldn't follow.

"How long do we have to figure it out?" I asked.

"A few days, maybe. I'm sure it won't be long before Egrette gives me all kinds of marching orders for it."

He sounded as thrilled about this as one would expect.

I wandered to the bed and sank down, eyeing an ostentatious painting of a very ill-tempered-looking nobleman. "At least this place is . . . nice?"

"You said 'nice' the way one might say, 'riddled with the carcasses of rats.'"

"I just didn't want to insult your childhood home."

He scoffed bitterly. "I was a prostitute's bastard. You think I was invited to come live in Raoul's steel palace? At any rate, we won't need to stay long."

The edges of my vision were growing blurry. I stared hard at the wall and noticed more of those writhing shadows I'd seen in the ballroom wriggling just outside my field of vision. They almost looked like . . .

"Asar," I said. "I think I'm seeing ghosts."

Apparently I didn't know Asar well enough if I thought this was going to be some kind of surprise to him.

"Probably shades of the dead," he said. "You're among them, so it makes sense you might be able to see the traces they left behind on this world."

When he put it like that, it almost made sense.

With another wave of exhaustion, I let myself fall backward onto a pile of velvet pillows.

Immediately, Asar was at the bedside, radiating concern.

"I'm fine," I said quickly. "Just . . . tired. Can wraiths get tired?"

I slipped one of my gloves off and stared at my hand. I wondered if I was imagining that it was more shimmery than it had been a few hours ago. How far would Asar's blood get me?

Asar perched at the edge of the bed and pulled back the blanket for me like a worried nursemaid.

"Your soul is working hard to stay here among the living," he said. "So yes, I imagine you'll be tired."

I didn't remember crawling beneath the blankets, but the next thing I knew, I was swathed in velvet. Luce wriggled into the bed beside me. I wrapped my arms around her and relished physical touch. Gods, I missed it.

Asar surveyed me carefully. His mouth thinned into a grim line, as if seeing me in this state had clicked a decision into place.

"Rest," he murmured. "I know where we can find what we need."

CHAPTER SIXTEEN

Asar

As a child, I'd been kept separate from my siblings. Egrette was close to me in age, and both of us were far younger than Malach, but we grew up worlds apart. When I first met her, she hadn't hidden how displeased she was to be presented with another sibling, especially given that she so clearly hated the first. Her resentment only grew as the years went on and I proved my usefulness to our father.

This had never bothered me. Sharing Raoul's blood set up me and my siblings to be natural enemies, like vampires and humans. It was just a matter of figuring out who would end with the empty throat and who would end with the full stomach. I'd had no doubts about what kind of king Malach would have been. Merely Raoul's inferior successor. Lazy and simplistic, interested only in the basest trappings of power.

But now, sitting in Egrette's office, I found myself surprised by what I was seeing. The room was a mess, every surface covered in letters and papers and maps marked with several different shades of ink. The windows were wide open, letting in a cold sea breeze.

She had actually *worked* in here. Worked like someone who really wanted to build something. And as she stood before those open windows, looking out over her kingdom, it occurred to me that she did, indeed, resemble a queen.

"What an incredible gift," she murmured. "Imagine what we could shape this kingdom into, Asar. I never imagined that we would do it together. But I will not turn down the help."

She returned to her desk and sat, looking me up and down.

"So, dear brother, tell me the truth now. How did you manage to escape the Descent?"

"You mean after you had Elias stab me in the back?"

She laughed softly. "I hear he stabbed you in the front. Your fault for not seeing it coming. Anyway, you can't hold it against me. What else could I do?"

She was right. I couldn't hold it against her. The rules of vampire nobility were simple. If she didn't secure the crown to her head, she knew she would be executed by the one who did. It was what Malach would have done, eventually, if he had survived. It was, perhaps, what she would still do to me. She looked like she hadn't made up her mind yet.

But for now, she needed me. My highly visible loyalty, and my skills, were more useful to her than my public death.

I looked out to the ships in the bay.

"Did Nyaxia appear to you herself?" I asked.

"She did. As, I hear, she appeared to the king and queen of the House of Blood. A great honor, to help the Dark Mother seize the world." Her eyes glittered with vicious delight. "Apparently the humans are quite riled. Even Shiket has been appearing to Atroxus's followers, the whispers say. Preparing them for war. It'll be fun to have a little fight."

Fun wasn't the word I would use.

I glanced at the papers on her desk, lingering on a pile of envelopes stamped with the crest of the House of Night. Curious.

"And the House of Night?"

Egrette looked smug. "It seems they did something to displease the Dark Mother. But we'll get our chance to flaunt in front of them soon enough, with the Melume so close. Perfect timing, isn't it? I didn't think it was due for another fifty years. Perhaps the recent shifts of fate have brought it closer."

She said it like this was a good thing. I was less convinced. But the mention of the Melume brought my attention back to the matter at hand—and its urgency.

"Indeed," I said. "Perfect timing. I want to go to Ryvenhaal immediately. There are spells documented in the archives that I can perform during the Melume. Uniquely suited to the wells open that night."

Her brow twitched. "And what would these spells do?"

"Give our soldiers access to more powerful magic. Help us forge stronger weapons. Protect our ships. The possibilities go on. You said it yourself. The timing of the Melume is a great opportunity. We need to capitalize on it."

She considered this. She had been raised to be everything a Shadowborn princess should, but she was never a particularly talented magic wielder, and she had little knowledge of the dark fringes of magical possibilities that I'd been raised in. I knew she had always romanticized such things, and she didn't know enough about it herself to know what was or wasn't possible.

At last, she said, "I suppose Gideon will be pleased to see you."

It was shameful that after all this time, his name still elicited a physical reaction—as if cringing against an incoming blow.

"I can't seem to get him out of Ryvenhaal much these days," she went on. "Perhaps it will be good to have someone else in court who can navigate the archives."

Sounded like Gideon. He had been intensely loyal to my father, but he'd never thought much of my siblings.

"I'm not surprised," I said flatly.

"Have you seen him since your exile?"

"No. I have not."

She held that look, one that made me think, just for a moment, that maybe she saw more than I'd given her credit for—that maybe she and I had more in common than I'd known, growing up.

"Gideon's skills are very important to this kingdom," she said. "And if Gideon himself is unwilling to provide them, then someone else should."

Now I understood.

Gideon wasn't willing to hand Egrette the loyalty that he'd given Raoul for centuries. So now, Egrette hoped that I could be her new Gideon.

Right here, sitting in a chair across from the desk that had once been my father's, as I had thousands of times before, I felt like I was peering into an alternate, horrible reality. It was so intrinsically repulsive that I had to force myself to stay in my seat.

If Egrette noticed my reaction, she didn't show it. "Fine," she said. "Go, and quickly. Let's seize every opportunity."

Then she rose and returned to the window, folding her hands behind her back.

"I can't believe I'm saying this, Asar, but I'm glad you returned. Goddess bless the daughters and the second sons. Imagine a kingdom built in our image. They always underestimate us, but they never understood. We are the ones who actually had to use our teeth."

Over her shoulder, she gave me a smile full of daggers.

CHAPTER SEVENTEEN

Mische

The rain pelted us sideways, slicing over my cheek like broken glass. The fastest of the drops passed right through me, like the strike of Elias's soldier had in Morthryn. Fitting, because the rainfall felt just as violent.

Our boat bobbed over choppy water. Distant thunder echoed from beyond the capital, highlighting the skyline against bursts of fog-softened silver.

"H-h-how much farther?" I wrapped my cloak tight around myself and Luce, who pressed her body to mine. I wasn't sure whether she was letting me shelter her, or if it was just her excuse to help shelter me.

I couldn't stop shivering. One might think that being dead would make me more resilient. No such luck. First, the exhaustion. Now, the cold.

"Almost there," Asar said tightly. Our boat, a tiny little thing etched with glyphs of protection, was piloted by a Shadowborn creation of smoke that barely took on the shape of a person. It was, even by my standards, a bit eerie. I thought maybe if we were going to make it through the storm in one piece, it might help to be guided by someone who at least had eyes. But what did I know?

We had been traveling for two hours now, and Asar had spoken about as many words. He warned me before we left the castle that though Egrette had not sent guards with us, we would undoubtedly be trailed by observation spells. Still, I knew his silence was about more than just caution. He sat with his back rod straight, his jaw tight, hands clasped in his lap. He would hardly look at me.

I barely remembered falling asleep after my conversation with Asar—it felt, actually, more like ceasing to exist. I awoke to Asar returning to the apartment with a set jaw and determined eyes. He told me that he'd maneuvered a plausible excuse for us to go visit the one place he knew we could find information about the mask, and potentially, the heart and eye, too.

"It's off the coast," he said, when I'd prodded for more information. "A place to keep things that are too valuable to stay in the city."

"Like . . . an archive?" I had asked.

He only said, "Yes," in a way that was clearly a lie, and then tossed a cloak at me and told me we needed to be going before the storm made travel impossible.

Travel already seemed impossible. But our window of time before the Melume was closing quickly, so off we went.

Now, our shadowy captain steered our boat through a narrow opening between two sheer stone cliffs. The stone had once been covered in ivy, though the leaves now had mostly fallen to the sea in wait for a sun that had never come. Still, the naked vines clung stubbornly to the rock, unwilling to let go even in death.

To my relief, the walls offered a reprieve from the rain. The tunnel continued for some time beneath arches of crumbling stone that looked older than Obitraes itself. When we finally passed through the final arch, Asar's very soul chilled. I knew it, because I felt it in my chest, too.

A castle now towered over us.

It was amazing that, large as the building was, we hadn't been able to see it from a distance. Perhaps that was the work of the storm, or perhaps it was the work of illusion spells. It was a striking structure, though I couldn't call it beautiful. Ebony cliffs curved around it on one side, the walls built into the glossy stone. The island itself was covered in greenery, which someone magically gifted had apparently worked hard these last few months to keep alive. A single pointed spire rose up from it in intricate black metal.

It was such a pristine example of Shadowborn architecture, all circles of stained glass and arches of twisted, decorative metal and ivy-covered stone. And yet, as our boat came ashore—at a small dock that seemed like it was very rarely used—I couldn't shake a deep discomfort. It looked more like a prison to me than Morthryn ever had.

With his work complete, our guide dissolved into the night without any further acknowledgment. A fresh sheet of rain soaked us. Asar stood abruptly.

"Don't speak to anyone," he said, as we climbed onto the shore. "Don't let anyone look at you too closely. And stay near me."

He seemed like he was questioning all over again his decision to bring me along.

I gave him a lopsided smile and a salute. "Yes, Mother."

Asar didn't even take the obvious bait of mocking my mockery—*I'm either a mother or a captain, pick your insult and stay consistent*—which made me even more concerned. Instead, he just let out a wordless grumble and ushered us down a flagstone pathway to a set of imposing doors. They opened for us like arms outstretched for a long-lost son.

With every step, Asar grew smaller.

Inside, a hush fell over us. The doors slammed closed behind us with a commanding *BANG* that made me jump forward.

We stepped into a large, circular room, open all the way up to the pointed spire above. Moonlight flooded in through stained-glass windows, and nightfire hovered in lanterns suspended in nothingness at the center of spiraling staircases. Tiny blurs flung from railing to railing, and it took a moment for me to realize that they were birds—flitting, agitated, near the windows. Balconies circled the walls, floor after floor, all of them lined with books—gods help me, I had never in my life seen *so many books*. Among them were shelves of artifacts. Surely a collection that rivaled any in Obitraes.

It dwarfed Asar's study in Morthryn, which had amazed me. Yet, it had none of its reverence. Asar had maintained his collection meticulously, with great respect for all the knowledge he held. Here, it was locked away behind bars and spells. I felt as if a cell door might slam closed behind us if we proved ourselves too interesting to let go.

"Where are we?" I found myself whispering.

"It's called Ryvenhaal."

Asar bit down on the word. Luce rubbed against his legs, and his hand absentmindedly stroked her head.

My steps faltered. I stared hard at Asar.

He paused, looking back. "What?"

"You grew up here."

It wasn't a question. It struck me with unshakable certainty. This place felt like Asar. It even smelled like him, though in an off-putting, twisted way, as if masking rot. And the way he wilted as we passed through these doors . . . I imagined that I might do the same if I ever stepped foot in the Citadel again.

Asar's throat bobbed. He continued walking.

"Better and better at mind magic every day, Iliae," he muttered.

My steps quickened to catch up with him. "Why here?"

"My father wanted to cultivate tools that could help him create the strongest kingdom in the world. And that meant cultivating Shadowborn magics that were on the wrong side of acceptability, even by Nyaxia's laws. Like necromancy. Ryvenhaal is technically outside the House of Shadow, which makes it less likely to attract unwanted attention."

Tools. A stab of disgust twisted in my stomach when he said that word. "You weren't a *tool.* You were a *child.*"

"If I had just been a child, Raoul would have executed me without a second thought. Being a tool gave me the chance to live."

He said this so simply. I hated how deeply I understood it. Because from the moment Atroxus chose me at eight years old, I'd had a function to fulfill, too. And like Asar, without it, I would have been thrown away. It was hard to question what kept you alive, even if it did terrible things with the life it gave you.

I seized Asar's hand, squeezing it under the safe cover of my leather gloves—even though I craved skin. The corner of his mouth lifted in a weak smile, but his businesslike pace didn't slow.

"If there is anywhere in the House of Shadow that holds information about ascension, it's here," he said. "It's one of the greatest archives of . . . sensitive . . . magical information in the world."

I looked up, to the floors and floors of shelves spiraling above us. Thousands of books? Millions? Tens of millions?

"I bet it is," I murmured.

Asar nudged my back, and it was only then that I realized I had stopped walking.

"I can smell your arousal from here," he remarked.

I choked a laugh, but I felt as if my cheeks had flushed—could that happen, as a wraith? My gaze met Asar's, then slid down and settled on his bare throat and the triangle of skin pointing down to his chest. I found myself staring at it like it was blood. With that same devastating, soul-deep hunger.

I imagined pressing my mouth to it. Dragging my tongue up his neck—

Asar broke the tension by turning to the hall, clearing his throat. "This way."

Sun fucking take me. *Get ahold of yourself, Mische.*

I tucked my hand—tingling beneath my gloves—into my coat pocket as we wound through a maze of bookshelves. Books and crates were carted around by formless shadows that almost—almost—resembled floating humanoid silhouettes. Still, I felt constant presences lurking just out of sight. The dead whispered in the back of my mind.

"They're loud in here," I murmured. "The dead."

"Remnants of dead souls are attracted to places where they sense they might be acknowledged. They've always lingered around here, but they're . . . active tonight. Maybe because the Melume is so close."

"Or because the veil is tearing."

Asar was ominously silent in response to that. We passed a mirror mounted against a brocade-covered wall. I could have sworn I briefly saw Vincent peering through it, frowning with impatience.

We came to a set of black double doors with glyphs carved in a circle at its center. Asar pressed his palm to the center of it, and the doors opened for him. But when I tried to step through, my head slammed against something hard.

"Shit!" I pressed my hand to my forehead. Gods, that actually *hurt*. It was almost refreshing to feel such a physical sensation.

Asar tried again to usher me through, only to earn me another throbbing bruise on my forehead.

"This room is spelled to keep out the dead," he said. "You must qualify."

"Why would you need to do that?"

"We were practicing necromancy, Dawndrinker. Why do you think?"

"You thought they might . . . break free?"

Asar gave me a pitying look, like my disbelief was very naive.

Fair enough.

I sighed. "Alright. Then you go get what we need, and I'll stay here."

"Right. Leave you alone to go explore and get yourself into trouble."

"I would *never*," I said, aghast.

"You expect me to believe that *you* are going to sit quietly in this room of ancient tomes without wandering off?"

His tone told me exactly what he thought of my self-control, which was a little insulting.

I threw my arm over Luce's back. "Luce will stay here and make sure I'm so, *so* obedient."

Luce let out a yip.

Asar sighed. "Fine. Five minutes."

And with another stern, "Be good," he disappeared through the misty door.

It was physically painful to remain still when there was so much to explore. But I was determined to prove Asar wrong, so I found a quiet spot near the door and sat against the bookcases, Luce beside me. I stroked her back absentmindedly as I watched the shadows lug stacks of books from one shelf to another.

"What about you, Luce?" I asked. "Was this your home once, too?"

I thought back to the glimpses I'd seen of Asar's past in our journey to the Descent—Luce in her previous life, dead and drained, a cruel punishment for the crime of Asar's existence. Then, Luce in the new life Asar had given her. It occurred to me that we had some things in common.

Luce sniffed in agreement.

A flash of lightning drenched the shelves in cold silver light, and a boom of thunder sent the birds fluttering around in a panic. I watched them fly in circles in the center of the spiraling staircases.

I mused aloud, "How do you think they got—"

CRACK.

THUMP.

A flash of gold hurtled to the ground a few feet shy of me.

I jumped up, startled.

A bird twitched and spasmed on the tile floor. Its head was twisted back, wings skewed at a gut-churning angle, yellow feathers bent and broken. I watched, horrified, as a slow pool of blood seeped through the tile grout lines as it fought through its final breaths.

"Poor creature."

The voice unfurled with the low, silken cadence of smoke from a candle.

I tore my eyes from the dying bird to see a man standing before me.

I hadn't heard him coming. Hadn't even felt him, even with my heightened senses.

The darkness bent around him in a way that made it difficult to focus on the specifics of his features. He had an angular face, handsome in that typical vampire way but otherwise unremarkable. His hair was light ash brown, slicked back neatly from his face. His frame, tall and slender, disappeared beneath finely tailored, simple black clothing.

He was, I knew instantly, very old. Vampires did not age as humans did, with wrinkles and gray hair. But I could sense his years in the way his skin stretched over his face, in the shade of his fair eyes as he raised them to mine.

"The endless night has them terribly disoriented," he said, nodding to the bird, now still. "They keep flying into the windows. Bring her to me, please."

Bring her to me. Bring her to me.

I didn't remember moving. But blink, and suddenly, I was several strides away from the door, a bloody, broken bird in my hands. The man and I both crouched close to the floor. The man now held a small retractable knife that looked oddly familiar to me, and he was scratching a circle into the floor.

"A ritual circle." My thoughts felt a bit gummy, sticking to each other like honey candy left out in the sun. "For necromancy."

"You've been taught well," the man remarked. "Place the bird where it belongs."

Luce curled against me, staring the man down warily, growling low.

But blink, and the bloody bird sat at the center of the circle. Items had been placed around its edges—a feather, a handful of birdseed, a little piece of a withered leaf, a broken twig.

"Good," the man said casually. "Now, help me bring her back."

Help me. Help me. Help—

But something that I saw in his icy stare made me slam the door against the sweet stick of his compulsion.

I rose abruptly and stepped back.

"Who are you?" I said.

The man smiled and passed his hand over the ritual circle. This smile belonged to a kindly grandfather, but his eyes belonged to a predator.

The bird spasmed gracelessly back to life and attempted to fly away, but the man caught it swiftly in one hand and tucked it, still twitching, into his breast pocket.

He said, "I suspect that we have a mutual—"

"Gideon."

Asar's voice was like a blade sliding from a sheath.

The man got to his feet and dusted himself off. He offered Asar a smooth smile.

"You came to visit," he said. "And after such a long time. Not even a letter now and then."

Asar's hand flattened against my back. Even across the bounds of death itself, I nearly jolted at his fear, so sharp it verged on panic.

I told you to stay put, he said into my mind.

I did, I just—

"She was merely helping an old man, Asar," Gideon said, with a warm chuckle. His gaze fell to the stack of books and scrolls in Asar's arms. "You won't find what you're looking for in those. Come."

He started down the hall. But Asar didn't move. His hand remained on my back.

And I knew—I *knew*—that he was considering turning around and leaving. And just because I knew he wanted to, I did, too.

We don't have to do this, I told him silently. *We can find another—*

"You came all this way," Gideon said over his shoulder. "Surely you must know that I can help."

Asar's throat bobbed.

Reluctantly, he lowered his chin. And without another word, we followed.

GIDEON LED US down several winding hallways, all lined with bookcases and shelves and doors leading to yet more bookcases and shelves. I couldn't imagine the information that was holed up in this place—gods, I could have spent a lifetime here drowning in it.

"Likely literally true," Gideon said—and I stiffened at how easily he had slipped into my thoughts without my even feeling it. "Even I have not read everything. Asar made it through a significant chunk of it, though. My most devoted student. Has he told you much about his time here?"

Asar was stone-faced as we walked, his hand still protectively on my back. "No need to bore her."

"Bore? You were brilliant." Gideon's gaze roved over me. "You must be too young to recall the Wraith Warden at his peak. But he was an unmatched talent. Did he ever tell you of his first mission for the crown? Barely more than fifteen years old, and he—"

"Gideon."

The name was a sharp rebuke. But Gideon laughed and plowed on through.

"Please, allow me to brag about my pupil, Asar. What was it called—ah, Farnelle. That was it. A little island near the channel to the House of Night, claimed and fought over by both kingdoms. Raoul tasked Asar with gathering intelligence, nothing too extreme for a teenage boy. But Asar, overachiever that he was, managed to topple the noble there himself. A city of thousands, taken down by a hundred spare soldiers. How might he have done such a thing?"

"Gideon," Asar hissed.

But Gideon just smiled at me.

"A marriage should not be built on secrets," he said. "Congratulations, by the way."

A chill danced up my spine.

"The House of Night knew that Raoul wanted Farnelle, and as such, they fortified it heavily. Asar quickly learned that the key to taking Farnelle was not to look within its walls, but within our own. He uncovered unflattering comments from one of Raoul's highest-ranking nobles, who just so happened to lord over Zeren, the territory closest to Farnelle. And in offering Raoul this traitor, he also offered the perfect punishment. Kidnap the child of Farnelle's lord and plant her in Zeren. And when the House of Night launched all their resources at Zeren, swoop in to snatch Farnelle from their jaws. All while allowing them to rip the sacrificial lamb to shreds." Gideon shook his head. "It was brilliant. He spent months laying the groundwork. Turn two enemies against each other and walk straight through the front door."

Asar avoided my gaze.

"A long time ago," he muttered, masking a hint of shame.

"You've always been too humble. Here."

Gideon opened a door and ushered us inside. The chambers seemed more a library than bedchamber, with four stories of bookshelves rising above us and great glass windows spanning floor to ceiling. Machine lifts ran from floor to floor, their golden gears gleaming under the firelight.

At those, I couldn't help but gawk. It had been decades since I'd seen work like this. Like most gods of the White Pantheon, Srana, the goddess of machinery, did not allow vampires to use her magic, forcing those in Obitraes to use manual or magical solutions to our practical problems. But rarely, very wealthy vampires could import human-made technology and use it until it inevitably stopped working, tainted by proximity to Nyaxia's magic. An expensive, endless cycle of repair and replacement.

Gideon noticed my staring and chuckled softly. "One small benefit of my role in the Shadowborn court." He ushered us onto one of the lifts and pressed a button. Gears creaked to life, and I watched the machinery work in amazement as we began to rise. "And, I will admit, they do last a little longer here," he added, "since we are technically outside the House of Shadow's borders."

"It's a farce," Asar said.

"A bad lie still fulfills its purpose so long as everyone agrees to believe it."

A booming thunderclap rang out. Lightning cut through the shadows, briefly illuminating the silhouettes of the dead before dissipating. A fresh wave of rain hammered against the large arched windows.

Gideon grimaced. "Vicious out there. I think you'll be spending the day. Even the shadows won't take a boat across the channel now. Here."

The lift ground to a creaky halt. He led us out onto the balcony landing, then into a nook within the shelves. Inside it was a small table, two armchairs, and three walls lined with books.

"Now, since we've all decided to trust each other, tell me, Asar, what you are really looking for."

I still wasn't entirely convinced that Asar wasn't about to end the conversation and walk out. But his gaze landed on me, and whatever he saw made his gaze soften.

He sat and gestured for me to do the same. Luce, begrudgingly, settled on her haunches.

"We are here," Asar said stiffly, "to find information about relics of Alarus. His mask. His eye. His heart."

Gideon soaked up those words with the delight of an addict sucking down smoke.

"Those aren't any relics," he said. "Those are remnants. How intriguing."

"I've been sent on Egrette's behalf," Asar said.

"Oh, of course. I would never imagine otherwise." A flash of sharp teeth. "It was always clear that there was something special about you, Asar. A pity that your father never truly recognized what it was."

He rose and looked to the bookcases.

"You know already, I'm sure, about the Mask of Vathysia, baked into the bones of the Shadowborn castle. What convenient timing for you to ask about it now, with the Melume so close. The eye and the heart, however . . . *that* is more interesting. There is great power in transitions. The transition point between life and death. Between mortality and godhood. The moment a soul is created, and the moment it is destroyed."

He laid a book on the table with a mighty *THUMP*. Tendrils of shadow opened it, sending up a puff of dust. When it cleared, it revealed an ink drawing.

It depicted the gods murdering Alarus.

Vitarus and Shiket held him down, one at each arm. Srana bore the blessed blade she had created to cut apart his body, already wet with his blood. Ix, who had lured Alarus to this meeting, stood in the background, mouth covered in horror but eyes bright with pleasure. Atroxus loomed over his captive brother, one hand cupping his face as if in affection, the other reaching for the blade that would take off his head.

My eyes lingered on Atroxus. It was a poor likeness, drawn by someone who had clearly never seen him. And yet, the triumphant smirk on his face made him look just like the god who had chosen me and bedded me and cultivated me like a fine possession. It was the exact same expression he had worn when he tried to raise an eternal sun over Obitraes, ready to kill millions to wipe away the inconvenient consequences of his betrayal.

He hadn't looked like that when I'd driven that arrow through his throat, though.

"Everything a god touches is a source of great power," Gideon said. "But the place of their death is the greatest of all. Even Srana could not craft a blade strong enough to dismember Alarus without some help."

He tapped the page. Asar and I squinted at it.

The drawing was so faded that it was difficult to make out the details. Srana's weapon appeared to be a cross between a blade and an axe, a curved blade on a long handle. And a knot of scribbled ink on the blade seemed to depict—

"Is that an *eye*?" I said.

"That is, some believe, *the* eye," Gideon said. "Torn from Alarus as the final step to creating the weapon that could dismember him."

I couldn't help but cringe. Asar winced, too. I squinted at the drawing to see the faded smear of blood on Alarus's hand, presumably where his eye had been ripped out.

"So we're looking for a crown that is a mask and an eye that is an axe," Asar muttered. "Gods are straightforward as ever."

"Some say that the White Pantheon could not destroy the eye when they dismembered Alarus. That the weapon was cursed in Alarus's final spite, unable to be handled by the White Pantheon. If it exists, it may still remain at the site of his murder in the deadlands."

"The deadlands?" I squeaked.

The deadlands—the realm that sat between the mortal and divine worlds—were accessible only through the House of Blood.

Great.

Gideon let out a *psh*. "You've always appreciated a challenge, Asar. Surely this is no exception."

"What about the heart?" I said.

Gideon's smirk flickered, and for the first time, I sensed just the barest edge of his emotions—frustration, like I'd hit upon a nerve.

"You aren't the first to ask," he said. "Many have searched for it. If it exists, it would be a remarkable source of power. Look at what the House of Night was able to do with a few broken teeth and a drop of divine blood. But alas." He leaned back in his chair. "The heart has not been written of in any scripture I can find, new languages or old. Perhaps it was destroyed. It has been two thousand years, and flesh is flesh, divine or no."

Even Gideon did not seem to believe this. Asar certainly didn't. If the heart had been destroyed, we were in trouble.

"And the mask?" Asar said. "Where in the palace is it stored? Theoretically. Of course."

"*Theoretically,* one would have to navigate the Palace of Vathysia at the height of the Melume. It has changed quite a lot in the last two-thousand-odd years." Gideon set aside the open book and slid another out from beneath it. "You might find this helpful. Maps of Vathysia, from before its fall, including what documentation still exists of the palace as it once was."

But instead of passing the book to Asar, he held it, long fingers caressing the scratched, aged leather.

His gaze fell to me.

"But enough business," he said. "Mische, it isn't often I meet someone that my stone-hearted protégée clearly is so fond of. Tell me more about yourself."

Tell me. Tell me. Tell—

I caught my answer halfway up my throat. I had never told him my name.

Asar was on his feet, his hand on my shoulder.

"That's enough," he snapped.

"It gets lonely here. Is it a crime to look for some conversation?"

"That isn't a conversation. It's an evaluation."

Gideon cocked his head. The birds flitted in a panic from window to window.

"You must be tired," he said. "I won't be offended if you have little energy for socialization."

He slid the book across the table.

A crack of lightning illuminated the harsh angles of Gideon's face, the purple glow of Asar's scars, the elegant skyline of the Shadowborn castle sitting upon the cliffs in the distance. Gideon gazed out the window, hands threaded in his lap.

"Beautiful, isn't it?" he said softly. "There is a certain peace in a tempest that you can only appreciate from its center. But it will pass soon enough. Your old chambers are ready for you, Asar, if you two would like to get some rest."

CHAPTER EIGHTEEN

Asar

In a striking display of arrogance, Gideon had not changed the glyphs protecting his private chambers. I had been the one to carve them there, all those years ago, one of many tests of my abilities. I'd apparently done such an impeccable job that Gideon had not seen fit to replace them. They recognized me instantly, though I still felt a tiny jolt as I ran my hands over them—as if even those little symbols saw that something about me had changed intrinsically, and perhaps not for the better.

The door clicked open. The scent of knowledge and death surrounded me.

I had doubted many times my decision to bring Mische with me to Ryvenhaal. Before, it had seemed like the least-bad option among bad options, compared to leaving her alone in the Shadowborn castle, surrounded by monsters. But once we were here, I found myself grateful to have her beside me. With her, this place seemed more pathetic than dangerous, as if the sheer force of her light illuminated all its drab dark corners.

But I had to do this part alone. I left her in the bedchamber—against all instinct—with Luce to guard her. Now, a tiny flutter of fear sparked in my chest—the fear of the eight-year-old boy I had been the first time I crossed this threshold. I saw it now as I had seen it then. A place full of monsters that would either consume me or help me consume the world, if I became enough like them.

One of those monsters now sat before the fire, a glass in his hand. I could smell the contents right away. Wyvern blood. Rancid stuff. Wyverns were extinct, and he had been parsing out his supply, glass by glass, for centuries.

Gideon did not look at me. He had known I would be back. He gestured to an empty chair, a glass already prepared beside it. "Join me."

I did. The chair settled beneath me in just the same way it had decades ago. And yet when I looked up at Gideon's face, now illuminated by firelight, I was struck by how different he looked. Vampires did not show age as humans did, but time had carved countless marks into my instructor, scars and wrinkles and the hollow darkness under eyes that had looked into the heart of death itself.

He stroked a little golden bird, which sat, lethargic and twitching, in his lap.

"Tell me, now that we can be honest with each other, how is Morthryn?"

"They gutted it. But I'm sure you knew that."

"It was useless as a prison without you. And what a waste to let your enviable collection sit in the ruins with divine war on the horizon."

"That's all it is to you? Millennia of history to be stripped for weapons?"

"Don't wag your finger at me, Asar. You are the one who came here looking for the keys to ascend to godhood."

I was silent.

He laughed softly. "Surely you don't think I'm stupid. An eye, a crown, a heart. I see that you've already brushed divinity. Now you're asking for the ladder to climb the rest of the way."

I took a sip of blood, the bitterness near painful.

"Did you know?" I asked. "What I was?"

It was one of the first questions that had come to me after I'd learned about the drop of divinity within my bloodline—a question I had only thought to ask in the quiet lulls of my imprisonment, when

I couldn't bear to relive Mische's death one more time. *Did Gideon know?*

"I've concluded that my father didn't," I said, thinking aloud. "Or he would have killed me."

"Don't be so sure. He was wiser than you give him credit for. Do you think he ever would have bedded your mother if he had not known there was something special about her?"

I'd only ever known my mother as a brilliant person enslaved to depraved hungers—blood, drugs, wine, power. I could count on one hand the number of kind words she had said to me, and yet, I jumped to her defense.

"She was beautiful and intelligent. He'd slept with lesser."

"Sometimes knowledge transcends logic. I suspect that your father was attracted to your mother's lineage. His magic saw it, even if his mind did not."

"And you?"

Gideon gazed into the hearth. Perhaps he was remembering the same night I was—when I had crawled from the swamp pit I called home to meet a man in a black suit who had offered me freedom from fear.

"After I met you, your father was trying to determine whether to keep you or if you were more useful dismembered for parts," he said. "I told him, *My king, if you cultivate him, you will have a greater weapon than the House of Shadow has ever seen.* No, I didn't know of your blood then, though I had my suspicions later on. But I saw something more valuable. Hunger. Even now, I sense it stronger than the divinity. Tell me, what has you starving so?"

In the fireplace flames, I saw a constellation of freckles and gold eyes and a perfect body falling beneath a blade of injustice.

"I don't know what you mean," I said, and Gideon chuckled.

"I know you better than anyone, Asar. Nothing would bring you back here but a mission to resurrect a dead lover that ends better this time around. It is remarkable. I have never seen a wraith like her. What did you do, drag her directly from the underworld? I could spend hours studying—"

"You will do no such thing."

Words ripped free. The shadows shuddered.

I had seen the way he looked at her, when they knelt together over the bird that now lay in Gideon's lap. I knew that look well. It was the look that had put me in dark boxes and lowered razor blades onto my skin and had begun the slow, methodical process of turning me into exactly what he had promised my father:

A weapon.

Gideon clicked his tongue. "So protective. That heart of yours, Asar, will be your downfall. You crave love like an animal craves meat. It destroyed you last time, just like I told you it would. Someone had to get you out of that trap."

When I left to go live in the city with Ophelia, Gideon's last words to me had been, *Happiness will be the worst thing that ever happened to you.*

I took another sip of blood, drowning my fury beneath the bitter flood.

"Someone," I said stiffly.

And even now, a part of me that had once trusted Gideon as a mentor—hell, a father—still wanted him to deny it.

Only now did I acknowledge perhaps that was why I had come here, too. To ask the question I never could in my exile.

I'd always wondered. Wondered how Malach was able to get past the wards in my house. Wondered whether he might have had some help, whether someone might have given him the key, or even just left it somewhere conveniently placed. I had been so careful.

But even when I hated Gideon, I had always trusted him. Until that night.

"Her death saved you," he said. "Your father was concerned. And you know you would not have survived it if Raoul had decided the risk of keeping you alive was greater than the reward. You are my pupil, Asar. I took your tutelage seriously."

My knuckles whitened around the glass of rancid blood. Darkness crept closer and closer to us.

In the hearth flames, I saw Ophelia's mangled body. Then, even more horrifying, the thing she had become after her failed resurrection. Decades of suffering. These images melted into Mische's final moments, her charred body, the tears rolling down her burnt cheeks.

"Your anger is far more valuable than your happiness," Gideon said. "I told you the night we first met that this would be a life in which your worth is measured by the blood you spill upon it. It is not a life for pretty little birds."

He gently stroked the twitching finch in his lap. The creature was dying again.

His greatest shame. After all this time, it still played out night after night.

Gideon had never mastered the art of necromancy himself. All he could do was claw his pets back for hours at a time, only to relinquish them once more to death. I knew he resented me for being able to do what he never could.

"They stay for a while," he murmured, "and then they are gone. All you can do is appreciate what you have while it lasts."

Once, Mische had told me of a dream of happy endings. And the hope in her face then had made me believe in them, too.

And yet, a small part of myself still believed that Gideon was never wrong.

I let this truth slide down into my stomach like the bitter poison of wyvern blood. Then I set my glass down.

"Getting the mask isn't as simple as following a few old maps," I said. "You didn't address the issue of the keyholder."

"I wondered if you would catch that."

"You'd insult me by thinking otherwise."

The mask would be protected by more than just the phases of the veil between the living and the dead. Harking back to our days as followers of the god of death, the Shadowborn specialized in keyforging—the art of keeping keys not as objects or even spells, but embedded into a person's mind and body. Usually a long-lived advisor whose loyalty was unimpeachable. Someone who had the tolerance to death magic to bear the weight of the spell for centuries.

"I will need the key," I said, "if I'm to get the mask on the Night of the Melume."

One by one, I undid the buttons of my gloves at my wrist.

Gideon's eyes gleamed. He had been waiting for this.

"I could help. For the right price."

Price. I knew what it would be. I knew the minute he laid eyes on Mische, he had started dreaming up all the ways he could test her. He craved knowledge the way he accused me of craving love.

Oh no. Certainly not.

"You taught me, Gideon," I said. "You know I have taken more powerful things from more powerful people."

I removed the other glove. Then I stood and slipped off my jacket, laying it across the back of a chair—far enough away that the blood spatters would not reach it.

The realization fell over Gideon too slowly. He had automatically reverted to the same roles we'd assumed for decades: he was the master, I was the student.

But that wasn't the truth anymore. Gideon was an old man, and I was a demigod.

By the time he had even started to move, with a *whoosh* of darkness, I had Gideon pinned to the wall. Shadows drowned the open air, my chair had been overturned, and the dead finch, discarded from Gideon's lap, lay belly-up at the edge of the hearth, embers gnawing at its tail feathers.

Gideon's icy eyes searched mine. My hand was pressed to his throat, leaving him fighting for breath—he was, after all, still merely mortal.

"You are making a mistake," he rasped out. "You don't understand what it would mean to make an enemy of me."

I laughed, the sound jarring.

"No, *you* didn't understand what it would mean to make an enemy of *me*."

He barked a scoff. He didn't resist me, not physically. But his talons sank into my thoughts. He knew better than anyone how to push past my mental walls and drag out the carcasses of my worst memories. They trailed their rotten guts all over the inside of my skull—Luce's body in my arms, Ophelia's, Mische's. Countless failures, countless small tortures, every rung that broke my bones in my fall from grace.

And in my distraction, Gideon lunged against me.

But I wasn't a child anymore.

I sucked up a lungful of the shadows he tried to use against me, and exhaled, our magic exploding against each other.

The crash made the ground tremble. Stacks of books toppled. Glass teetered from shelves. A flash of lightning rang out. And when the darkness cleared, I was standing, chest heaving, hands shaking, and Gideon was crumpled up against the wall opposite me.

"Shame on me for underestimating you." He said it with a sneer of hatred. And yet, there was a hint of pride in the words, too. "If you kill me, Egrette will know."

Gideon's life had been sworn to the crown of the House of Shadow, and that meant that if it ended, whoever held it would be alerted immediately. Just one more protection given to him in exchange for his loyalty.

But it was Gideon himself who had taught me that death could be wielded in so many ways. Taking a life was merely the bluntest, clumsiest use of it.

"I will not kill you," I said.

A laugh, wet with blood. "Of course I couldn't be so lucky."

I approached him, step by step. "Get up."

Get up. Get up. Get up.

"Oh, psh." He started to rise, but his right leg gave out beneath him at a grotesque angle.

I watched him struggle with a confusing pang in my chest. For so much of my life, Gideon had seemed untouchable. More god than man.

At his third unsuccessful attempt, I seized his arm and slung it over my shoulder. He was shockingly light. The intimacy felt right and revolting in equal measure. Few vampires cared for their ailing parents, just as few vampire parents truly nurtured their children. And yet, as I helped my mentor across the room, it seemed like a natural end to a natural cycle. Perhaps Raoul had sired me. Perhaps Alarus's blood had made me worth saving. But it was Gideon who had created me.

"Over there." I gestured to a clear patch of hardwood—plenty of room for glyphs. I helped him to it, then lowered him. Tendrils of darkness slithered around his arms and ankles, pinning him.

His icy eyes speared me.

"Will I feel it?" he asked.

When I was done with him, I would have popped every stitch in his mind to pry out the combination of spells that would allow us to access the mask. I would have carved countless glyphs into his skin, and some on bone. I would have ripped out the secrets he'd been committed to death to keep and scrambled his memory of my visit.

Excruciating, brutal work.

I could offer him mercy. Seize his consciousness before the worst of the pain. Did he deserve that much? He had believed in me when no one else had. He'd given me blood and shelter and, above all, knowledge—the very power that I would tonight use to destroy him.

But then I thought of an unlocked door in a little townhouse.

I thought of the way he had looked at Mische.

I said nothing. But Gideon heard my answer, anyway. He jerked against his restraints. "There it is," he sneered. "That hunger. That will end you, Asar. If you think this will be the last step of our dance, you are mistaken."

I drew the knife from my belt, then stepped over Gideon and stared down at him. Years ago, sometimes people would comment that we looked alike, even though we weren't related. I never saw it. Not until now.

"It's what you would have done," I said.

He laughed softly. "You are right, boy. You are right."

I knelt beside him. *Thwip,* as the blade sprang free.

"Your woman is lovely," he murmured. "You'll ruin her."

Probably, I thought.

I made the first cut.

CHAPTER NINETEEN

Asar

The work took hours. Gideon didn't scream at first, but before long, he was grunting and hissing like a rabid animal. It took a long time for him to lose consciousness. But in the end, I had what I needed—the combination of the glyphs that would allow us into the mask's tomb etched carefully into my own mind. I tucked Gideon back into bed afterward, the bloody glyphs healed to the best of my ability and hidden beneath his clothing. His maid might notice them tomorrow, but after decades in his presence, I doubted she would care to tell anyone.

Still, what had happened to him wouldn't stay a secret for long. I'd done my best to scramble the memories of our visit, though I couldn't excise them completely—not from a magic wielder as advanced as Gideon. The risk of this was not lost upon me. But so close to the Melume, consumed by her great mission from Nyaxia, Egrette would be too distracted to notice Gideon's absence for at least a few more days. Enough time for Mische and me to get what we needed and get out of the House of Shadow for good.

Before leaving Gideon's chamber, I changed my bloody clothing and threw it into the fire. Still, I felt the wet cling of his blood on my fresh shirt. Worse, I felt the innards of his mind spattered all over mine—much harder to scrub away.

I had gotten soft. It had been too long since I'd done this.

Though I was expected, I couldn't bring myself to return to my old bedchamber. I wasn't ready to see Mische—or rather, I wasn't ready to let Mische see me. I felt like my shame was smeared all over my face.

Instead, like a ghost, I walked the path of my previous life. This night could have been countless others. Another night returning exhausted after another task. Another cascade of screams in my ears. Another soul added to my collection at the expense of my own.

I found myself wandering past tireless shadow archivists engaged in their endless work, down familiar paths, until I arrived at the doorway to an atrium. This part of the library was somewhat removed from the rest, separated by a narrow hall. The windows here, rising several stories, revealed the churning sea and raging stormy sky. Lightning reflected over a cracked mosaic floor. Curved bookcases stretched up to the ceiling, punctuated by several tall bronze ladders. And—

A crash came from the alcove.

"Shit!" a bright voice hissed.

I whirled around to see—

"What are you doing here?" The words came out harsher than I'd intended.

Mische stopped mid-movement and peered over her shoulder.

She was on top of a piano, two books poorly contained in one arm and another pages-down on the floor, clearly having just evaded her grasp. One bare foot was on the keys. She was wearing something silky and black that didn't exactly look like clothing.

Beside the piano, Luce's tail thumped the ground as if to tell Mische, *I told you so.*

Mische gave me a nervous smile.

"Uh. Nothing. I just thought that instead of wasting time in the room, I'd—"

"How did you find this place?"

I was practically snapping at her. Inwardly, I cringed at the sound of my own voice. But the sight of Mische in this place, seeing me with Gideon's blood still on my hands, yanked something to the surface that I hadn't been prepared to confront.

Her smile faltered. "I don't know. It just . . . called to me. Asar, what's wrong? What happened?"

Because of course she saw it.

Turn around, I told myself. *You can't be near her like this.*

But against all good judgment, I stepped closer, closer. My fingertips caressed the dusty piano keys. Then, because I couldn't help myself, I played a few notes. It was horrifically out of tune. Poor neglected thing.

"Was this yours?" Mische said softly.

Her foot, elegant and bare, still touched the keys. I had hardly seen her skin since Morthryn, and now, it transfixed me. In the moonlight, it was nearly impossible to see the silver sheen to her form, even if one was looking for it. My gaze slid up the curve of her ankle. Her leg. Her calf. The black silk around her body, draping between her cleavage, revealing her bare chest, collarbone, throat. Then, at last, her face, and those eyes—cutting through me just as I had cut through Gideon.

"What in the Mother's name are you wearing?" I said.

"My clothes were soaked. And they stunk. I had to make something else work."

"You went wandering around Ryvenhaal in a sheet?"

Because, upon closer examination—goddess help me, it *was* a sheet. An actual bedsheet, that she'd tied to herself with a too-large leather belt around her waist and a few pins.

"I couldn't find anything else," she said defensively with a shrug. "I think I did a decent job."

I stared at her shoulder, where the sheet had slipped to reveal a fresh expanse of smooth brown skin. My eyes followed the swooping folds of fabric—*very thin* fabric—with the fresh, torturous knowledge that it was just a single piece that was probably barely hanging on to her body.

I yanked my eyes away, back to the piano keys.

A beat of silence. Then she asked, "Did you get what we need?"

I thought of the sensation of Gideon's mind snapping.

"Yes." The less said, the better.

Luce let out a low whine and gave me a sad look. Then she slunk off into the library shelves, as if to offer my complicated emotions their privacy. She had seen the worst of what I had been, and even then, she had known when I needed her and when I wanted to be alone.

My fingers, as if of their own accord, played a few slow notes. All my favorite ones, assembled into a song I'd played once, in Esme's living room.

A reminder of a place that seemed, in every way, the opposite of this one.

I felt Mische's delight bubble up, even without looking at her. "I remember that song."

But the melody was awkward and off-tune. For some reason, it hurt my heart here. I let the melody fade off into silence.

"I told you," I muttered, "to *stay in the room*. This place is dangerous."

Mische looked up to the windows.

"I think it's quite beautiful here. But . . . sad. Even the ghosts here are sad. It was probably a difficult place for a child to grow up."

My jaw was so tight that my ears rang with the tension.

"I think that maybe," she said softly, "that child might have had to find peace in little places like this one. Maybe that was how he learned to see things that no one else paid attention—"

I jerked several steps backward.

Hurt flickered across Mische's face, which gutted me. "I'm sorry, I—"

"Don't apologize," I snapped. "*Never* apologize. I'm just—I shouldn't be here."

"Be here?"

"Be near you."

The words slipped free before I could stop them, and I winced at how harsh they sounded. No sooner were they out of my mouth than I was drifting closer to her again, like ivy reaching for light.

Her eyes searched my face.

"Yes, you should," she murmured. "Stay."

I swore I could feel the ache of compulsion in that command—*stay, stay, stay*.

"You don't want me to do that, Mische."

"Why?"

I barked a laugh—because it seemed *ridiculous* to me, actually ridiculous, that she didn't understand.

"Because I can't be near you and not—" The sheet slipped farther down her shoulder, revealing more forbidden skin.

My trousers strained painfully.

I drank in the glint in her honey-brown eyes. The way her nipples, beaded beneath the tantalizingly thin fabric, rose a little faster. When had that started? Her body, mimicking breath?

Gideon had told me my hunger would be my downfall. Perhaps he was right, because now, it was so devastatingly powerful that I could think of nothing else. And I had thought nothing could be more powerful, until now, when I felt her soul reaching toward mine, and I realized:

She was just as hungry.

She whispered, "Stay."

One word, and my self-control shattered.

The keys squealed a dissonant chord as I leaned over her, pushing her back to the piano. The sheet around her body twisted, revealing a glorious expanse of lines and curves like no artist had ever managed to assemble, framed by silk like gift-wrap. Full breasts, that freckle rising and falling. Her stomach, a hint of dark hair where her thighs met, and the soft flesh of her legs.

I thought to myself, surely it would be worth it. Surely it would be worth it to die by that skin, and let those thighs cradle me down to the underworld.

Instead, I yanked the belt from her waist. My blood ran hot when the rest of the sheet, barely clinging to her, fell open in its absence.

And it took all my self-control to pull that sheet back over her before I lowered my mouth to her skin.

My tongue found that freckle right away. My memory was good, even without a visual guide. I hadn't been sure how much Mische could feel of physical sensation now. But she drew in a delicious, sharp breath when my teeth closed around it. A sharper one still when I moved down to her nipple.

That was what I needed tonight. Not my own satisfaction, but hers. I needed to paint over Gideon's pain with Mische's pleasure.

"That," I groaned. "That is what I need, Mische."

My hands found her hips, fingers digging into her skin. Her form was solid, but not quite right to the touch, a little more nebulous than it should have been. If I had let myself pause, it might have been a reminder of how much work I had left to do.

But I was not going to let myself think.

I was going to touch her, in whatever way I could. Even if it wasn't enough.

"I thought you didn't—that maybe you—"

Her words were weak and choppy. I lifted my head. Through my haze of lust, I had to blink incredulously at her.

"What?" I said. "You thought that I didn't want this?"

She smiled weakly. "When I'm like this."

Incomprehensible.

"Don't say stupid things." I jerked my chin to the ladder against the bookshelf. "Hold on to the bars. They will keep your hands where they need to be."

And I didn't give her time to answer before I slid down between her legs. A dissonant, beautiful chord rang out as her feet struck the keys. Her back lifted from the polished wood at the lightest brush of my lips. That first taste was so immaculate that I couldn't even resent the fabric that separated us.

My tongue pressed the sheet to her, tracing her folds, first on one side, then the other. I lingered at her bud, outlining it through the sheet, before closing my teeth around it gently and sucking—a little harder, a little rougher, than I would have if I'd had the divine privilege of her bare skin. Just to make sure she felt me.

And oh, she felt me.

Her back arched, a mewling gasp slipping between her lips. I loved this about Mische—she reacted so intensely to everything, every joy or sorrow, every pain or delight. During sex, her pleasure radiated from her every expression and movement and muscle, mapping my path to tread. The first time I'd witnessed it, with my mouth on her throat and her hand between her legs, I thought I would die to feel it again.

When I had finally had the chance to make love to her, I'd been patient. Systematic. I didn't have the self-control for that now.

I ground against her, teeth and lips and tongue, my hands holding her thighs firm as she squirmed. With her next moan, fractured with want, I smiled against her in satisfaction.

"I'm glad you can feel it," I said.

She laughed roughly, and the sound morphed to a moan as I pressed my tongue against her again, slower, deeper—teasing at the entrance I could feel through the sheet but couldn't enter. I yanked her closer, fingernails biting into flesh, grinding against her as if to punish us both for my frustration.

"Asar," she gasped. Her want was maddening. It was in the note of her voice as she said my name, in every cord of her muscles as she writhed against me. Still, not enough.

"Louder," I commanded.

And in the next stroke, Mische, ever the star pupil, obeyed. Her cry echoed from the ceilings now, loud enough to shake through the thunderclaps. I wanted her voice to scar the rafters. I wanted it to scar me.

"Good," I said. "Again."

I moved one hand from her thigh to assist at her slit, caressing with my fingertips what my mouth couldn't reach. Her whole body shuddered, writhed, twisted.

"Gods help me," she moaned. "I—"

My eyes flicked up. One of her hands still gripped the rung of the ladder. The other had traveled down, reaching for me, as if on instinct.

I barked, "Bars, Mische."

She returned her hands to the ladder rung, and I had to pause to admire the way she looked—her body stretched out, so impossibly beautiful even beneath that sheet that revealed every swell or dip of her flesh.

"Push against the ladder," I said. "And scream for me."

And then I made her come.

I buried my face between her thighs, tongue and teeth working at her bud, while my thumb slid down to knead at the wet slick of her entrance, and goddess help me, I wanted nothing, nothing, nothing more in my entire pathetic life than I wanted to slide into her.

Instead, I thrust her over that edge alone.

Mische did scream when she came, just as I told her to. The piano keys sang along with her as her foot slipped. Her body arched, trembled, fought against her grip on the ladder—though she didn't let go, not even as I nipped and sucked her through every shuddering aftershock. I seared the sound of her pleasure into my bones. A song beautiful enough to wash away Gideon's wails.

I found myself joining her atop the piano. My hips fell naturally to hers like the moon to the horizon. A wave of devastating desire fell over me as my cock aligned, through my clothing and the sheet, to the wet slick of her. I ground against her in one slow stroke, just because I couldn't stop myself, and her legs positioned around my hips as if to hold me there.

I held myself above her, careful not to touch her skin—torturous—and looked at her.

She still held on to the ladder, though her muscles were looser now. Her eyes were bright, lips parted. She looked so *alive*. Right down to the quickened heave of her chest, and the tint to her cheeks that looked almost like a flush.

She looked at me with such abject, undeserved affection. It made me think of how a sunrise I'd never witnessed must feel.

A lump rose in my throat, and I pushed it down. I leaned back, straightening.

A smile curled her mouth. She released the ladder in favor of me.

"I can do that, too," she said, reaching for my cock through my trousers.

But I looked at this flawless, incredible woman, and I heard Gideon's voice:

You'll ruin her.

Through the sheet, I pushed her firmly back to the piano. "Bars," I commanded. "I'm not finished with you."

Her honey eyes slipped over me, seeing, as always, every complexity I didn't reveal. But she didn't push.

Her fingers closed around the ladder.

"Good girl," I said. And I set back to work, painting over the bloodstains with her gasps of pleasure, as the storm wore on, and on, and on.

WE DID, EVENTUALLY, make our way back to the bedchamber, where Mische quickly sprawled out on the bed like some kind of amorphous slime fungus, utterly spent. Luce returned from her wanderings sometime later, curling up before the fire.

But I didn't rest.

Instead, I pored over the books I'd taken from Gideon's office and my transcription of the glyphs I'd ripped from his mind, trying and failing not to relive what I'd done to get them.

Eventually, the storm passed. When Mische awoke, I was struck by how wraithlike she seemed, compared to the glow of her aliveness in the library. The passage of time hung a little heavier.

Somewhere in these halls, Gideon likely still lay in his bed, bloodstained and moaning, but Mische and I didn't so much as acknowledge him as we returned to the castle under a silken, silent, endless night.

CHAPTER TWENTY

Mische

Vincent stared at me from my bedchamber mirror, looking annoyed.

It was really, really not what I had been expecting to see.

I let out a yelp and lurched backward, nearly toppling over an ottoman. Luce let out a low growl, crouching back on her haunches.

Shortly after we returned to the Shadowborn castle, Asar disappeared again to go meet with Egrette. She was demanding of his time, with the Melume nearly here—though a suspicious part of me wondered if that was because she was nervous about what he might do with it if left to his own devices. He'd barely spoken on our way back to the city. I was no fool. I knew our trip to Ryvenhaal had stuck with him, even though he refused to talk about the details.

That left Luce and me by ourselves with the notes we had retrieved from Ryvenhaal. But I found it difficult to focus. My exhaustion now clung stubbornly, no matter how much I rested. When I closed my eyes, I dreamed of the underworld.

Eventually, I had to drag myself upright. There was too much work to do to waste time.

That was when I saw the Nightborn king.

When I caught myself and turned back to the mirror, I half expected to see myself staring back, like the ghost had just been a stress-induced hallucination. And I did see myself, too—albeit a transparent version of myself. But beside me, sure enough, there was Vincent.

Not a hallucination, apparently.

"Sun fucking take me, Vincent," I gasped, hand to my chest. "What are you doing there?"

"How many times must we discuss this? I said I would follow you. The Melume is near." He gestured at the window—to the full moon hanging beyond it, tinted foreboding red. "The underworld is very close to the House of Shadow right now. I'm sure you feel it, too."

Uneasily, I realized that I did, indeed, feel it.

I adjusted my robe around myself, closing the gap at my neckline. "That doesn't mean that you should just go sneaking up on people in their bedchambers," I grumbled.

"I am the greatest Nightborn king in Obitraen history. I go where I please."

I felt another wave of deep sympathy at the thought of Oraya's upbringing.

"I take it that your journey to Ryvenhaal brought you what you need for the Melume." His face hardened. "Shame that I did not realize a century ago the kinds of things that the Shadowborn were hiding there. Quite a treasure trove, it seems. I could have made great use of that information in life."

I disliked it when Vincent waxed romantic about that kind of thing.

"You were watching us in Ryvenhaal?" I said.

"I observed in the ways that I could. Ryvenhaal is close to the dead. You sensed that, surely."

That was undeniable. Upon more consideration, it was unsurprising that Vincent had been able to peer through the veil there.

But then, at another thought, I frowned. Crossed my arms over my chest.

"What else did you . . . uh, *observe*?"

He scoffed. "Don't flatter yourself. We are discussing matters that could lead to the destruction of the mortal plane and you're concerned that I'm leering at you like a common—"

"Gods, *stop*. Please." The mere sound of Vincent saying the word "leering" in conjunction with the memory of what Asar and I had done in the Ryvenhaal library made me want to peel off my own skin and bury myself in the dirt.

"Alright, alright." *Leering.* Ugh. "That's enough of that. What's so important that it made you turn up in my bedroom mirror?"

Vincent's form wavered, slipping away and reassembling, as if I were seeing him through the snow-leaden gusts of a blizzard. I had to strain to barely make out the words *the House of Night*.

My brows shot up. "Wait. What?"

Now he enunciated clearly. "You must go to the House of Night."

I had hoped I had heard him wrong. "Why?"

"I cultivated Alarus's blood in my time as king," he said. "Blood that, at one time, had pumped through Alarus's heart. I realized it when you were in Ryvenhaal. If any kingdom in Obitraes is powerful enough to find and house the heart of Alarus, it is the House of Night. Go there. Take the blood. Use it to find the heart."

There was a certain note to his voice that made a pit form in my stomach. I'd heard it so many times, from so many different kings—even from Atroxus himself. Vincent spoke like a king faced with the opportunity to seize a powerful weapon.

But when I thought of the House of Night, I wasn't thinking of god-touched weapons. I was thinking of my best friends, and the dangers that followed Asar and me wherever we went—angry gods and beasts from the underworld and all other manner of terrible things that I refused to bring to their doorstep.

"The House of Night doesn't have the blood anymore," I said. "Oraya gave it to Nyaxia."

To save Raihn. But I left that part out.

But at the sound of her name, indecipherable emotion flickered over Vincent's face, before he pushed it away.

"There is always something left to cultivate," he said. "Our work to find and distill the blood that went far beyond that. She—" His voice caught, ever so slightly. "Any Nightborn ruler would know that. They will have the blood. Mark my words."

Our work. Vincent spoke of Alana, Oraya's mother—a follower of

Acaeja who had used her spellcasting knowledge to help him distill the blood of Alarus.

But a lump rose in my throat. Elias had said it, too, when we were in the Descent. That the House of Night was holding some powerful divine weapon. I hadn't wanted to believe it then, and I didn't want to believe it now. Not after I'd seen firsthand in the Nightborn war what terrible things weapons created from Alarus's remains were capable of.

I didn't want to believe that after all that, Raihn and Oraya would turn around and leverage that power again.

I swallowed hard.

"Raihn and Oraya are already outside of Nyaxia's favor," I said. "She didn't even call upon the House of Night for her army. They're already in danger. I can't bring them this."

A wrinkle flitted over Vincent's nose. "And I am supposed to adjust our plans just because that Turned traitor is unworthy of keeping Nyaxia's favor?"

Turned traitor. Raihn.

"The *Turned traitor* is the king of the House of Night."

"Do not try to endear him with what he stole," Vincent sneered.

"He is your daughter's husband," I snapped.

Vincent's cold rage fell over me like ice. "He is my *murderer*. And if I was alive, he would pay for it."

I stepped abruptly back. It was rare that I felt naive—I was an optimist, but that didn't make me unrealistic. Still, now, I felt suddenly foolish for ever thinking that Vincent could be motivated by something greater than his desire for power.

"Think like a vampire," I said coldly. "Is that what that means? I won't bring this to their doorstep. They won't survive it, and I won't be the reason for that."

"You don't have a choice," he shot back. "*We* do not have a choice. If you fail, the House of Night will cease to exist. We don't have the luxury of cowardice—"

"Cowardice." I choked a laugh. "You're trying to tell me that you're doing this to protect your kingdom. But you won't even speak

Oraya's name. She deserves that much from you, after what you put her through."

Vincent stilled. He was silent for so long that I wondered if perhaps he had begun to fall back to the underworld.

But at last he said, between gritted teeth, "My words are useless to her. My actions may not be."

"Words are never useless. And neither is compassion. This isn't just about us."

"You cannot be afraid to use the power you have at your disposal. Not with this much at stake."

"We should all be afraid of power. Anyone who isn't doesn't deserve to wield it. This could *destroy them,* Vincent." When I blinked, I saw it so vividly. The House of Night was already weak. They would crumble if the House of Shadow came for them, or worse, if the White Pantheon did. Nyaxia might not bother to protect them. And then what?

Perhaps Vincent might see that outcome as Raihn's deserved punishment. But it was my greatest nightmare.

Vincent had started some argument I barely heard, but I shook my head. "No. There are other ways to find the heart. I'm not going there."

And then I grabbed the blanket from the bed and threw it over the mirror, cutting Vincent off before he could say another word.

"THIS WILL ALL need to go *perfectly,*" Asar said.

His tone did not sound particularly confident.

I gave him a bright smile. "I'm not worried at all."

I was definitely worried.

He gave me a look that said he knew I was, too.

We sat in the middle of our chamber floor, books and papers scattered around us. Most were maps and illustrations of Vathysia, including those of the palace as it had existed in those days. Others were diagrams and documentation of spell work, glyphs thousands of years old, predating the existence of Obitraes.

Luce, bored of us, slept belly-up by the fire. I sat cross-legged among the piles of parchment. And Asar stood rod straight, arms crossed, and paced with the exacting relentlessness of a military commander.

"Show me the path again," he barked.

I sighed, but closed my eyes and recited the directions to the mask yet again, for the hundredth time. The layout of the palace would be confusing at the height of the Melume, when the past would be fully transposed over the present.

I would have to make the trip alone. Asar and Egrette would need to conduct the spell to usher the beginning of the ceremony into the castle. It was traditionally performed by the Shadowborn heir, and since Asar also bore Heir Marks, Egrette was not willing to risk the possibility that she might try alone and fail in front of allies and enemies alike.

The Melume would last all night, but the window that would open the castle up to the past, when the veil was thinnest, would last only for a few minutes.

Which meant that, while Asar was conducting the ceremony, I would need to go ahead and start unlocking the way to the mask.

By myself.

The tricky thing was, we weren't completely sure which path would end up being the correct one. The maps were very, very old, and the Melume's illusion was not always consistent. Which meant that I'd have to rely not only on my impeccable rote memorization skills—trained, of course, on a lifetime in the church—but on my magic.

Asar was, apparently, satisfied with my performance, because he said nothing once I finished, just continued pacing.

"You are connected to the dead," he said. "Use that if you get lost."

I watched the ghosts out of the corner of my eye. They had grown more visible, and more active. I could now almost make out their humanoid shapes. Still, they didn't seem especially helpful.

"What if someone stops me?" I asked. "I still can't quite get compulsion right."

There was nothing "quite" about it. Every time I tried it on Asar, he had barely managed to hold back his laugh. I sounded ridiculous, and not at all convincing.

"You're just thinking about it too hard," he said. "You'll get it eventually. Compulsion is easy when it's right. But trying and failing is worse than talking your way out of a bad situation if you get into one. Use your charms instead."

"Or my magical death touch?"

Asar gave me a flat stare. He did not like joking about my death touch. He did not like joking about my death at all.

He hadn't been the same since we returned from Ryvenhaal. Like he was perpetually tensed to protect an infected wound.

"I'll make it to you as soon as I can," he said. "The ritual shouldn't take long."

And then we would go to the mask itself, step between the veils that separated time and space, and take it.

This was where the plan began to fall apart. We didn't know what to expect when we reached the mask itself. And worse, we didn't know what would happen once we attempted to leave.

"The mask is protected by complex layers of magic, and we'll be disrupting them at their basest level," Asar said. "No matter how careful we are, and how distracted Egrette is, she will feel it when we take it. We'll need to leave immediately."

And that was the final, crucial unanswered question: where the hell would we go?

"They can't follow us to the deadlands," I said quietly. But even as the words left my lips, they sounded ridiculous. Few mortals had ever managed to get into the deadlands, and fewer still had managed to survive long enough to make it out alive. We had barely twenty-four hours before our grand escape. Not enough time to uncover yet another grand divine mystery.

"We could go to the forest," I suggested. "I managed to wander around in there for a few months."

"Until Egrette captured you."

I threw my hands up. "Well, I don't know how she managed to do that."

It still bothered me that I didn't know who had told her of my location. Clearly, someone had.

"They'll be determined to find us," he said. "If we can't go straight to the deadlands, we'll need to find a safe place to map out our next move."

I knew Asar detested having to say this. His impatience was palpable. He wanted to complete this mission as quickly as possible, divine dangers be damned, and he didn't care what that entailed. It made me uneasy.

I glanced down at my hand. Was it more transparent than it had been?

That night in Ryvenhaal with Asar, my body had felt closer to life than it had since my death. But that had only made its absence since we returned unbearable. I felt cold and empty. The whispers of the dead were louder. I could sense them lingering just beneath the surface, reaching for me—reaching for Asar.

Asar, too, was looking at my skin, likely calculating whether it was closer to death than it had been.

And then, he said something that I had been dreading:

"We may need to consider going to the House of Night."

He spoke carefully, and his tone said he knew exactly how grave a suggestion this was for me. I had told him of Vincent's theory, and I had also told him that we were absolutely not under any circumstances dragging the House of Night into this.

"I don't say this lightly," he said. "We will need an alternative option. But it is your decision. I respect it either way."

I was quiet.

It was hard to think about Raihn and Oraya. I missed them so fiercely, but I loved them even more. I loved them enough to recognize that the best thing I could do for them was ensure that they never saw me again.

I shook my head. "I can't bring them into this."

And gods help me, I loved Asar so much for the way he did not hesitate when he said, "Fine. Not the House of Night. We'll find another way."

But neither of us knew what that could possibly be, and the walls were closing in.

Tick, tick, tick, the clock warned.

HOURS PASSED, AND we had no better answers. My frustration grew, and so did Asar's impatience. It increasingly seemed like we were about to be backed into a corner we couldn't get out of.

Soon enough, Asar was summoned, yet again, back to Egrette, who seemed to enjoy having him at her beck and call. Though I knew Asar would disapprove, I couldn't bring myself to sit in this room and continue bashing my head against the wall. So with Luce at my side, I slipped out into the halls. Maybe a walk would trigger some inspiration.

The castle was abuzz with activity. Travelers from all over the House of Shadow—from all over Obitraes, it seemed—had come for the Melume. I kept my hood up and was careful to guard my thoughts. Some of these people were among the most powerful Shadowborn nobles in the kingdom. And though with all the commotion, I largely slipped by unnoticed, some intrigued gazes followed me.

There she is, their thoughts would whisper. *The Wraith Warden's bride.*

Asar had been right. Claiming me as his wife offered a level of protection far greater than any weapon. No strategically minded noble would risk touching me, not when Asar still bore Heir Marks on his arms and had the Shadowborn crown within his reach.

"Too many people," I whispered to Luce. "Let's find somewhere quieter."

We climbed the grand staircase until the crowd thinned. Eventually I reached what appeared to be a large dining room. It was empty, the polished black table set with untouched crystal glasses and porcelain plates. Iron-framed windows offered expansive views of the city on one side and the bay on the other. Even Morthryn was visible, far in the distance, its crooked spires reaching to the blood-tinted moon and great glass eye peering from another world.

From up here, it was clear that there was not a single place that war had not touched. The bay was full of ships—so many more than I'd seen when we first arrived. The city below was overrun with soldiers bearing the white uniforms of the House of Blood or deep green of the House of Shadow. Tents had been erected outside the city to house the influx of new soldiers. And the entire skyline was alight with the hearths of booked-up boarding houses and the billows of roaring armorers' fires.

Once, before we embarked into the Descent, Atroxus had shown me a vision of a world devastated by a war between vampires and humans. Now, those images crashed over me, too vivid. It all seemed so close to reality.

"I have to admit, I never expected that I'd see you here, of all places."

A voice I hoped I'd never hear again came from behind me. The scent of smoke drifted across the ballroom.

I turned.

Luce growled low in her throat, and Septimus chuckled.

"How loyal. You know, the Shadowborn nobles say that the Wraith Warden's pet is notoriously finicky. Apparently you've—"

My hand was moving before I could stop myself.

When Septimus stepped closer, I struck him straight across the face.

The slap rang out with a satisfying *CRACK*.

He lurched backward, fingers flying to his cheek. I gasped and pressed my hands over my mouth. Sun fucking take me, why did I just do that? I didn't even know that I *could* slap someone, though I was grateful my hand didn't pass right through him, which would have triggered all kinds of uncomfortable questions.

It was a stupid thing to do. Yet I couldn't bring myself to regret it.

Septimus stared at me, startled. I stared back, equally startled. Between us, his lit cigarillo rolled slowly across the floor, giving off a lazy plume of smoke.

And then, he laughed. It was a slick, elegant sound, like blood over marble.

"And to think I wasn't sure if you would remember me at all."

He leaned down to pick up his cigarillo. Apparently too precious to waste. Yuck.

"I hoped I'd never have to," I snarled. "We thought that if we were lucky, you were dead."

"That's not very holy of you, priestess."

Stop talking, Mische. The scolding in the back of my head sounded too much like Saescha's. But the words, as they so often did, just poured out of me.

"What the hell did you expect? You tried to overthrow the House of Night. You tried to kill my best friend. And you—"

The sight of Septimus made those memories crash back over me. Lilith and Vale's wedding. Me wearing a beautiful gold dress that I'd once felt so lovely in, meeting the eyes of the man who had Turned me.

And then everything falling apart. The Bloodborn soldiers and Rishan soldiers turning on Raihn. Cairis's betrayal. Simon's men dragging me up to that bedchamber and locking me up, a gift to buy a prince's favor.

"And you were going to *give me to him,*" I ground out.

Those words weren't terrible enough to describe it.

I didn't like to think about what Malach would have done to me if Oraya hadn't freed me when she did. But those possibilities had visited me in my nightmares ever since.

Septimus adjusted a button at his wrist.

"I will take full responsibility for the first two things," he said, "but not the third. That was all your friend's doing. What was his name—Cairis? Even I thought it was terribly cold."

A stab of betrayal twisted in my gut.

Cairis had nursed me back to health after I'd nearly died in the Kejari. He had been a friend when I had needed one most.

I'd liked him. Trusted him. We all had.

"I don't believe you," I said.

But perhaps the darkness had already taken its toll on me, because secretly, I did believe it. Cairis had always known what people wanted and had always been so shrewd in using it.

Septimus half shrugged. "Suit yourself, dove. I have never been afraid to bear the mantle of the villain."

He stared out the window beside me. An exhale of smoke rolled against the glass. "Quite a sight, isn't it?"

"How did you even manage to worm your way into another castle, after what happened in the House of Night?"

Not long ago, the House of Shadow had so disapproved of the House of Night's decision to ally with the Bloodborn that they almost went to war over it.

A smirk curled Septimus's mouth. "When a goddess calls, you answer. There's an eternal night to be seized. Haven't you heard? Of course the House of Blood is honored to heed her call, and if doing so means allying with the Shadowborn, then perhaps we shall all let bygones be bygones." His brow twitched. "Though I confess, I was surprised that the House of Night doesn't appear to be involved. Tell me, how are Raihn and Oraya these days? Are they pacifists, I wonder, unwilling to answer Nyaxia's call? Or did she not call upon them at all?"

"And yet she called upon the Bloodborn?" I asked. "After two thousand years of hating you?"

"A surprise to us, too," Septimus said. "But we are such loyal subjects. Happy to go crawling back after centuries of getting kicked in the face. Like a good little dog."

His fingertips brushed the bruise on his cheekbone—a little too dark for the strike I'd given him. His eyes slid to me, sparkling with a smirk.

"Your husband knows that, it seems. Crawling back to his sister. Unless his intentions aren't as straightforward as her arrogance would have her believe."

What the hell was I doing? This was a dangerous conversation to have. I could feel Septimus picking me apart like a splayed-open carcass.

"I have to go," I said and began to turn away.

But behind me, Septimus said, "I hear that you need to get to the deadlands, and quickly."

I stopped short, whirling around. I bit back the words before they made it up my throat: *How did you know that?*

"That's ridiculous," I said plainly.

"No disagreement there. The deadlands are notoriously dangerous, and besides, it would take a newcomer decades just to figure out how to gain entry to the damned place." Septimus slid his hands into his pockets. "So yes. It's ridiculous. And yet you're still standing here."

He was right. I should walk away.

But I thought of the ticking clock, and our rapidly diminishing options, and just how desperate I was to protect the House of Night.

And I did not move.

"I know someone who has been there, actually," he said. "My cousin spent years doing the bidding of our Dark Mother. It so happens that he's in Obitraes now. If you *were* looking for passage to the deadlands, and if you *did* need to find it quickly, he may be willing to guide you."

Responses swirled in my head.

Denial—*I don't know what you're talking about.*

Dismissal—*I would never take your help.*

Disbelief—*I don't believe you.*

I said none of them.

Instead, I only asked, "For what payment?"

"Call it a favor."

I scrunched up my nose, and he chuckled. "My, what a reaction."

"Well, I'm not stupid. It's just such an obvious lie."

"Look into my mind if you wish, Shadowborn. I'm not lying to you. Perhaps our interests align in this particular scenario."

I was silent, staring at him hard.

He was a handsome man, objectively, though all his features were a little too sharp, like touching him might draw blood. An acquired quality, I knew. He'd been broken until his edges were jagged.

Most of Obitraes looked at the Bloodborn like they were animals. But it had always struck me as cruel and reductive. No one outside the secretive Bloodborn inner workings even knew what the original disagreement between the House of Blood and Nyaxia was that had earned their ire, nor did we know the details of the curse that ate away their sanity and lifespans. But I knew they had suffered immensely for something that had happened long before their birth. Whatever the truth was, it couldn't justify what had happened to them.

Still, none of that meant I trusted Septimus. The opposite, actually. Most vampires fought for glory. Septimus fought for survival. That made him twice as dangerous.

He gestured to his temple, cigarillo between his fingers. "Go ahead. Really."

I hesitated. I had never looked into a mind on my own, at least not with any specificity. But I could feel Septimus's mind, a door cracked open for me.

I had insisted that we couldn't go to the House of Night. I didn't exactly have the freedom not to explore every other possible option.

I wasn't actually sure how to do this, and I tried not to let Septimus know that. I closed my eyes and concentrated. I could sense his presence beside mine, carefully guarded, save for that single opening left for me. I reached into it. And then, with all my strength, I flung it open.

An avalanche of images crashed over me.

First, I saw myself as he saw me. I felt the offer on his lips, and glimpsed a man with long white hair before a cold empty gate, and felt the genuine hope that his gift might be accepted.

But I kept pushing, pushing.

I saw a palace of red and gold and white, snow-dusted, cradled in stone. Saw a severed head, a blond man, eyes wide open, black blood congealing around the ragged cut at his throat. Saw claw marks running down stone, leading to a crumpled form on the floor. Heard a million screams of decimation.

And I felt *rage*.

Here, as he stood over the army he'd summoned at Nyaxia's call. Here, as he stared into my face, staring into his, looking into all his secrets. And—

Septimus jerked away. The door in his mind slammed closed.

"Eager, aren't you?" he said coolly. But his fingertips rubbed his temple, and I sensed that perhaps he hadn't been expecting me to pry quite so deep.

I stared at him, brow furrowed.

Because I really hadn't sensed any lie in his offer.

"Why?" I asked.

"I heard that you used to be a missionary. We have some things in common, then. I, too, greatly enjoy being the solution to a problem."

I said nothing. My eyes narrowed.

"You still think I'm lying." He let out a puff of smoke. "Even after I opened my mind to show you I'm not."

"No. I think you're telling the truth. I just don't think the problem that you're talking about is mine."

"I will admit it, dove, you had me fooled. You are more perceptive than any of them give you credit for."

"I've traveled to a lot of places and met a lot of people. After all that, you learn that everyone is the hero of their own tale."

Septimus chuckled to himself. It was an oddly sad sound. "Some tales don't deserve a hero. I think your husband knows that, too."

He sank down into a chair by the window, then gave me an expectant look and gestured to the empty one across from it.

"So," he said, "will you be joining me?"

For a long moment, I did not move.

Septimus had attempted to kill my best friends. Had stood by as I was chained up and presented as a gift. Had come alarmingly close to destroying the House of Night.

But it was now mere hours before Asar and I would have mortal and divine enemies alike at our heels, and we had no options for our next move save for the one that I refused to make.

I sat down.

CHAPTER TWENTY-ONE

Asar

There were some things I missed about exile.

Yes, I had lost everything. But the thing about losing everything is that it's surprisingly easy to adjust to having nothing. It turned out that I often didn't mind being all alone save for Luce, prisoners that I rarely had to interact with, and as many books as I wanted.

On the Nights of the Melume, I would take a glass of blood wine, climb out onto the roof of Morthryn, and watch the sky with Luce beside me. In those early years, Esmę would join us, too, and we'd drink ourselves into a stupor together as I played her song after song until even the dead were exhausted.

It had been a much better party than this goddess-damned ridiculousness.

"Magnificent, isn't it?" Egrette said to me. "An embodiment of a new era."

We stood upon the dais together, looking out over the grand celebration. She had practically turned herself into a living recreation of the Shadowborn crest, with a gown of deep green velvet accented with bronze. Her cape was heavily embroidered with copper thread, giving the impression that she was wearing the metalwork that the Shadowborn were so well-known for. Her hair was bound in an elaborate braided updo, with the Shadowborn crown woven into it as if it grew organically from her head.

Yet, despite her admittedly impressive appearance, she stank of anxiety. She guarded her mind well, as any well-trained Shadowborn should, but she was less adept at keeping the signs of her nervousness from her body. Her hands were clasped tight in front of her, white-knuckled.

"Magnificent," I repeated, deadpan, and took a sip of wine.

During his rule, our father had decorated the castle in immaculate finery for this event, all roses and ivy, stained glass and patriotic crests. But Egrette had taken another path. She had the expensive decor and the beautiful flowers, yes—the overflowing feast tables and orchestras of the most talented musicians. But instead of covering the walls in stuffy, formal decor, she had covered them all in sheets of black silk. She'd removed the velvet drapes and thrown open all the doors and windows, allowing the chiffon to sway in the gentle sea breeze. It gave the entire castle a ghostly, mournful cast, like a veiled widow at a funeral. It was grand and breathtaking, and, I knew, would only be more so once the ceremony began.

It was also a clear message: *We fear nothing. We have the night that never ends.*

It was striking. Powerful. I had to admit it, even though I was here to tear it all to pieces.

The ballroom was already full of people—Bloodborn in uniforms of red and white, Shadowborn in deep velvets or impeccable military finery, and even a few Nightborn nobles, swathed in flowing silks of blue and purple and silver. Like the Kejari, the Melume was one of the rare Obitraen events that transcended Houses—the House of Shadow's one opportunity to fling their doors open to flaunt our power before all our rivals. The ships, Bloodborn and Shadowborn, crowded the bay, covering the glittering silver sea with fluttering sails of green and black, red and white. Even the music was ominous, bows drawing over strings with the slow promise of a shadow falling over our enemies.

Yet, I scanned the crowd for only one face.

Typical. Late. I found myself doubting the decision to leave Mische to prepare alone.

"Not much longer now," Egrette remarked. She nodded out the window, to the moon, which was tinted red. The ring of crimson behind it now gleamed unmistakably. At the height of the Melume, the moon itself would be just as bright, as if covered with spilled blood.

Then she glanced over her shoulder—at the frame that stood behind us, shrouded in gauze that faintly rustled with a breeze that was not coming from the sea.

The Dusk Window.

It was one of the few relics of the age of Vathysia that remained openly displayed in the castle. A breathtaking piece of work. Some people—uneducated people—referred to it as a "mirror," but that didn't do it justice. The first time I'd seen it up close, I'd found it so difficult to look away that I almost stumbled into the middle of Raoul's Melume ceremony, which he'd appreciated about as much as one would expect.

The design of the frame itself was pretty enough, with its intricate bronze swirls and flowers and thorns. But the real beauty of it lay within. At first glance, it did indeed appear to be a mirror, albeit one that was barely usable—the surface was foggy, spotted with silver and red-black, and fractured by cracks that arced corner to corner like lightning strikes.

But if one looked closer, they might notice that the image in the glass didn't quite match up with a reflection. They might notice that it offered, instead, a glimpse into the world in which it was created. This same palace, but far in the past, before Obitraes existed at all—Vathysia, a dead House, and the dead souls that had once walked its halls.

Most of the time, the images in the Window were impossible to make out. But they became clearer as the veil drifted closer. On the Melume, for a few beautiful minutes, we would use the Window to open the door between the past and the present.

This required a ritual to be conducted by the Heir of the House of Shadow—the king had the connection to the castle and the land,

and so, it would be the king to draw upon the magic etched into the history here to draw back the veil. Egrette didn't care to hide just how much she resented having to conduct this spell together, though not enough, apparently, to risk trying it by herself and failing. To make up for this blow to her public image, she seemed committed to making sure that she was as visibly royal as possible. I was more than happy to allow her to keep the stage.

Soon, Egrette flitted off into the crowd with Elias and his pack of guards at her heels, ready to flaunt her power in front of her audience of nobles. I was grateful to have my own excuse to slip away into the ballroom. Standing at the dais, so highly visible, made my teeth grind.

I strode through the party, scanning for Mische. One hand massaged my temple. I had a horrible headache, like something was pressing up against the inside of my skull—too much awareness of too many sensations, too many whispers of too many different minds, and too many looming shadows of too many possible fates.

And every minute that passed without Mische here was another minute that something could be going catastrophically—

"Hello, Warden," came a low murmur from behind me, right into my ear.

The words slithered up my spine. Goose bumps rose where they darted over my skin.

I turned around. "Where have you—"

Mische stood before me, grinning, hands clasped behind her back.

I forgot what I had been saying.

She wore a gown that was so distinctly Shadowborn that on anyone else, it would verge on stereotype. And yet, contrasted with her lightness—lightness that transcended even death itself—it was elevated to something interesting, something different. The gown was crafted of dark green velvet, nearly black, which hugged Mische in a series of swoops that ran over her body like water. The bodice was a corset, with a neckline that revealed generous cleavage hoisted up by the boning, framed in gathered fabric that slipped off her bare shoulders. She wore long black gloves that ran all the way to her upper arms. A gauzy black veil—traditional for the Melume—was pinned to her honey-brown curls. The hood was a blessing. It made it nearly impossible for a casual observer to notice the odd shimmer at the edges of her form.

She looked stunning. A perfect image of a Shadowborn lady. No, a Shadowborn queen.

And yet—it still didn't quite suit her. Like all that heavy fabric and overdesigned finery just constricted her ethereal beauty. Even the shadows of the dead, already beginning to collect in the periphery like cobwebs, seemed drawn to her—all of them moving as she did, as if orienting themselves around her north star.

At my silence, her brows rose.

"I actually startled you!" she said proudly. "Look how good I'm getting at that Shadowborn stealth."

Luce, who had followed close behind her, yipped in an approval that made Mische beam.

"It's acceptable," I said.

She scowled. "You're quite a critic." Then her eyes fell to my fingers, still pressed to my temple. "Are you alright?"

I slipped my hands into my pockets.

"Yes," I lied.

"You're nervous."

"I'm not nervous."

Her smile faded. "It's alright. I am, too." Then she extended her hand. "Dance with me, Warden. Let's distract ourselves."

I scoffed. "We don't need to start what will already be a difficult night with that kind of humiliation."

She actually looked a little hurt, which made me instantly, violently regret my words. Then she leaned closer, eyes sparkling. "Isn't a Shadowborn royal expected to dance with his wife?"

I briefly forgot what I was doing and where we were and all the many unpleasant realities upon our shoulders. I forgot everything except for her.

"Dance with me," she said again, her voice comically low, and I stifled a chuckle.

"Was that supposed to be compulsion, Iliae?"

"What, it didn't work?"

Maybe it had. I wondered whether Mische had figured out yet that I would never—could never—say no to her. It was the kind of powerlessness I'd been taught to fear my entire life. And yet I was so eager to run headfirst toward it. Even now. Especially now.

I took her hand. Even through the velvet of her gloves, through the not-quite-right sensation of her form beneath them, the touch sent a jolt up my spine.

"Shame the music isn't as good this time," I said, deadpan, nodding to the orchestra, entrenched in a grand waltz.

I'd meant it sarcastically, but Mische was completely serious as she said, "Not even close. But we can make it work."

I swept her out onto the dance floor, and together we swirled and dipped to the rolling swells of the music. We were, at best, average dancers, especially compared to the other nobles on the floor, all determined to outmatch each other. Yet, as I watched genuine joy bloom over Mische's face, I couldn't find it in myself to care.

"See?" she said. "We're not bad. Except, I'd be better without this thing." She motioned to her dress. "How do Shadowborn women even breathe in this?"

"You don't need to breathe, technically."

"Yes, but I *like* to."

"The dress isn't the biggest challenge you'll face tonight."

"Easy for you to say. You try wearing a corset and twenty pounds of velvet while pulling off a grand heist."

I dipped her, and in the movement, I caught the faintest inhale of her scent—spice and ash and, I was certain, even though I'd never experienced it myself, sunshine.

"I will if you want me to," I murmured in her ear, and Mother help me, I felt drunk, literally drunk, on her burst of laughter.

"Oh yes, Warden. Please, please, *please* do. You'll make me the happiest girl in all the underworld."

But at our next twirl around the ballroom, Mische's smile suddenly disappeared. Her eyes snapped over my shoulder.

"What?" I asked, attempting to follow her gaze.

"I just—nothing. I thought I saw—nothing." She shook her head.

Then she looked at the dais, where the Window stood. The gauze over it rippled faster, and mist clustered around its base. The shadows at the edges of the room now more closely resembled humanoid forms, mostly arms and hands, reaching down. I wondered how Mische saw them. For her, they were probably much clearer than they were to me.

How much longer? she said into my mind.

I eyed the moon outside—now a rosy hue, with shadows undulating across it.

Just a few minutes, I said. *Egrette will be after me any minute.*

A knot of anxiety pulled tight in my stomach. I could handle the unknowns of magic, even unknowns that defied mortal understanding. But tonight, we were relying on lots and lots of luck, and I didn't trust it.

You remember the paths? I asked Mische. *Try the northern ones first, and then—*

And then the east. Yes, I know, Warden. Just like I knew the last three dozen times you quizzed me on it.

Yet, she said this with affection.

I ushered her through a twirl, the movement giving us another excuse to survey the room. I noticed the spirits lingering in the dark seemed . . . more active than I'd remembered from Melume celebrations past.

Mische followed my gaze, her brow furrowing.

It feels . . .

She trailed off. Yet, she didn't need to finish.

Wrong.

Something didn't feel right. The dead were always hungry. But here, they seemed ravenous. Panicking, even.

Before I could answer, a cold burst of air rolled through the ballroom. The orchestra's song rose to a deafening climax, and the shapeless shadows of the dead rolled down the walls like dripping paint.

Outside, the moon was now bright red.

It's time, brother, Egrette said into my mind. I looked up to the dais to see her staring at me expectantly. *The Night of the Melume is beginning.*

Mische and I had stopped dancing. We stared into each other's eyes. Both of us felt it—the impending collision of worlds. Everything was about to get very complicated, and very dangerous, and suddenly the prospect of letting go of her, safe in my arms for this final moment, seemed impossible.

She gave me a weak smile. "Good luck—"

"Mische!"

A booming voice rang out behind me.

Mische's eyes widened, lips parted. I felt, in my own heart, the cold spell fall over hers.

I whirled around.

A towering man wearing Nightborn finery stood before us. Dark red hair fell to his shoulders, its messiness standing in stark contrast to the neatness of his clothing. His stance was rigid, and the sheer intensity of his emotions—a knot of shock and anger and breathtaking *relief*—were so intense that they burst from his mind without me even having to reach for them.

I stepped in front of Mische, wary.

Finally, she managed a single word:

"Raihn."

CHAPTER TWENTY-TWO

Mische

The look on Raihn's face destroyed me. Utterly destroyed me.

Because after that initial wave of shock, he looked so damned *happy*. His entire massive form just sagged in a full-body sigh of relief.

"Mische," he breathed. "I can't believe it's—thank the fucking Mother."

I blurted out, "What are you doing here?"

I spoke too quickly to temper my tone, and it struck Raihn like an open palm. His mouth closed. His emotions went cold. His gaze darted between me and Asar, who had stepped protectively in front of me.

Raihn? Asar asked into my mind. *Raihn, the Nightborn king? Here?*

And then, when my silence gave him the answer: *Is he stupid?*

Yes. Yes, he was. He had to be. What was he thinking?

"Who the hell are you?" Raihn snapped at Asar.

Asar bristled.

Stop— I started to tell him. Not quickly enough. Because he smoothly answered, "I'm her husband."

It was the absolute worst thing he could have said. My entire body folded into a cringe.

"Husband?" Raihn bit out.

"What are you *doing* here, Raihn?"

He could not be here. *He could not be here.*

A cold gust of wind cut through the ballroom, this time with a low, mournful whistle that sounded like a choir of bodiless voices. The room was dark. The spirits were restless, now gathering at the outskirts of the ballroom, staring at the guests with blatant jealousy. The guests' attention had turned to the dais and the bright crimson moon hanging over it through the window, oblivious to what was unfolding here—oblivious to the presence of Nightborn royalty. Raihn wore no crown, no royal garb, nothing to mark him as king. What the hell had his plan been? To march out into the middle of the Melume ceremony, reveal his identity, and demand my release? Sun fucking take me.

I knew that Egrette must be screaming into Asar's mind right now, calling him to the Dusk Window. They had only minutes to conduct the ceremony. Yet, he didn't move, one hand on my lower back, his stare piercing Raihn.

"What the fuck do you mean, *what am I doing here*?" Raihn said. "I'm here for you."

He stepped closer, and Asar hissed, "That's enough."

Raihn shot him a seething glare, which dragged from head to feet. I knew the calculation he was making. I knew that he was thinking of another party and another Shadowborn prince, and I knew exactly how all those pieces fit together from where he stood.

"Asar!" Egrette's annoyed voice cut across the ballroom. She paced the dais, cape swishing behind her. "It is time."

But Asar didn't move.

Go, I snapped at him.

I'm not leaving you alone with—

You need to do the ceremony, and you need to do it right now. Just go.

"Mische," Raihn said, voice low. "What the fuck is going on?"

Asar didn't want to—I could practically taste his reluctance—but in the end, he had no choice. We wouldn't be going anywhere if he never managed to bring the Melume on at all. So with a final wary stare, he acquiesced.

"Get over here," I hissed to Raihn, ushering him to the corner of the ballroom. My chest was tight with the ghost of a quickened heartbeat. The dead were swarming at the edges of my vision, urging me on.

"You can't be here," I whispered. Then, a particularly terrible thought struck me. "Is Oraya here? Please tell me Oraya is not here."

The thought of both of them, *together,* placed in this danger was devastating.

"No. Jesmine is waiting, though. The invitation was technically hers." His eyes were already darting between the exits. "They'll all be distracted for a few minutes. Let's go. We'll be halfway to the House of Night before—"

"The House of Night?" I repeated, and Raihn gave me a dumbfounded look—like my confusion was perplexing.

"We haven't heard from you for nearly a year, Mish. A fucking *year*. We knew you had been captured by the Shadowborn. Did you really think that we wouldn't come for you?"

He said it like this was not only obvious, but downright offensive to consider otherwise. And I did feel foolish that it hadn't crossed my mind they would come for me. Because of course the Nightborn spies would have heard of my very public capture and sentencing. Of course he and Oraya would think that I was off in Morthryn. And of course they would think that the only reason I was still alive—*if* I was still alive—would be because the Shadowborn had some worse torture planned for me.

My eyes burned. Strange that I had no beating heart, and yet, it was hard to think of another word for the pain between my ribs.

I said, "I'm not going anywhere."

His gaze shot to the dais, where Asar stood beside Egrette, who addressed the crowd with grand, royal exuberance. The ceremony had begun, but Asar still looked only at us.

Raihn's eyes darkened. "Mische, if you're being forced into something—"

"I'm not," I said quickly.

"—we will burn this kingdom to the fucking ground. I don't care what wars we—"

"Raihn, stop. *Please.*"

Again, I started toward him, only to stop myself. He took in that hesitation, a line between his brows.

"I'm so relieved to see you," he said. "You have no idea how worried we were."

I did have some idea. Perhaps it even verged on the worry I felt for Raihn right now, as worlds inched toward collision.

Luce, who I had barely noticed return, rubbed protectively against my legs, staring Raihn down. The dead slithered from the shadows. One of them, a faceless silhouette, wrapped its arms around Raihn's shoulders. He didn't react—didn't see it. But I had a hard time hearing anything over the whispers. My head throbbed.

On the dais, Asar and Egrette now turned to the Window. Egrette pulled off the veil, revealing the gleaming silver surface, reflecting an inverted image of this very ballroom, millennia ago.

"You don't understand," I said to Raihn, struggling to lower my voice. "You need to leave."

"Then help me understand." He stepped closer, and I jerked away.

Hurt flinched over his face. A physical reaction, like I'd slapped him.

I couldn't remember the last time I had greeted Raihn with anything other than a hug. Gods, he gave the best hugs. They had rescued me from so many nightmares. So many long days spent so close and so far from the sun. They had reminded me that I had someone to live for in the long years when I felt like I'd lost everything.

Now, I couldn't even let him look at me too closely. He knew me so well; he, of all people, would see the difference in me.

And in this moment, I felt so, so dead.

"Please," I begged him. "Please just go."

Raihn's anger had now fallen away.

"Help me understand, Mish," he said again, and that note of helplessness nearly broke me.

I opened my mouth—

—and doubled over, hands pressed to my forehead.

A wail vibrated my bones. No, not one wail, but thousands—millions. I forced my head up again to see that the Window was glowing bright, and the reflection within it no longer depicted the ballroom.

I understood the purpose of the black fabric on the walls. Because now, another world was superimposed over this one—another castle. The architecture was beautiful, ornate columns and sweeping arches, all rendered in translucent, ghostly paint strokes of the past. Silhouetted figures swept around the ballroom, playing out a mirror image of what they had done here thousands of years ago, weaving through the delighted vampire guests.

This was what this place had looked like in another age, when Alarus had still ruled it. A ghost's breath warmed the back of my neck: *Now. Go now.*

Beside me, Luce paced anxiously, as if to say, *Let's go. Let's go.*

We only had a few minutes. If we missed this opportunity, it would be over. I was already supposed to be making my way to the mask's holding chamber.

Things were about to get bad.

And I couldn't even bring myself to look at Raihn's face—that stupid, sweet, sad puppy dog face. Gods fucking damn him.

"You shouldn't be here," I blurted out as I turned away. "I have to go."

"Mische—" he called after me.

But I was already running down the halls.

CHAPTER TWENTY-THREE

Asar

The past and the present merged. I'd thought that my nervousness over what we were about to do would keep me sharp. But when I was at the Window with Egrette, conducting the spell to lift the veil between the past and the present, everything had gone hazy. The ritual was more ceremonial than anything—it was no great magic. Yet, as I walked the past, step by patient step, toward the present, I felt myself slowly submerging into a deeper, more powerful well of magic. As if I was returning to a natural base state I hadn't even known I had.

Bit by bit, the House of Shadow, the home that had never wanted me, fell away. And in its place rolled in Vathysia. An ancient kingdom of death.

It reminded me of how I'd felt the first time I had successfully conducted necromancy. Like I was operating on instinct, not logical knowledge.

As soon as the ritual was over, I swept down the stairs of the dais and out of the ballroom. I felt disoriented, the ground too light under my feet, my head swimming. The nearness of the past—the dead—was thrilling.

Mische had taken too long to leave, distracted by her argument with the Nightborn king—the fucking fool, walking straight into the

Shadowborn court. Another unpredictable factor we didn't need. Still, I felt for him. His worry had been palpable—a feeling I knew, firsthand, all too well.

I hoped he had listened to her. For his sake and for hers. I was acutely aware that the line between success and failure was perilously thin, and already, I felt our balance wobbling.

I strode down the hallway. The hum of the party faded behind me—unnaturally so, as if I were now underwater. A quickening breeze blew through the open windows, sending the sheets of black chiffon undulating. It was oddly mournful, superimposed over the ghostly outline of the past. There was no living soul here, only the dead, pacing the grounds in rote repetition of lives more than two thousand years past. A maid bearing an armful of folded table linens passed by, and I found my steps faltering.

The visions of the Melume weren't ghosts. It was an image of the past—not the same as wraiths in the Descent or the souls in the underworld. And yet, I could have sworn that, just for a moment, that maid's eyes slipped toward me. When her intangible form barely clipped my shoulder, I felt her presence jolt through me the way I felt it when I touched a wraith. The same desperate hunger.

But I didn't have time to analyze what could be off tonight.

"Asar."

I bit back a curse.

Elias.

I turned to see him standing at the other end of the hall, half a dozen of his men behind him. His green guard's cloak rippled in the breeze. "You shouldn't be out here alone. Lots of enemies within our walls tonight."

I wished I could have ignored him. But he would follow me if I didn't throw him off.

"Noted. I'll be so very careful," I said. "Egrette knows I have work to do tonight."

I started to walk away, but he said again, sharper, *"Asar."*

"Go back to the party, Elias. I'll be—"

"We found Gideon."'

And with that, I stopped.

Shit.

I knew Gideon would be discovered eventually. And I knew that when he was, it would be obvious who was responsible. I just thought we'd have more time until that happened. Who had alerted Elias? The maids despised Gideon. Surely not them.

Unless he had recovered faster than I'd expected. His eyes in those last moments flashed through my mind, dark with a fury far more powerful than his physical strength, and I tamped down an uneasy chill.

I kept my face blank and turned around.

"Found him? Found him where?"

Elias laughed softly. "This is your problem, Asar. You think everyone around you is stupid. You know, Egrette actually believed in you. Actually thought you could do great things together. I told her, *Bullshit. Asar is too arrogant for that.*"

More footsteps. I glanced down the hall to see six more Shadowborn soldiers rounding the corner—cutting me off.

Messy, messy, messy.

"You know this is a losing game for you," I said. "Let's not play it."

But I knew that no matter what I said, Elias was not going to let me walk away. He was, as much as I disliked him, a good soldier. He was devoted to Egrette, and that meant he was going to make me kill him before he'd let me go.

Sure enough, Elias sighed and drew his sword. But I saw through his performative resignation. He would enjoy this.

So goddess-damned close.

I hadn't yet been able to retrieve a sword. I had no blade save for the little knife I kept in my belt, the same one that had carved the glyphs into Gideon's skin. It was no weapon.

But I didn't need a piece of metal to do the work for me. I had something better.

I stretched my fingers at my side, opening my palms to the past—to the dead. The darkness swelled beneath the swaying sheets of black.

Maybe a small part of me was grateful to have the opportunity for payback.

"Let's get this over with," I muttered.

And Elias smiled as they descended upon me.

CHAPTER TWENTY-FOUR

Asar

I knew how to kill. I once had wielded death like an artist wielded a paintbrush. But I'd never been a warrior the way Elias was. My killing happened in the curtained quiet of the daylight hours, in quiet locked rooms or sound-dampened dungeons.

Yet, I could see the appeal of this, loud and messy.

I had no time to calculate. This was all instinct. The darkness flooded me, stronger than it had ever felt on even my best nights as my father's second.

Behind you, they warned, as one of Elias's men dove for me.

This one, they whispered, wrapping around the throat of another at my slightest command.

For even the most talented Shadowborn magic wielders, it was nearly impossible to hear the thoughts of more than a couple of other people at once—let alone other Shadowborn, who had been trained since birth to guard against the unwitting betrayals of their own minds. But now, though I had more than half a dozen soldiers coming for me, I sensed them all—every one of their unrealized intentions.

I grabbed one and shoved him into his comrade's impending strike, sending both careening to the ground in a blood-drenched pile. Tendrils of darkness flooded from the walls and strangled the next, buying me enough time to grab a sword and send it through one man's heart, and then another before he had time to adjust.

With each of my heartbeats, I ended another, another, another. And I felt my mind grow deliciously hazy, the dead draw closer, the darkness encroach.

But I was so connected to my magic that my own body became a liability. It couldn't move as fast as my mind did. One of the soldiers' blades caught my arm, the burst of pain making my steps fumble at a critical moment.

The next strike drove through my torso.

The dead let out a screech and clawed at my assailant, and I swung back around, sword bared, to skewer him through his chest.

I sagged back against the wall, breath heaving. I paused just long enough to take in the scene around me—what I had done. Bodies cluttered the hall. Some still twitched, their slurred thoughts of pain nagging at the back of my mind. Blood collected around my boots.

Elias encroached upon me like a wolf upon cornered prey. The expression twisting his face was half smile, half sneer. Each death I'd doled out to his men had driven him deeper into his bloodlust.

"I should have done a better job finishing you off in the Descent," he growled. "But better late than never."

My knuckles tightened around my sword as Elias prowled closer.

I let a sliver, just a sliver, of my pain slip through my mental walls.

I let my blood-slicked hilt slide from my hand, the blade falling to the ground with a pathetic *CLUNK*.

I let him approach me with his raised sword.

I let him take in this situation for what it looked to be. An easy win.

And then, just as the smirk of certain victory rolled across his lips, I reached into the darkness and threw open the doors to all the parts of myself I didn't yet understand.

The parts of myself that I had cultivated in Morthryn. The parts of myself that I had gained when Mische pulled me out of that ritual circle.

The veil to the dead was so thin. I tore through it like it was a woman's lace lingerie, and let the dead rush through me.

Dark silhouettes crawled from under the flowing chiffon, from the dark corners of the ceiling, from within the ghostly silhouettes of Alarus's past kingdom.

And they leapt upon Elias like starving wild dogs.

Was it cruel of me, I wondered, that I'd saved him for last?

His eyes went wide. But instead of surprise or fear, his final look to me was one of pure rage. He threw himself at me with his final burst of strength.

But he was just a mortal, in the end.

The dead crawled over him like ants to a carcass, pulling him apart. It reminded me of what Ophelia had looked like in her failed resurrection. Reminded me of how she must have flailed and fought when Malach had first killed her, with Elias by his side.

Elias didn't suffer as she had. Not quite.

But at least it was close.

No, I decided. It was a fitting end for him.

To his credit, he really did try not to scream.

Try.

I turned and disappeared down the hall, Elias's final, guttural wail echoing behind me.

CHAPTER TWENTY-FIVE

Mische

Where the hell was Asar?

I bolted down hallway after hallway, Luce keeping pace beside me. I tried to think about the task that lay ahead of us instead of Raihn and his puppy face and the fact that he was here when the world was ending and, and, and—

I squeezed my eyes shut.

Focus on what's under your own two feet, Mische.

I had repeated Saescha's words to myself too many times to count, but now, they weren't particularly comforting. Maybe because I so often heard them in her voice, and that came with its own slew of anxieties.

My sword, which Luce had retrieved for me, slapped clumsily at my side. Somehow, on a night of ghosts and lost gods, it didn't feel very useful. I whispered the path I'd memorized like a religious chant—*left, right, left, left, right, two doors down, right, down the stairs* . . .

With every step, I fell deeper into the past. I was in another version of this world, thousands of years ago, before vampires existed, before the god of death had been killed. Before Nyaxia had torn the world in two with her vengeance. Soon, I didn't need to whisper at all. I just felt the path calling to me.

And all of it seemed impossibly real, impossibly tangible. I passed a woman carrying baskets of folded cloth, and I could have sworn her eyes met mine.

Eventually I reached a door, rendered in translucent silver, three thick iron bars across it. It was magnificent, ornate in a way that reminded me of a warped version of Shadowborn architecture.

I reached out, expecting my hand to pass right through. Instead, I met twisted metal and smooth wood—solid.

I was already behind, and seconds were ticking by. This needed to be open by the time Asar got here. I pressed my fingertips to the frame. I could feel the glyphs, the elegant little carvings buried between the twisted decorative whorls. Even those seemed slightly unfamiliar, as if written in a language too ancient to understand.

I closed my eyes.

Just feel it, Mische.

What a fucking joke. How many times had I given Oraya that advice? Now, it seemed ridiculous.

Luce gave my legs an encouraging nuzzle, which I appreciated.

I reached deep into my magic, then threaded my awareness through the glyphs.

And though the magic that had once forged this lock wasn't Nyaxia's at all . . . it still felt so familiar. Like a melody someone had played for me once, drawing to mind a soft fleeting smirk, a deep brown eye, the scent of frost-dusted ivy. The keys were different, but I knew the song. And perhaps it knew me, too, because one by one, the glyphs unfurled like blooming flower petals.

The door swung open.

Slow applause rang out behind me. "I never doubted you, Dawndrinker."

I turned around and the sight of Asar's blood-covered body had my heart leaping to my throat.

"What the hell happened?"

He gave me a wan smile and approached the door. He was good at hiding his pain, but I sensed it anyway.

"We don't have much time," he said. "Someone up there has probably already discovered them."

"Them?"

"Elias. Some of his soldiers."

Shit.

I drew in a gasp through my teeth. "You killed him."

"They came after us. I didn't have any choice."

Shit. Shit. Shit.

Elias was Egrette's closest confidant. Not some nameless guard who could go missing without attracting any notice.

Upon seeing my expression, Asar conceded, "It's . . . not ideal."

He leaned against the doorframe and peered into the room beyond it.

"I haven't seen this," he murmured, with a note of admiration, "in a long, long time."

Together, we stepped inside. The room was circular, the walls lined with ornate arches and stained-glass windows revealing stark nothingness. A shallow pool of water filled the center, mirror-still.

Except . . . no, it wasn't water. It looked like the veil between the mortal world and the Descent. But this seemed a little more solid, glittering silver, as if covered with luminescent algae. Dark forms moved beneath the surface, though I couldn't make out what they were. I narrowed my eyes, leaning closer—

Then leapt back with a curse.

"Shh," Asar hissed. "They're likely already looking for us."

"Sorry," I whispered, hand to my mouth.

But really, could he blame me?

The shark circled the perimeter of the pool, just under the surface, rendered in the same translucent strokes as the ghosts and the rest of the room. It wore a gleaming metallic skull.

A guardian.

If it noticed us, its steady, unbroken path showed no sign.

"It's not real," Asar said. "Just a ghost of Alarus's old guard."

"Would we really call the ghosts 'not real'?" I said, thinking of the way the woman I had passed in the hall had really, *really* seemed as if she had been looking right at me.

Asar paused in that way that I knew meant he wasn't sure. Then he gestured to the center of the pool.

"The mask is there," he said.

I'd been so distracted by the shadows—and the shark—that I'd somehow managed to miss it, which now seemed ridiculous, because it was one of the most beautiful things I'd ever seen. It sat just under the water, staring up with an eyeless gaze. It somewhat resembled a jawless, humanoid skull, bearing two pointed canines. The shifting light played over intricate carvings that covered its copper surface. I realized, upon closer examination, that they were glyphs—thousands of tiny, tiny glyphs.

Even separated by thousands of years, the weight of its presence was staggering. No part of me questioned that I was witnessing something powerful.

Some deep, primal discomfort pushed me half a step backward.

"We just . . . walk up to it?" I found myself whispering. Suddenly everything seemed very, very quiet.

"For a few minutes. Yes."

I watched the shark as it made another pass around the pool. It was so close I could've reached down to touch it. "And the guardian?"

"It shouldn't bother us."

"You just hesitated before you said that."

"No, I didn't."

Yes, he fucking did, but fine.

The dark forms wriggled beneath the water like fish in a frozen pond. Were they a trick of the light? Something . . . more? I couldn't tell, but I didn't love that they grew more numerous, now, slithering toward the surface.

Asar took his first steps into the circle. The water only came up to his calves, as if he stood upon an invisible sheet of glass.

I followed, shivering as I stepped into the water. The shark passed below us, seemingly unbothered. But the shadows seemed restless, pressing up against the underside of the surface like faces to a window.

"Come," Asar said. "We don't have much time."

This eclipse between the past and present would only last for a few minutes. Asar and I waded deeper, to where the mask stared at us with gaping black eyes.

This was the crown of the god of death. The king of the underworld. The urge to kneel before it, bury myself in its power, was overwhelming.

Asar crouched down. "Here."

The circle of glyphs was tiny, nearly invisible, floating suspended around the mask. There were empty spots in the pattern, like puzzle pieces lost.

"That's what you got from Gideon?" I said, and Asar nodded.

The shark passed beneath us again, and I couldn't help but admire it. The guardians that still remained in the Descent were starving and battered. But this—a guardian at its peak—was one of the most majestic creatures I had ever seen.

Luce danced back and forth at the shore, not bothering to hide her urgency.

"Ready?" Asar peeled his gloves off, and I did the same. Under this light, my hands had a ghostly, silver sheen. Before I even touched the surface of the water, writhing forms were collecting beneath them.

"Ready," I said, even though I wasn't sure I was.

Asar and I began our work. He used the glyphs that he'd taken from Gideon, integrating them into the seal like the missing threads into a grand tapestry, his needle perfectly placed. And just as I had over so many broken gates in Morthryn, I helped him complete each stroke, the spell stronger for every time we passed it between us.

A bead of sweat trickled down his brow, plastering a whorl of dark hair to his temple. The white of his scarred eye grew searing bright.

With each glyph we snapped into place, the water slowly rose—or was the floor falling? The surface was soon around my thighs, then my hips. The mask grew clear, its haunting call louder. A roar built in my ears.

The shark passed again. Now, it swam around us.

More and more shadows pushed to the surface. They had become unmistakably humanoid, hands outstretched, mouths open. An uneasy realization clicked into place:

Asar and I had spent months closing gates to the underworld.

Now we were tearing one open.

But the mask, rising nearer, commanded my full attention. The dead gathered around us, all of the ghosts of the palace's past gathering in wait around the edge of the circle.

Three more glyphs.

"Be ready," Asar ground out between clenched teeth, as he moved to the last keys.

Two more.

But then he paused. I sensed his concentration flicker, and then realized why.

There were two glyphs left in the key he had gotten from Gideon. But only one remaining slot in the spell.

After a brief hesitation, he wove in the final glyph, only to wince and hiss a curse. I felt the jolt, too, like an unyielding lock's tumbler crashing back down.

With a grunt of exertion, Asar withdrew the incorrect glyph. At first, I thought that mistake would send our entire spell, so carefully woven, spinning out of control. The momentum of it was overwhelming. The dead crowded us now, uncomfortably attentive.

But Asar slid the final glyph into place.

Our spell was complete. The door snapped open.

Suddenly, the mask was here, solid and real, ready for the taking.

Asar shook with the effort of holding the gate open.

"Now!" he commanded.

I reached for the mask—

Too late, I saw another shape approaching behind the wall of ghostly figures. Its body was long and serpentine, eyes bright white sores, and mouth open to reveal gaping nothingness.

A souleater.

Rushing straight for the door we had just opened.

The creature leapt up from the underworld, tearing through shrieking souls like they were wet paper, coming right for me.

I had seconds.

Asar's widening eyes settled on the souleater. I saw his decision before he had time to make it. He would slam the door closed to protect me.

But we had one chance, and I wasn't about to waste it.

I grabbed the mask.

At its touch, a gasp ripped through me. Its ancient stare peered into my soul, seeing more than I revealed to it.

Immediately, I flung it toward Asar.

The souleater grabbed me, just as Asar's spell collapsed, and the door between the living and the dead crashed closed again.

The last thing I heard was Asar screaming my name.

CHAPTER TWENTY-SIX

Asar

I threw myself after Mische, and was met only with a sheet of glass. Beneath it, more souls collected so quickly that they crowded out my view of Mische and the souleater that had taken her. The mask landed beside me with a crash and a cascade of water, thrown in Mische's final act. I barely looked at it. Instead, I clung to her rapidly fading presence.

The fleeting collision between the past and the present was fading.

I couldn't use Gideon's glyphs again. By the time I finished, Mische would be gone forever.

I lifted my hands and slammed them against the glass. I'd already broken through one veil to retrieve Mische. I would not hesitate to do it again.

CRACK.

Fractures exploded like lightning from my hands. The souls shivered with desperate delight against them.

From what felt like a million miles behind, Luce barked a frantic warning, just before an impact from behind sent me flying away from the cracks. The trapped souls beneath moaned in protest.

You are unwise, fallen one. The voice washed over me like a wave against the rocks. *The underworld has taken her back to where she belongs.*

The shark circled me, vacant eyes seeking my own. Its body was now dark and defined, nearly as solid as Luce's.

"Unacceptable." The only response, as Mische's presence rapidly faded. "Retrieve her."

There is only one who may command the guardians, and you are not he.

No. Not yet.

But I would be.

I was a well-read, well-studied person. I was well aware of the many dangers of handling god-touched items directly. Acaeja's warning was never far from my mind, and I had no doubt that it had been a serious one.

I knew this.

But I did not care.

I spun to the mask, which lay upon the battered veil. It floated atop the water, perfectly still, producing not a single ripple. As if its power reduced all natural rules to mere suggestion.

I did not hesitate as I seized it and put it on.

The pain was extraordinary.

The pleasure was unbelievable.

{At long last,} a voice whispered, with piqued interest, *{a new heir.}*

The mask settled around my face as if molding to my skull, latching to my forehead and cheekbones and the angle of my nose. I gasped, and my lungs filled not with air—not with life—but with death. I could see the entire underworld. I could feel every soul that wandered there, every souleater that hunted them. I could sense the turn of every path, the swing of every gate, every mountain peak or river current or wandering soul. All of it at once, unencumbered by mortal senses or fallible flesh.

Someone was screaming, strangled and rough, and it took me a long moment to realize it was me.

I was doubled over in the water, head lowered against the glass.

I blinked away a fleeting memory of a woman with galaxies in her hair.

No. Freckles like cinnamon. Honey-brown eyes.

I pushed myself up to my hands and knees. Then to my feet. The cracking veil bowed beneath my weight. The guardian still circled me.

"I am the heir," I said. "I bear the crown. Retrieve her."

The guardian regarded me, continuing its path.

The voice snarled. *{Remind them that one does not disobey the crown.}*

"I bear the crown." My words did not sound like my own. "Retrieve her."

The guardian hesitated, precious seconds slipping away.

She is already lost, it said ruefully. *And the veil cannot bear more damage.*

{Give them no option!} the voice commanded.

"I am the king of the dead," I boomed, "and *I command you to retrieve her."*

Retrieve her. Retrieve her. Retrieve her.

The veil shook with my command. The compulsion reached into the past, across realms.

The guardian passed beneath me again, eternity groaning beneath its fins.

As you wish, Highness, it said, at last.

It raised its great head, and dove deep, deep, deep.

And then the glass shattered.

A rush of sound, of emotion, flooded around me. The wailing dead screamed in pain and joy, released into the land of the living. The guardian parted through them as if they were nothing, scattering bodies through the weightlessness of the water or slicing them into smoke.

I dove after it. My movements were strange—neither swimming nor striding. Reality simply accommodated my will. The weeping wounds of the broken underworld, freshly wrought, throbbed in my heart.

A great wail shook the room. I pushed through the dead to see them—the guardian and the souleater engaged in a vicious battle. The guardian had grabbed the souleater's snakelike tail in its golden jaws, and the souleater now twisted itself around to claw at the guardian's body. The guardian was quickly fading. It was a creature of the past, a mere shade of what it once had been at its peak, and I'd dragged it back into the present by force.

But it was still a product of divinity. Even a shade of its power, long dulled by time, was enough to shatter worlds.

The guardian sawed its teeth into the souleater, forcing it to open its jaws. Mische's limp body floated free, and I dove for her.

I wrapped my arms around her as the souleater, its jaws and claws now both free, ripped the guardian in two. Its death cry echoed as I lunged for the surface, dragging Mische up to the shattered veil.

I dragged us to the edge of the pool. The cold air of mortality struck me like a wall. The two of us crumpled in a heap upon the tile floor. The woman beneath me felt so fragile. Weaker, even, than a living mortal.

I rolled over. A spectral depiction of a palace hung above me in flickering silver. No—not *a* palace. *My* palace.

My brow furrowed.

{Much has changed,} the voice said thoughtfully, *{in all these years.}*

"Asar."

The woman's voice was small. I sat up and turned to her. Her body wavered between solidity and ghostliness. She was slowly rolling over to push herself onto her hands and knees.

She looked so urgently, naggingly familiar. But I couldn't remember—

Mische.

Her name shattered the dam. Reality washed back over me as if I'd been plunged into ice water.

{Wait—} the voice started.

But I tore the mask off my face with a sickening *rip*, wincing as it took flesh with it—like it had been burrowing into bone. I knelt down next to Mische as she lifted her head. When I took her face in my hands, I didn't care that it chipped away at my already pathetically depleted strength.

"You are such a fool," I said.

"Just have to keep you alert," she said with a weak laugh. She carefully extracted herself from my touch. Then she looked to the veil, and her face fell.

The pool that had once held the mask now swirled with glittering oblivion, framed by the razored shards of what little remained of the gate. Hands reached from within it, the dead on the cusp of figuring out how to pull themselves through.

The man who had spent centuries healing the hurts of the underworld wanted to weep at this sight. For a moment, I thought to myself, *What have I just done?*

I turned to the mask, which lay beside me. My own power now felt dull and useless, my body weak and unremarkable. But I had studied magical artifacts long enough to know that drunken cravings for power were generally a bad sign.

I used the edge of my cloak to slide the mask into my pack.

"Let's go," I said. "We have minutes before all this collapses, and less, surely, before Egrette sends the entire Shadowborn army after us."

I got to my feet, wincing as a fresh waterfall of blood soaked my shirt. Mische stood, too, wavering slightly. She grabbed her gloves and pulled her hood back up, covering her wet hair and hiding the worst signs of her condition. Which, I realized with an uncomfortable jolt, looked much more dire than they had minutes ago.

She stared back at the shattered gate, roiling with the desperate dead.

"We'll fix it," she whispered. "Right?"

"We will fix it," I vowed. Even though I was looking only at her.

The dead let out another distant wail, growing closer.

"Come," I whispered. "We have to go."

Mische wiped her eyes with the back of her hand, and together, we fled back into the tunnels before they closed up behind us.

CHAPTER TWENTY-SEVEN

Mische

Asar, Luce, and I were no longer trying to be subtle. We flat-out ran through hallways, staircases, tunnels. The collision of the past and the present was now over, only a sliver remaining. The ghosts of the palace this had once been now were barely visible against the rippling chiffon. Yet I still felt so far from life. The ghosts that had once occupied these halls still watched me as we ran by. These ones were still only faint shadows, but once that wall of wraiths got through the broken gate we had torn open, things were about to get much more dangerous.

As we spiraled up another set of stairs, shouts and running footsteps pounded from above. Steel clattered. It was hard to make out the exact sounds, but it certainly wasn't the boisterous commotion of a ball, that was for sure.

"Egrette's guards?" I rasped out. Even though I didn't exactly breathe anymore, I still felt like I couldn't catch my breath.

Asar winced. "Probably."

His gait, typically so graceful, was choppy. One hand pressed to the wound on his torso. I had my sword ready, but it seemed comically useless. At least I supposed I could grab onto one of Egrette's soldiers and suck the life out of them with my wraith touch if I really had to. The thought struck me with an unpleasantly visceral delight that instantly made me feel dirty. The idea of touching skin, using that warmth to drag myself closer to the mortal world, felt more tempting than blood after starvation.

When we had nearly reached the ballroom, Asar flung out his hand to stop me before we rounded a corner. Sheets of silk enveloped us as a cool ocean breeze slithered through open doors. He pressed his finger to his lips, listening to the sounds beyond. His shoulders rose and fell heavily. The scent of his blood was distracting. I found myself staring at the thin, bloody fabric clinging to his torso. The urge to reach out and touch the wound, and the muscular flesh beneath it, was so overwhelming I found it difficult to think about anything else.

Asar glanced at the hall. Then me. Then the hall. I could see him making a mental calculation.

"We double back to the back entrance," he whispered at last. "I can't count the guards, but there are too many, and they're getting closer."

Luce let out a whine of protest. I agreed. This was a risky plan. We would need to cross the entire castle again, and then loop around the grounds to make it to the shore.

I eyed his bloody shirt. "It's too far. And they'll find us before we make it out, anyway. Look at yourself, Warden."

"What exactly are our alternatives, Dawndrinker?"

Another clatter echoed down the hall. They were definitely getting closer, and quickly. Gods, what the hell was going on down there? It sounded like the entire party had devolved into chaos.

The thought of Raihn flitted through my mind and I felt sick.

Gods fucking damn it.

Asar's hand hovered at his pack—just above the mask within it.

"No," I said.

"What?"

"You aren't using that."

He gave me a wry smirk. "Some might say it's rightfully mine, anyway."

But I was not in the mood to joke. The call of the mask reminded me of what I'd seen in the House of Night, when Septimus and Simon tampered with weapons made from Alarus's teeth. The memory of Simon, twisted beyond recognition, terrified me. It was too easy to imagine Asar in his place.

"No," I said firmly. "You don't use it. I've got—" I wiggled my fingers.

Asar stared flatly at me. "What?"

"Death touch! Magical death touch!"

He looked unimpressed. "Forgive me if I'm not exactly eager to throw you out there to go tickle the Shadowborn military to death."

I opened my mouth to argue, but another wave of shouts echoed from down the hall. Closer now.

I stopped, brow furrowing. Asar's did, too. Because we both now realized that this was not *just* the sound of a military mobilizing. This was the sound of actual battle.

"Wait," I said. "If we're here . . ."

My voice trailed off. But I saw the question in Asar's face, too: *Then who are they fighting?*

We pressed ourselves to the wall and shuffled closer to the sounds—and to our freedom—under the cover of billowing black chiffon.

"Maybe it's the Bloodborn," I whispered. "Maybe they turned on Egrette. Maybe—"

"Shh," Asar hissed.

I realized it was now silent.

Suddenly, utterly silent.

Now, the only sounds were clashes that echoed much farther away—perhaps from the ballroom?

I barely stopped myself from whispering, *What the hell?* How could that be? Seconds ago, it had sounded like a flat-out battle was happening around this corner. That couldn't just disappear.

Asar pressed his finger to his lips, then, before I could stop him, he slipped around the corner.

"Wait—" I started.

But instantly, he straightened. He stared down the hallway, no longer bothering to hide himself.

When I joined him, my mouth fell open.

As we'd suspected, we had indeed been hearing the Shadowborn military. Apparently Egrette thought highly of Asar and me, because there were easily more than a dozen guards here.

At least, I thought so. It was hard to count, because so many of them weren't in one piece anymore.

Limbs and torsos and a few stray heads littered the ground, scattered from wall to wall like broken, discarded dolls in the wake of a child's tantrum. Black blood pooled on the marble tile. The corpses were fresh. They still smelled painfully of life.

Luce let out a growl as she sniffed the encroaching tide of blood.

My first thought was that the Bloodborn had turned on the House of Shadow. The Bloodborn were as skilled at killing as the Shadowborn were at spy craft. They were certainly capable of this degree of bloodshed.

But something about that possibility didn't add up. An uncanny scent hung in the air, like the faintest trace of a campfire's smoke, or the warm afterglow of a sun that had just set. It made the hair prickle on my arms even across the chasm of death. The strikes that had taken apart the soldiers were clean, but vicious. Someone had kept going long after these men were dead. That seemed incongruous to the Bloodborn, who were too efficient to waste that kind of time.

"I suppose we got lucky," Asar muttered. But I heard the trace of sarcasm in his voice. Nothing seemed lucky about this.

We stepped gingerly through the pile of bodies. A disgusting jolt of pleasure ran through me when the blood touched my toes, exposed in my now-pitifully-unhelpful dress shoes.

We darted down one hall, then another.

Freedom was so damned close.

We were almost to the final hall. At the last branch, we started down one path, then stopped short when we heard incoming voices. Shit. Other way.

I whirled to the other direction.

But the Shadowborn were masters of stealth and manipulation, and the guards that Egrette surrounded herself with would be the most skilled the House had to offer.

We sensed them far too late.

As we were about to round the last corner between us and the ballroom, Asar stopped short. Grabbed my wrist.

Too slow. They already heard us.

The guards stood before us in a wall of green and black. They stared at us, as if shocked that we had actually stepped right into their path. I couldn't blame them. It shocked me, too.

Then the captain thrust a long finger at us. "In the name of the queen, we order you to surrender yourselves."

But of course, they were already lunging for us by the time the words left his lips. The next seconds unfolded in slow motion. I saw Asar's eyes dart from the soldiers to me. Luce crouched as she coiled to lunge.

And then blood spattered across my face.

That was all I felt at first—the blood, distractingly hot and sweet and wonderful on my life-starved skin.

Then—

CRASH.

Broken glass rained down over us.

A streak of gold plummeted from above. My skin prickled. The scent of fresh-kindled fire filled my nostrils.

CRASH. Another streak.

Asar pushed me forward with a wordless command: *run.*

We had only one path available to us, leading us straight back into the ballroom.

And before I could choke out a *what the fuck was that,* my question was answered.

Another window shattered in front of us. My arms flew up to shield my face. And when I lowered them, a figure in pristine white robes and brilliant gold armor stood before me.

A Sentinel.

CHAPTER TWENTY-EIGHT

Mische

How?

The Sentinel cocked their head. My own dumbfounded face stared back at me, reflected in smooth gold, bisected by a single jagged scratch.

Not just any Sentinel. The one who had captured me at the veil.

How?

Sentinels were warriors of Shiket. Soldiers of the White Pantheon. They couldn't enter Nyaxia's territory. Never, in *two thousand years,* had they *ever* done so.

Another streak of gold careened to the ground beside them—a second Sentinel, this one standing silent behind their partner. Behind me, the final gasping gurgles of the Shadowborn guards rang out from the next hall.

"I told you that I would find you if you ran," the scratched Sentinel said. "But how very typical that you would not believe me."

We would lose, if we fought.

We would lose.

I shot Asar a glance and I saw the same certainty reflected in his eyes.

His hand moved to the mask—

But before I could think better of it, I grabbed his pack and threw it to Luce, who snatched it from the air and bolted.

Asar looked at me like I was a fucking idiot.

What in the Mother's name are you—

But the scarred Sentinel whirled around, distracted. What had been their orders? What did they want more—the mask, or us? It turned out, in the moment, even they weren't sure.

I gave Asar a shove. *"RUN!"*

Luce knew what was going on immediately. Ever the best girl, she galloped through the ballroom like a phantom, weaving and bobbing through utter chaos, so fast even god-touched soldiers couldn't catch her.

The party had devolved into gory pandemonium. Tables and chairs had been overturned. The floor was slick with blood. The sheets of chiffon that had looked so ethereally elegant at the beginning of the night were now singed and tattered, whipping with each vicious gust of wind. Vampires hissed and battled, attempting to seize their glory against warriors of the White Pantheon.

But the Sentinels were methodical machines of death. Their swords, blessed with the divinity of the White Pantheon, burned vampire flesh at even the slightest touch. Ash scattered the floor, creating a gummy paste with the pools of blood.

I craned my neck up, to the open windows and the eternally dark sky above them. The heavens swirled with wisps of purple and teal, like fish circling a pond. A sign that the gods were watching.

Nyaxia would come, surely. The White Pantheon had entered her territory. That was a slight that would not go ignored.

At least her rage would keep the Sentinels from following us. But we certainly couldn't be here when she arrived. I couldn't imagine that she'd be happy to see us.

Asar eyed the sky, too, mapping the same calculations. Luce zigzagged ahead through the ballroom, headed to the back door that led to the ocean. Two Sentinels flew after her.

Asar and I wove through the party, following her. But we weren't as nimble, and we attracted far more attention. One of the Shadowborn guards—apparently ever committed to his mission—attempted to grab me, and without thinking, I grabbed his face between my palms. The rush of euphoria that came with his cry of pain, even from a touch that lasted mere seconds, was intoxicating. It felt like the first swallow of blood after far too long.

I let the soldier fall and continued to run.

But then a crash ahead. A Sentinel stood atop an overturned table, cutting off Asar. Before I could move to help him, a grip seized the back of my dress—gods fucking damn it, I *knew* this dress was going to be my downfall—and dragged me away as I flailed.

An onslaught of sensations consumed me. The gold-streaked sky. The swaying leaves of trees. Feathers and blood. The scent of the ocean. Vostis. The Citadel.

I felt more alive than I ever had been, and deader than I had since the night I was Turned.

I crashed into a wall. My sword flew from my grasp. A metal vise clutched my throat. I kicked and kicked and managed to wrest myself free through sheer determination, falling in a heap on a pile of broken glass.

I lifted my head to see the Sentinel, with that same scarred face, bearing down on me.

I tried to stand and immediately fell back to my knees in a wave of overwhelming dizziness. Whatever meager scraps of life I'd drained from the soldier, the Sentinel's touch had taken it all away and more.

Asar. Where was Asar?

Disoriented, I scanned the crowd. I couldn't count how many Sentinels there were—a dozen? More? My gaze locked on the opposite side of the ballroom, where Asar fought. Gods, he was breathtaking. The shadows wrapped around him like wings. He'd claimed a sword from some dead soldier somewhere, but no matter how skilled his movements, the piece of metal was nothing compared to the way he wielded the darkness. Like an artist.

But he was wounded, and I was dead. We couldn't get out of this through brute force.

Think, think, think—

I needed time.

The dead wailed in my ears, begging, *We need time.*

My gaze flicked to the Dusk Window, which still stood at the abandoned dais. Hands pressed to it, the dead pushing against a veil that was already tearing.

The Sentinel encroached, and I blurted out, without thinking, "I'm nobody."

Think, Mische.

The Sentinel paused.

"I'm nobody," I said again, breathlessly. "I'm—I'm already dead anyway. Trust me, you don't want me."

I was talking, but I didn't know to what end. It was a directionless stalling tactic.

"Look," I babbled. "I'm a priestess of Atroxus. I'm—I'm loyal to the White Pantheon."

I grabbed my sleeve and yanked it up, prepared to show off decades' worth of burn scars and an old phoenix tattoo that had marked my loyalty.

Instead, I revealed a smooth, unmarked, slightly translucent arm.

Shit.

The Sentinel stared, unmoving.

"You no longer wear the tattoo." At first, their voice sounded oddly small. But then they said, with seething divine rage, "That is a small justice. You should not bear the mark of the one you murdered. Not even in death."

Why were they talking to me instead of killing me?

I rose on wobbly legs. Stepped backward once, twice.

"I can help you," I said. "I can—"

"You, Mische Iliae, murdered the king of the White Pantheon," the Sentinel roared. I staggered backward as they stalked closer. "You tore the sun from the sky. I have seen your past and your future. A million lives will end due to what you have done. And you have the nerve to stand here and bargain with me? As if I can be won over by petty bribery?" They threw their head back and laughed.

Another step back. The edge of the dais now dug into the backs of my thighs. I cast a quick glance back at the Window. The whispers of the dead had grown deafening, drowning out the sounds of the ballroom battles. The veil was so, so weak.

"I just thought—I thought—" I stammered.

"You do not think," the Sentinel hissed. "You have never thought. I do not do this for the games of the gods, Mische Iliae. I do this for justice. I do this because those you have made suffer, and the countless you will make suffer, deserve your suffering in return."

Where are you? Asar's mind called into mine. More Sentinels and soldiers alike had descended upon him.

But I couldn't answer. The Sentinel pushed me roughly to the dais, then crawled on top of me.

I gasped as another set of memories raked through me, my own past fed back to me. Prayers at the Citadel beside Saescha. The sweet scent of incense. My young self, going into the bedchamber with Atroxus, in service of the very god I would one day kill.

"You have *always* known," the Sentinel breathed.

I splayed my hand flat against the floor. My fingertips brushed my sword.

Where are you? Asar barked. *I can't see you.*

I'm alright, I managed to get back to him. *Prepare yourself.*

I felt his flash of confusion, but he didn't have time to respond before I grabbed the sword and swung it with all my strength against the Sentinel's face.

The Sentinel released my throat. The instinct was surprise more than pain—the blade bounced awkwardly off their armor, leaving a fresh nick in the gold.

But I didn't need to kill them, or even hurt them.

I just needed a few seconds.

I leapt up and threw myself against the Window. The dead reached for me. *You're one of us,* they begged. *Let us out. We're so hungry. We're so thirsty.*

Through the morass of empty, desperate eyes, I saw a familiar face—Vincent.

You'd better help me here, I told him, momentarily regretting that I was so rude in our last conversation.

When I pressed my hands over the glyphs around the edge of the mirror, still burning with the remnants of the spell that Egrette and Asar had cast, I felt the veil part for me like an open embrace.

It really was dumb fucking luck. To think that I could possibly conduct a spell that could be, supposedly, done only by the heirs of the House of Shadow.

Apparently I was just that good.

Or maybe I had just enough help from the other side.

Or maybe it was simply easier to destroy things than to repair them.

I swallowed a pang of sadness as I grabbed onto a gate to the underworld that was hanging on, barely, by its twisted hinges. I thought of Raihn, and prayed desperately that he was already long gone.

The Sentinel's hands closed around my shoulders.

I ripped open the door to hell.

CHAPTER TWENTY-NINE

Asar

I felt Mische's magic before I saw it. Even the Sentinel I was fighting felt it, because they paused halfway through their strike to turn to the dais.

When I looked to her, I knew I would remember that image for the rest of my life.

Mische, standing in front of the Dusk Window, her torn dress billowing out behind her, black silk hood pinned around her face, hands outstretched like a mother's waiting arms as the shadowy forms of the dead poured out around her.

I thought, *Damn masks and eyes and hearts and divine missions. This is what a true goddess looks like.*

A sight so stunning that it made the entire damned world stop mid-breath.

And then, it all crashed down around us like a toppled wine glass.

The dead were eager. The veil was already damaged. And now, they had been released straight into a room full of blood and flesh and sex and death. Everything they craved.

The Sentinel didn't know what to make of it. I seized upon its distraction, driving my blade through its gut—a strike that would do little to hurt them, I knew, but it would buy me time. Mische toppled from the dais, her form swallowed beneath the avalanche of writhing shadows. Wraiths, when released into the world above, were even further removed from their mortal selves than they were in the Descent. The creatures that poured into the ballroom were wretched mimicries of what they once had been. Their limbs were twisted and deformed, bending the wrong way or not at all. Their faces were distorted, eyes too large, mouths too wide, some missing features altogether. They moved more like shadows through leaves than living beings.

And they were hungry. Starving.

The light of divinity, the contrast in every way to the darkness of the Descent, was the most appealing to them of all.

Brilliant, Mische. Absolutely fucking brilliant.

I didn't intend the thought for anyone but myself. But I still heard her amused reply:

I think that might be the nicest thing you've ever said to me.

Goddess help me, I was proud of her. My chest hurt with it.

The Sentinel lurched away from me as a slew of dead piled upon it. I seized this window of freedom and ran.

To the door, I told her.

I had to dodge and weave to avoid the wraiths. But Mische slipped free of them easily. Indeed, sometimes it seemed almost as if they were *protecting* her, which was intriguing. She was, after all, already dead. She had offered them a bridge to the living, and now that they had an entire buffet of life spread out before them, they were more than happy to gorge themselves on that offering instead.

The open door, agonizingly close and yet frustratingly far away, loomed ahead of me. The sky was brighter now, swirling with approaching divinity. Nyaxia would be here any moment.

It was then, when I was inconveniently distracted by impending divinity, that she found me.

A wall of darkness rose up before me. And within it, stepping through the chaos with cold, singular focus, was Egrette.

She was utterly calm, in eerie contrast to the tumult unfolding around her. Her dress was torn and bloody, her elaborate hairstyle half-undone, the crown crookedly clinging to her head. Her exposed Heir Marks were covered with the black of vampire blood. And though her kingdom collapsed around her, she looked only at me.

I felt her rage. More surprising, her pain, fresh and deep. It startled me just how familiar that feeling was.

I had felt it after Mische's death. I felt it even now.

Egrette knew how to shield her mind. She didn't care to. I understood that, too.

She stood firmly between me and freedom.

"The mask is already gone," I said. "Let me pass without trouble and I won't bring any more to you."

But even as the words left my mouth, I realized that this had nothing to do with the mask.

"All our lives, we have been playing a game, Asar. We fight over a chair, over a crown, over a kingdom. Fine." Her mouth, full of blood, twisted. "But it is not a game anymore. I will never forgive you for killing him. Not tonight. Not a thousand nights from now. And not the night I stand over your corpse."

After all this time, it really never had occurred to me that Egrette had actually loved Elias.

But here, on this night of mirrors, I saw another version of myself reflected in her grief—the villain in her story. The resentful bastard brother who had betrayed her, butchered his own mentor, slaughtered her lover, and sacrificed his own kingdom and hers.

I raised my blade. Reached to the darkness, which now so easily met my call, swirling around my sword.

"Just let me walk away," I said.

But I knew in this moment that she would never stop hunting me.

I bit back a silent curse. I could handle Egrette, but it would take time we didn't have. Out of the corner of my eye, I saw Mische running through the crowd. And behind her, an odd movement upon the dais—

Egrette lunged for me.

Just as a souleater burst through the Dusk Window.

Its body squeezed and contorted through the frame. The metal snapped, sending the Window toppling. The beast flapped and writhed as it tumbled onto the ballroom floor like a beached shark, so drunk on its gluttonous luck it didn't even care it was on dry land.

The wraiths scattered in panic. A wave of the dead rose up in perfect timing to Egrette's distraction, pushing her across the floor. Mische seized the opportunity and barreled toward me, gown streaking out behind her, and for a moment I thought maybe she actually was flying, because she looked every bit the phoenix.

"Come on!" she shrieked, dragging me toward the door.

But I hesitated.

Egrette freed herself from the dead and whirled to me. She was several strides away, and even surrounded by such death, her stare found me immediately.

End her, a part of me insisted. *She will never stop coming for you. End her right now.*

But Mische gave me another rough push, punctuated with Luce's frantic bark from ahead. "What the hell are you waiting for?"

The gods and the dead alike were at our heels. There was no more time.

I turned away and fled into the night.

CHAPTER THIRTY

Mische

We ran and ran and ran until we had fallen back to the docks. The screams of the living and dead alike echoed behind us. We found a quiet side street and pulled up our hoods. Guards ran past us, rushing into the burning palace.

I was shaking. The voices of the dead still echoed in my ears.

Ahead, a man in a white suit smoked a cigarillo, the one little dot of ember-orange glowing like a lone north star.

I chanced a glance over my shoulder, back to the palace, steps slowing as Asar continued briskly ahead.

A streak fell from the sky directly in front of me, making me stagger back. At first, I was certain it was another Sentinel, but—

"Get over here. Quick."

Raihn was frazzled, his hair messy, his once-fine clothes stained. He landed so hard on the cobblestones that he stumbled a little, his hand thrust out to me.

I could have wept for the sight of him. Thank the gods. *He's alive, he's alive, he's alive.*

He lurched closer, urgency in every line of his form. "Come on, Mish. We need to get out of here. Let's go home."

I took a half step back.

I was drowning under difficult realities tonight. The consequences of my actions hadn't yet set in, though I knew they would soon. But right now, the consequences to Raihn—a king of a rival House, a king who had been spurned by Nyaxia, a king who already was on the precipice of war—were staggering.

I managed, "You have to go, Raihn. Right now."

"I'm not leaving without you."

Gods help me, I couldn't do this.

"You have to. Nyaxia will come, and—"

"You've given me no good reasons to believe that you're safe," he spat. "Not a single fucking one."

We have to go, Asar said gently into my mind. I glanced over my shoulder to see him several strides ahead, watching protectively, unblinking, but waiting to intervene unless I asked him to.

Raihn followed my gaze. His voice lowered, the words intended only for me. "Please. Whatever is happening, we will work it out together, at home, where you're safe. Let us *help* you."

And there it was. The gods-damned sad puppy face.

He meant every word of it.

I could tell him everything. He would understand. He would give us every resource. Right now, I could change everything.

But what a cost he, Oraya, and their entire kingdom would pay for it. Here, doused in the smoke of what we'd brought upon the House of Shadow, that was more inevitable than ever.

Tears burned in my eyes. I blinked and one slithered down my cheek.

Yes. Three letters that would lead me to a comfortable embrace from friends who I longed for so fiercely.

Yes.

One syllable. So easy. So close.

My lips parted to let it free.

And I said, "You will leave the House of Shadow."

You will leave. Leave. Leave.

Asar had been right. Compulsion, when done correctly, was just another instinct. I hated myself for just how easy it was to use it against Raihn. I knew his mind so well. I could slip into it like a familiar pair of gloves and snip away every possibility of rejection.

Raihn's eyes went blank. He fell under the spell immediately. He was a Nightborn king—he knew how to steel his mind against Shadowborn intrusion.

But not with me.

He never saw it coming.

"You will leave right now," I said. "You will go back to the House of Night. You will not come back here looking for me. You will hug Oraya and tell her that you love her and you'll—you'll stay *safe,* alright? You will *go stay safe.*"

Go. Go. Go.

My voice cracked, on the verge of shattering. Raihn's mouth had closed. He looked down at his outstretched hand, like he'd forgotten what he was doing with it.

"So *leave,*" I commanded.

Leave. Leave. Leave.

I was better at this than I ever thought I could be. Raihn didn't even resist it.

I blurted out, "I love you."

He didn't hear me. He was already leaping into the sky.

IT ALMOST BROKE me. It really did.

Asar's hand skimmed my lower back, the touch too light and too dull beneath layers of clothing that I resented. I had never so badly wanted to let someone pull me into an embrace, and I had never so little deserved one.

A smooth voice rang out in the darkness.

"It turns out that the House of Shadow apparently knows how to throw a hell of a party." Septimus exhaled a plume of smoke, gesturing to the palace with a lazy hand, cigarillo between his fingers. "I knew it would be an eventful evening, but I have to admit, this exceeded my expectations."

In this moment, I *hated* him.

I hated him almost as much as I hated myself.

"Where's the boat?" My voice was practically a croak.

Septimus raised his palms. "No need for that. I uphold my promises."

He gestured to the dock. Unassuming among the warships was a little rowboat with two men within it.

"They have been instructed to take you to the House of Blood. My cousin will come meet you at the rendezvous point, then escort you to the deadlands. Try not to be too put off by his appearance. I swear he's perfectly personable." Then, after consideration, "Well. Somewhat personable. Here."

He tossed something to us, which Asar caught mid-air. He opened his hand to reveal two small vials, each containing shimmering silver liquid.

"A little something to knock you out for the journey," Septimus said. "A safety measure for the House of Blood. I'm sure you of all people understand the value of our privacy. Besides, I'm sure you need some rest, anyway."

Asar bristled. We exchanged a glance.

I told him silently, *It probably won't even—*

Septimus cocked his head. "It will work," he said. "Trust me."

"That is quite some *trust* you're asking for, if it does," Asar said.

"I promised you safe passage. You will get safe passage." Septimus exhaled a plume of smoke. "It's a condition of the deal, I'm afraid. Outsiders are not allowed within the House of Blood. We're already bending rules for you, but I can't allow you to sightsee on the way there." He gestured to Luce. "Your companion will remain awake as your guard, if you prefer."

This did make sense, even if I resented it. With the destruction raging behind us, we didn't have time to argue.

Asar gave Septimus a critical once-over. I knew he was rummaging through Septimus's mind—looking, one last time, for evidence of betrayal.

But Septimus just smiled, a hand over his heart. "By all means. Help yourself to whatever's left inside my skull. My intentions, as I'm sure you know by now, are honest."

"Forgive my skepticism," Asar muttered. "You deal in betrayals like a moneylender deals in debt."

Septimus laughed softly. His fair gaze lifted to the Shadowborn castle. Plumes of smoke, shimmering with divinity, now poured from the broken windows. Terrified screams still echoed from within. An inferno burst with a sickening crash from one of the spires, glass twinkling to the ground like razored rain.

Utter carnage.

The grandest place in the House of Shadow had been destroyed by the person who had once been chosen to guard it.

"Well, that's a bit hypocritical of you," Septimus said. "Don't you think?"

PART THREE

An Eye

INTERLUDE

Years passed, then decades. The boy grew. He became a prince, and he became a monster.

I will spare you the details of his rise and his fall. It is, after all, a tale you have heard before. Just know that both were extraordinary. In his mentor's hand, the prince was honed into exactly the weapon that his father dreamed he could be. He became more legend than man, and he thrived on it, because only a legend could cross into the unknowns he still longed to conquer. And yet, his hunger for knowledge remained insatiable. No matter how far he pushed himself, he still found that promise he had been offered all those years ago—a life beyond fear—evading him.

His downfall, fittingly, was a painful tumble from the height of his success. When he came home that night to find his lover's body, he knew it was over. He knew it even before he sealed his fate himself.

His attempted resurrection of his lover—a Shadowborn noble—was forbidden. He was, after all, a weapon, and weapons should not strike without the hand of their master on the hilt. But the prince knew that his true crime was not conducting the necromancy, but failing at it. What damned him were the fresh scars on his face, still seeping, and the fact that they would mark his failure forever.

The prince did not care. Not about this, or anything. He sat in his imprisonment, awaiting sentencing.

He thought his mentor would come to visit him, but he did not. Instead, one night, a guard delivered a single folded piece of parchment.

The prince almost refused it. A lifetime of abuse had stoked hatred in his heart.

Yet, in this vicious world, hatred was independent of admiration, and the prince still, after all these years, admired his mentor deeply.

So, he took the letter and unfolded the parchment. It held only a single line written in familiar script:

Remember this feeling.

The prince stared at that sentence. Then, in a fit of rage so violent it sent the guards lurching away from the bars, he crushed the paper in his fist, decimating it with a burst of darkness.

Something within him snapped in two.

The implication that this could one day be something that drove him to become a greater weapon enraged him. The prince had spent a lifetime hauling strength from the worst of his memories, forging rage into destruction. And it was, always, always, destruction. The only thing he was capable of. The only purpose he could fulfill.

Upon his sentencing, the prince was officially cast into exile. He was sent to the prison to rot away with everything else the kingdom did not wish to look at. For a long time, the prince resented this place. It echoed his rage and pain back at him. He saw himself in the prisoners, in the ghosts, in the bowing beams that moaned their death wails, and he hated them all.

Weeks passed, then months.

He had stopped counting the nights of his exile when the prince, at last, wandered the halls of his new home with fresh eyes. He realized how deeply it was hurting. He noticed the stress fractures in the doors, windows, beams. He heard its voice, so quiet he had dismissed it before, begging for his help.

He paused at a gate in the prison's lowest levels, close to the boundary to the veil. Jagged cracks fanned out through the bronze metal.

He looked down at his hand, and the scars that echoed those cracks so perfectly.

Help me, *the prison moaned.* Help me.

The prince touched the cracked metal and could have sworn he felt an exhale of relief.

The prison, he knew, was not a prison at all, but a temple repurposed. It had once been a place of spiritual solace, but in the eyes of the Shadowborn king, it was fit only to be a place of pain. It occurred to the prince only now that it was so deeply misunderstood.

He thought of all the times he had been told that his greatest purpose was to become more effective at inflicting suffering. He thought of all the times his mentor had told him that his life was only worth the blood he spilled upon it.

The prince reached for the broken gate, and slowly, methodically, tenderly, patched each and every wound.

When he was done, he stepped back and surveyed his handiwork. It was immaculate.

For the first time in months, he smiled—satisfied in his defiance.

CHAPTER THIRTY-ONE

Mische

I had been skeptical that the tonic would work on me, all things considered. But I remembered nothing after stepping onto the little boat. Just dark and dreams.

I dreamed of Saescha's face—her face in her final moments of life, and then as a wraith, desperate for Atroxus's light in the Descent. I dreamed of Asar's, his eyes distant and unfamiliar. I dreamed of Raihn's, agonized and relieved, before I betrayed him. I dreamed of a vision Atroxus once showed me, a beach covered in corpses, myself kneeling among them.

And I dreamed of a god I'd never met, bearing a mask of copper, watching me with skeptical interest.

Tell me, he murmured, leaning close, *who are you?*

I opened my mouth to respond—

And let out an ugly groan.

That certainly was no dream. The sound startled me, because it was too real.

Sun fucking take me. I felt terrible. Absolutely terrible.

"—home for the next few hours," a gruff voice was saying.

I forced my head up. My vision swam. I couldn't make out anything through the soupy smudges. I felt like I was splitting in two across worlds. One foot in death, one in life.

A hard, cold nose nudged my face.

Time to wake up, Luce urged.

I blinked hard. The smog cleared slowly. The ghosts scattered like fish in a disrupted pond.

I was slumped on a low, dusty couch. Asar was beside me, groggily dragging himself back to consciousness, with Luce now on top of him nuzzling his cheek.

We were in what appeared to be a small, run-down apartment, or perhaps a boarding house room. Instantly, I knew we were in the House of Blood. The furniture was far different than the ornate velvets and metals of the House of Shadow, or the sleek silks of the House of Night. It was all carved from wood with accents of bone and tarnished metal. The chairs were low to the ground, covered with slightly malformed red pillows. A small dining table and two chairs were in one corner of the room, a door to a modest washroom in another, and a bed surrounded by a wooden platform sat against the wall. None of it seemed to have been occupied in the last fifty years. A fine layer of dust coated every surface.

Our Bloodborn sailor knelt by the hearth, summoning a fire, which doused the cobweb-dusted interior in light. Still, I shivered violently, and the fire didn't seem to help at all.

"You can wait here for your escorts," he said as he rose. "My time with you is done."

He sounded relieved, which was a little insulting considering that we were unconscious the entire time. Surely our company couldn't have been *that* terrible.

Still, I noticed that his clothes were now much dirtier than I remembered. How long had our journey been? I found it difficult to unscramble my memories.

While I could barely sit up, Asar was already standing. We were both still wearing our torn, bloodstained finery from the ball. His hair was smooshed up on one side at an angle I might have teased him about if I'd been less groggy. He patted it down as his gaze shot to me, taking quick assessment of my condition, then Luce's, and then, finally, landing on the pack—which held the precious mask. He stared at it for a long moment, then ripped his gaze away, only for it to linger—as if involuntarily—on me again. Whatever he saw made a line of worry form between his brows.

"How long will we wait?" he asked our escort.

The man was already halfway to the door. "A few hours. A few days. I was your keeper, not theirs. Don't worry, Shadowborn. You'll be safe here. We have our ways of keeping the gods' eyes from things better left unseen."

He smiled, revealing sharp, bloodstained teeth. "Good luck!" Then with a wave that somehow seemed a bit sarcastic and the *click* of a lock, he left us alone.

Asar tried the doorknob, only to confirm what we already knew. We were locked in.

I stood, swaying slightly. Maybe it was a blessing that I was feeling more dead than I had, because even in this state, spending gods-knew-how-long unconscious in a corset made my ribs brutally sore.

I went to the single cracked window and peered outside. We were surrounded by water. Jagged mountains and snow-dusted hills rose against the horizon. A cluster of small buildings stood at a distant shore, barely more than shacks. The moon was silver again, nestled comfortably among the stars. Still, all of it seemed a bit duller than it once had been, as if still mourning the dance partner of the sun.

"We're very far north," Asar said, looking out beside me. "We've traveled a long way."

We had. Yet the events of the Melume felt like they had just happened. I could still feel the hands of the dead on my skin.

Luce trotted into the next room and flopped over in front of the hearth, letting out an exhausted groan, like she hadn't slept in days.

"You've guarded us a long way, Luce," I told her. "You deserve some rest."

She grunted her agreement, rolling belly-up, already halfway to snoring.

Asar placed the pack on the table. It was a standard Shadowborn bag, in plain black leather, fine enough but unremarkable. No one would ever guess what it held.

He unclasped the flap.

"Don't touch it," I said quickly.

He nodded, lifting a hand to show me his gloves. Then he slid the mask from the bag and placed it on the table.

A shiver swept over me. The shadows lurched forward, as if reaching for it.

Maybe part of me had felt that it would simply evaporate when the Melume was over, like all the other ghosts of the past. But no. There it was. Alarus's face stared up at us in decorated bronze, engraved with countless ancient glyphs that swirled over it like churning waves. They moved across its surface so slowly that I found myself questioning if I was imagining it. The carvings gave off a very slight glow, which seemed to subtly shift from white to silver to black to purple.

It reminded me of something that I couldn't place.

Not until I looked at Asar and saw his scars gleaming with that exact same light.

Then my gaze drifted down to his Mark, visible between the hem of his sleeve and the edge of his glove. The organic strokes of ink were a near-perfect sibling to the flowing lines of glyphs on the mask's surface.

"For thousands of years, even the scholars thought that this could never be retrieved," Asar murmured. "And yet. Here it is."

The crown to Alarus's lost kingdom. The crown to the House of Death.

A yawning hunger opened up in my chest, and I tamped down hard on it. Another wave of dizziness struck me. My mouth was dry.

Gods, I was *starving*.

"Sun take us," I muttered. "I can't believe we pulled that off. I can't believe we *did all that*."

I swayed a little, leaning against a table, and I could feel Asar's gaze, sharp and protective, taking in every wobble.

"You need blood," he said.

"No, I need to get this dress off." I attempted to reach for the laces, first by reaching from above, then by twisting around my waist. It was no use. I'd been tied into this thing by a small army of shadow servants, provided so generously by Egrette, and it seemed like it would take magic just as advanced to get me out of it.

"Here."

I felt Asar's presence behind me. The comforting scent of ivy fell over me.

His hands worked at my back, and the pressure released. I wished I breathed, so I could celebrate with a fresh gulp of air.

"Thank the gods," I muttered.

But as soon as the words left my lips, they just reminded me that we were in no position to thank the gods for anything.

I swayed slightly.

"Hold on to the couch," Asar said, sensing my weakness immediately. "This will take a minute."

He continued working at the laces. I leaned over the couch to grip the back.

My voice was rough as I said, "We just made so, so many enemies."

My head spun at the thought of it. Shiket, who had gone so far as to cross into Nyaxia's territory. Nyaxia, once she inevitably learned that we'd stolen the mask. The House of Shadow, ready to take their vengeance.

"Fine," Asar said. "Let them come for us."

He loosened another loop.

Then he added, more softly, "You were incredible, Iliae. Absolutely incredible."

Incredible felt like the wrong word for it. Yes, I had felt powerful standing in front of the Dusk Window, the entire realm of the dead ready to heed my call.

But any pride I felt in that disappeared when I thought of Raihn's devastated face. I had succeeded in wielding the power that had evaded me for so long, but it felt like such a cruel victory.

I just shook my head. "No. I don't think so."

Another loop.

I knew Asar saw exactly what I was thinking.

"You were protecting him."

"He'll never forgive me. Never." And could I blame him? I had violated him, and the only reason the compulsion had even worked was because I knew his mind so well. A lifetime of friendship, weaponized.

But I didn't regret it, and that felt the worst of all.

I turned my head slightly. I could barely see Asar out of the corner of my eye, head lowered, brow creased in focus. He worked at my corset laces the way he had worked at the broken gates of Morthryn.

I had seen the way he'd looked at the House of Shadow burning. I had felt his guilt, just as he had felt mine.

"I'm sorry," I said softly. "About what happened to the House of Shadow."

A barely there flinch rippled. "It will recover. Probably with a vengeance, largely directed at us."

"I know. But it was still your home."

"It wasn't. It had never wanted me. But . . ."

His voice trailed off. He undid another tie of my corset, and I now had to hold the dress up to keep it from falling.

"A long time ago," he said, "when I was a child, and then a young man, I had dreamed that maybe one day, it could have been. Instead, I left it worse than I found it. And that version of myself mourns what I have done. Even if I don't regret it."

I understood this. It was the part of me that still mourned what died when I thrust that arrow into Atroxus's throat. The belief, the faith, the dream. Not the god.

Another loop. Almost done.

He said, wryly, "Are you going to tell me it's not my fault?"

I shook my head. "No. I've learned over the years that people think they want absolution. But that's not what they really need to hear."

"What do most people need to hear?"

For some reason, I had to speak past a lump in my throat.

"They need to hear, *'Even if it is your fault, I will love you anyway.'*"

He was quiet, thoughtful. He pulled through the final loop of the lace and straightened. "There," he said. "Done."

Slowly, I turned around, holding my dress against my body. I swayed, still, and I knew he was tracking that sign of weakness. He was so close that I could feel his breath against my lips. And gods, how I wanted to close the distance.

The scent of his blood was overwhelming. Hunger twisted in my stomach.

His gloved hand swept over my cheek, wiping away a smudge of dirt.

"For whatever of your mistakes, Mische Iliae," he said, quietly, firmly, "for whatever of your faults, for whatever unintended pains you may bring this world, I will love you anyway."

Love. That word sank deep into me, twisted around my still, cold heart.

I knew Asar loved me, and I knew that words were the least valuable currency to show it. And yet. His voice wrapping around that word made me shiver. I wanted to capture it and hold it in my soul forever. A gift I could never deserve.

I swayed again, wordless.

"And I will never stop telling you that you were incredible, because you were, and you are, and don't you dare ever be ashamed of it," he went on. "Now stop arguing with me and drink, so I can keep watching you bring the world to its knees."

Sun take me. This man.

I was so tired. I was so weak. My heart hurt. And when he put it all like that, I didn't have it in me to resist anymore.

I let the dress fall. It was so heavy that it hit the ground with a satisfying *thump.*

Asar's smile faded. His gaze raked over me, inch by inch, feet to head. I relished that stare. I felt it almost like I felt his touch.

"Sorry," I murmured. "It was heavy."

"Oh," he said, slowly, deliberately, "don't you dare be sorry."

"I'm sure there are some clothes in here some—"

But Asar had already gone to the bed and, with one vicious movement, threw back the blanket, then the sheet. He raised his brows at me expectantly.

I swallowed thickly. "That's not—it's not safe for you."

"There's a sheet. Perfect protection."

I started to protest, but another wave of dizziness struck me.

"Sun take me, Mische, just get into the bed and drink."

Through my headache, I thought to myself, *What a wonderful collection of words.*

I obeyed, going to the bed and lying down. I sank into the mattress, lashes already fluttering, world tilting. For all my protests, Asar was right. I was fading fast.

He gently smoothed the sheet over my body, then lay beside me on top of it. I reached for his wrist, but he shook his head and lifted his chin instead.

My brows rose. "I can't."

"You need it faster than a wrist can give it to you."

"I'll hurt you. And there's no magical bathtub here."

"I'm feeling . . . invigorated. I think I can handle it."

Invigorated. That seemed like one way to describe how he'd looked holding that mask. Like the god we had set out to make him.

My gaze traced the angle of his perfect jaw, then the elegant lines of his throat. Found the steady beat of his pulse there, right under his skin, and couldn't tear my gaze away.

A lifetime in a church, and yet, I'd never had my self-control tested so much as it had been since I met Asar.

I truly meant to protest more. But his gloved hand found the back of my head, guiding it down.

And I found myself lowering my lips to his skin.

My fangs slipped easily through his flesh. His blood flooded my mouth, sweet and rich.

He let out a groan of pleasure that I felt vibrate against my lips, and gods help me, I almost lost all coherent thought right there. The last time I'd fed from his throat, he'd been inside me, the two of us writhing through our hungers together.

I was grateful for the sheet between us, because my body rolled against him before I could stop it, the carnal impulse overwhelming.

"Good," he whispered. His hand fell to my waist, sliding down, and his touch burned, even through the fabric between us. His fingers dug into my hips in a way that reminded me too vividly of how he'd held me there when I rode him.

My palm flattened against his stomach, enjoying the way the ridges of his abdomen tensed under my touch.

I was so hungry.

So hungry.

And he tasted so, so good. Better than he had in the Descent, or in Morthryn. How was that possible?

I wrung out that next swallow.

And I was so drunk on my desire, on the sheer life that Asar offered me, that I couldn't help myself. I followed the ridge of the V that led into his trousers. Lower, to his length, hard and throbbing already.

He drew in a delicious, sharp breath as my palm wrapped around it through his clothing. I knew he was considering pulling away, as he had in Ryvenhaal. But I extracted my teeth just enough to whisper, "No. I want you."

His cock twitched at those words. As if my hunger alone was pure pleasure for him.

"Then you'll have me," he said.

And I felt a door opening for me—a door into his mind, coaxing me inside. I realized what he was doing: giving me an opportunity to reclaim the power that I'd used to destroy. Paint over the pain with pleasure. The gift I hadn't even known I needed.

With a gloved hand, he gently lowered my head back to his throat.

"Perfect," he murmured. "You are perfect."

I drew in another mouthful and pushed my hand up his length. I felt his spark of pleasure in my own body, his thoughts intermingling with my own. My thumb swirled around his tip, and gods, I resented the layers of fabric between us for dulling the details, the folds of skin, the silky texture.

My mind slipped further into his. He was thinking about my body pressed against his. He was thinking about my hand around his cock, and just how desperately he wished it was inside me instead. His desire made me dizzy with want, and I fed that back to him as I pumped him harder, faster.

He thrust against my hand as I drew another agonizing swallow. I sensed him driving closer to the end. I wanted to wring it out of him.

But with my next drink, I sensed a wave of weakness. A jolt of pain.

Immediately, I tore myself away from his throat.

His blood dribbled at the corner of my mouth, and my tongue

darted out to capture it. He stared at me with half-shuttered eyes, soft in their dreamy exhaustion and sharp in their vicious hunger.

I said, "Did I take too—"

But Asar just gripped my waist through the sheet and pulled me on top of him.

The weight of my body, the sensation of my thighs opening around his hips, sent his wild pleasure—his hunger—through us both.

"No," he growled. "No, you've never taken enough."

His hips thrust sharply up, dragging his rigid cock against my core. I let out a fractured moan.

I rolled against his length, faster, shifting with the constant feedback of his mind. I watched the blood roll down his throat, still glistening with the remnants of my kiss, and I had to throw my head back and bite down on my own lip to stop myself from going back in.

"Look at me," he commanded.

Look at me. Look at me. Look at me.

His voice reverberated with the power of compulsion.

I did. His gaze was glazed over and predatory.

"Tell me what you want."

His hands ran up and down my body through the sheet. One paused at my breast, circling my hardened nipple.

I slowed my movements, then stopped, and watched his entire body go taut in protest.

I said, "I want to watch you lose control."

His mind answered, *I've done that for you long ago.*

Aloud, he said, "Then make me."

Beneath the haze of my pleasure and his, I understood what he was offering me. The opportunity to reclaim the power of compulsion.

I was greedy. I was selfish. I gladly took it.

"Come for me," I breathed.

Come for me. Come for me. Come for me.

Oblivion crashed over him first, and as his hand found my core, the wave barreled over me a moment after. Asar gripped fistfuls of the sheet around my body, and when I collapsed against him, I had to bite down hard on the pillow just to keep my mouth from finding his bare skin again. Base, feral euphoria, mine and his combined, erased my senses.

Asar swiftly grabbed me and pressed me to the bed, the sheets still between us. He lowered his head over me, his nose nearly brushing mine, lips so close I could taste his words.

"You are an event, Mische Iliae," he murmured. "God slayer. Dawndrinker. Shadowborn queen. And I would die to taste your skin."

His gloved hand was tight around my wrist, pressing my palm to his chest, right over his heart. Like he wanted me to feel just how much he meant it.

And a terrible part of me, right now, wanted to throw back this sheet, open my thighs around him, and let him.

But I choked a breathy laugh, the tension breaking.

"I think it's best if only one of us is dead at a time," I said.

Slowly, a smile spread over his lips. I withdrew from his mind and wriggled from under his grasp as he settled beside me. Lust still throbbed between us. But the exhaustion came, too. Mine from the aftereffects of my feeding. His from all he had given up.

"Feeling better?" he said.

My eyelids were very heavy. I forced them open to look at him. "Mm-hmm. And you—"

"I'm perfect." He smoothed the sheets down over me and extracted himself from the bed. "I'll clean up. You rest."

I wanted to protest. I really did. But my lashes fluttered. When I forced them open again, Asar was back, wearing fresh clothes, lying on top of the sheets while I lay beneath. I resisted the urge to curl up against him, and settled instead for the weight of his body beside mine.

I dreamed of skin, and want, and all the ways the two collided.

CHAPTER THIRTY-TWO

Asar

I did not sleep.

The last time I'd let Mische drink directly from me, it had sapped my energy so much that I hadn't even been able to hold off Elias's common guards. Now, I wasn't nearly so affected. The weakness faded quickly. When I changed my clothes, I noticed the smooth skin on my torso—the wound Elias had inflicted in his last moments was gone. Fast healing by even vampire standards.

It surprised me. No matter what I said to reassure Mische, I'd been sure her feeding would affect me. But I wouldn't question a blessing, especially not with a Bloodborn stranger showing up at our door any minute.

Still, I wished I could rest. Mische sprawled out on the bed, snoring—and I loved that horrific, deafening sound, because it was so messily alive. It was honestly charming to me that, wraith or no, Mische still snored. She had gotten up some time ago to throw on some fresh clothes—despite my protests—only to immediately fall back into bed. Now, she wound herself around Luce, who had gotten up sometime in the day to join her.

Mische looked healthier now. The snoring, at least, was a good sign. She had desperately needed the blood. Still, I noted with some concern that she hadn't seemed to gain quite as much life as she had the last time she drank. She was still faintly translucent.

I turned back to the table before me.

To the mask that sat atop it.

It was everything I had expected an object that captured the very essence of a god to be. Which was to say, beautiful and horrifying. The kind of thing that, under any other circumstances, I would insist should never be handled by mortal souls.

And yet. Here I was.

{Here we are,} a voice whispered, fleeting as a distant wind. *{Seizing destiny.}*

I pushed the voice away.

God-touched artifacts were known to be dangerous, not just for their power to destroy, but also to those who wielded them. Mische and I had both witnessed that firsthand over the years. I was prepared for what I was dealing with.

I could have sworn I heard an amused laugh at that.

But I stood abruptly, sliding the mask back into the bag. My attention turned to an approaching presence outside the door. Then heavy footsteps.

A powerful knock rang out—two decisive raps.

Mische flew upright, curly hair so messy it formed a halo around her head. Luce jumped up and bolted to the door, barking like mad.

"I prefer to only knock once," a low voice came from the other side.

I went to the door, Mische close behind.

When I opened it, a Bloodborn man stared back at me.

I knew, instantly, that this was Septimus's cousin. They shared similar angular facial features, but while Septimus's were cold and elegant, this man exuded unfinished ruggedness. He wore fine, traditional Bloodborn clothing like Septimus did—a white suit with red accents—but while Septimus's appearance was immaculate, this man's was wrinkled, the collar unbuttoned, the sleeves pushed up to his elbows. His stare was hard and piercing, his hair long and silver, messily half bound up. A heavy sword was strapped across his back.

Most interesting of all, he had horns.

They were black, and started shortly above his hairline, curling back toward his skull. The scholar in me couldn't help but stare at them. I'd spent a lifetime studying magical curiosities, but I had never seen anything like this before. How, I had to wonder, had he gotten those?

The man swept a cold, analytical gaze over me. From that look alone, I'd bet he was some kind of military leader, because he assessed me like I was an opponent to be dismantled.

I slipped through his mind as if shuffling a deck of cards. He was well trained against Shadowborn magic, keeping the sharpest specifics of his thoughts guarded beyond my reach. But I saw enough. He was, indeed, a general—countless images of battle and destruction confirmed that, so engrained into his psyche that he couldn't have hidden them even if he'd tried. I saw an island and a rocky shore, a palace nestled in the snow, and—

I paused in surprise.

The faces of goddesses. Nyaxia, which was not surprising, given what Septimus had told us. But Acaeja, too, which was *very* surprising.

Interesting. A Bloodborn who had encountered the White Pantheon.

"Atrius," the man said stiffly. "Your guide."

He didn't exactly seem pleased to be here.

Mische started to introduce herself, but Atrius said, "I know who you are." Then, as if that was all the greeting he needed, he went on, "Forgive me if I'm not much for pleasantries. We have a long journey ahead. Our boat is waiting."

THE BOAT WAS smaller than the one we'd arrived on, little more than a dinghy. It turned out our temporary holding cell had been on a small island, within a lighthouse.

"Not far to shore," Atrius grunted, and we bobbed along on the choppy surf. It was a cool night. My breath and Atrius's froze to ghost-pale plumes with every exhale. Mische's did not, and I found myself lingering on it.

She looked out at the lights dotting the approaching shore. The moonlight illuminated a few buildings. The House of Blood's style of architecture stood in stark contrast to the smooth marble domes of the House of Night or the twisted iron spires of the House of Shadow, all red-painted roofs with sloping, curved peaks and gold accents that glittered under the icy moonlight like streaks of blood. The House of Blood had the harshest climate of the three Houses, the terrain largely rough and mountainous, and progressively colder and snowier as one traveled north. Few had anything positive to say about the House of Blood, but the few times I'd been here, I did have to admire it. I'd always thought it was beautiful in the same way that Morthryn was—a little ugly, a little marked by all the ways it had been dragged back down to the dirt, but forever standing in defiance.

"Is that the capital?" Mische asked.

Atrius scoffed. "No. That's an outpost town. The capital makes this look like a village."

"What's it like?"

"I haven't been there in a very long time." He said this flatly, but I felt a hint of longing with the words.

"Why not?" she asked.

"Traveling. We'll stop here to get supplies. And then we will start our journey north."

I glanced at Mische, and the faint, faint glimmer of night I could see through her skin.

"How long will it be?" I asked.

"Are you concerned about time?"

"We don't have much of it to waste. Certainly not enough for detours."

I eyed his sword, which he'd laid across the bottom of the boat as he rowed.

Mische and I had taken every measure to ensure that Septimus wasn't lying about his promises. But I was no fool. No matter how well constructed a deal was, I knew there were countless ways Atrius could manipulate the bounds of an agreement.

He laughed softly. "I'm not planning on killing you, if that's what you're concerned about. I have no reason to do such a thing."

"You don't have much of a reason to help us, either."

"I have always left the silver words and pretty deals to my cousin. He calls me when he's ready to act, and I do."

"So you really have been to the deadlands?" Mische asked quietly.

"Yes."

I knew the onslaught of questions was coming before she opened her mouth.

"Why were you there? What did you do there? What was it like?" She said them all so quickly, as if they all warred for dominance.

"I was there by the bidding of the Dark Mother," he said flatly. "We did whatever she requested of us. And you will see what it's like for yourself soon."

The bidding of the Dark Mother. Interesting.

The chill in his presence left no mystery to how he now felt about it. It had gone poorly. No surprise to me. The House of Blood's relationship with Nyaxia had always been fraught. That was the tricky thing about worshipping the one who had damned you.

We arrived at the docks and Atrius handed over the boat to some waiting workers. "Put your hoods up," Atrius said. "The Bloodborn aren't kind to outsiders."

No objections here. It was better if we didn't attract attention.

The town smelled of salt and iron—the sea and the mountains and blood. It was built closely packed together. The moment we stepped onto the shore, I sensed that this was an old place, a city that certainly long predated the existence of vampires. The Bloodborn had clearly tried to maintain its former glory, but it still showed the strain of millennia of struggle. Stone walls were cracked and patched and cracked again. The gold metalwork that trimmed the red-painted peaks of the buildings was chipped, and in some places, missing altogether. And though we kept our hoods up like Atrius commanded, we still earned wary stares. Villagers stopped in the middle of their sweeping or cleaning or forging or feeding to watch as we passed. The Bloodborn, some said, could smell outsiders.

Atrius led us deep into the city, to an unmarked door in an unmarked stone building. When he ushered us inside, the scent of blood struck me with such intensity that it made my steps falter. The hunger that I'd been tamping down—shockingly strong, despite the fact that

I'd practically gorged myself at Egrette's party in preparation for this journey—roared back with a powerful surge.

It was a pub. White stone tables were dotted with years' worth of blood droplets, now browning and crusted. A handful of tables sat scattered around the room, occupied by Bloodborn men and women hunching over mugs and wineglasses and, in one corner, a single aging human blood vendor, who stared blankly at us as a Bloodborn woman suckled at her neck. There were other humans here, too—I could smell them immediately—but they must have been upstairs, perhaps entertaining their patrons in other ways alongside their sustenance.

Everyone stopped to stare at us.

The man behind the counter, a thin, pale creature with dark circles beneath his eyes, straightened.

"Atrius. Mother's tits." He cackled. "When the boy told me you'd been here, I almost took off his head for telling tales."

Atrius shot the man a pointed look that clearly said that the errand boy's head was not the one at risk.

"I'm meeting someone," he said. "The room we requested?"

The barkeeper shut his mouth and raised an arthritic hand to the back of the pub. "Of course. Second door down."

Atrius strode through to the back of the pub, and we followed. The stares did, too.

"Why does everyone seem so surprised to see you?" Mische asked.

"I've been away."

"Away where?"

Atrius gave her an exasperated look. "Isn't it considered rude in the House of Shadow to ask so many questions?"

"Oh no, it definitely—" She clasped her hands in front of her. "It definitely is."

We were taken down a narrow hallway, fleeing the gaze of a fascinated scullery maid. Atrius opened the door to reveal a small room with a single card table, four chairs around it. A woman already sat in one of them. Her scent instantly told me she was human. She had long dark hair that was braided over one shoulder. She wore plain traveling clothes that matched Atrius's—and, most interestingly, a deep red cloth tied over her eyes.

Mische stopped short.

"You're an Arachessen," she blurted out.

The woman chuckled. "Such a polite greeting." Her Obitraen was good, but she spoke with a thick accent. Though she wore a blindfold, her face tilted to us as we spoke, as if making direct eye contact. "I prefer to be called Sylina, thank you."

Mische gave her an apologetic smile. "I just—wasn't expecting it."

I hid my surprise better than she did, but I was equally taken aback. The Arachessen were acolytes of the goddess Acaeja, a small but well-known cult with sects across the human lands. They took their recruits young and destroyed their eyesight in offering to their goddess—supposedly, a method of showing commitment, as well as a way of helping the recruits learn how to see via the threads of fate instead. Depending on who you asked, the Arachessen were viewed as deranged lunatics, dangerous cultists, or wise sorcerers. They were known to be skilled assassins, but far more dangerous was the organization's habit of manipulating world events to align to what was Right by the threads of fate—or at least, what they claimed to be.

I stared down the newcomer, careful to keep my thoughts still. The Bloodborn were unable to look into minds, but the Arachessen could.

"Please, sit," she said, as Atrius took a chair beside her. She shot him a smirk. "It sounds like a joke, doesn't it? Two vampires, a seer, and a ghost walk into a pub . . ."

And a ghost.

Mische's face stilled. I froze mid-step.

"If we're going to survive this together, you'd better stop underestimating us," Sylina said. "I see through the threads of fate. Whatever you've done to disguise her true nature from prying eyes, it wouldn't work on mine. Now please. Sit."

But I didn't move. I glanced between Atrius and Sylina, piecing together my theories.

"Now I see," I said. "Typical Bloodborn. You've kidnapped a seer to guide us. Or to spy on us?"

The Bloodborn were known for leveraging human magic wielders, especially seers. Most of them were not taken to the House of Blood willingly.

But Atrius and Sylina shared a brief, amused glance. It was uncanny, the way her face moved as if she saw straight through that blindfold.

"Kidnapped?" Sylina chuckled. "Trust me, I'm no prisoner."

"But you are a spy."

"Would you blame me, if I was?"

"You'll appreciate having the help of the seer when we're navigating the deadlands," Atrius said gruffly, already visibly irritated with this discussion.

Beside me, Mische frowned thoughtfully.

"Your accent," she said. "You're from the human nations. Where?"

Sylina cocked her head. A glint of pleased surprise. "Rare that any vampire even asks. I am from Glaea."

Glaea. Where had I heard that name before?

The realization hit Mische first.

She said into my mind, *That's the country Elias said was conquered by the House of Blood.*

Of course. He'd said it on our journey through the Descent. That the House of Blood was moving against the human nations in Nyaxia's name, even before Mische had ushered in the eternal night.

The images I'd seen of Atrius's past—battlefields and swords and fallen cities—now took on a new light. I turned my attention to Sylina, pushing toward her mind. I saw mountains and cliffs, a stone temple in the mountains, a palace with spires like knives—a throne—

My brow furrowed in confusion.

A throne with *her* on it.

A wall slammed down, snapping away the prying fingers of my magic. Sylina was now on her feet, her pleasant mask gone.

Atrius sighed and rubbed his temple.

"Stay out of my mind, vampire," Sylina hissed. "And keep your insulting surprise to yourself. I told you I was no prisoner. I rule Glaea as Atrius's equal."

As Atrius's equal.

Oooh, Mische said silently to me. *They're* together *together.*

But this revelation was not any more comforting to me.

"You're telling us that you rule your country," I said. "But even though it is still recovering from a war, you're here, an ocean away, leading us into the deadlands. Why?"

It didn't add up. It was one thing for Septimus to send us off with some expendable general. But why would an important couple come all this way, put themselves in this kind of danger, when they had so many reasons to stay where they were?

"We aren't doing this out of goodwill," Atrius said. "Septimus told you as much. This shouldn't be a surprise."

Sylina gave me a piercing stare from behind her blindfold. The directness of her stare was unsettling.

"No need to give me that suspicious look, Prince Asar," she said. "Our reasons are none of your concern. Just as the reason why you're looking for the eye of Alarus is none of ours."

The eye of Alarus.

That was information that we had not provided to either Septimus or Atrius. Information that no one but Mische and the gods should know. She was taunting me with it.

Atrius shot Sylina an annoyed look, growing wearier of this conversation by the second.

Mische said silently to me, *She's testing us.*

I knew it. It was a familiar game. Push, elicit emotions, and use the distractions to learn your opponent's mind.

It could be typical distrust between Houses. Or it could be something more. I thought uneasily of the gods at our heels. The Arachessen were acolytes of Acaeja. But Glaea had been conquered in the name of Nyaxia. I couldn't say who these two answered to now.

"It is my concern when our enemies know more about us than we do about them," I said.

"Respectfully, it sounds to me like you aren't in a position to be making demands," Sylina said.

"You must be desperate, too, since you're here instead of lording over this country you supposedly care so deeply about."

Her face darkened. "I am here because I read the threads of fate and I can feel it when they're all converging. And more importantly, I am here because I was not about to allow my partner to wander into the deadlands alone with someone who is inevitably going to stab him in the back."

Under the distraction of our argument, I felt Sylina pushing into my mind, and prepared to push back harder. But Mische slammed her hands down on the table. A burst of darkness rolled through the room, making the lanterns shiver, pushing Sylina's magic away. It was, I noted with a twinge of pride, very skillfully done.

"This is ridiculous," she said. "We're about to journey into the gods-damned deadlands together. We aren't going to survive it unless we trust each other." She shot me an annoyed look. "Like it or not."

Atrius let out a wordless grunt and waved her away.

"Let's not waste each other's time with games. We both need to make the journey. If you stay out of our business, we'll stay out of yours."

Mische gave them a bright, sweet smile. "We're grateful to have the help."

And she was still holding that lovely smile when she said into my mind, *They are probably going to betray us, huh?*

Probably, I agreed.

Aloud, I said, "Yes. We're so grateful."

CHAPTER THIRTY-THREE

Mische

Our guards seemed eager to set off immediately, and Asar and I were in no position to object. The Bloodborn had an entire stable of horses, which delighted me. The Nightborn rarely used mounts—wings were much more efficient. The Shadowborn did occasionally, though they were a luxury reserved for the upper class, seeing as horses were naturally (and understandably) quite wary of vampires.

When I saw the herd—herd!—of horses in the pasture, my eyes nearly bugged out of my head.

They looked like entirely different creatures than the flighty beasts I'd seen in other Houses. They were heavily muscled, white with black noses and cropped manes that stood straight up. Unlike the other horses in Obitraes, they didn't seem nervous in the presence of their vampire masters. Even when Luce trotted up with us, they merely gave her several uneasy snorts before returning to their grain.

"They're gorgeous," I breathed.

"You've seen horses before, Iliae," Asar said, amused.

"Not like these." I threw my hands out toward a big white horse who trotted curiously closer to me. "Look at this beauty!"

"She bit me when I arrived," Atrius grumbled.

But he stroked the horse's nose, anyway. It was an instinctual movement, the type that came only from genuine affection. It gave me no choice but to like him.

The horse turned to me, and I reached out on instinct before I caught myself and clasped my hands behind my back.

No touching the horses, Mische. No touching anyone at all.

"Sorry, girl," I murmured to the horse. "I would if I could."

The horse nickered in a way that said, *I understand,* which I appreciated. When Luce nuzzled me instead, I stroked her head in thanks.

Still, I was selfishly delighted when I was given the mare as my mount. I was careful to layer large blankets under her saddle, shielding her from my skin. If Atrius and Sylina noticed my fussing over this peculiar task, they were mercifully silent about it. "What's her name?" I asked Atrius as we set off.

He looked at me like this was a strange question. Then he glanced down at the mare.

"Six Six."

I followed his stare to a brand on the horse's shoulder: VI VI. Six Six.

I frowned. "That's a terrible name."

How judgmental, Asar said into my mind. *Some horses probably think Mische is a terrible name.*

I wrinkled my nose at him.

"These are war horses," Atrius said. "They're loyal and fearless partners in battle. Not pets."

"She can be a loyal and fearless partner while still having a name."

"A formidable name like Luce?" Atrius said drily.

Luce growled.

Asar looked legitimately furious.

"Luce *is* a loyal and fearless partner. And she *does* have a formidable name."

Luce sniffed in agreement.

Maybe the Bloodborn were just bad at names. Septimus was the seventh Bloodborn prince, and *his* name sounded like his parents simply ran out of inspiration by the time they got to him.

"Agreed," I said. "You could have been a little more creative."

"And what would you have suggested?" Atrius said.

"Something majestic. Like . . ." I didn't even think before the word was leaving my lips. "Saescha."

Immediately, I snapped my mouth closed. Why the hell did I just say that?

I could feel Asar's stare burning into the side of my face, though I looked straight ahead.

It hurt—actually hurt—to say Saescha's name aloud. I wasn't expecting it. When was the last time I'd spoken her name? Was it in the Descent, when I'd begged her forgiveness? Or was it when I killed Atroxus and damned her for the second time?

But Saescha was a beautiful name. The horse was powerful and strong and majestic, just like she had been. There were worse namesakes. Right?

"Saescha," Sylina repeated slowly. "Pretty."

"It is," I murmured.

It is, Asar agreed softly into my mind, and he reached out to brush my thigh with a brief, comforting touch, as we kept on riding.

I HAD THOUGHT that one upside of this whole ordeal might be that I'd finally get to see the House of Blood. I was, despite myself, very curious. Raihn had been there before we met, but had always objected to traveling there during our years wandering together. When I'd asked him what it was like, he'd just said, "Fucking bleak."

But to my disappointment, the city we'd arrived in was the only town we passed through. Our first escort had apparently brought Asar and me to the northernmost bounds of Bloodborn society.

Still, what little we did see of the House of Blood did not strike me as the depressing place Raihn had described. We hugged the coast at first, where the mountains met the sea, and then veered inland. The land rolled out in endless plains, stark against the distant peaks of the mountains. The grass was silver and the dusty earth white. Even the mountains were white, like bleached bone. Sometimes, we could see the distant skylines of one Bloodborn city or another, out there shielded by the ivory cliffs, red silhouettes bloody beneath the moonlight. But mostly, there was nothing out here. Nothing but the cold and the silence. Still, though it wasn't the grand magnificence of the House of Night's rolling dunes and grand marble towers or the House of Shadow's lush flowers and metal spires, it held a sad, ethereal beauty.

Time passed like that, nights blending into each other beneath the moon that never changed and the sun that never rose. Eventually, when we gathered to rest, Atrius drew a clumsy map in the dirt with a stick. It looked like a crooked, convoluted maze.

"We're close now to the maze of arches," he said. "That's where Nyaxia tore her passageway through the deadlands back into the mortal realm."

He dragged a path through his drawing, then tapped the end of his streak. "We'll encounter the Keeper here."

"The Keeper is actually r-r-real?" It was now nearly impossible to hide my shivering. The air was frigid, but the cold seemed to come from within, and no amount of cloaks or blankets eased it. "I thought he was a myth."

"Most do," Atrius said. "And he's very good at keeping himself hidden so it stays that way. Thus . . ." He tapped the drawing with his stick. "The maze."

"Why didn't the gods just seal the passage?" I asked.

"The gods weren't concerned with the passage. The Keeper took it upon himself to safeguard it. The gods probably forgot it existed at all. I'm not sure why anyone would expect differently."

The bitterness in his voice was palpable, but before I could press further, he went on, "The Keeper is a lesser god. One of the few that still lives. If we challenge him in battle, he'll reward our victory by opening the door to the deadlands. But defeating him is no small task."

"*One* lesser god?" I said cheerfully. "That's nothing."

I sounded more confident than I felt. I had to work to keep another shudder from my voice.

Atrius did not look convinced. "I had an army of elite Bloodborn warriors the last time I did this."

"Right. But this t-time, you have us."

He glanced between us, unimpressed. "Mm-hmm."

What is that look on his face? I said to Asar silently. *I'm a god slayer!*

Even though the god slaying still felt like a bit of a fluke.

But Asar was quiet. His brow was drawn low over his eyes. I glanced at him and noticed that his hand was at his waist, drifting closer to the pack slung over his shoulder, as if by instinct. When I reached for his presence, I felt a peculiar, unfamiliar fog clustering around the mind I now knew so well.

Asar? I nudged, and he jumped slightly, like I'd startled him. He blinked, turning his attention to the map.

"Once we get past this Keeper," he said, "what then?"

Atrius said simply, "Then we'll be in the deadlands."

"And once we're in the deadlands," Asar said, "how long until we reach the execution site?"

"That depends."

Trying to get information out of Atrius was like trying to drink blood from stone.

Asar did not hide his annoyance. "*Depends* on what?"

"It depends on how injured we are after our encounter with the Keeper. It depends on how difficult the passage is through the door. It depends on what adversaries are waiting for us on the other side. It depends on the skies and the winds. It depends on how much has changed since I was last there. I hear you know the Descent, Shadowborn. Does it ever remain the same for two minutes at a time? The deadlands are even more unpredictable."

Sylina smirked, lifting her shoulder in a half shrug. "It depends on fate."

Asar scoffed.

She cocked her head. "What? You don't believe in fate?"

I felt Asar's stare take stock of the shivers I hid, the transparency in my skin, the way I no longer even mimicked breath.

"It doesn't matter if I believe in it," he said. "I certainly don't trust it."

CHAPTER THIRTY-FOUR

Asar

I would begrudgingly admit that we were indeed fortunate to have Atrius. The maze was already nearly impossible to navigate, even with him at the head of the group guiding us. The stone was sheer white here, reminding me of the bone cliffs of the Descent, though this was perhaps some kind of polished marble. Once, maybe it had been a grand building of some kind, but those days were long behind it now. The stone was worn and crumbling, reclaimed by the harsh wind of the northern Bloodborn territories. The only thing left that hinted at what it had once been were the broken gold doorframes, signaling each new potential turn, and the slippery cracked staircases.

When Atrius had described a maze, I'd been expecting sprawling, flat hallways. But this one climbed up just as much as out. There were no straight angles. Each path spiraled and twisted, and all of them were virtually indistinguishable from each other.

Up close, I had to admire the artistry of the wall. The glyphs carved into the stone had been long sanded away by time—at least, I thought they were glyphs, though they looked nothing like any I'd ever seen. I could feel the ancient remnants of their magic pulsing through the stone—probably predating not only Obitraes but also Vathysia, going back to the magic that the gods used to create the very bedrock of this world. It was fascinating. Even my collection didn't contain artifacts this old. So few remnants of this magic existed in the mortal world at all. I could've set up camp here and studied it for hours.

Mische, too, stroked the stone as we traveled through.

Do you hear that? she said into my mind. *It's talking.*

She peered over her shoulder at me and gave me a weak smile. She was exhausted, and she couldn't hide it anymore, but I could see the same eager curiosity in her face that I felt. It was exactly the same look she'd get when she came with me to fix the gates in Morthryn's halls, and the sight of it made my heart hurt.

I'd give the Bloodborn this: they trained impeccable horses. I'd learned that the beasts would be willing to follow us anywhere, through swamps or mountains or, now, up narrow, rocky, ancient paths that shifted under their hooves. They did it all without complaint. I stroked my gelding's neck as he passed over a particularly tricky crack in the road. I had no idea how far up we were, but the wind made it seem like we were very high. Luce darted happily ahead, more energetic than she'd been in days. Atrius took up the front, then Sylina, then Mische, then me. Mische's horse had grown slow, and she slipped and stumbled over even small rocks, her neck swaying. This much time this close to death was not agreeing with her.

"H-how did you find your way through the first time?" Mische asked. The weakness in her voice made my heart twist. The effects of the blood I'd given her had waned quickly.

The mask in my bag pulled at me, as if drinking down that glimmer of fear—an uncomfortable sensation.

Atrius was silent for a moment. I heard the ghosts crawling behind the bone walls in the quiet, as if rising to answer the question. I wondered how many of them had once been Atrius's comrades.

Atrius said stiffly, "Trial and error," and urged his horse onward.

AFTER HOURS IN the maze, Sylina cocked her head in concentration and raised her hand silently. Atrius paused beside her, peering around a corner. We stood before an open arch, towering five or six times our height. Still, for all its grandness, at first glance it looked no different than the countless others we'd passed on our way here, framing a sheer drop down into the cliffs. It was only when I looked more closely that I could sense something off about this particular passage—that the image we were staring at didn't quite match up with the others, the stars a little misplaced, the skyline of the mountains in the distance not quite matching up with the view through the arch beside it.

An illusion. And a well-made one.

Atrius turned around in his saddle.

"He is here," he said quietly. "This door will pass through to his bridge to the deadlands. It will seal behind us, and our only option will be to move forward. But the opposite door won't open unless he opens it for us."

Atrius drew his sword. His horse, ever loyal, pawed the ground, as if ready to charge into battle.

Mische and I drew our weapons, too. She frowned down at her broken blade.

"Do we *have* to fight him?" she said.

Atrius looked at her like this was a foolish question.

She spread her hands. "Could we maybe just ask him nicely to let us pass? I can be very persuasive."

"It's not an outrageous question," Sylina said to Atrius, who seemed annoyed.

"If you want to go try to seduce the Keeper, by all means, do so," he said to Mische. "If you die, at least we can go home."

It was only at this dry joke that the terrifying possibility occurred to me that perhaps a lesser god *could* kill Mische. Mortal blades didn't hurt her, but the Sentinels' blessed weapons had. I had to imagine that a god's would be just as dangerous.

Mische scowled. "I didn't say anything about seducing him."

I examined the arch. The illusion to hide the door was difficult to push past, even for me. But I could sense, albeit vaguely, a presence beyond it—undeniably divine.

Strangely enough, though, it didn't feel sentient. I sensed no emotions. No mind.

Curious.

"Gods respect nothing but dominance," Atrius said. "Be ready to move as soon as we pass through. If given the opportunity, he'll kill us all before you have the chance to speak. And I know this because I've witnessed it."

I rubbed my fingers together at my side, testing my magic in preparation. On the Night of the Melume, I'd been close to the underworld, the greatest wells of my power right at the surface. Now, I had to haul it up like water from a drying well.

The Mask's power thrummed beside me in a way that felt deliberate, reminding me of its existence. As if I could ever forget it.

At Atrius's instruction, we arranged ourselves in a set of four—Atrius and I taking up the front, Mische and Sylina behind, Luce at the center.

And at Atrius's command, there was no time for hesitation. We all surged forward as if one entity.

For one terrifying moment, as our horses dutifully charged through what seemed like an open, empty door to a bone-crushing drop, my stomach fell out beneath me. Every survival instinct screamed. It occurred to me to wonder, *What if he picked the wrong door?*

Time slowed. I watched the cliffs below in slow motion. The wind whipped my hair back.

And then we crashed into darkness.

Our horses hit the ground, hooves screeching against stone. A bridge stood before us. It was dark, save for a cold white glow from what looked like luminescent snow beneath it. My horse slipped on something as he recovered, though I couldn't quite identify what. Stone surrounded us on all sides, and above us. At the end of the bridge stood a door, the twin to the one we'd passed through, bricked over and full of glowing mist. Silhouetted before it was a hulking figure.

The Keeper.

My sword was already raised. Shadows swelled around me.

Mische was surrounded by darkness, her blade high above her head. Atrius's battle roar echoed in the dark as we charged ahead.

Only to be met with silence.

My brow furrowed as logic clawed through adrenaline.

Atrius had the same realization. He pulled his horse to a skidding stop, fist raised to signal a halt. The rest of us followed, our horses snorting and dancing with anxiety, whitened eyes staring at the creature before us.

Atrius had been right. The Keeper was a terrifying being. He was at least the height of three men atop each other. He had the body of a tiger, with paws the size of my head. The torso of a man, bare and scarred. The head of a bull, eyes glowing white, one horn missing. A broadsword that was nearly as tall as I was lay beside him.

And he was already dead.

He was slumped against the frame of the gate. His gut had been ripped open, humanoid torso split chest to navel to reveal a mess of guts. I realized the liquid my horse had slipped on, thick and silver, was his blood, which spread across the bridge.

We stared at him.

Then at the gate behind him. Stone. Closed. With no one to open it.

Silence.

Sylina at last said, "That's inconvenient."

I dismounted and knelt beside the corpse. It smelled terrible, but I was fairly certain the stench belonged to the Keeper and not to rot. The decay hadn't progressed far.

Mische joined me. She pulled off a glove and laid her hand over his arm. It looked comically small in comparison.

"I don't think he's been gone for long," she said.

"I thought it was impossible for him to be killed at all," Atrius said. "He has guarded this passage for thousands of years."

He actually sounded a bit sad.

I eyed the wound. The skin around it was scorched. Up close, I could see faint whorls of smoke slowly rising from it.

Godlight?

"Perhaps it's possible if a god does it," I said.

"His threads were cut suddenly. I can still sense it." Sylina turned slowly, taking in the rest of the room. "Asar may be right. A mortal didn't do this. Perhaps someone who wanted to make sure that no one passed into the deadlands."

Mische and I exchanged a glance.

Nyaxia? Mische said silently to me. *We've definitely caught her attention by now. Or maybe Shiket? She sent the Sentinels after us. Maybe she suspected we could come here next.*

It could have been any of them. It was probably easier to count the gods who *didn't* want to find us than the ones who did. I had been betting on Shiket and Nyaxia being so distracted by each other that they would let us slip away. That hope now seemed naive.

Mische stepped gingerly past the Keeper's corpse and went to the gate behind him. She reached into the mist. Beyond her, her palm flattened against solid stone.

"No one else can open this?"

"If anyone else ever has," Atrius said, "history never recorded it."

We all stared at each other, at an impasse.

Then I turned back to the Keeper's corpse, which Luce was sniffing suspiciously. It wasn't in bad condition. Fresh enough. And this was his home, which would make it easier—more of his essence to draw from. There was the small complication that he wasn't mortal, but Mische and I hadn't let that stop us before.

It was actually a little invigorating to have a challenge.

I neatly folded up my left sleeve to the elbow. Then the right.

"Well," I said. "It's a good thing that we're necromancers."

CHAPTER THIRTY-FIVE

Mische

When Asar had said *necromancers*—plural—I'd been hesitant. I had, after all, only conducted necromancy once, and it hadn't exactly gone well. But when Asar had extended a hand to me like my participation was just a natural given, I found myself sliding into the spell work like it was a second skin.

Ironically, conducting necromancy made me feel more alive than I had in days.

Sylina observed us work with fascination, and Atrius sat back with considerably more wariness. Necromancy, apparently, was too much for even the Bloodborn's well-trained horses, who clustered at the other end of the bridge, as far away from us as they could get.

I sensed the Keeper's soul nearby, a blurry presence lingering just out of sight. It was easy—instinctual, even—to craft the glyphs that would lead him back. Still, the logistics of the spell were challenging. We didn't have a lot of space considering the size of the Keeper's body, which was so heavy that it took all four of us—plus Luce—just to drag him away from the wall. None of us had known much about the Keeper in life, which made it difficult to choose the five components of his ritual circle, especially since we were limited to what we could find in this room.

"The components are more symbolic than literal," Asar said, at my trepidation. "As long as we're able to sense their connection to him in some way, they can work."

On the surface, this was not a helpful answer. But once I began working, it made perfect sense. Some innate, intangible part of me was able to tell which items were close enough to the Keeper's essence and which weren't, even if I couldn't explain why.

In the end, after much trial and error, Asar and I crafted a complete ritual circle around the corpse. Body was represented by a bloody piece of stone where he'd fallen. His sword, which was so heavy Asar and Atrius had needed to drag it across the bridge together, represented breath—the thrill of battle. Psyche had been challenging, but after many failed attempts, I found a beaded bracelet tucked away in the pocket of his belt—so small it nearly disappeared into the seam. A relic of his past, clearly. For secrets, we took a lock of Atrius's hair to represent the shame of battles lost.

That left only soul. This had been tricky. The others rummaged through every little stone, every possession on the Keeper's corpse, in search of some trinket that would work, but I shook my head at each one.

Finally, on a hunch, I crouched at the edge of the bridge, staring down at the snow beneath it, glowing faintly.

"Why do you think this is here?" I asked.

"It's preserved by magic." Sylina knelt next to me. She reached out to take a handful. "I can tell it has come a long way. The threads are different from everything else here."

I reached into it, too, letting it sift through my fingers. The ghostly almost-shadow of the Keeper's soul, still just out of sight, stirred. I felt a tug on some intangible link between them.

Even though I couldn't explain how I knew it, I sensed that this snow had been precious to someone. A connection to a previous life.

"I think," I said slowly, "that maybe it's here because it came from his home."

Atrius said that the Keeper had taken it upon himself to guard this gate to the deadlands. He had confined the rest of his endless, immortal life to this tiny room. Perhaps he had wanted to bring one piece, however small, of his old life.

What was soul-deep, if not that?

A handful of enchanted snow became the final piece of our circle, the spokes of the wheel now complete.

When it was done, Asar and I surveyed our handiwork in satisfaction. I was beaming so hard my cheeks ached.

"Beautiful work, Dawndrinker," Asar said.

"Not bad yourself, Warden," I said. "Not bad at all."

A map to help a soul to walk back to life. Stunning.

Atrius, who'd been lounging against the wall looking bored, rose and picked up his sword. "Yes, wonderful. Now bring him back, we'll defeat him, and then finally be on our way."

I looked at the Keeper's slackened face and felt a little sad for him. "Seems impolite to drag someone back from death just to immediately start hacking at them."

"I'm certain he won't have as many qualms about coming after us once he's back," Atrius said.

"He'll likely be . . . unhappy to see us," Asar agreed. "I've resurrected my fair share of warriors, and they usually come back angry."

"At least he'll be alive afterward," Sylina said. "A fair repayment for a little humiliation."

Still sounded like a very bad day for the Keeper to me.

I turned to Asar. "Alright. Then go ahead."

But he just stared expectantly back at me and gestured to the ritual circle.

My brows arched. "Me?"

"If the Keeper is as enraged as I suspect he will be, we'll need to be prepared, and whoever conducts the ritual will be distracted."

Which meant Asar—and his drop of god blood—would be more useful ready to fight than entangled in the spell during those crucial seconds when the Keeper awoke.

Still, I was uneasy.

How do you even known that I'm capable of doing it? I asked him silently. *I'm dead myself.*

You have a stronger grip on your magic than you ever have. The dead will happily follow you anywhere. The corner of his mouth twitched in a smirk that made my not-heart flip in my chest. *As they should. They have exquisite taste.*

Gods damn this man. What could I even say to that?

I sighed. *"Fine."*

I KNELT BY the ritual circle, staring down at the etchings in the stone. I was acutely aware of everyone's stares, especially Atrius's—mildly interested—and Sylina's—deeply interested.

How do I start? I asked Asar, too embarrassed to say the question aloud.

He gave me a knowing look before unsheathing his sword.

Let's not ask stupid questions, he said. *You've done this before. You already know.*

You're such a frustrating teacher.

As if you were any less cryptic in your day, missionary of the "You Just Have to Believe in Yourself."

Gods above, he really *did* know me.

I closed my eyes and pressed my hands to the glyphs. Last time we'd conducted a ritual like this, Asar had been beside me—he was the needle and I the thread. Now, I held both, but the pattern before me was so simple. Each glyph, each offering, was a plot on a map from death to life, designed for a single soul.

I no longer was conscious of everyone watching me, nor the bridge nor the door. Instead, I peered past the veil, into the realm of the dead. I could sense the bounds where the underworld should be, like indentations in a copper gear, but none of them fit together properly. The veil was tattered, bleeding. The souls of the dead wandered in chaos. Once they felt my presence, they rushed for me.

Please help—

—looking for—

—so lost—

My heart ached for them. It was a terrible, endless fate. *Soon you'll be at peace,* I promised them.

But none of these were the soul I was looking for. I kept returning to the offerings we'd collected and the map we'd drawn.

And then, at last, there he was.

He was unmistakable. I'd already familiarized myself with him in the creation of the ritual circle—the only solution to the puzzle we'd created. He hadn't been gone long. Some of the dead that reached for me had degraded beyond recognition, but he was still whole.

I cast the web out for him, and pulled, thread by thread.

In another world very far away, his body twitched, sending the ground trembling. "Be ready!" Atrius commanded.

As I urged him closer, the Keeper's life rushed by me in a thousand fragmented glimpses—a birth in a place of snow and stone, a life in a grand bustling city, years of loyal watch.

His soul was difficult to grasp once it approached, big and unwieldy. He rushed closer to life, first slowly, then faster.

Faster—

The ground shook. In the physical world, the Keeper's body flailed. Shadows looped around his limbs, Asar's attempt to pin him down, but they wouldn't hold for long.

In the realm beneath this one, the Keeper's eyes snapped open and met mine.

He resisted me. He didn't want to return. But I had him ensnared now, triangulated between all these pieces of his essence. I pulled harder, a roar of exertion escaping between my teeth. Darkness spilled from my fingertips, flooding through the glyphs.

The images sped up. Years and years of watch here, upon this bridge. Countless battles, won and lost.

And then—

Death.

I felt the blade in his gut. Felt his skin tear, his intestines ooze free. Tasted something sour, felt the unmistakable whisper of a god's breath over his skin. A metallic, rhythmic tick rang in time to the final beats of his heart—*click click click click*—

A realization dawned on me, as I lived that last breath with him—that when he died, his sword had been left untouched, and he had felt nothing but grim resignation.

The Keeper's soul barreled toward me, faster, faster. Greater than that of a mortal. Greater than I could control.

I tried to shout a warning to the others. Tried and failed.

Because the sound drowned beneath the Keeper's bellow as he crashed back into the land of the living.

I flew back against the wall. The ritual circle exploded in a burst of darkness. The ground trembled.

And the Keeper's massive body rose, and rose, and rose, as he stood and let out a bone-trembling roar.

CHAPTER THIRTY-SIX

Asar

"What have you done to me?" the Keeper thundered. His voice was the shifting of mountains, greater than that of any mortal. He thrashed like a fish on a line, massive limbs flailing. I shouted a warning as his tail nearly swept Sylina away, though she stepped into nothingness and reappeared safely afar seconds before it struck her—an impressive Arachessen skill.

Mische pushed herself up with Luce protectively at her side. She had been stunning in the throes of her ritual, her eyes glowing bright white, licks of darkness pouring from her hands. Now, the final ebbs of her magic faded.

I let out a breath of relief when she met my eyes and nodded a silent, *I'm alright.*

The Keeper clutched his torso—now whole again—as if feeling for his death wound. He swung his head up, eyes glowing white, infuriated steam puffing from his nostrils. He seized his sword—a weapon so massive it had taken two men to move it—and raised it over his head as if it were a child's plaything.

I threw all my strength into calling the shadows, sending tendrils of them winding around his limbs, but I knew that there was no holding him.

Just as the Keeper prepared to fell his weapon, Atrius called out, "We challenge you, Keeper, for passage into the deadlands!"

Mid-strike, the Keeper froze. Recognition flickered through his rage.

"You," he growled. "I remember *you*."

Atrius lifted one hand, the other still firmly on his sword. "I thought perhaps you'd like a rematch."

For a moment, the Keeper was still. "Challenge me," he repeated. Then his rage returned, slow and inevitable and terrible, voice rising with every word. "Fools. *Fools!* You ask for passage? You know not what you seek. You are already merely ants on a carcass. As are we all."

I sensed something different in him now—something stronger and yet more tender than anger. Beneath his rage, his words cracked as if he was on the verge of tears.

Pain. Grief.

Sylina's brow furrowed. Her head cocked slightly. She felt it, too.

"We have given you a second life, Keeper," I said. "It's what you deserve, after your years of service."

Asar, Mische said into my mind. *He—*

But apparently my words had been the wrong ones. "A second life?" the Keeper roared as he whirled toward me. The blade rose, glinting eerily against the light below. I tensed, ready for it to fall.

Mische let out a wordless shout and dove for me, even as I hissed, *"Don't."*

But when she collided with me, and the Keeper's gaze fell to us, he stopped. His stare picked me apart, narrowed with interest.

"It has been many years," he said bitterly, "since I have seen your kind here."

He lowered himself, slowly, until he was nearly at eye level, his great claws digging into the stone.

"They killed all the others like you," he said. "Just as they killed all the others like me. Now there is nothing left. For too long, I have been a naive fool."

They. "You're speaking of the gods," I said.

"The gods that remain. The ones who live by sweeping away all else. And now they plan to do so again." Smoke plumed from his nostrils. "They swore to me once that it would never happen again.

But they are liars. Go, if you know what is good for you. The gods prepare for war. I have already lived through such an atrocity. I will not live to witness it again."

"If you let us pass," Mische said softly, "we'll stop it. That's why we've come here. Why we've asked for your help. Please."

Into my mind, she whispered, *He didn't fight, when he was killed. He just let it happen. I saw it.*

Whatever he had witnessed in his final moments had made him choose death over the future ahead.

The Keeper regarded us in silence. Then, with his free hand, he reached down and scooped up a handful of snow. Cold flakes fell over my head and Mische's. It occurred to me that they resembled ash.

Atrius and Sylina watched, tense, unblinking.

I thought Mische's plea might actually work.

But then the Keeper lowered his head.

"They always claim they will be better," he murmured. "And even now, I am a fool for dreaming it could be true."

When he moved again, it was so swift we didn't have time to react.

He let the snow fall, then raised his sword high. Fire flashed in his eyes.

"You wish to challenge me?" he roared. "Very well. Challenge me."

Flames burst up the walls, dousing us in red light.

Atrius and Sylina lunged. I reached deep into the shadows. Luce snarled.

The Keeper brought the blade down—

—and thrust it into his own gut.

Silver blood spattered over my face. Mische gasped and jerked backward, narrowly avoiding him as he sank onto his knees.

"Go," the Keeper gurgled out. "The snow will offer you passage home. If you make it that far. Even the monsters have fled."

He splayed out his hand against the closed gate.

"Do not ever bring me back," he said.

And with a sickening, wet, agonizingly slow crunch, he dragged the blade up, up, up, splitting himself in a twin to the wound that had killed him.

The door burst open. A gust of wind sent us sprawling to the gaping frame, so strong it was as if the world had tipped sideways. The horses snorted and pawed the ground, frantic at first, then fearless as they charged forward, the first to dive into the open arch. I narrowly managed to grab onto Mische's arm, her hand clutching a handful of snow. Luce tumbled against us both, and we all went careening into Atrius and Sylina, sliding through the door, and then we were falling, falling, falling.

As I plunged into nothingness, I watched the Keeper slump over, his blood dripping over the edge of the stone, rapidly shrinking in the distance.

And then, nothing.

I OPENED MY eyes.

An inverted version of the world stared back at me.

I knew, logically, that the land of the gods did not follow the physical rules of the mortal realm. But to see it laid out in front of me was disorienting, even after the time that I spent in Ysria. There was no sky, only upside-down terrain hanging overhead, like a shattered mirror in which each shard offered a glimpse of another world—white dunes, lush forests, majestic mountain ranges. In one shard, I recognized a glimpse of the House of Shadow. In another, a sliver of Vostis, Mische's homeland. The fractures between them glowed with ethereal gold, little bursts of light streaking back and forth like shooting stars.

For a moment, I couldn't hear anything because I heard *everything*—the monotonous din of thousands or millions of voices whispering at once.

I sat up too fast. My head throbbed. The hum faded. Luce sniffed my face, concerned.

Beside me, Mische rubbed her eyes as she got her bearings. Atrius was already on his feet, leaning over Sylina, who was on all fours, her forehead pressed to the ground. The horses, shockingly, had not bolted after our unpleasant landing, though they stood in a tight circle, snorting in irritation.

I stood and took in the scene around us.

Mische whispered, "Holy fucking gods." An ironic choice of words.

The deadlands were rarely depicted, or even mentioned, in religious or historical texts, save for their occasional reference as the place of Alarus's dismemberment. I hadn't realized that I'd even had a mental image of what they looked like until now, when it was so clear that it certainly had not been this.

We were in the middle of a city so incredible it defied mortal comprehension.

Or what once had been one, long, long ago. Now, it was in ruin.

Great buildings that rivaled what I'd witnessed in Ysria towered over us—just as incredible, and just as utterly foreign. A triangular tower stood beside us, countless stories high and slightly tilted, jutting up into misty clouds. Hundreds more disappeared into the distance, shrouded in a haze of gray dust. The ground, beneath a thick layer of dust, was crafted of large marble tile. The streets ran in perfect, endless blocks in all directions, interrupted by occasional crumbling ravines. Stairs circled up, up, up, to nowhere.

I turned to find myself staring into the monumental face of a fallen statue. It was so large that I needed a moment to take in the entire thing. I realized that she had swords on her back, jutting into the hazy sky—or once had. Now, four were broken off, several small buildings crushed where they had fallen.

Shiket. Albeit an unfamiliar depiction of her—with different armor and her hair free in undulating stone waves.

Other statues lorded over the ruins, too. I spotted Vitarus, with a building that might have once been a hanging garden dangling from his outstretched hand; Ix, dancing over a murky distant harbor, her long-chipped thorny arrow glinting in the sky; Zarux, toppled over in the distant sea, half his briny face peering over the horizon. Acaeja stood upon a distant hill, wings outstretched and only slightly chipped, staring directly down at us.

I hadn't believed it was scientifically or magically possible to build a city so grand. Any society that could do so had to be far more advanced than ours.

But this place also reeked of death. The stench seeped from every building, every ruin, like rot from fermented fruit.

"*This* is the deadlands?" Mische whispered. She turned in a slow circle, around and around, eyes wide, like she couldn't take it all in at once.

"What were you imagining?" Atrius said drily. "Desolate tundra, a few cursed mountains, maybe some divine beasts?"

She paused, then said, "Well. Yes."

Atrius kept his thoughts guarded. Still, I sensed his tension. I suspected that his last visit here had not been pleasant. Beside him, Sylina had managed to stand. She now steadied herself against a wall, swaying slightly.

Atrius let out a humorless scoff. "That was what I had expected, too, once. But no. The deadlands were once a world much like ours." He gazed wryly up at Shiket's looming visage. "The gods' pleasure garden, before they turned their attention to our world. Now it's just another place they hide what they have discarded."

My gaze lowered to the streets ahead of us, long abandoned. Despite the ruin, it was all shockingly well-preserved after what had to be thousands of years. In one corner, a small, overturned cart sat, remaining wheel spinning lazily in the breeze. It could have easily been any Obitraen child's wagon. The mundanity of it was jarring against the backdrop of the grand ruin.

And somehow, I knew what had happened here, as if from the hazy memory of a long-forgotten dream.

"They destroyed it," I murmured.

{Bones upon which to build a stronger kingdom,} a voice whispered, so faint and brief I thought I'd imagined it.

"Seemingly so," Atrius muttered. "I don't know how or why. Maybe a war among themselves. Maybe they just got bored. The gods are cruel, and they care about nothing."

He said it with the bitterness that could only come from one who knew it firsthand.

"It's horrific," Mische whispered.

There was no other word for it.

I'd never known of this, not even in the books I'd dragged out of Ryvenhaal's deepest shelves. The existence of such a tremendous past was staggering. *Illumination into all the dark corners of the world,* Gideon had promised me, the first night I'd met him. To think there were so many places even his promises couldn't reach.

Mische looked up at the fractured sky, reflecting the glimpses of the mortal realm and the arcing light between them. "And what is that?"

"Perhaps the closest we'll ever come to seeing the world as the gods do," Atrius said. "They witness everything at once. And they travel through the cracks between them."

The spira. It looked more impressive up in the sky than it had from within.

I caught movement out of the corner of my eye, and turned, hand on my weapon, to see a little smear quickly ducking behind a crumbling building. A deep crack ran down that street, weaving through the ruins. It looked different—fresher—than the rest of the carnage. Silver smoke puffed from it.

Mische pointed into the distance, where slips of silver wound over the landscape. "Are those *wraiths*?"

They were faint, and amorphous even by the standards of the Descent in its worst condition—barely identifiable as humanoid. Yet, they were unmistakable.

Impossible, my logical mind protested. *They can't be here.*

The deadlands were a completely separate realm, farther from the underworld than even the mortal plane. It was terrible enough for the underworld to break through to the mortal realm, but if the damage was spreading so far that it seeped into the deadlands as well . . .

It would mean that the condition of the Descent and the underworld was so bad that those trapped there were now clawing their way out any way they could.

Sylina still kept one hand on the wall. "The threads here are . . . twisted. Torn."

"Were those here before?" Mische asked Atrius. "The cracks, and the wraiths?"

His brow was low over his eyes, wary. "No. And it was not this quiet."

I realized he was right. It was completely silent.

Atrius had told us to expect countless dangers and beasts, but there were none. Only abandoned ruin.

"Even the monsters have fled," Sylina murmured. Some of the Keeper's final words.

Another gust of wind sent dust and debris rolling down the abandoned streets. Above, the gods' pathways flashed across the sky, like the lightning of a distant, deadly storm.

"We should be going," Atrius said at last. He shushed his horse, stroking its nose, then pulled himself up onto it. "At least we'll move quicker without unwanted company."

He jerked his chin to a hill in the distance—what looked to be another abandoned city rising up in a series of jagged spires. "The execution site is that way."

Perhaps we were all wondering whether it was wise to go toward whatever had chased far worse beasts than us away.

But none of us said it.

CHAPTER THIRTY-SEVEN

Mische

The ruins were a museum of horrors. This had once been a civilization that dwarfed any I'd ever seen—when we left the city we'd arrived in, we traveled through sparser townships, then sprawling space that had perhaps once been farmland, now dry and shriveled. Yet, even after all this time, all the discarded remnants of mundane lives still remained. A tipped-over garden table. A dented cauldron rolling lazily down a hill. A little piece of twisted metal crunched under my horse's hooves that I realized, upon examination, had once been eyeglasses.

At one point, as we traveled through a narrow alleyway, I paused at a strange stain on the wall, the stone scorched in a shape that was oddly, terribly entrancing.

Sylina paused beside me, staring at it, too, with her blindfolded gaze. Then she reached out to touch the wall, before quickly withdrawing her hand.

Only then, at her reaction, did the shape suddenly make sense:

It was the shadow of two people, crouched down, clutching each other. One leaned against the other, whose face was raised to the sky, now seared in silhouette against the stone. The shape was too distorted to say whether it was a couple, a parent and a child, or perhaps two strangers who didn't want to die alone. None of these options seemed any better than the last.

I felt Sylina's cold horror, too—just as sharp as mine.

"I spent a lifetime worshipping the White Pantheon," she murmured. "I never imagined . . ."

Her voice trailed off. But she didn't need to finish. I understood her implicitly. It felt like the most shocking, gutting betrayal, even now.

The Arachessen worshipped Acaeja. But Sylina was now with Atrius, and the country she ruled had been claimed in Nyaxia's name. Perhaps Sylina's relationship to the White Pantheon was almost as complicated as mine.

I looked up into the distance, where a monumental gold statue of Atroxus peered through the mountains.

I thought of countless dawns and dusks on my knees before his visage, in stone or in flesh. I thought of the countless times he or the priests or Saescha had told me that my faith was my greatest virtue. That I was only worth whatever tiny sliver of Atroxus's divine wonder that I could bring into the world.

Divine fucking wonder. From the being who had done *this.*

Did these people think that, too, when they built such incredible monuments to their gods? Did they think it when they were on their knees, begging for mercy?

"I was a missionary of Atroxus," I said quietly. "I saw so many times how faith could help people who had nothing else. I believed it. I *lived* it. How do you reconcile that?" My throat clenched. I shook my head. "I didn't think that it would still hurt to think of it all as a lie."

Lies that I not only believed, but that I *told.*

"I was always taught to defend what is Right by Acaeja's fate, not moral goodness," Sylina said. "I was taught that Rightness was simple, when morality was complicated. But I've learned there is no such thing as a single truth. The threads are often contradictory." She flattened her hand against the stone. "Maybe multiple things can be true. Your saved souls found solace in your god, just as mine did. But even in the biggest lies, there is something real. I found a home with my sisters of the Arachessen. Not just with my goddess."

It was a kind thought. I understood why Sylina wanted to believe it, because I wanted to, too. Faith wasn't just about a church and a god. It was about your connection to those who shared that belief with you.

Yet the memory of Saescha in her final moments, her face raised in adoration for the sun she craved more than anything, twisted in my heart.

What if losing one, I wanted to say, *still means losing the other?*

But Sylina had already urged her horse on, pushing her emotions back into a controlled box in a way I sensed she'd likely done many times before.

"Come," she said. "We have a long way to go."

BEFORE LONG, MY horse was swaying beneath me. I was shivering near constantly, now, though during our brief rests Asar offered me sips of blood from his wrist. It barely helped. My hunger was agonizing. Asar saw it, even though I denied it.

Eventually, we came to a broken gate. The execution site loomed ahead. Closer, it now somewhat resembled a colosseum, tall and circular with columns of stone and gold. Leading up to it was a streak of ruin, cutting through buildings and towns and terrain. Splashes of liquid gold glinted over the wreckage at seemingly random placement—a pile of collapsed stone here, a crushed building there, and other patches falling off into the distance.

It was a clear path, albeit a scattered one, as if something massive had barreled straight through the landscape. It didn't seem like part of the original ruins, but it also was clearly much older than the fresh cracks leading to the underworld.

Asar pulled his horse to a stop beside me, staring up. I followed his gaze to a towering, twisted arch of metal, now broken. A gate, maybe? *Clink, clink, clink,* as a chain dangling from it swayed in the breeze. The chain gleamed faintly, and I found myself inching away from it.

"Is that godlight?" I asked.

Asar stared at that chain, unblinking.

"Nyaxia was here," he said, his voice distant.

My brows rose. I looked to the path of destruction, stretching miles, with fresh eyes. The splashes of gold.

Nyaxia had fought through every god of the White Pantheon in her rage after Alarus's death. We came through the hole she'd torn between worlds when she escaped. And now we were seeing the path of enraged carnage she'd ripped through her fellow gods.

"Observant of you," Atrius said. "This is Nyaxia's battleground. Leading right up to the execution site."

His finger traced the line of wreckage into the distance, all the way to our destination.

Sun take me. I touched the twisted metal, and I could *feel* the past crashing over me, two thousand years later—Nyaxia's grief, tender as mortal flesh, and her rage, stronger than that of greater gods.

Every Obitraen knew this story well. Her victory over the White Pantheon was immortalized in every church. But this seemed so much more raw. More sad than victorious. Like her grief had seeped into the ground with the blood.

How had she felt, when she fought through them? When she went back to the mortal world to create her own kingdom? The vampires spoke of their creation as a triumph. Here, it seemed more like a desperate attempt to fill the hole her loss had left.

"She must be so lonely," I murmured.

Asar was still staring up at that chain, *clink, clink, clink*-ing against the gate.

"She must be so angry," he said.

CHAPTER THIRTY-EIGHT

Asar

We were close to the execution site now, stopping for one final rest. The horses were tired, especially Mische's, which now lagged far behind the others. Mische had slid off her mount like gelatin off a tipped plate. She shivered constantly, and she was exhausted. She no longer snored. Her body did not mimic breath, even when she slept. It was growing harder to deny that I could feel her slipping away.

I wasn't tired, even though I couldn't recall the last time I had really slept. While the others rested, I wandered the ruins. We had crossed through remnants of cities and towns and farmland, and now were on the outskirts of the city that held the execution site. All were empty save for the wraiths, so lost they didn't even know to follow us. And all reeked of pain.

I hated this place. It felt deader than the underworld ever had. The underworld had been built to be a place of peace. This was a place of suffering.

{Such sacrifices are necessary to build greatness.}

The voice flitted through my mind, and I closed my eyes to push it away. But the darkness offered no reprieve. Every time I blinked, I found myself slipping into vivid daydreams of the things that had happened here.

Now, I saw Nyaxia chained against the wall in those godlight restraints, marks carved into her skin, blood on her naked body. I heard her guttural scream of grief—

Gravel crunched. My eyes snapped open.

A little wraith girl peered at me from behind a pile of stone. She crouched slightly, as if debating running away.

I smiled softly. "Ah. You again."

I had spotted her several times during our travels. The child was in better condition than the other wraiths here, which were so far gone they barely even resembled people. She was a wisp of a thing, with blunt, straight hair, perhaps ten years old when she died. Her body was faint, dissolving into nothingness after the flow of her long skirt. But her eyes were alert, a sign that her soul was still intact.

"No need to be afraid," I murmured. "You've been following us for quite some distance, haven't you?"

The girl smiled, glowing slightly with the acknowledgment. Wraiths craved the attention of the living. I shouldn't have been encouraging her. She would continue following us if I did, and who could say what dangers that would lead her to. But her loneliness was tender and familiar. Eternity was such a terribly long time to be alone, and no soul—especially not a child's—deserved such a thing.

Still, as she hesitantly moved from her hiding spot, I lowered myself to her eye level.

"What is your name?" I asked.

The girl spoke, but no sound came out. I scooted closer, straining to hear. But her voice was lost to death, and she was so far from the underworld. With her name, I might—might—have been able to guide her back. Without it, I could do little for her.

The girl's eyes lifted over my shoulder, and she took half a step back.

Collecting strays again, Warden?

Funny, how I'd never experienced the sensation of the sun falling over my face. But every time, I was so certain that it must feel something like Mische's presence.

Apparently I can't help myself, I answered.

Mische shot me an affectionate glance that made my heart stutter as she knelt down beside me. Then she turned to the girl and gave her the brightest, warmest smile.

"Hello, beautiful," she said softly. "What is your name?"

The girl spoke soundlessly again, and Mische cocked her head, listening.

A knot of pride and worry tightened in my chest as I watched her. Pride, because the dead so adored Mische—rightfully—and worry, because she was so much closer to them than I wished she was.

"Celie," Mische repeated. "What a lovely name."

Celie. The child's name was the string that bound her to the identity she'd held in life. With it, I saw fragments of her past, albeit vague, scrambled ones—glimpses of a childhood somewhere very cold, warm fires and empty stomachs, carefree games and grieving tears and the affection of a very fat orange cat. She'd had a too hard, too short life.

She had deserved a fairer death.

Can you help her pass? Mische asked the question I was already asking myself. The logical answer was a cascade of objections. We were far from the underworld. I had no idea how the broken paths back—the paths that shouldn't even exist—would work. I could fail and lead the girl somewhere else entirely. Pushing her through could weaken a veil that was already disintegrating. Or she might just continue to follow us instead, perhaps even creating a path for worse beasts in her wake.

And yet. That stubborn hope still shone through. That nagging desire to right this one unjust wrong.

I looked to the child. Then to the nearest ravine, pulsing with the underworld's sickened light.

I stood and went to the crack, Mische and Celie close behind. We knelt before it. I touched the stone and closed my eyes. This time, instead of unwelcome visions of past pain, I sensed the underworld spread out before me—a tangled, broken web, barely holding itself together. I drew Celie's path back, though it was imperfect, full of hopeful guesses.

And then I opened the door for her.

"I can offer you, Celie, the peace you should have gotten five hundred years ago," I said. "If you want to attempt the journey."

But the child was frightened. She stared down into the mist, shying behind Mische, who gave her a gentle, encouraging smile.

"You're going to be safe," she promised.

It was a promise we couldn't truly make. But she always made it so easy to believe her.

It was Mische, in the end, who ushered the child's soul through the door. Celie stepped into the ravine, her body disintegrating. I felt the strain on the path I'd drawn out for her go slack. Quickly, I swept the retractable knife from my pocket and etched glyphs around the crack, attempting—imperfectly—to seal it again. Mische caught on quickly, working beside me.

When it was done, we sat back on our heels. Light still seeped through the crack, but it was dimmer now.

"Do you think it worked?" she said softly.

I didn't answer. I hated verbalizing uncertainty and hated verbalizing hope even more.

Instead, I just murmured, "Thank you for helping."

"It's a little selfish. In my nature, apparently. Just like I know it's in yours, as much as you grumble about it." She playfully nudged my shoulder, her clothed arm to mine, though the touch still sent a jolt through me. "Feels good to fix something again, doesn't it?"

Goddess, it did. Like a drug. I hadn't realized quite how much I had missed it. I eyed Mische's profile, shimmering, translucent. Her hood was down now, but lately, it was easy to tell that something wasn't right even when it was raised.

"I can fix more than that," I said. "Soon enough."

Mische's smile faded. She turned to look at me, worry etched between her brows.

"Atrius said that the gods don't care about anything. Do you think that's true?"

{Do not mistake ambition for callousness,} a voice whispered, before I shuttered it back.

I looked out over the majestic, terrible ruin. The long-gone world the gods abandoned. The fresher ruin of Nyaxia's grief.

"Alarus cared about the underworld," I said. "He cared about Vathysia."

I was certain of that. I'd felt his care in my decades overseeing Morthryn and the Descent, doing all I could to match it with my own.

"But was that just pride in his work? Or was that love?" Mische drew her knees up to her chest. "Maybe he could only love it once he knew what it was like to have something to lose. He built the Descent on his story with Nyaxia. It was all a monument to her."

I considered this. She could be right. Perhaps the underworld, the Descent, Vathysia—all of it was just a game to Alarus before Nyaxia came along. Perhaps it only started to mean more to him once he realized he was building it for her. A legacy to protect them once he'd turned away from everything else he had.

And he lost her in the end, anyway.

What an uncomfortable thought. I didn't want to look too hard at it.

"This is all uncharacteristically bleak of you, Dawndrinker."

Mische shivered. "It's hard not to feel bleak here."

"Gideon used to tell me that life was only worth the value of the blood you spill upon it. I imagine that much like powerful vampires, powerful gods probably feel the same way. Open to sacrifices."

Her expression hardened. "Maybe greatness should come not from the sacrifices you make, but the ones you refuse to."

Her eyes were dimmer than they had been in life, but I still sank into those threads of brown and amber-gold.

Yes. I agreed with her. There were some sacrifices I would never make.

She searched my face. Leaned closer. A breeze blew, but it barely rustled her hair, and though I drew in a breath, I couldn't smell even a hint of spice.

"Are you afraid of what you'll become, if you succeed?" she said.

{Only a coward fears greatness,} the voice hissed.

My answer was immediate, with Mische's skin so close and so far. "I'm more afraid of what will happen if I don't."

She stared at me for a long moment, her eyes peeling me apart, the wrinkle deepening between her brows.

"No matter what's ahead, never sacrifice the messy parts of your mortality, Asar. I like those the best."

My gaze fell to her mouth. I so desperately wanted to taste her.

Slowly, I raised her hood. Then I laid my hands on either side of her face through the fabric. I pressed my lips to her cheek. Her jaw. Her throat.

"Then take them," I murmured. "They're for you."

"Yes, please." Her words were warm with a smile. "I'll have it all."

I lowered my head, kissing her shoulder, her collarbone, her chest.

I prayed to find breath. I prayed to find a heartbeat.

"Tell me you feel it," I whispered.

Silence. Then, "I feel it."

But we both knew it was a lie.

And I found only silence.

CHAPTER THIRTY-NINE

Asar

"We're close now," Sylina said softly. "The threads are converging."

The only sound was our horses' hoofbeats over cracked stone paths as we wound through what once had been bustling streets. This city was more condensed than the one into which we had first arrived, the roads narrow and buildings flowing into each other, as if the entire town had once been a single continuous structure, rising into the sky like a mountain. Alarus's death site stood at the top—even more grand, and even more mournful, than it had looked from a distance. Up close, the building did indeed resemble a colosseum.

What a humiliating cruelty. To execute Alarus on the grandest stage of a discarded world, in front of an audience of ghosts. It was the kind of spite that was left out of scriptures and history books.

{The cruelty of small minds,} a bitter voice sneered. *{They will pay for it one day.}*

Everything had gone deathly silent, as if the ruins themselves held their breath in anticipation. Even the dead did not follow here. The horses walked slower, perhaps to navigate the narrow, cracked streets, or perhaps because they had no interest in going to the death site of a god. Mische's horse trailed farthest behind, head low, hooves dragging.

Soon, the road narrowed in front of us to a single stone gate. A towering wall stretched out on either side, circling, it seemed, the colosseum. Atrius craned his neck and squinted up at the columns looming over us, then swung his leg over his horse.

"Time to dismount," he said.

"Why?" Mische said, as we all obeyed. Her horse let out a groan as she slid off her body.

Atrius didn't answer. He drew his sword, then stroked his horse's nose, murmuring something to it in a language I didn't understand—the lost tongue of the Bloodborn, perhaps. With gentle hands, he slid his steed's bridle off, letting it fall with a melodic clink to the ground.

Then he stepped back, lifted his blade, and drove it through his horse's chest.

I jerked backward as a spray of blood spattered our faces. Mische let out a wordless cry of horror. Even Luce flinched in surprise.

Atrius still whispered under his breath, and he didn't let go of his hilt, even as the animal fell slowly to its knees. He twisted the blade. Thickening red mist, the horse's blood under the control of Bloodborn magic, hovered around them both. He was, I knew, manipulating blood within the horse's body, too, using it to enhance his strike.

"Rest, my friend," he murmured, as he finally pulled his sword free. Blood gushed from the wound, but when Atrius lifted one hand, it smoothed into a silky wave as he guided it from the animal's body. The horse moaned as it sank to the ground, but it didn't thrash or fight. Atrius had been efficient.

Sylina bowed her head as if in prayer. But Mische cried, horrified, "What are you doing?"

The horse had stopped twitching. The blood now circled Atrius in a steady, floating river, and he uncapped the canteen at his hip and guided the stream into it.

"The gate demands a blood sacrifice." He gestured to the stone door. The carvings that adorned it, sure enough, had begun to fill with red, as if the door was hungrily sucking up what had spilled. "And besides, where we are going is no place for horses. They've served us well, but their journey is over."

But Mische shook her head, stepping protectively closer to the mare. "They went to hell for us. And in reward, we just kill them?"

"Each of us needs to make a blood sacrifice to pass."

"She deserves better than to be somebody's sacrifice." Her fingers dug into the blanket beneath her saddle, like it was taking all her self-control not to throw her arms around the horse. The poor creature barely seemed aware of her surroundings anymore, swaying, knees nearly buckling.

The hard truth was that she was not going to last either way. All this time with Mische on her back, sapping her life bit by bit, had taken its toll.

Atrius capped his canteen. I watched, ready to step in if he reprimanded her, but he looked at Mische with genuine pity. Apparently, she could melt even Bloodborn hearts.

"You were Turned, yes? In some ways, the Bloodborn have more in common with humans than we do with other vampires. We understand impermanence." He knelt and stroked his dead horse's neck, lashes lowered in respect. "The curse that the Dark Mother placed upon us takes much from us. We're born knowing that we will die too young, and with little dignity. This is why the Bloodborn see no shame in death. The greatest gift we can offer is a life that serves those who come after us, and the greatest gift we can be given in return is a death with dignity. There is no sadness in that. I'll give her a quick, painless end. As she deserves."

Tears welled up in Mische's eyes. "She deserves better than any of this."

A humorless smile twisted his mouth. "So do we all. And yet, here we are, making the best of the hand we were dealt."

I laid a comforting hand at the small of Mische's back. She wiped her tears with the back of her hand, but she didn't protest further. She would mourn her companion—Saescha, as she had dubbed her, a name that I knew held such painful significance in this moment—but she understood reality. Atrius held true to his word. Mische stroked the mare's face as he killed her, and Mische and I led her soul through the open door to the underworld.

Quick and painless.

But still unfair.

THE GATES FOUND our sacrifices acceptable. We gave some of the horses' blood to the deadlands, saved the rest for our own stores, and continued on foot. The roads were steep, and in worse condition than the ones into the city. Sparkling white frosted the rocks and the long-abandoned iron fences lining the road. Above us, the shards of different worlds in the sky all seemed to point toward us—all those glowing cracks leading right to this spot.

Atrius frowned up at them, suspicious.

"Can any of you explain that?" he said.

"Magic flows," Sylina said. "It has to pool somewhere."

"And what better focal point than the death site of a god," I muttered.

I had a terrible headache, and it grew worse with every step. A garbled buzz rose in the back of my head—like an angry avalanche of words rushing by too quick. The mask at my side nagged at me. Soon, sweat rolled down my back. Heat throbbed from under the earth. Odd, considering that the deadlands had, until now, been so cold.

Atrius was the first to crest the top of the path leading into the colosseum. When he did, he stopped short. Sylina joined him, then Mische, Luce, and I.

We all stared down. I shielded my face from a burst of heat.

The pit below resembled a spoked wheel. Stone lined with arches encircled a large, sandy floor. The spectators' stands were now crumbling, stepped seats reduced to piles of brick, but the stage itself was in surprisingly good condition. Statues guarded over each of the towering columns along its edge, their hands outstretched. Some were blindfolded, and others wore masks that covered their entire faces. I didn't recognize the figures. Perhaps they were some other lesser gods from thousands of years past, now long discarded like this realm had been.

Yet, for all the building's beauty, it was hard to look at anything but the damage at its center. Massive, glowing cracks all ran down the spiraling stairs to the center of the stone floor, where they converged in a twisted silhouette that almost resembled a figure, limbs spread, lying flat on the ground.

No, not just lying. Held down there by force, as his kin dismembered him.

A strange metal structure had been built over the cracks. It didn't match the architectural style of the rest of the majestic, ancient building. It was crafted of gleaming copper, arching over the widest of the cracks. The flames surged beneath it. Fresh smoke plumed from towering bronze chimneys.

"What . . . is that?" Mische asked.

No one answered, because no one knew. But the voice in the back of my head hissed, *{Desecration.}*

I rubbed my temple and muttered, "Let's just go." I was suddenly very eager to get this over with.

We started down the stairs, walking gingerly as the decaying steps wobbled beneath our feet. With each one, the heat grew more unbearable. The faces of long-forgotten gods stared down at us, doused with a fiery red glow.

At the bottom, a grand arch opened up before us, leading into the sands of the pit.

I paused for a reason I couldn't identify. My hand pressed against the rusted metal gate.

And suddenly, I was two thousand years in the past.

I should not have come.

The gravity of this decision strikes me now. Gods do not often admit their own mistakes, not even to themselves. But I feel that certainty now: I should not have come.

Vitarus and Shiket hold my hands down, binding them with blessed chain. Ix watches silently, bloody tears streaming down her cheeks, but her lips are twisted with a hungry smile.

I came unarmed, like they told me to. My left hand bleeds, gold blood seeping into the sands. They pried away my only remaining weapon. And now, the flames of her forge behind her, Srana forges her blessed axe. She meets my gaze, clockwork eyes tick, tick, ticking in calculation.

I think, perhaps she will be the one to speak in my favor.

But she looks away, and she pulls the blade from the fire—a blade she had prepared for this specific task, a blade that is now strengthened with the great power I have.

Atroxus takes the weapon from her. He leans over me, the smile bright and hungry on his face.

"You were always so arrogant, brother," he said. "I warned you. You gave up your crown, your heart, your eye. All for her. And now look at all you have destroyed."

He is so foolish. He believes he is destroying a threat. But he is too arrogant to see that he is creating a greater one.

I think of my wife. Her kiss goodbye still burns on my mouth. Somewhere far away, she holds my final gift to her. I grieve that I will never get to see what she will become, and the fact that she needs to become it at all.

One day, Atroxus will regret this.

He brings the blade down—

"Asar!"

Pain.

For a moment, disoriented, I thought that I was feeling Atroxus's killing blow. Instead, I realized that the sharp throb was from Mische's touch, pressed to either side of my face.

Her eyes were worried, but when I blinked, she relaxed and released me.

"Put that down," she said.

I looked down to see the pack in my hands. The flap was open, like I'd been about to remove the mask.

I blinked in surprise. "When—"

"I turned around and you had it." She stepped back, sliding her gloves back on. "Sorry about your face. I had to get your attention."

I touched my cheek. The remnants of Mische's touch still stung. "No need to apologize."

That was unnerving.

{You will need me,} the mask whispered.

You're growing tedious, I told it, and let the bag hang at my hip again.

We were now in the pit at the center of the stands, though, unsettlingly, I didn't remember walking there. The metal structure now stood over us. I raised my eyes and briefly saw this view as Alarus had in his final moments—with Srana standing there, his eye in her hands, making his greatest asset into the weapon that would end him.

"It's a forge," I said.

A forge for Srana's magic, designed to harness the power that convened at Alarus's death site. It was far more advanced than any built by human practitioners of Srana's arts, and a much more complex structure than what I had seen in my vision. So much so that at first I didn't even recognize it as a forge at all.

The outskirts of the pit were cluttered with statues, though not ancient ones like those carved into the stone. These were gleaming metal with too-long limbs of gears and pipes, like marionette versions of Shiket's Sentinels. Other creations were scattered, seemingly discarded, in the sand, too—blades, knives, crossbows, and a pile of cylindrical machines that I'd never seen before, like bladeless spears.

Mische touched one of the copper columns of the forge, only to let out a hiss and yank her hand away. It was blessed by the White Pantheon. Toxic to her, as a wraith.

"This hasn't been here for two thousand years," she said. "I think this is newer."

Atrius was quiet, striding along the edges of the pit, gazing at the weapons. Sylina's hands ran over the walls, like she was searching for something.

My eyes narrowed as I watched them. They seemed unsurprised by any of this. As if they'd known what to expect when we got here.

But before I could speak, a blinding light flashed. No, two lights—one, bright orange, from the cracks beneath the earth, and another from the sky, as the lines of the spira lit up with blinding white. Wisps of ethereal colors swirled overhead, blotting out the glimpses of the mortal realm.

The hair prickled at the back of my neck as I watched the sky.

{You were warned,} the voice remarked.

Luce barked a warning and dragged Mische backward just as a burst of flame surged from the forge. Behind me, Sylina let out a gasp, and when I tore my gaze from the sky, she was leaning heavily against the wall.

"I can't—I can't see," she choked out. "The threads are gone. I can't see."

What did it mean if the threads of fate themselves had gone dark?

A distant sound quivered in the air, quiet at first.

Tick tick tick tick . . .

Atrius whispered something to Sylina, helping her upright, shooting an alarmed glance to the sky.

"Arm yourself," I barked, drawing my sword. Mische did the same. Luce growled at the sky.

The ticking grew faster. Faster.

Ticktickticktick tick . . .

I knew that sound. I'd heard it before.

The sky roiled with wisps of rainbow light.

A god.

A god was here.

Click click tick, *click click* tick, as the machinery above us shifted, collapsed, reformed.

And when all that gleaming copper snapped into a perfect circle, at its center was Srana, clockwork eyes observing us with methodical precision. A smile spread over her face, revealing teeth of polished brass as mechanical limbs opened behind her—wings, legs, a terrible combination of both.

"Hello again, fallen one," she said. "How fascinating that after everything, you would still come to this spot."

CHAPTER FORTY

Asar

Get back! I told Mische as Srana encroached. Sylina and Atrius pressed themselves against the wall, and Mische, dragged by Luce, shrank back beneath the forge's beams and gears. Srana did not seem to notice any of them. Her attention remained solely on me.

"What a delight to find you here." Her voice was comprised of the echoing ticks and clicks of metal against metal, hot like the flames of their forging. Limbs of steel and copper collapsed and reformed to her body as she lowered herself. The entire forge shifted as if an extension of her body. This was the palace she had built, a temple to the creation of weaponry and technology, and now, it all bowed to her.

Srana vaulted down like a spider flinging itself from thread to thread of gleaming steel. Heat blasted my face as the flames of her forge rose up to meet her, eager to please its mistress.

"My siblings are so shortsighted," she purred. "I told them that you could be so useful. But they did not listen. How they underestimate me. Srana, sweating over forges and clockwork. As if I was not the one to create all that made them so very great."

*Tick*tick *tick*tick *tick*tick—as her fingers unfolded, gear by gear.

"Such potential. I have created so much from so much less. If they allowed me to, what a beauty I could craft. Your flesh is the least interesting thing about you."

Her fingers clicked and twitched, as if she was already mentally acting out all that she would do to me if she had been given the opportunity. I thought of the demigod I had met in Acaeja's care—the one with the copper arm and face. Now I understood what she had been. A creation intended to strip her for her most useful parts and discard the rest. A failed one.

I looked at the polished structure around us with fresh eyes, and realized that the metal figures lining the walls were not statues.

They were weapons.

This had been the site where Srana had forged her greatest creation: a blade that could cut up a god. And now, she used the power of what had happened here to create more weapons, all designed to be perfect foils to the creatures born of what had once been Alarus's power.

"You are building an army," I said.

"Building an *army,*" she scoffed. "You sound like Shiket. As if I am merely a creator of tools. No, godling. I am an artist, painting a new world. And what a gift we have been given, on a canvas so blank." She gestured to the windows to the mortal world above. All of them beneath an eternally black sky.

I found myself laughing, and my voice did not sound like my own.

Srana. Of course. She was not one of the most powerful goddesses, or the most worshipped, like Atroxus or Shiket or Acaeja, who promised power, glory, intelligence. But she had created the tools that the gods relied most heavily upon. And if someone was to take the crown of the White Pantheon from Shiket's hands before it made it to her brow, she could be the one.

And now, I understood why I was still alive.

This was a secret. Srana had managed, somehow, to keep her machinations from the attention of her distracted siblings. She'd slain the Keeper to keep us, or anyone else, from finding her forge, but avoided closing the door to keep from attracting the attention of her cousins.

But my presence here—well, that was either a gift or a complication. She seemed as if she hadn't decided which yet.

Either way, I was in trouble. I had nowhere to go, with her attention so completely focused on me.

"Tell me, god slayer," she purred, "how useful of a soldier could you be?"

I needed a distraction. I needed—

"If you want a god slayer—"

My heart went cold. *Mische, no—*

"—then it's me. I'm here." Mische stepped out of the shadows. She smiled, even though I could sense her fear.

"Do you remember me?" she said. "I remember you. Even though I was almost gone by then."

Tick, tick, tick, tick. Srana drew back, turning her attention to Mische.

I watched Atrius out of the corner of my eye, slinking through the shadows with Sylina. He stood among a store of god-forged weapons. I wouldn't be able to kill Srana, but perhaps between the blessed weapons and my shred of divinity, I could hurt her enough that she'd rather flee than risk alerting the other gods, or at least keep her distracted enough that the others could find the eye. It could be our only chance.

Atrius! I shouted into his mind, hand outstretched.

We had one opening. One moment of Srana's distraction.

Atrius met my gaze.

But then, he looked to Sylina, feeling her way along the stone, clearly still unable to see. Something that I couldn't make out was clutched against her body.

He looked to the copper blade he now held in his other hand.

And then he looked to Sylina's bag, which held the vial of snow that would grant us passage back to the mortal realm.

My heart fell as I saw him draw his final conclusion.

He just shook his head, presenting his thoughts to me as he and Sylina slipped back into the shadows:

I said I'd guide you, Shadowborn. I didn't say I'd die for you.

Goddess fucking damn it. I *knew* they were going to betray us.

Gears ticked and ground as Srana took in Mische from all angles.

"So you are the one who killed Atroxus," she mused. "And yet, so unremarkable! So common. Barely even a mortal warrior. How could—"

A streak of light arced across the sky, reflecting in Srana's metal face. She stopped and peered above.

Another god? It didn't quite feel like it. Still, it distracted Srana.

In that opening, Luce—brilliant Luce—sprinted for the weapons stores and flung one across the sands to me. I dove for it, grabbing the glowing copper sword. My palm burned as it closed around the hilt—it was a creation of the White Pantheon, and hurt like it.

Get back, Mische, I hissed into her mind. Her eyes met mine across the forge.

But before we could move, golden light blinded us.

A stroke of white and gold smashed through the top of the building, careening straight into Srana.

Srana let out a cry and drew back with a collection of clinks and ticks.

A Sentinel, I realized, as she flung the figure away. Even though they should not have been able to follow us here.

But I didn't have time to question it. For now, it was a blessing.

I lunged for Srana.

But I was too slow.

Too slow to reach Mische as the forge flames roared up again.

Too slow to readjust as the Sentinel skidded in the sand, turning on her like a lion locking onto its prey.

And too slow to stop them before the two of them collided with the force of a shooting star, sliding straight into the forge flames together.

CHAPTER FORTY-ONE

Mische

As a small child, I had once seen an entire house go up in flames. Saescha had I had been sheltering in a barn in a drought-stricken village. We didn't see what had started the fire in the farmer's cottage, only that it had spread so quickly that by the time we smelled the smoke, the little house had been consumed. As we fled into the night, Saescha had to choose whether to cover my eyes or my ears. She chose eyes, but it had been the wrong choice. I'd had nightmares about the sounds for a long time.

Later, as a priestess, I learned how to find refuge in the flames. I knew that fire could bring pain, but it could also provide comfort. It brought light and warmth to those who needed it. I had no need to fear what I could control.

Still, even into adulthood, I dreamed of those flames.

Now, I realized: maybe I had been dreaming of my own future death at Atroxus's hands all along.

Those nightmares felt just like this.

The Sentinel dragged me down, down, down. The heat was unbearable. Flames surrounded me. They hurt me, but couldn't kill me—couldn't kill what was already dead. The Sentinel's fingers dug into my shoulders, the two of us thrashing together like rabid dogs as we tumbled into damnation.

"Your arrogance knows no bounds," the Sentinel snarled. "Did you think that I would not find you? Did you think that you could escape justice?"

I stared into the Sentinel's smooth mask. In my reflection, I saw my face burning, melting, as Atroxus killed me. My face, young and innocent, under the light of Atroxus's divinity the day he had chosen me. My face, mouth open and teeth bloody, as I had descended upon Saescha.

We crashed down together onto jagged stone. The impact snatched the ghost of breath from my lungs. The flames, bright orange and searing white, obeyed the laws of the divine world, not the mortal one. I couldn't see anything through them. Everywhere I looked, I saw only licks of metallic gold.

"Get up," the Sentinel snarled as they hoisted my limp body upright, pushing me against the wall. "Meet your justice standing."

I couldn't sense Asar down here, or Luce. I couldn't feel much of anything at all. The pain of a two-thousand-year-old betrayal was so thick in the air that it stifled all my other senses. I managed to look up, and through the flames I realized that I wasn't just seeing the fire reflected on the walls—the stone was streaked with brilliant metallic, too. Like spilled paint.

No, not paint. Blood. Alarus's blood, still staining this spot all these years later.

The Sentinel's fingers dug into my skin. The agony was unbearable. My scream tore up my throat without my permission.

I realized, through my screams, the Sentinel was commanding, "Repent. *Repent*. Tell me if you can be saved. Is there anything left in you to salvage?"

I flailed against their hold. I could barely make out the shape of the terrain through the flames—could barely think through the pain. My sword was gone, slipped from my grip as we fell, leaving me lashing out with bare hands and feet.

"You damned a million souls," the Sentinel breathed. "Confront it."

When they leaned close, I lunged and sank my teeth into their neck.

Pain. An onslaught of images—every sin, every betrayal. My teeth hit only metal, not flesh. Still, it seemed to affect the Sentinel in some way, because they lurched backward in surprise and dropped me.

I rolled against stone and clumsily recovered. I managed a glance up. I could see, through the fire, a sliver of the world above. Gods, it looked so far away. The earth vibrated with the force of whatever was happening up there. I could see Srana's gearwork shifting, and flashes of movement.

Asar couldn't save me.

I got to my feet, but the Sentinel struck me again, sending me flying against the rocks. I rolled over, coughed, sputtered. I looked down at my hands to see that they were nearly invisible against the ground. I was fading away. Desperately, I grabbed at the rocks, trying to pull myself up. My hand touched a smear of gold.

Sensations crashed over me.

Atroxus's voice in my ear: *You made the wrong decision, brother.*

The pain of a blade cutting through muscle, bone.

I gasped and squeezed my eyes shut. In the darkness, I saw a familiar face. Vincent.

Do not yield, he snapped. *You are so close to what you need.*

What?

Everything blurred. The Sentinel dragged me back as I thrashed. When I slid down the stone, again, my hand pressed to a smear of Alarus's blood.

My smile was weak and ugly across my face.

No, it is you who has made a terrible mistake, I whispered to Atroxus in my final breath.

You have ended me. But you don't know what you have just created.

What you have just created.

My lashes fluttered. A blunt impact struck my ribs—a kick from a metal boot. I was lying in the dirt, doused in fire. I rolled over to my side.

Get up, Mische, I told myself, *Get up.*

I forced my eyes open. Perhaps they had adjusted to the light of the flames, because now, I could make out the shape of the ravine.

It seemed that the cracks in the earth ran beneath the surface, too, not just above it. I could see little alcoves in the rock, blazing white.

My brow furrowed.

"What do you have to say for yourself?" the Sentinel demanded as they loomed over me.

But I was not listening to the Sentinel.

I was looking at a figure of silver, hiding in a stone crevice behind the flames. A wraith, albeit one that had no features. How could they be here? Perhaps the forge held another fissure to the underworld.

The wraith placed a finger over their lips. *Shh.*

And then they pointed down, to an object at their feet. A long, silver handle, and a delicate curved blade. An axe. Glowing upon its blade were two concentric circles of luminescent red, nestled between carved eyelids.

Alarus's eye, ripped from him and forged into the very weapon that was used to dismember him.

It was as Gideon had theorized. The gods couldn't take or wield the axe again. But they could still harness its power here, to create more weapons to be used in their holy war.

I sucked in a breath, suddenly reinvigorated. I looked up, up to the shifting, glinting gears of Srana's creation above.

I needed to get Asar down here—get him to the eye.

But a grip locked around my ankles, dragging me back, and the Sentinel hoisted me up, hand to my throat. My own face, neither alive nor dead, stared back at me.

Why were they playing with me this much?

"What do you want with me?" I ground out. "Kill me already, if that's what you want."

They paused, like they didn't expect this from me. "You think all I want is petty violence? No. You must be brought to justice. You murdered a god. You murdered *the sun*."

"I saved millions," I spat. "*Millions*. Atroxus was going to raise a dawn over the vampires that would burn them all to ash."

"Them," the Sentinel hissed. "As if you are not among *them*. So you traded one sacrifice for another. That is not the mark of a savior. How did you decide which soul deserved to be lost? *How?*"

There was something in the Sentinel's voice that seemed . . . oddly vulnerable then. Oddly human. I stared into my own reflection.

But the Sentinel flung me away with a snarl. "I will not allow your justifications. They are a disgrace to all who had once trusted you."

My consciousness flickered. *Perhaps they're right,* a cruel voice whispered. *Perhaps you are.*

I gritted my teeth as I caught myself on my hands and knees. Even in death, my body, or whatever of one I had, couldn't hold out much longer here. Desperately, I lifted my head to peer again into the shadows. The wraith was still there. Others, perhaps drawn by the influx of divine power in this spot, clustered behind them now. All barely shades of who they once were. Souls who deserved peace, too.

A familiar face emerged, clearer than the others. Vincent. He pushed through them and knelt before the axe.

His lips moved, and I could only barely make out the words:

Take it.

Was he out of his mind? I couldn't touch it, let alone wield it. Not without Asar.

I shook my head.

Vincent insisted, *Take it.*

Another earth-shattering blow had my vision going white. I barely clung to the rocks. With every touch, the Sentinel sapped away more of me.

Above, I glimpsed Srana and Asar locked in a battle that he would, inevitably, lose.

Take it.

The Sentinel loomed over me, raising their sword.

You hold a piece of Alarus, too! Vincent bellowed. *Take. The. Eye.*

I had no choice.

My hand closed around the silver handle.

Breath swept through me. Blood roared. An ancient stare snapped to mine.

{Who are you?} an intrigued voice whispered.

I lifted the axe and swung.

CHAPTER FORTY-TWO

Asar

Luce let out a howl and bolted across the sands. Even in the presence of a goddess, the sight of Mische toppling into those flames made everything else inconsequential.

I threw myself after her, but a grip caught me mid-stride. Srana lifted me up and examined me like a captured specimen. She now barely looked humanoid at all, just an endlessly expanding being of metal arms and ticking gears, unfolding ever further.

"It seems we have attracted some attention," she said. "We shall have to make quick work of you with the time we have."

The forge would, undoubtedly, kill any mortal instantly. But Mische was already dead. Perhaps she had a chance. I reached for her presence through our tenuous link. I could sense her, barely. But she was weak and far away.

Srana drew me closer, eyes *tick, tick, tick*-ing faster with interest. Her knife-sharp fingers dug into my skin, drawing blood.

I raised my blade and struck her across the face with a wretched *CLANG*.

Luce lunged at her.

Srana let out a hiss of annoyance. I hit the ground and rolled as she jerked back, batting Luce away like an inconvenient insect. She struck the wall with a high, pained squeal, then slid down in a flailing heap.

The sound sent a bolt of fury through my blood.

{You are capable of much more than this,} the voice urged in the back of my mind.

My attention snapped to my pack, which now lay in the sand on the other side of the forge, the mask humming with power within it.

It was true. I had the blood of a god in my veins, and here, in the spot where he had been murdered, I had his vengeance, too. His power lurked right beneath the surface, ready to be seized.

Shadows gathered around my hands, bubbled up in my chest. When Srana reached for me again, I stepped through them, evading her grasp.

But this only amused her. I leapt from shadow to shadow, slipping from her as we danced around the arena. *Tick*tick *tick*tick *tick*tick, as metal reformed around me, keeping pace.

"You wish to play a game." Srana's voice echoed through her web of metal, trembling like the chords of a pipe organ. "Very well. Perhaps we shall craft a bargain."

I evaded one metal grasp only to nearly run headfirst into another. Her limbs multiplied faster than I could elude them. Even with Luce's help, distracting Srana as she darted around each reaching hand, I was losing ground.

Again, I pushed my magic out into the searing heat of the forge.

Mische.

Nothing.

"There is a war coming," Srana said. "Would you like to rule the White Pantheon? Or perhaps you would like to create something new entirely. Either way, you will want to be on the winning side."

A wall of copper sprang up before me, and I skidded around it. Too slow. Srana seized the back of my jacket, dragging me to her.

Again, I pushed toward those flames.

MISCHE, I bellowed.

"I could make you great," Srana purred. "Greater than your watered-down blood ever could. Alarus was so powerful, they said. So great, they said. But who created the weapon to best him? Not Atroxus. Not Ix. Not Acaeja. Not Shiket. *Srana.*"

Scalpel-sharp fingers turned me around to face her—five, ten, twenty, until I was suspended in a web of metal.

Her gleaming face twisted into a smile. At the edges of the room, the clockwork soldiers quivered, then groaned to life with a grand symphony of ticks and hisses and mechanical squeals. They moved with immortal grace in perfect synchronicity. Dozens of them. Hundreds.

Sun take me. They were horrifically incredible.

Srana's glee gleamed like polished steel. "Look at what I have already built from nothing at all. Imagine what I could make of you."

The pack still lay in the sands, barely out of reach. The flap had fallen open, a sliver of bronze peeking out.

In one last, desperate attempt, I lunged after it.

Pain, as my skin split against Srana's lancet grip.

My fingertips brushed the mask.

And then, with a rush of scalding heat, the forge burst into flames.

CHAPTER FORTY-THREE

Mische

Everything was suddenly simple.

A second stretched to an eternity. I could see it all at once, life and death and every rung in between, sprawling out before me like a spider's web. Complex, chaotic, and yet so easy to understand.

{See how beautiful it is,} the eye murmured. I did not hear the words but felt them in my soul. Everything became distant. The challenges that had once felt insurmountable now were merely pieces moving across a game board.

Was this, I wondered, what it was like to witness the world as a god?

A shiver ran through the axe. *{This is nothing, mortal. You cannot dream of such a thing.}*

The flames of the forge were now white-hot, engulfing the walls, the floor, the stone. It was in my lungs, in my eyes, in my hair. But it didn't hurt anymore. It flowed into me with the euphoria of blood.

A fresh crack now ran through the ground. Reaching hands and gaping mouths of the dead pushed through it, desperate for life.

{They attempt to escape a painful fate,} the eye observed. *{But it will not work.}*

And yes, I could see that now, as if another world was superimposed over this one—that the fissure in the underworld they'd come from was crushed and mangled, like the rusted jaws of a steel trap. Yet I noted this distantly, with no emotion, as if it was merely the color of the sky.

The Sentinel had staggered away from me, pressing themselves to the wall. A second, fresh gouge, now ran across their smooth helmet where they had barely evaded my swing. It created an X across their face.

They no longer seemed so frightening. They were a collection of scraps. A few threadbare remnants from a tattered lost soul and a blessed suit of metal. That was all.

I sensed a drop of satisfying hesitation.

"What have you done?" they breathed.

The wraiths broke free. I saw every single individual soul, even within the writhing, decayed morass. They grabbed the Sentinel, winding around their legs and arms.

I watched, unmoved, as the dead pulled the Sentinel back toward the crack.

But then, in this sea of soft, hazy indifference, I felt something hard:

Fear.

Raw, mortal fear.

The Sentinel's hand flew out in a desperate lurch—reaching for a savior. Reaching for me. Their heart, or whatever remained of it, pounded with animal panic.

{Leave them,} the eye said. *{They are inconsequential.}*

But there was nothing, nothing, that could quite prepare you for the way someone looked when they were truly desperate not to meet death.

Let them go, all rationality commanded.

But I was moving before I was thinking.

I grabbed the Sentinel's outstretched hand and pulled them back.

At that touch, I felt so much: my life flashing before my eyes again. But this time, I watched the moments pass by like leaves in the autumn wind. I was bigger than that now. More than the past events of the girl I had once been.

I stared at my face reflected in the Sentinel's mask. My eyes were bright white, my body framed by ink black. Whorls of shadow poured from my eyes, my nostrils, my hands.

The Sentinel clutched my hand. Time slowed.

And then they did exactly what I knew they would.

They raised their sword.

I knew it was coming. They were a divine warrior. They had nothing but their single task.

But here and now, I was a fucking god.

I raised the axe to block their strike. Their blessed sword bounced off it with a harmless *cling*. I pushed the Sentinel away with a defiant thrust. The flames of Srana's forge surrounded me in a welcome embrace.

It was nice, I thought, to feel warm again.

I looked up, to the opening of the forge. What had seemed so far away minutes ago now was laughably simple. The journey from death to life, like everything else, was merely a path to walk. You only had to know the steps.

Life and death surrounded me. It all seemed so damned easy now. A web to be scaled.

I raised the axe, and I started climbing.

CHAPTER FORTY-FOUR

Asar

The blast sent the ground trembling. Gearwork soldiers stumbled and clattered against each other. A wall of white flame burst from the crack. Srana dropped me and snapped upright with a symphony of ticks and chimes.

Mische rose from the forge.

She was doused in the white of the flames and the darkness of the shadows. At her heels, the dead climbed from the crack. Her hair flew out behind her. Her eyes were bright white, her skin glowing a bronze that rivaled the sun itself. The flames of the forge and the shadows of the dead whorled around her like a ball gown of divinity. She didn't walk, she simply ascended.

In her hands was the axe—a creation of steel and hatred and divine power, with the eye of Alarus forged into its center, glowing red, staring straight into the heart of the underworld itself. A relic beyond anything any mortal had ever witnessed. Once, the sight of it would have brought the collector in me to my knees.

But when my knees hit the ground now, it wasn't for the eye.

It was for her.

I wanted to bury myself before her. I wanted to cut myself open for her, let her take whatever she wanted, and treasure the scars for the rest of my pathetic life.

Her glowing gaze met mine.

Then reality crashed over me—the fire, the dead, and Srana, her face drawn into divine rage, rushing to close the space between us.

I would worship later. Now, I leapt for her. My hands opened, and I called to every force, living or dead or divine, who cared to answer.

Mische extended her hands to pass me the axe.

My hands fell over hers, and for just a second, I was startled by just how *solid* they felt.

Then she pushed the axe into my arms, and I was no longer thinking at all.

{Ah,} a new voice whispered. *{Now, you . . . you look familiar.}*

It was said that the eye of Alarus was all-seeing—that it allowed him to map the paths between the living and the dead. What the legends didn't say was how overwhelming it was to see everything, *everything,* all at once. Inflating lungs and decaying flesh and would-be fetuses growing in the womb, nothing but a few wisps of tissue. Bones and breath and burial tears. All of it, *all of it,* rushing through me. So much meaning that it became meaningless.

It was like I was waking up for the first time in my entire life.

Or like a part of me was dying, crying out in the dark.

Mische released the weapon and fell backward. The bright light drained from her eyes, leaving behind that golden brown.

Srana, with a roar of rage, dove for me. "I grow tired of this," she snarled.

TICKtick TICKtick TICKtick, as gears and gears and gears built beneath her, raising her up.

With a careless shove, she threw Mische aside.

I watched her form, so newly fragile, tumble against twisted metal of the forge.

My grip tightened around the handle of the axe. My blood filled the rivulets of the design that spiraled up its length, leading to the eye.

{Srana does not yet fear you,} the eye whispered. *{But she will.}*

I let Alarus's power overtake me.

Yes. She would fear me.

"Do not touch her."

The words shook the columns, the metal. They made the flames surge and dance in this monument to a two-thousand-year-old betrayal.

I lunged for Srana, and brought the axe down upon her.

Metal dented, twisted, crumpled. She fell back, righting herself in a cascade of glinting light. But I saw her shock. Her eyes *click, click, click*ed as her pupils adjusted, reevaluating.

{She has always done that,} the eye said. *{Analyzed what she is too small to understand.}*

She had looked that way when she had cut out this very eye and forged it into a coward's weapon. A weapon she wouldn't even wield herself.

And she had the gall to believe she could rule the White Pantheon.

No. She was a weak traitor. Just like the others.

Srana fell back, attempted to collect herself. But I raised my hand, and the dead surged for her, dragging her down to the sand.

Only now did her curiosity give way to true fear.

{Good,} the eye hissed.

"Release me!" she shrieked, as I stalked toward her.

I laughed.

How powerless she now looked.

TI-ti-TI-ti as gears jammed, locked.

Shadows fell in waterfalls down the bloody walls. A screech rang out as Srana attempted to claw across metal to drag herself free.

I saw Srana standing over the body of a dead mortal woman with all the indifference deserving of a dead pest.

I saw Srana's face looming over mine, those eyes *click, click, clicking* away, holding out the weapon crafted from her betrayal.

I saw Srana forging the chains that would bind a girl with galaxies in her hair through her torture.

"No," I snarled. "No, Srana. I will not release you."

The darkness whipped around us both, suspending me over her. She sprawled out in a mass of twisted metal. With a jerk of my hand, the shadows dragged her across the floor, inch by inch, until she was directly beneath me.

The heady elation of revenge flooded me. My smile was so tight it hurt my teeth.

"What shall I do to you?" I said. "Shall I cut out your eye, too?"

I moved the tip of the blade to her face, right next to her eye, where the broken gear *cli-cli-click*ed in a futile attempt to turn.

"Shall I stand by and let them rip you apart gear by gear, just as you stood by and watched your kin commit such injustices?" I gestured to the dead, who jammed their desperate fingers into screws and coils, digging for a taste of divinity.

I leaned closer.

"Or, perhaps I shall take a finger for every link of the chain you forged for her?"

Srana's confusion delighted me.

"Oh, cousin," I breathed. "You think I do not know the things you did to Nyaxia in her captivity?"

And there, at last, was delicious fear.

{Now she sees you,} the eye purred in satisfaction.

"You," she gasped.

But there was nothing she could say to earn my forgiveness, let alone my mercy.

I saw those clockwork eyes watching over the murder of a woman in the ashes of a dead god.

Watching over the torture of a woman with galaxies in her hair.

These two memories twisted, tangled. I didn't care to separate them. Srana would suffer for either crime.

I raised the blade and brought it down.

CRACK, as metal split and shattered. Srana wailed. Her right arm screeched as it dragged across the floor, pulled apart by the hungry dead. The skies churned above, lightning spearing the web between worlds.

"They will come," she screeched. "The others will come for you!"

{Let them,} the eye taunted.

"I don't care," I replied. And I did not.

I raised the blade again.

But then, a sound pushed through the haze.

A voice screaming a name.

"Asar!"

I paused.

I knew that name, that voice, though I could not place them.

"Come back to me." The words slipped through me like smoke, sweet with a familiar compulsion.

Come back to me. Come back to me. Come back to me.

I lowered the axe. There was now sand under my feet. I turned.

A beautiful woman approached me slowly, arm outstretched. She had eyes of amber and smelled of cinnamon.

Smelled of cinnamon . . . and blood.

The scent made my heart stutter. A cacophonous clatter rang out behind me as Srana collected herself and made her pathetic escape into the ether.

{Do not let her go!} the eye cried.

But I barely noticed her departure.

The woman stepped closer. Her hands slid over my shoulders, gingerly reaching past the axe. There was blood on her face, smearing over freckles. Blood on her clothing. She swayed slightly.

"We have to leave, Asar," she said. "The gods are coming. Come back."

Come back. Come back. Come back.

All at once, her name struck me.

"Mische," I gasped.

I dropped the axe, reaching out to catch her as her knees buckled. Blood cascaded onto the ground. Luce circled us in anxious urgency.

She was bleeding so much. When had this happened? How had I not seen it?

How could a wraith bleed like this at all?

But she didn't feel like a wraith when I drew her up in my arms.

"We have to go," she murmured, lashes fluttering.

Everything fell away but the panic.

I looked up at the skies above, shattered shards of a hundred worlds, now swirling with divine interest. Moments, and the gods would be here.

But we had no passage back. No way to run fast enough. Nowhere to hide. My mind raced through countless impossible choices, arriving at only one conclusion:

I refused to live this again. I would not hold Mische's dying body as the gods watched.

My gaze fell to the axe, with the eye pulsing at the center of its blade.

Then to the mask, lying in the sand.

I couldn't save her as a mortal. But a god was not confined to the bounds of time and space. A god could step between worlds.

Luce whined a warning, as if she knew what I intended to do. But it was easy to ignore her, faced with Mische's death. Easy to discard a piece of my mortality I knew I might not get back.

"Hold on to me," I told them both.

I pulled Mische close. I grabbed the mask and slid it over my face. Then I held the axe.

The divine power threatened to sweep me away all over again.

But I anchored myself to Mische. I looked up at the spira, a shimmering web that connected worlds.

I needed to take her somewhere safe. Somewhere we could hide, if only for a little while.

I had seconds to decide, and when I arrived at our only answer, I knew she would hate me for it.

But at least if she hated me, she would be alive.

I gathered her up in my arms, Luce at my side, and jumped.

PART FOUR

A Heart

INTERLUDE

Let me tell you now about the night the prince learned he was a god.

It was not the first time he had met the goddess—he had seen her once before, the night she gave him the mission that brought him here, into the belly of the dead kingdom he did not yet know was his birthright. He had traveled through the Sanctums of the Descent to the underworld alongside the acolyte that he had become so fond of.

And with every level, every Sanctum, every healed hurt, he fell deeper in love.

When the goddess came to him, he still had his lover's blood on his lips and her scent on his skin. He fell asleep entwined in her naked body, and he woke up alone.

The goddess looked at him with disgust.

"So this is what you have been doing with the mission that I have given you," she sneered. "You have been bedding sun-tainted harlots."

The prince scrambled upright. The goddess threw clothing at his feet.

"You are foolish to trust her," she said. "And more foolish still to love her."

Perhaps this was true. His mentor had taught him to trust sparingly. Bed who you want, he had said, but always keep the knife beneath your pillow.

The prince had known that any vampire who continued to wield the power of the sun after Turning was a rare being. He had known how deeply she had once loved the sun, and how deeply she mourned its loss. If she had ever believed she had hidden this from him, she was mistaken. And in the beginning he had indeed wondered: What might she be willing to do to reclaim it?

But the Dawndrinker had become a partner, and then a friend, and then a lover. She had become a twin soul, burning alongside him on the path to death. He did not doubt that she had told him lies. But the truth in every wound they healed together was absolute. A connection so intrinsic that it rendered all else meaningless.

He had not answered the goddess. But perhaps she saw his true feelings, and they enraged her.

"Mortals," she seethed. "You are so ungratefully sentimental. You made an oath, and now you believe you will use it to seize the ending that was stolen from me. Do you think I chose you for this task because you are so great, so powerful? No. I chose you because your blood already carries my husband's. Because your soul already belongs to the underworld. When you fulfill your oath to me, it will take it back."

The prince was silent.

Your soul.

It should have been a shock. If he had not already had his suspicions, he would not have even understood what she meant.

But he had been wondering. Sometimes magic knows even what a mind does not. Something within the prince that surpassed logic knew that his connection to the underworld ran too deep to be mere coincidence. That the dreams he had of the god of death were more akin to visions.

You are a king, *his mother had said.*

The prince understood, now, that he was not a divine champion. He was a sacrifice. A relic merely as valuable as the ones he had been collecting on his journey.

"It is in me," he murmured. "My bloodline. The relic of soul."

"Do not be too arrogant. You are no demigod. Merely the product of some mortal tryst, centuries before my birth, that survived through generations. Useful for nothing but a sacrifice."

He stared down at his hand, marked with tattoo and scar and flesh. Mortal, with a single drop of a god.

Staring down upon his impending death, he was not angry. He was not frightened.

But he did grieve.

In his journey to the underworld, the Dawndrinker had made him believe he could be capable of healing the hurts of the world. With every broken gate they mended, every lost soul they freed, every wound they stitched, he had let a little more of that hope shine through. It had happened so slowly he had not even realized how fiercely he had wanted to believe it, until now, when it shattered beneath the ugly truth.

The prince did not grieve his own life. He grieved that dream.

Because the prince was not a healer. He had been crafted from a young age to destroy. Life was only worth the value of the blood one spilled upon it. And the blood would always, always spill. The only thing he could control now was whose.

There was always a sacrifice to be made.

The kindest thing he could do, the only good he could offer, would be to ensure that it was his.

He accepted this. A simple truth.

And then he turned to the goddess, and he crafted a deal.

CHAPTER FORTY-FIVE

Mische

It didn't feel like this the last time I died. That had been quick. I hadn't been fighting anymore.

Now, I fought.

Colors and shapes and sounds smeared around me, all the messy runoff of a life circling a drain. I saw Asar's face close to mine, and he looked so beautifully mortal—the scars painting history across his cheek, lines and scars and battle marks. Nothing like the terrible, blank version of him I had seen when I handed him the axe.

I tried to say, *Good, you're back.*

But I couldn't speak. The world tipped backward. I clung to that blurry image of Asar's face. It was crumpled with dismay, then smooth with determination. I had only ever seen him look that way one other time.

A tear hit my cheek. Not mine.

We were moving. The world bent, twisted, faded to darkness and then extreme light.

I dreamed of Saescha, standing before the dawn, doused in gold. She looked so much more real than she had in my dreams, and so much happier. For a moment I thought maybe this was really her, maybe she had passed to the afterlife. I tried to call her name, but she wouldn't hear me, anyway.

We were falling. I smelled ivy and frost. Asar held me tight as we hit the ground. Pain, as we fell to the rocks.

No—snow.

No—sand.

Sand?

Shouting. Movement. We were running. I was fading. I dreamed of the Citadel. I dreamed of a kingdom of sand and night skies and some friends that I loved there very much.

Asar's voice echoed: *I need—*

I need—

I need her, he had said the last time, and I wanted to stroke his face and tell him it wasn't true. He was a god, and I was no one. He would be just fine without me.

It's up to you whether you choose to believe me—

Asar's words cracked. He never sounded this way. So undone.

—but I will not allow her to die here. I will not allow it.

My lashed fluttered. Reality fell away with the retreating waves upon the shore.

I saw the underworld flicker around me. Deep cracks now opened in the sky. Souleaters circled. Blood poured through the gaping wounds. A million invisible voices screamed out.

I couldn't speak, and he was already gone, anyway.

The underworld. Crumbling mountains. Morthryn tumbling from the sky.

Pain. A wave of pain that ripped apart the seams between worlds. Everyone was shouting.

Someone screamed. Was it me?

Raihn. His face leaned over me. He was wearing that face I hated so much—that big dumb puppy dog face. But I was still so happy to see him.

I smiled weakly. "Hello, you."

And he returned my smile. It was the same smile he had given me when he'd pulled me from the burning Moon Palace. "Hey, you. Everything is going to be fine. Alright? Everything is going to be fine."

I don't think so, I thought, but I let him say it, anyway. He always needed to hear it more than I did.

The voices blurred together. Shouting.

—the fuck did you do to her?

I *didn't do anything to her—*

Raihn. Oraya. Jesmine—was that Jesmine? What a strange dream.

Eyes closed. Opened. Closed.

Vincent stood over me.

"At last," he said, "you've finally listened to me."

What?

He grabbed my shoulders. "We do not have time. Go. Take the blood—"

She doesn't have time—

—No time, no time,

no

time—

Saescha turned around to stare at me, her smile growing colder, colder, colder.

You are out of time, she said.

Asar leaned over me. Gods, he was so beautiful. More beautiful than the sunrise.

"Asar," I whispered.

A sad smile twitched over his perfect mouth.

"I told you I would never let you go again," he murmured. "I won't."

He slid the mask down, and suddenly, it was the god of death staring down at me.

I didn't like that. I mourned Asar's perfect, imperfect face.

But the pain began, and the darkness rose up, and dreams and reality and death and life all crashed together into a single overwhelming cacophony—

And that was all.

I FELT HEAVY. Like rocks had been strapped to my wrists and ankles. Everything ached. The pain was oddly tangible, solid, in a way I hadn't experienced in a long time.

Was I dead? Dead*er*? I had already died once, and it hadn't quite felt like this.

I opened my eyes.

The sight that greeted me was familiar. Blue ceilings painted with stars. Silver filigree. Purple-stained windows.

Where had I seen . . .

Panic crashed over me.

I sat up sharply, or tried to, and mostly ended up flopping around like a fish.

I recognized this place. I was in the Nightborn castle.

"Mische," a familiar voice gasped.

My head whipped around to see Raihn and Oraya at my bedside.

Raihn had stood so abruptly his chair nearly tipped over. He breathed my name in a single exhale of relief.

I barely heard him, because I was too busy just staring at them. They were real, not a dream.

I shouldn't be here. I shouldn't be here. I shouldn't be here.

And yet, I was so, so happy to see them.

Oraya smiled. "Hello, Mische."

My eyes burned. "Hello."

But then Raihn's expression darkened.

"You have," he said, "*so* much explaining to do. *So. Much.*"

CHAPTER FORTY-SIX

Mische

Raihn was furious. I could smell his rage like wildfire smoke. He approached me, one step after the other.

"What," he breathed. "The hell. Have you been *doing*? You turn up at our doorstep, half dead, in the arms of a prince of a kingdom we're practically at war with—"

My heart clenched. "At war?"

"No," Raihn snapped. "I get to ask questions now. Where the hell have you been? Do you have any idea the things that we have been doing to find you? You couldn't send us a letter? A few fucking sentences saying, *Hello, Raihn. How's the weather? I'm alive!*"

I wasn't alive.

I squeezed my eyes shut. Gods, I felt *terrible*.

The bleak reality of our situation slowly rolled over me. Angry goddesses and vengeful warriors. A broken underworld. Wraiths. Divine war.

The litany of horrors that followed Asar and me wherever we went.

And we were here. Here, in the home of some of the most precious people I knew.

We couldn't be here.

My eyes darted around the room—empty aside from the three of us.

"Asar," I blurted out. "Where's Asar?"

"Asar?" Raihn repeated. "You mean the fucking Wraith Warden, Mish?"

I winced. "He's—"

"Oh, I know who he is, and I can't believe that we've just let him within our castle walls."

"The only thing he has going for him," Oraya said quietly, "is that he saved your life. He's locked up."

"You *locked him up*?" I yelped.

"This is us being *nice,* Mische," Raihn said. "Because we wanted to talk to you, alone. Without a Shadowborn prince here manipulating your mind."

I choked a laugh. "Manipulating? No. No, that's not—"

"Don't laugh at me," he spat, "like it's some kind of ridiculous proposition."

"I remember the last time I found you in this castle with a Shadowborn prince," Oraya said. "Won't ever forget it."

I glanced at Oraya, and then had to force myself to look away. Because the look on her face reminded me far too much of the night she had rescued me from a bedchamber just like this one, where I had been imprisoned as a gift for the man who had Turned me.

I'd always been able to feel Oraya's emotions so strongly. Right now, her hurt cut deep. I had once worked so hard to earn that trust, and now, I felt every crack as I destroyed it.

My chest hurt—gods, my chest hurt. My heart thumped against the inside of my ribs in an odd, distracting way, and I frowned as I looked down at my hands.

They looked different. Felt different, too. Burn scars peeked out from beneath my sleeve.

Scars.

What the hell?

"I need to see him," I said.

I threw back the covers, already halfway to standing up, but Raihn raised his hands. "Wait. You're not going anywhere."

I gave him as cheerful a smile as I could muster. "I can walk."

"I don't care if you can fucking walk. You need to tell us what happened to you." He flung a hand to the window, revealing the eternally dark sky. "You disappear and then the world is fucking ending and now you show up with some Shadowborn—"

"He shouldn't have taken me here," I said.

"I'm glad he did. At least now you can't just force me to turn around."

The compulsion. My face heated with shame. I could barely bring myself to look at him.

"I'm sorry," I said. But even that tasted like a lie. Because I wasn't sorry. I would do it again. Even now, I found myself testing the edge of his mind, considering whether I could make it work. I could ensnare Raihn or Oraya, but probably not both, and in their own home, it wouldn't get me far, anyway.

Raihn would never forgive me. I knew it. I didn't blame him one bit.

"I don't care," he spat. "I don't care, Mische. Mess with my head. Twist my thoughts. Fine. If that's what you need to do to feel safe, do it."

"Feel safe?" I bit out. "That's not what I—"

"That's not what pisses me off. What pisses me off is that you felt like you *had* to do that. I've known you for nearly a century, Mische. Nearly a hundred goddess-damned years. Haven't I earned your trust?"

The words cut. But it was the look on his face—genuine, vulnerable, beneath the rough edge of his frustration—that pierced my heart.

Oraya sat at the edge of the bed. She reached for my hand, and instinctually, I jerked it away. Hurt flickered over her face. I stared down at her open palm against the bedspread.

When I first met her, Oraya had been so afraid of the world that she wouldn't even let anyone get within five feet of her. The first time she'd let me hug her, I felt like I'd won the Kejari.

And now I was the one to push her away.

"We can't help you until you tell us what's happening to you," she said, her voice hard and soft at the same time in that particular way of hers. Tenderness beneath steel.

I looked at her and saw her as Vincent did. I thought of the House of Night collapsing beneath the weight of what I brought to their doorstep.

I said, "I need to see Asar."

Their disappointment crushed me.

A muscle feathered in Raihn's jaw.

"You will stay here until you recover," he said. "I'll bring Asar to you. But you stay here."

I started to protest, but Raihn cut me off.

"How many fucking times now have you made decisions about my life without my input, Mische? Entering the Kejari. Forcing me to—" His jaw tightened, and he swallowed the words. "I'm making this one for you. Just one. Three days. And then if you want to walk out of here, fine. Go. But I'm not going to let you die in my kingdom. I'll give you anything you ask for. But I refuse to give you that."

Tears stung my eyes. The weight of the secrets that I was keeping from them threatened to smother me. I could barely keep them down.

They went to the door and Raihn threw it open.

"Wait," I blurted out.

They stopped, turned. They actually looked hopeful.

All of it sat at the tip of my tongue.

But the best I could choke out was, "I really, really missed you."

Raihn's face softened. But he still looked so brutally, heartbreakingly sad. "Us too," he said, and closed the door behind them.

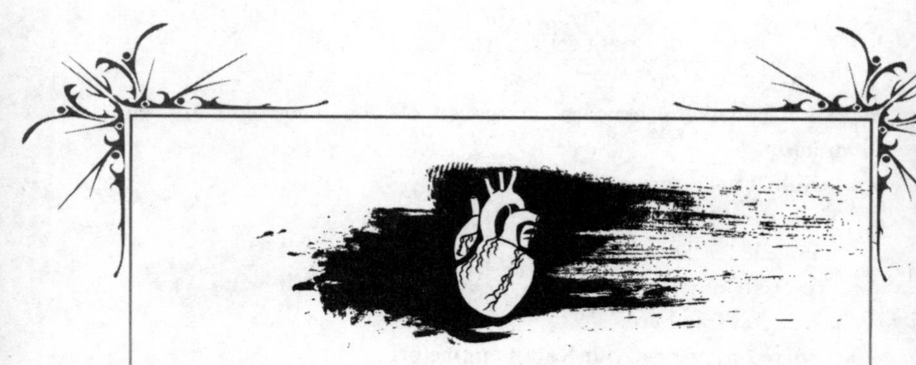

CHAPTER FORTY-SEVEN

Asar

My forehead pressed to the wall. My eyes were closed. Visions of the present and past smeared by.

I remained in the room that the Nightborn locked me in for a long time.

The chamber was fine enough. It was, of course, a prison cell, but it was one that for all intents and purposes looked like a bedchamber. In vampire society, the line between "guests" and "prisoners" was often very thin, and places intended for one could easily be swapped to suit the other. The Nightborn made no secret of which one I was.

I had gotten out of rooms more heavily fortified than this one countless times. I could have the door off its hinges or some poor guard beheaded on the carpet in minutes.

I didn't. I sat patiently.

{An insult, that they dare to imprison a king,} a voice whispered.

{They will be inconsequential in the end,} another added. *{Just like all the rest.}*

In the darkness, I saw Srana's face. Felt the metal of her body splintering under each blow. *C-cl-c-cl-c-cli—*

I remembered how she had leaned over me and smiled when she handed Atroxus the—

No, not me. Alarus.

Alarus.

Something warm and hard nudged my arm. A low whine interrupted my thoughts. I opened my eyes to see Luce nuzzling my hand. She looked both worried and disapproving. A familiar expression by now.

I rubbed the top of her head.

"Don't give me that look," I grumbled. "I did what I had to."

Luce continued giving me that look.

I scoffed. "You've been spending too much time with her. Such preachiness."

I didn't even have to name Mische anymore. She was just *her*—a constant presence.

Luce rubbed against my knees. I ran my hand over her soft, shadowy body. For the first time in a long time, I thought of the first time she'd let me do that—back when she was so different than what she was now. I'd sat so still, not even breathing, for fear that I'd scare her away. But inside, my heart was leaping.

It was the first time in my short life that I had experienced true affection from any other living being. And I had known from that moment, when that frightened dog decided to trust me, that I would never, ever betray that trust. Luce had a friend in me for life. And, it turned out, for death, too.

Luce let out a whine and glanced to the door. I'd lost track of how many hours we'd been waiting here. Time moved strangely, though I wasn't sure if that was because of my worry, the aftereffects of traveling through the spira, or because everything still felt vaguely dreamlike since I removed the mask.

"She is going to be alright," I murmured. It was a reassurance to myself, too—even though I knew it was true. I wouldn't have agreed to leave her otherwise.

Mische, Luce, and I came through the spira directly onto the Nightborn palace grounds. I remembered that, though not much else. Just flashes. Shouting, meeting the royals, bringing Mische into the palace. The way she just kept *bleeding*.

Even now, I couldn't quite recall what I had done to help her. I'd brought us through the spira. I had used the power of the mask and the eye to heal her wounds. But all of it had felt so far away, like I was watching my own actions from a great distance.

By the time I let the axe fall and removed the mask, I had brought Mische back to the cusp of life. And when the Nightborn had ordered me imprisoned, I let them take me away without a fight, even though every shred of me resisted leaving Mische's side.

We needed their trust. She was out of danger. And when I saw them fall to their knees at her bedside, I knew they thought her life was just as precious as I did.

I touched my cheek. The scars hurt more than they had in decades. My left eye stung. I still felt the imprint of Alarus's mask on my cheekbones—the ghostly weight of a crown of the dead. Blood beaded at the outline where it had lain against my face.

The hum of indecipherable whispers rose again. I glanced at the bag across the room, the mask tucked away within it. The axe stood beside it, propped against the wall and wrapped up in a makeshift sheath of fabric, but the eye at its blade glowed straight through it.

Luce let out a low growl, and I tore my gaze away.

A presence approached down the hall. Then footsteps. I was waiting at the door by the time it opened.

The Nightborn head of war stood there—the lithe woman with an ash-brown braid over her shoulder. She looked me up and down with a piercing violet stare. She was better than most at guarding her thoughts, but she didn't bother hiding her distrust.

"Against my professional recommendation," she said drily, "you have been allowed to see Mische. I'm here to bring you to her chambers."

Allowed. Cute.

But ever the grateful guest, I simply rose and followed.

MISCHE LOOKED SO alive. She looked so alive that it struck me across the face when I walked into her chambers, closing the door firmly behind me. The color was back in her cheeks. Her hair flew about her in wild curls. She wore clean Nightborn clothing, a silky purple blouse and trousers.

"We have to leave," she said, without looking at me when I arrived. "We can't be here. Between the Shadowborn and Nyaxia and—and Shiket—"

She was gasping between her words, like she wasn't used to having to catch her breath when she was talking this fast. She rummaged through the piles of discarded clothing on an armchair, throwing them into a bag.

A fresh wave of the scent of her blood—intoxicating—hit my nostrils. "Mische, just—"

"We *cannot be here,* Asar. We—"

She stopped mid-sentence, doubling over, her whole body clenching with pain, and I'd had enough.

"Stop," I barked. "Sit down. We are not going anywhere right now."

She collapsed against the edge of the bed, head hanging. But just as quickly, it snapped up again, and the fire in her eyes startled me.

"I told you," she ground out, "that I did not want to come here. And you still brought me here. They can't afford—"

But then her eyes fell to my face. They widened. "What is *that*?"

It took a moment for me to realize what she was talking about. She lurched forward, touching her own cheek as if a stand-in for mine, and I realized that she meant the marks the mask had left on my cheekbone.

"Is that from the mask?" she gasped.

{She should be grateful,} the mask whispered, insulted.

{A small price for greatness,} the eye agreed.

I winced, pushing away the voices. To Mische, I said, "It's nothing."

"It's not *nothing,* Asar." She swallowed, and I watched the flex of her throat. It seemed so deceptively alive. "I looked into your face and I didn't see you there at all. That was terrifying."

"I came back," I said.

{Did you?} the eye mused.

Holy hell, I wished they would shut up. The relics weren't even with me. Why was I still hearing them?

"They are dangerous. You told me that, and I've seen it before." She shook her head, eyes glistening. "You promised me you wouldn't sacrifice your mortality."

I'd had enough.

"What was my alternative, Mische? I needed to bring you somewhere safe. Somewhere to save your goddess-damned life. There is no sacrifice I wouldn't make for that. Not mine, not theirs. And I have known these people for all of a few hours, and I can already tell that the thing they 'can't afford' is to let you die because you were too prideful to let them help you."

A flicker of hurt, then anger, wrenched over her perfect, alive face. But I kept going, approaching her step by step. "I already told you that I would never watch you die again. I made that decision in an Ysrian prison. Have more respect for me than to think I'd break it so easily."

I blinked and in that split second of darkness, there she was: Mische, in my arms, flesh charred, life draining from her drop by drop, destroyed by the god who had once promised to protect her.

She was not arguing anymore. Her mouth was closed. Her bright, deep eyes searched mine. My hand seized hers before I could think about it.

"I don't regret it," I said. "I would do it a thousand times over. A thousand times, if it means that I get to hear you berate me for it here rather than imagine those words over your corpse. You are the sacrifice I will not make, Mische. *You.* Don't ask me to apologize for that."

Silence.

Mische stared at me. Her lips were slightly parted. Her chest rose and fell with breaths that she couldn't quite seem to catch. The scent of her blood hung in the air, beading at her stitches.

And then, I realized.

We both realized.

Slowly, her gaze slipped to my hand.

Her hand.

My hand holding her hand.

No pain. No burning. No drain of energy that came with the hungry touch of the dead.

Mische tried to snatch it away, but I curled my fingers tight around hers.

"Don't," I whispered.

It was the only word I could get out.

Her palm was warm. Her flesh was soft. Her skin was solid and imperfect and wonderful and fucking *alive*.

Our eyes locked. Hers grew slowly wider.

"Do you feel—" she started.

"You," I managed. "I feel *you*."

I couldn't bring myself to unlock my fingers, as if I feared that letting go of her would mean I would never find her again. My other hand reached for her cheek. I flattened my palm against her face. Her cheek was soft, the curve of her chin firm. My thumb brushed the underside of her lip.

"How?" she choked out.

"I don't care." The easiest answer I'd ever spoken. Perhaps the only time I, a man obsessed with answers, had ever said it.

I don't care. I don't care. I don't care.

I stroked her cheek. Her jaw. The soft slope of her nose. Her breath was shaky. Her lashes fluttered. I didn't blink. Didn't breathe. I felt like I'd been offered something so precious, so fragile, that I didn't want to even look too hard lest it fall apart in my hands.

She was real.

She was solid.

Her eyes fluttered closed. She lifted her chin, letting me trace the exquisite contours of her features.

I still was holding my breath.

This, I realized, was prayer.

Her knees were against mine, her body so close I could feel the warmth of it—warmth, actual warmth. My head lowered. Her chin lifted. Her breath warmed my lips.

"I don't regret it," I said again.

"Which part?" she murmured.

"Any of it, Mische."

And then I kissed her.

CHAPTER FORTY-EIGHT

Asar

I had once believed that there was no feeling more intense than being in the presence of gods. But kissing Mische, touching her skin again after all this time, dwarfed it. And yet, in the same measure, kissing her made me feel so weak, so fallible, so deeply mortal. She let out a little gasp against my mouth, and I sucked it into my lungs. Her lips parted for me and her tongue, silken smooth, slipped free to meet mine. She tasted like redemption.

Her arms wove around my neck, and I pushed her to the bed. We undressed each other frantically, clumsily. Our hands struggled to abandon skin in favor of undoing buttons or clasps. I wanted, needed, to be touching her at all times. Each kiss, each breath, each stretch of exquisite flesh made me hungrier.

He hands slid under my shirt, flattening over my stomach, while I slipped her blouse over her head. At the sight of her body, bare and beautiful and so real, I whispered a curse with the reverence of a prayer.

She clumsily yanked my shirt off me while I pushed her flat to the bed. My mouth traced her jaw, her throat—pausing there, at the steady beat of blood under the surface, and goddess help me, it hurt to drag myself away. But there was too much to touch, too much to taste.

I kissed her shoulder, her collarbone. Traveled south, to the swell of her breasts—lingering. One hand reached up to cup the right while my mouth refamiliarized itself with the left. Her skin smelled like cinnamon and tasted of the sun. Her knees parted around me, and her hands raked down my bare back, fingers tracing muscles, bones, scars—like she, too, was trying to memorize me all over again.

I pressed my tongue against her hardened nipple, relishing the way I could feel her inhale in her gasp, pushing up against me. Her shock of pleasure zapped between us—she let me feel it, opening all her mental doors. I threw my mind wide open for her, too, like windows on the first warm summer night, letting in the solace of the moonlight.

Peace.

For a moment, I breathed against her. Then I kept going, undoing the button of her trousers and peeling back the fabric as I moved down to her stomach, which tensed as she huffed an almost-giggle. "Tickles," she breathed, and she sounded drunkenly euphoric in a way that made me feel it, too.

I slid her trousers off, revealing the soft flesh where her waist met her hip. I remembered the first time I kissed that curve. I had dreamed of it a thousand times since. Now, the wound from Srana's blow slashed across it, neatly stitched and bandaged, beads of black blood dotting the gauze.

I stared at that. The wound that had almost ripped her away from me again. But that same wound marked her as closer to life than she had been in months.

I slid one of her arms from around my neck and kissed her palm, her wrist. Then I observed her bare skin—bare skin once again covered with scars, as it had been in life. She even had the tattoo, the finch-like phoenix smoldering beneath decades' worth of burns.

Mische stared at it, too, a furrow between her brows.

"How—" she started.

But my answer was still the same.

"I don't care." I kissed those scars one by one, just as I had the first night she had shown me them. Then, I had hated them because of the pain they represented to her. Now, I loved them, because they meant she was here.

Every thrum of my blood hummed that refrain: *You're here, you're here, you're here.*

"I don't care," I whispered again, and I slid her undergarments down. She kicked them away, and the scent of her desire, thick and sweet, overwhelmed me.

I wanted to touch every part of her that I'd separated myself from via cotton or silk or the fucking frayed threads of my self-control.

I sank between her legs and drew in a deep inhale. I tasted her slowly at first, getting reacquainted with her skin, the way her inner thighs met the soft lips of her pussy. When I kissed her slit, rolling my tongue softly against her, her hips bucked. Her fingers dragged through my hair, as if, even beneath the distraction of pleasure, she couldn't stop touching me.

My mind emptied of all thought. All that remained was lust.

She let out a fractured moan. Her blood rushed. I felt it throbbing just beneath the fragile flesh of her inner thighs. My fangs ached, and I ran them along her skin, tongue slipping out against the goose bumps they called to the surface.

Mische let out a whimper, the most beautiful sound. My gaze flicked up, my head rising just enough to watch her over the swells and dips of her perfect, naked body. She was watching me, breath bated, hands still clutching at me.

Her want vibrated in the air between us, so pure and unashamed. I loved the way Mische wanted. And I was in no position to deny her now.

So when she attempted to pull me back up, I let her. Let her hands slide over my body as mine slid over hers, taking in every curve, scar, dip, press of bone or fat or muscle. Let her unbutton my trousers and push them away, leaving only skin between us.

How easily our bodies aligned around each other. Like the sun and moon meeting in an eclipse.

Her thighs opened. My cock found her entrance. Last time I'd teased her, relished her. I couldn't now. I was too desperate for her. I wanted to sink so deep inside her that I no longer knew the edges of my own soul.

"I missed you," she whispered against my lips.

"I missed you," I murmured, and pushed into her.

She let out a trembling cry and pulled taut around me. Everything disappeared—gods and wraiths and death, war and betrayals, magic masks and cursed axes and all the fears I tried to tell myself I did not feel. Everything but her.

I was whole, entwined in her skin and soul alike.

Wordless moans and whimpers tumbled from her lips, smothered by my kisses. I pulled away just enough to look at her as I withdrew and pushed back into her, slow, savoring every strain of her muscles.

A wince of pain flickered over her face. I halted mid-stroke. Of course. Her bandages. The wound was fresh—

But she breathed, "No. Don't stop." A lopsided smile spread slowly over her lips, and her ankles hooked around my hips, pulling me slowly—agonizingly—back inside her.

"I love it," she murmured. "Even the pain. It feels—it all feels—"

I couldn't resist. I pushed deep, deep into her, her hips rising against the movement as we ground against each other. I wanted to kiss her, but I also wanted to watch her—watch the way that pleasure spasmed across her face, so full and free.

"I want it all," she managed, fractured with an almost-moan.

I understood now. The pain, the pleasure, the hunger. All were markers of the gift she had somehow, miraculously, reclaimed.

"Then you'll have it, Dawndrinker," I murmured against her mouth, and pushed into her again, again, again.

And yet, as her pleasure grew, so did her hunger, building in her mind and mine.

"More," I commanded. "Take more."

I rolled over, clutching her body, so that she was on top of me. The angle pushed her deeper against my hips, dragging a low, wordless groan from between my teeth.

I lifted my chin and cradled her head, guiding her to my throat.

I want it all, she had said.

Take it, I said silently to her. *It is all for you, Mische Iliae.*

And Mische—beautiful, hungry, sex-drunk Mische—did not even protest. Her teeth broke my skin with an exquisite stab of pain.

The purr of silken, honey-sweet bliss that shivered through her body and mind alike nearly pushed me over the edge.

Her fingers interlaced with mine as she drank deep, her hips rolling with each swallow. My world narrowed to the divine mission of meeting each unspoken demand of her body, feeding her every hunger. I felt a soft but firm pressure slide over my shoulders while her hands ran down my body, and I opened my eyes to see that the shadows had slithered from the corners of the room down to meet us, putting me exactly where she wanted me.

I smiled.

"You're a stronger Shadowborn every day, Dawndrinker." My newly freed hands kneaded her thighs. "Quite a talent."

She extracted her teeth, lips curling into a smile. "I'm committed to my craft."

My fingernails dug into her hips, and goddess help me, I couldn't stop myself. I thrust up into her, seeing stars as her walls clenched around me. She reared up, offering me an awe-inspiring view of her body, head thrown back.

I wanted—no, needed—to feel her come. It became my singular purpose.

She was right there, trembling with its proximity. I wanted to hurtle her over the edge, feel her every muscle inside and out vibrating with my mark on her.

Instead, she slid free of me.

I let out a growl of frustrated disapproval that was downright animalistic.

But Mische just gave me a sly smile and lay down, curling against me so her back was pressed to my torso. Her thighs opened, offering me entrance again.

The position offered me access to her entire body. I couldn't bring myself to resent that. My fingers slid around her inner thigh, holding her open as I pushed back inside her from behind. She was so wet that there was no resistance, as if our bodies begged to be reunited.

She let out a shaking keen. My hands greedily slid down her exposed skin—her breasts, her stomach, the hips that arched and pushed against me, and finally, her slick, swollen bud. As I circled it, her whole body shuddered. She whimpered my name through clenched teeth.

I kissed her ear, her cheek, her jaw. "Tell me what you want."

She turned her head to shoot me a knowing look. Then she lifted her chin.

Suddenly, I understood why she had shifted positions.

To offer me her throat.

If I had been thinking logically, I might have hesitated. What if there was still some wraith left in her? Worse, what if I took what she wasn't prepared to give?

But I was not thinking logically anymore. Every instinct had realigned to a single gluttonous, carnal goal, which was to relish in Mische's pleasure. Our minds were intertwined, her hunger and mine inextricable. I felt how much she wanted it.

I wanted it, too. More than anything.

So I kissed her throat, and as I thrust deep into her, I bit.

The first time I had tasted Mische, I had known I'd made a mistake. I would no longer be able to resist her. I had given myself a single taste of an addiction I would never again be able to satiate.

Now, as her blood flooded over my tongue, thick and sweet and rich, I was perfectly content to be ensnared.

I had barely felt hunger lately, disconnected from my mortal impulses. Now, faced with the exquisite taste of her, they were all that remained.

My fingers dug into Mische's soft flesh, pulling her close, as I drank deeper. Whatever remained of finesse or self-control disintegrated. Mische writhed desperately against each thrust, curses and prayers tumbling from her lips.

She was everywhere. My tongue, my skin, my stomach, my cock, my heart. Everywhere.

"More," she begged. "I need—I want—"

She couldn't get the sentence out. But she didn't need to. We were beyond words now.

I rolled her over, pushing her between the bed and my body, offering myself the freedom to drive into her faster, frantic, desperate. My hand slid down her body, between her legs, circling her bud.

"Take, Mische," I murmured in her ear, my voice rough. "All of it. All for you."

Her fingers seized my free hand, like she wanted me with her as she hurled herself over the edge. I clutched her as she detonated—like the sunrise exploding over the horizon.

I had no choice but to go with her. I wrapped myself around her and pushed deep, her pussy clenching around me as we came together. Empires rose and fell as we held each other through the aftershocks.

And only three words cycled through me: *It is her. It is her. It is her.*

The world went silent save for our serrated, heaving breaths.

I kissed her hair, then the curve of her ear. When I reached her cheek, I tasted salt.

I slid from her and she rolled over in my arms, so we lay face to face. Her skin was flushed and hot. A tear streaked down her cheek.

I kissed it away. "What is it, Dawndrinker?"

"I just—" She drew in a ragged breath and let it out. "I feel so *alive*."

My embrace tightened around her. Something sharp skewered my heart. I couldn't quite identify whether it was pleasure or pain.

She did feel so alive. It was a gift so precious I didn't even have words for it.

Yet, a warm body was one that could so easily go cold. A beating heart was one that could be pierced. Rushing blood could so easily be spilled.

"How?" she whispered. "Did you—did you resurrect me?"

How wonderful it would be, if the answer was yes.

But I knew it wasn't that simple. She felt alive, looked alive, tasted alive. But I could still sense death clinging to her, ready to sink its claws into her, drag her back to the underworld. And Mische, I knew, from the disbelief on her face, could feel it too.

{She still belongs to the dead,} the eye said dismissively. *{Soft skin or no.}*

I flinched. The voice was gone so quick I hoped I had imagined it.

Mische frowned. "What?"

I shook my head. "I just— Nothing." Then, after a moment, "Perhaps the mask and the eye were powerful enough to pull you closer to life, when I healed you."

Closer. Not all the way.

Her brow furrowed. "But in the deadlands, I was already hurt *before* you healed me."

Her hand moved to her abdomen. Together, we touched the gauze, and the beading blood beneath it.

A mortal's wound.

I didn't have an answer, which frustrated me. I hated unknowns at the best of times. Now, when the fate of something so precious sat between their teeth, I couldn't tolerate them.

Mische flipped her hand to wind her fingers through mine, sensing my frustration. "Sometimes, magic is dancing to a tune that mortal ears can't hear."

"I'm not a mortal," I grumbled.

Her thumb ran over my hand—tracing my scars.

"I like your mortality," she said softly. "Don't wish it away."

Mische did not have to know that I had already signed away my mortality. And that price was nothing compared to hers.

{You will not miss it in the end,} the mask said dismissively, and I slammed my mental doors against it.

A wrinkle formed between Mische's brows.

"We can't stay here, Asar. I mean it. I know you came here to protect me, but—"

"Frustrating, isn't it, when someone forces help upon you against your will," I said pointedly.

"That's completely different."

"Because you're the missionary, so *you're* the only one allowed to make everyone else accept your sacrifices and then leave?"

"That's not f—"

"I think it's very fair. I know you."

Those three words left my lips with more weight than I'd expected. *I know you.*

Her scowl was so charming that I couldn't stop myself from kissing the wrinkle over her nose in an offering of penance.

"Forgive me," I said. "I can't help it."

"Can't help what?"

"Arguing with you so I can listen to you breathe."

She made a face. "You are such a sap, Warden. Such a sap."

But she was smiling, anyway.

"Shh." I pressed a finger to her lips. Then replaced it with my kiss.

"Stop talking," I whispered into her mouth, "and let me touch you."

A man only has so much self-control.

Her tongue slipped against mine. Her limbs wound around me. We melted back into each other like two rivers converging.

"Fine," she sighed dramatically, and I touched her, and touched her, and touched her.

And for a few more beautiful minutes, in my reverence, the voices were silent.

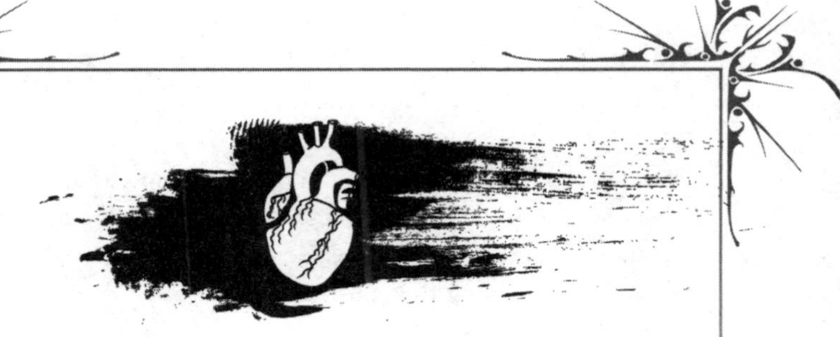

CHAPTER FORTY-NINE

Mische

I was now in a much better mood.

I loved feeling. Feeling was wonderful! Feeling Asar's skin, feeling his breath, feeling his cock inside me. Feeling him tense when he came and relax in the moments after. Feeling him breathe, long and slow, beside me when we dozed to sleep. Feeling his kisses when we awoke, and then feeling all of it again and again.

Now, I felt tired and sore, and I loved that, too. It was not the emptiness of wraith exhaustion—though I could sense that looming in the background. It was a very alive kind of tired, like I'd just run a long way. Or, maybe, had sex five times in one night.

Five! Really!

I sat up, wincing as my stitches stretched. Between the blood and the medicine, the wounds were now shallow, my vampire healing restored, though it would be some time before it was fully gone. I didn't mind. I liked the pain. I liked it the same way I liked the sore ache between my legs or the faint burn on my chin where Asar's stubble had scratched against it. I didn't even realize all the sensations I had been missing until they had returned to me, a precious gift I swore I'd never take for granted again.

I felt so alive.

And yet—

And yet, death still loomed over me.

Still, I could ignore that for a little while.

"I didn't know it could feel this way," I said.

"Hm?"

Asar looked half asleep. It occurred to me now that I couldn't remember the last time I'd seen him sleep. Yet, when his eyes met mine, a soft smile bloomed over his lips.

Gods, I could watch that smile forever.

"Sex," I said. "It's so . . ."

Asar waited expectantly. Eventually, I settled on, "Fun!"

A stifled laugh. "Fun," he repeated.

"You don't think it is?"

"Oh, it is. It's just not the word I was expecting you to use."

"What were you expecting?"

"Devastating. Transformative. Spiritual."

He was being sarcastic, but I wouldn't deny that with Asar, it was all those things, too.

He caught a stray curl between his thumb and forefinger. "It wasn't fun before?"

Now it was my turn to laugh.

Asar did not. "That shouldn't be a funny thought."

"Of course it wasn't fun. It was . . . you know, an offering."

As soon as the words came out of my mouth, I regretted them. His face hardened.

"You are not, never have been, and never will be an *offering,* Mische."

I was already laughing it off, already turning away. But he caught my hand.

"Look at me," he said.

There was no compulsion in the command. But I obeyed, anyway. Asar's stare was steady—and yet, so painfully gentle. He always had seen too much of me. Even on that very first night.

"You are not an offering. Not to Atroxus or any other god. Any of them would be lucky to kneel before you." He pressed his mouth to my bare shoulder, tongue briefly tasting skin. "As am I."

It was a more sobering thought than he meant it. Thoughts of gods led us to thoughts of ascension, and thoughts of ascension led us to thoughts of war, and thoughts of war led us to why we were here in the first place.

Asar pressed a kiss to my fingertips. "I see your thoughts turning."

"Mm." It was all I could manage to put into words.

"You're thinking about the House of Night?" he asked.

I let out another unhelpful, wordless noise, which was all the answer he needed. He kissed me again, this time on the back of my hand.

"The decision is yours," he said.

"We don't have many options, Asar."

What would we do, if we left? Go wander the seas or the forests, waiting to be captured or killed or gods knew what else? Sacrifice Asar's sanity to the mask and the eye in long-shot attempts to find the heart? He'd wielded them once and survived it, but I wasn't convinced he would be able to again.

My gaze traced the black-red marks that ran along his cheekbones, over the bridge of his nose, and circled his eyes. They were faint, but I still saw them every time I looked into his face. And though he tried to hide it, I was certain they were far from the only marks the mask had left on him.

I knew that Asar treasured time, because he knew how little of it I had. And so, I knew just how much of a sacrifice it was when he said, "We'll find another way if you want us to."

He genuinely meant it. Warmth suffused my chest at that.

But I let out a reluctant sigh.

"I think I know what we have to do."

"So THAT'S WHY you covered it," Asar said as I pulled the sheet off the mirror. "I had been wondering."

"I didn't wany any unwanted ghosts peeking at me." That close call in Ryvenhaal was enough to inspire caution.

"Understandable. Still, a shame. I would have enjoyed watching you from all available angles."

When I turned to the mirror, I startled slightly at my own reflection. My hair was a mess, my skin flushed. My mouth was slightly swollen, and the scabbed-over marks left by Asar's teeth dotted my throat and shoulder like little blackened flower petals. The sight made my thighs clench at the memory of his lips on my skin, and the exquisite, physical, mortal pain of his teeth.

I briefly considered dragging Asar back to bed. Just one more time.

Through the mirror, he returned my lingering stare.

I knew he was considering it, too.

Sun take me. What was wrong with me? I shook my head and adjusted my shirt to hide most of the bite marks, then returned my attention to my task.

It occurred to me that I'd never summoned Vincent. He always just seemed to turn up, usually when I didn't want him around. But now, the mirror showed me only our own reflections. I realized that since we'd arrived here, I barely saw or heard the ghosts, though I could sense their presence lingering like mice in the walls.

"Vincent?" I said, feeling a bit foolish. I leaned closer to the mirror, tapping on the glass. "Are you here?"

"You have finally listened to reason."

I jumped and whirled around. The voice was distant. Through the half-ajar washroom door, Vincent's ghostly face peered back through the mirror above the basin.

"Why are you over there?" I asked as I pushed the door open.

He looked irritated. "I don't get to choose."

His voice was weak, and even up close, sounded as if he were speaking across a great, windy distance. His form was fainter than I'd ever seen it, and sapped of color entirely.

"Are you alright?" I asked.

His lips thinned. "The underworld continues to decay. It has been . . . challenging here."

That word alone told me plenty.

I glanced at Asar over my shoulder. "You see him, too?" I asked. He nodded, visibly fascinated.

Vincent's hard gaze darted between us. He said something, but his words were too faint to hear.

I leaned closer. "What?"

He said, more clearly, "You finally came to the House of Night." Then his gaze flicked over me, feet to head. "You survived the forge. I'm pleased to see it."

Sun take me. Was that a hint of relief on his face? That was almost sweet.

"You told me that god blood could be used to find Alarus's heart," I said. "Do you still think that's true?"

"It is a part of a whole. I suspect it could be." His silver eyes settled on Asar. "If wielded by someone powerful enough."

"Find it how? Like . . . on a map?"

"You expect blood to point to a map?"

"Well, *no,* but—"

Vincent sighed. "You are Shadowborn. Have you conducted an anchor spell?"

I nodded. Asar had cast one to bind us together before our journey to the Descent. A straightforward way to magically link two objects or people.

Then it hit me. "You mean that you believe the blood could be used to find its other half. Like an advanced anchor spell."

Asar leaned forward, brow furrowed. "When I was in Ysria, Acaeja bound me to Mische as a way of opening a passage to her, through the spira. Could the blood be used to do this?"

I shot Asar a sharp look. The spira was not mortal magic. Asar had just used the eye and the mask to traverse it to save me. I didn't like that he was already so quickly talking about using it again.

Vincent considered this. "I had always been a better warrior than sorcerer. But perhaps. If one was capable of opening such a passage."

"You're talking about opening a door before you know where it will go," I said. "And using the blood would attract the attention of the gods."

If we hadn't already.

Maybe we were lucky enough that the protection of Nyaxia's territory shielded us, even temporarily, from Shiket and the White Pantheon—and even that seemed like more and more of a stretch lately. But Nyaxia surely had noticed Shiket's attack on the House of Shadow. She must know by now that we had taken her husband's crown.

So where was she?

This question hung heavily. Maybe she was distracted by something far worse than us. Or maybe we had even less time than we thought.

The look on Asar's face told me he was thinking this, too.

"The Nightborn palace has hallways that are underground," Vincent said. "We—I had conducted my more . . . divinely sensitive work there. It's as hidden from the eyes of the gods as one can be in Sivrinaj."

Still, my stomach twisted in unease. I had a reputation—earned, maybe—for being reckless. But there were some things I was just not willing to risk.

Vincent now looked past us, peered through the open door into the Nightborn palace. Even across such distance, I sensed a potent, sad longing. I wondered how much of it he could see, peering through from the underworld.

When he spoke again, his voice was distant, almost inaudible. "You have only one chance. We cannot waste it."

I stepped closer to the mirror, leaning over the basin, so I was staring right into his eyes.

"This is Oraya's home," I said. "Oraya's kingdom. I need to be able to trust you, because I can't gamble with her life."

A pained wince flickered over Vincent's face.

"Nor can I," he murmured. "It is far too precious."

And with the next wave of mist, he was gone.

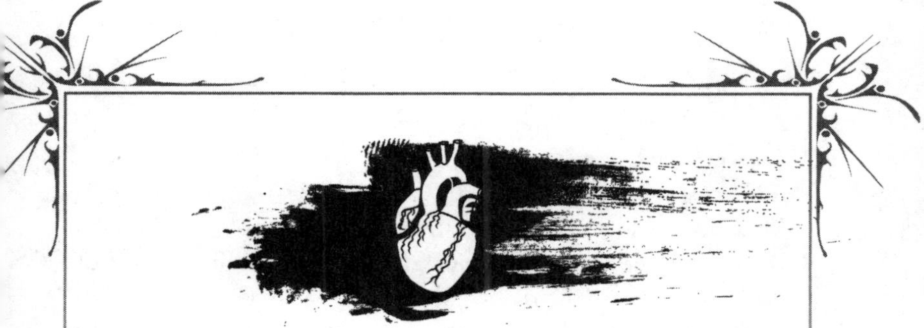

CHAPTER FIFTY

Mische

Raihn and Oraya sat across from us in the sitting room of my chambers. Raihn's arms were crossed over his chest, his face hard. Yet despite his expression, bordering on angry, his hurt radiated from him like the pain of an open wound.

I was so nervous that my entire body ached. If I needed any more confirmation that I was, indeed, still a wraith, the fact that I didn't vomit all over the carpet was proof enough.

When they'd first arrived, I had nervously introduced them to Asar just because I didn't know what else to do with myself, and Raihn had just snapped, "I know. We've met."

It was already off to a great start.

The clock *tick, tick, tick*ed. Raihn and Oraya waited. I was silent. Asar sat beside me, one hand on my knee. Luce curled up at my feet, having been returned to my bedchamber when Oraya and Raihn arrived. Now, she nuzzled my legs as if to remind me, *We're with you.*

The silence was getting awkward.

Oraya, at last, leaned forward. "Whatever you have to say, we're ready to hear it."

Just start at the beginning, Asar said into my mind.

But even that seemed insurmountable. What would that even sound like?

I was a bride of Atroxus.

I killed a god.

I shattered the sun.

I broke the underworld.

And by the way, I died.

That last one loomed the largest, heavy with dread. I could talk to Raihn and Oraya about ancient magic and grand divine wars. But I could not bear to see their faces when I told them of my death.

At my continued silence, Raihn stood with a huff of annoyance and began pacing.

For fuck's sake, say something, *Mische,* I told myself in a burst of frustration.

I blurted out, "I didn't write to you because I died."

Raihn stopped mid-step.

I could feel Asar giving me a bewildered look that said, *You're choosing to lead with* that*?*

I regretted it immediately.

Raihn's confusion soured. "Is that supposed to be some kind of fucking joke, Mish?"

Words poured out of me like a soggy mudslide. "No, but it's not as bad as it sounds. I'm alright. I mean, I'm alright for now, at least. It's not as bad as it was. I can even touch people now."

Sun fucking take me. Stop talking, Mische. Stop talking.

I closed my mouth. Then I sighed and lowered my hood.

Raihn and Oraya stared at me.

And I saw it, *felt* it, the moment they realized. Raihn's anger faded to terrible, wide-eyed shock. Oraya's lips parted.

I looked more alive than I had since coming back. So alive that maybe they didn't notice it before, when they were distracted by our surprise arrival, when they could have attributed my odd appearance to my fresh injuries. But now, they were looking for it. Now, they could see—sense—that something was not quite right about me.

Raihn sank slowly into his chair.

It was that look. The very look I'd been so desperate to avoid.

I wanted to curl up on the floor and die. Again. It would hurt more this time.

I gave them a weak smile and said what came most naturally: "I'm alright. I promise."

But I wasn't alright, and now they knew it.

Asar squeezed my knee.

"I think," he said, "that we should start from the beginning."

The beginning. The thought was staggering. The weight of all I'd left unsaid over nearly a century of friendship filled me with shame. I was about to cut myself open and show them a collection of failures.

But I opened my mouth anyway.

NO ONE EVEN asked questions. They all just listened. And the more I talked, the more the words just poured out of me. By the end, I was borderline manic, tripping over an onslaught that I didn't know how to stop.

"And now, we're here," I said. "With you. And that's—I think that's most of it. I mean, for now. There will definitely be more. I know it sounds unbelievable. And I know that—"

Gods above, I sounded ridiculous. I just couldn't make myself stop talking, because if I did, I knew that I'd have to listen to whatever they had to say. They were both so agonizingly quiet.

It's alright, Iliae, Asar said gently into my mind. *You can stop.*

I shut my mouth. Let out a shaky breath.

"So. Right. That's it."

No one moved. No one spoke.

"So this is you?" Oraya said at last, gesturing to the night sky. "*You* did that?"

I nodded.

"We saw it. The sun rising in the middle of the night, and then . . ." She splayed out her hands in a demonstration: *CRASH.*

To them, it must have looked like the end of the world.

Hell, maybe it had been. I supposed that was still to be seen.

Raihn's jaw was so tight that a muscle twitched in his cheek. His arms were crossed stiffly across his chest, like he was physically holding something back. My eyes drifted back to him every few seconds. I desperately wanted him to say something.

"It explains some things," Oraya said. She and Raihn exchanged a knowing, uneasy glance that made my stomach clench. "We've been having some unusual incidents over the last few months. Earthquakes. And these . . . I don't know what to call them. Creatures. We thought they were some kind of demon that we'd never seen before. There was another one today."

"Two," Raihn corrected.

Oraya winced. "Two. They're coming faster."

Wraiths. And if the Nightborn had thought they were demons, I could only imagine how terribly disfigured they must have been. I glanced at Asar, but he was staring at the night sky through the window with a blank, empty expression.

My brow furrowed. I nudged him.

He blinked and looked at me, and for a strange split second, there was no recognition in his eyes. But he recovered so quickly I questioned whether I'd seen it at all.

"The collapse of the underworld means that the dead are seeping through the other realms," he said. "You're seeing the effects."

"Vincent told me that the House of Night sits on a weak point of the veil," I said. It was reassuring that he'd been right about this. Made me trust him a little more.

At the mention of his name, Oraya's face went still, just as it had every other time. She hadn't reacted when I told her that he had helped me. I knew that it was because she couldn't let herself unlock that door.

Finally, Raihn spoke.

"So I take it, since you're finally deciding to tell us all this, that you've decided you'd like our help avoiding the end of the fucking world."

He was angry. He was *so* angry.

"Yes," Asar said. "If you're willing to offer it."

"What would you need?" Oraya asked.

I swallowed thickly.

Another difficult question. Another question to which I dreaded the answer.

"Is it true that you've been refining the blood of Alarus?" I asked.

Even now, I hoped they'd deny it. I had seen the way this power had been used to terrible ends during the Nightborn civil war. I'd seen what it had created of Simon, Raihn's rival.

But their silence was answer enough.

"You are." I couldn't keep the disappointment from my voice, even though I recognized the hypocrisy of it. Because here I was, next to Asar—trying to claim a power a thousand times more dangerous.

"We have too many enemies not to, Mische," Oraya said. "I won't be ashamed of leveraging what few advantages we have." Her gaze turned to the window, and the endless black skies beyond. "Especially if the gods are preparing for war now, too."

"Nyaxia never came to you?" I asked.

Again, an uneasy pause.

Then she said, "No. She didn't."

So it was as I'd feared in the House of Shadow. Even when preparing for her great war against the White Pantheon, Nyaxia had come to the Houses of Shadow and Blood to fight for her, but not the House of Night. If Nyaxia could not be bothered to ask the Nightborn for their help with a mission so sweeping, she probably wouldn't offer them her protection, either. Or worse, she'd give them her spite, instead.

"How can the blood help you?" Oraya asked.

"The theory is that we could use it to find the heart of Alarus," Asar said. "I could open a door into the spira and use the blood to direct it to the heart. We could do it here."

"Spira?"

"It's how gods travel," I said.

They did not seem to find this answer comforting.

"But you don't know where this thing is," Oraya said. "Or who could have it in their possession. It could open to anywhere."

"I'm not denying that it has risks," Asar said.

At last—at last—Raihn spoke. He leaned forward.

"So let me make sure I understand. You want us to create a magical god door to who-fucking-knows-where in our palace, wide open to who-fucking-knows-what, so that you can go through, grab the heart of the god of fucking death, and ascend to divinity." He gave Asar a pointed look. "You. The Wraith Warden."

Asar, always wonderful at reading a room, just said, "More or less."

"If you don't have the protection of a god, might as well make your own, right?" I said, in a too-cheerful attempt to break the tension.

It did not work.

"And what if you fail?" Raihn asked.

I opened my mouth, but I couldn't even bring myself to give voice to the worst possibilities. I was grateful when Asar answered instead.

"The underworld collapses," he said. "The souls of the dead no longer have anywhere to go, or are destroyed completely. The House of Night falls. So does much of the mortal realm."

Raihn's gaze fell to mine. "And you? What happens to you?"

I swallowed thickly. "I'll be gone." My voice was smaller than I'd intended. "Like the rest of the dead."

Asar's fingers squeezed mine, as if in steadfast reassurance: *It won't happen.*

Raihn glanced between us. Then to Oraya. Then back to us.

"It's all fucking madness," he said. "You must know that."

Asar let out a dry laugh. "Yes. I do."

But Raihn's eyes locked on mine.

"You had our help from the minute you got here," he said. "It was never a question, Mische. Not for a Mother-damned second."

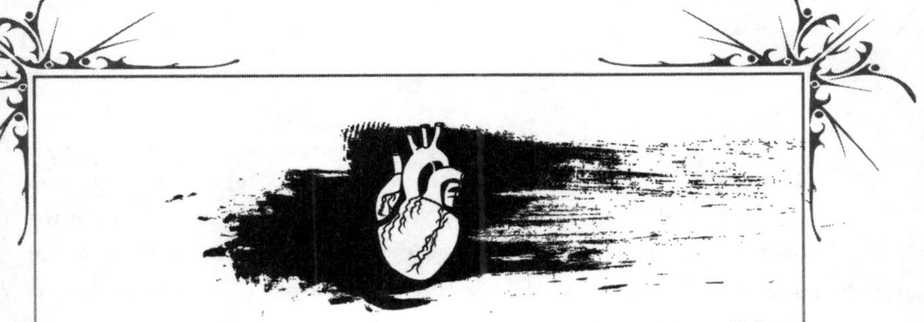

CHAPTER FIFTY-ONE

Mische

The gears ground into motion. We began our work of doing the impossible.

Oraya told us that they had been distilling the blood from the tiny particles remaining from Simon's body and the materials left behind from Vincent's work, with the help of Lilith, Vale's wife, who had apparently built up some knowledge of such things in her previous life. They carefully guarded what little they had, and in light of the recent earthquakes and wraith appearances in Sivrinaj, they had moved it farther from the city, to a location guarded to all but their closest inner circle. They sent word to Vale, who was already traveling, to retrieve it.

In the meantime, we had plenty of work to do. Necromancy was crafting a passage between worlds—opening a door through the spira was like that, but a thousand times more complicated. Asar and I would need to build a ritual circle capable of doing it.

But as we fell into planning and theorizing, I noticed Raihn quietly slip from the room.

I went after him.

"Raihn. Wait."

He stopped, peering at me over his shoulder.

"Just need some air." The corner of his mouth twitched into an almost-smile, and gods, I was grateful for that expression. "You coming?"

What kind of question was that?

THE TWO OF us went out into the hot night. After the cold damp of the House of Shadow and the downright freezing desolation of the deadlands, the House of Night's dry heat was almost stifling. Or maybe I just wasn't used to feeling temperature so acutely anymore. A small price to pay, I supposed.

Raihn and I wandered through the palace grounds. It was quiet out here. White marble paths wound through neatly trimmed gardens. The skyline of Sivrinaj glittered silver beneath the moonlight, a sea of smooth curves and delicate spires against the distant dunes.

We passed by an area that had been isolated with a series of makeshift metal gates. I paused. A hole had been torn through the marble path and the sandy ground beneath it. Though the crack was empty and dark now, I shivered when I passed by, the stench of the underworld at my nostrils.

"Unsettling, isn't it?" Raihn said.

"What came through this one?"

"I'm not sure if *people* is the right word."

Wraiths, then. Twisted wraiths. At least it wasn't souleaters, which would have been worse.

"We were able to put them down," he said, starting again to walk. "But they get a little more difficult every time."

"Asar and I can seal the cracks."

"They're quiet now."

"Right, for now. But not forever. Watch the human districts. The wraiths like humans best. More alive, I think. Asar and I can show Jesmine how to stop them more easily, too. It's not that hard once you know what to do . . ."

My voice trailed off. I felt Raihn's eyes boring into the side of my head.

"Why are you looking at me like that?"

"You just sound . . . different."

"Different?"

"Stronger."

A lump rose in my throat. I didn't feel stronger. And I didn't feel like I deserved the note of admiration in his voice.

We reached the garden hedges, and Raihn turned to me expectantly. When I recognized where we were, I groaned.

"Really?"

"I figured I'd take you to the last place I managed to force answers out of you."

This was the same place where I had told Raihn I would be leaving the House of Night. When he'd given me that stupid fucking puppy dog face and I'd felt like I was going to die on the spot.

This felt like a cruel and highly specific torture.

"Fine," I said, splaying my hands out. "I'm ready. Do it."

"Do what?"

"I don't know. Yell at me. Stomp around. Tell me what an idiot I am. I deserve it. Go ahead."

I was half joking. But the sadness on Raihn's face was so sharp it cut my heart open.

"Is that what you think this is? You think I brought you here, what, to scold you? You—You just told me that you died, Mische. *You died.*"

Gods, I felt his pain when he said those words. His grief, even though he was looking right at me. It devastated me.

I gave him a weak smile. "It's alright. I'm right here."

"It is not alright, Mische. It is not alright. *You fucking died.* And yes, a part of you is here. But the rest is . . . where? Down there? Like them?" He gestured to the crack in the distance.

I didn't like to think of myself that way. As a wraith. I rubbed my fingers together, as if to remind myself that they were now solid.

"In a way," I said quietly.

"Was that why you wouldn't let me look at you, in the House of Shadow? So I wouldn't see what you were?"

There was no accusation in his voice. Just genuine sadness.

I couldn't speak, so I nodded.

Somehow, his sadness actually intensified, and I felt it like a knife twisting. He sank onto a bench.

"Were you alone, when it happened?"

He was just torturing himself by asking this question.

I didn't like to think about those last moments. But now, I blinked and I was there again, lying in the ashes of Atroxus, Shiket's sword through my heart, listening to Asar's screams as they dragged him away.

"It didn't hurt," I said quietly. A comfort for him—*it's alright, I didn't suffer, you never have to worry about me.*

Even though it was a lie. No, I had been so far gone that I didn't feel Shiket's blade through my chest. But I did feel the ache of Asar's absence, the cold bite of my fingernails clawing for life.

Raihn sagged, his head in his hands. "Fuck, Mische."

I sat next to him.

"I didn't want you to know," I said. "Not about any of it."

"You never even told me about Atroxus. About what you were to him."

"I never wanted to talk about it."

"I'm sorry, Mische. I just—I am so sorry."

"You don't have to be sorry. You didn't do anything wrong."

He didn't believe me. And I understood that. *You didn't trust me,* he'd said to me. But it had never been about that.

"It's just . . ." I struggled to word it. "It's you and me, right?"

I found it so hard to explain my relationship with Raihn, sometimes. Even to myself. It always came back to those words: *It's you and me.*

And yet, Raihn nodded, like this made perfect sense to him, too.

I pulled my knees up to my chin, wrapping my arms around them.

"You kept it all from me, too, for such a long time. And then when you finally trusted me enough to tell me the truth about who you were, I—"

The shame now was unbearable. I thought of when Raihn had told me the truth about his Heir Mark and his past, on that terrible, tear-filled night.

And what did I do, after being entrusted with something so precious?

My eyes burned. "I forced you to do something you didn't want to do. I ran off and joined the Kejari and I—I manipulated you, not despite but *because* I knew how much you cared about me, and I knew you would do anything to protect me. And I thought by the time it killed me, it wouldn't even matter. Because you'd have what you really needed."

I knew how much that question had haunted him—*why, Mische? Why would you do it?* I knew that he would follow me into the Kejari to protect me, but I knew just as well that he always wondered what my end game had been. I'd always laughed it off. *I knew it would all work out,* I'd say. *That's faith!*

The truth was, no, I hadn't known it would all work out.

I had been ready to die to help Raihn become what I knew he could be. To *force* him to become what I knew he could be.

Now, this seemed so unforgivably cruel.

He shook his head. "You thought you were helping me."

"I did. But it doesn't matter, Raihn. It was wrong. And I'm sorry." Tears slithered down my cheeks. "I knew how badly you needed to know you could save someone. But the truth was, I needed to save someone, too. And I manipulated you because I was trying to fill that hole that—that Malach ripped out of me when he Turned me."

But when I blinked, it wasn't Malach I saw in the darkness. It was my own face, bearing down on Saescha, covered in her blood.

Even now, coward that I was, I couldn't share that with Raihn, either.

The tears just kept coming. I was sobbing now.

"And gods, what a tragedy that would've been. Because you're—you're so *good,* Raihn. You're so kind and nice and a really, really amazing cook and—and now you have Oraya and she's so perfect and you love her so much and you're such a good king and one day you're going to have such cute little winged babies and—"

"Ix's tits, *breathe,* Mish—"

"—and I never ever ever want to jeopardize any of that for you. Not *ever.*" I drew in a deep, shaky breath and let it out. "That's why I didn't tell you any of it. Not because I didn't feel safe to. Not because I don't trust you. But because you have earned such a good life. And I'm—"

"You are a part of that life. Not just a stepping stone to get to it."

He let out a long, rough sigh and pushed his hair back from his face.

"You and me, right?" he murmured. "Two fucked-up people getting through the worst of our Mother-damned lives together. We were just trying to survive. And I wouldn't have done it without you. That's just the truth of it."

I nodded and wiped my tears with the back of my hand.

Because he was right. We were just surviving for so long together. I'd lost everything. But when I met Raihn, there it was. Purpose. A reason to think, every day, *Well, I have to wake up again now, because what would he do without me?*

And I knew he had done the same for me.

"I think that we learned how to live a certain way to survive," I said. "And now we have to unlearn it."

Raihn laughed softly. "Maybe. Maybe so." He looked up at the sky. "I think the key to survival will be a little more complicated now than just you and me learning how to enable each other's madness."

I shuddered, even though the breeze was warm.

Raihn's gaze slipped back to me, his red eyes shining in the moonlight.

"Never think for a second, Mische, that you were the one who brought this upon us," he said quietly. "We're all just trying to do what we can to save who we can, all while the gods play games with us. But as long as we have to go up against them, I'll be damned lucky to do it with someone as fierce as you by my side."

I choked a laugh. "Fierce?"

But he was stone serious. "Yes, fierce. For nearly a century now I've seen you protect the people you love. That's ferocity."

I wasn't so sure that he was right. But gods, did it hurt to hear it—because I knew he believed it. I'd know it even without my Shadowborn magic, just by the way he looked at me.

I was so, so fucking lucky.

Before I could stop myself, I threw myself against him, wrapping him up in a hug. Gods, I had forgotten what it was like to hug Raihn. Like throwing yourself against a wall. But he wrapped his arms around me, enveloping me in a cocoon of warmth.

It made me think of the countless times he had hugged me after my nightmares, all those years ago. And in the same breath, it made me think of how different I was now.

We parted, and I stared up at the night sky.

Raihn's eyes slipped to me. "So. This Asar character."

I stiffened. "Mm-hmm?" I said, too casually.

"Just how hard have you fallen?"

"I don't know what you're—"

"For fuck's sake, Mish. That entire apartment reeked of sex."

My face heated. "Gods, *Raihn,*" I squeaked.

"And the man follows you around staring at you like you're a goddess. And when he came to us, when we all thought we were losing you . . ." His face darkened. "I know that look. Like his entire world was ending. No wonder the man is about to go rip apart the fabric of the universe for you."

"The apartment *did not* reek of sex," I repeated, because for some stupid reason, it was still the only thing I could think to say.

"Yes, it did. And good for you." He jabbed my arm with his elbow. "I don't want to think about it or hear about it, but I hope you had a great time."

"Oh gods, *stop*—" I gasped, burying my head in my hands.

"I know what it looks like when a man is gone. And he is so far gone for you."

I peeked through my fingers at Raihn, then lowered my hands. I couldn't stop the smile from pulling at my cheeks.

"He's just—I really—"

I kept reaching for words and coming up short.

Raihn's brows rose. "Are you actually *speechless*? Ix's tits. You must like him."

I thought of Asar, kneeling next to the broken gates of Morthryn, committed to his eternal watch. Asar, lying in bed beside Luce, lazily scratching her head. Asar, head bowed over the piano. Asar, head bowed over me.

Yes, I was speechless. Because what words existed to describe that?

I said, at last, "He makes me want a happy ending."

When I finally forced myself to look at Raihn, he was giving me a quiet, serious stare.

"Is that silly?" I said.

He shook his head. "No. It's not silly at all."

CHAPTER FIFTY-TWO

Asar

When Mische and Raihn left, Oraya watched me like a cat watches a bird flitting in the rafters. Her silver eyes were sharp as the blades she carried—even here, in the bowels of her own castle. One of them sat on the table between us, the carvings along its length glowing red.

Eventually, she spoke. "Raihn won't say it, but it needs to be said, so I will." She dug the tip of her blade into the table and leaned across it. "You're welcome here as long as Mische says you should be. But let's be clear. If you ever hurt her, in any sense, I will peel your skin off and make you eat it."

She said it like she was discussing the weather. It was probably the only time I'd had to suppress a smile at such a blatant threat.

And yet, I heard the echo of Gideon's voice: *You will ruin her.*

{No matter,} the mask whispered. *{There will always be others.}*

I barely disguised my flinch. The mask and the axe were in our chambers, locked away on the other side of the palace. And yet, their voices hadn't diminished.

"If I ever hurt her," I said, "I'd hand you the blade myself."

{How presumptuous of you,} the eye remarked, and I violently pushed it away.

Oraya seemed tentatively satisfied with this response. She sheathed her blade and leaned back in her chair.

"I'm glad we're aligned," she said. "Now we can get to work."

ORAYA AND RAIHN brought us to the rooms that Vincent had described in the basement, in what had once been the king's private, secret wing. The room we chose had at one time been a study of some kind, but we haphazardly pushed all the furniture out of it, piling it unceremoniously in the hall. Emptied, the room was so sadly unassuming—a scuffed tile floor, four brocade-papered walls that peeled slightly at the corners, a dangling spider or two.

{But imagine what it will be,} the eye murmured. *{A path to completion.}*

Mische introduced me to a woman named Lilith—the wife of their general who was retrieving the blood, and, apparently, the one responsible for most of their work distilling it. When she had pushed her wire glasses up her nose and stretched out her hand to grasp mine, she'd paused and cocked her head.

"Have we met?" she asked.

We hadn't, though she did seem oddly familiar. She was blunt, straightforward, and trusted the intelligence of her listener to keep up. All qualities I appreciated. I liked her immediately.

With the help of the Nightborn, Mische and I collected an assortment of notes and books and supplies—chalk and razors and paint. It would be a daunting spell, one that would require us to nest ritual circles atop ritual circles. By the time we were done, this entire room would be covered in spell work.

The thought, in some ways, excited me. In others, it unnerved me. It was hard not to remember that the last time I had done this, etched glyphs into every corner and crack of the mortal world in a desperate attempt to make the impossible possible, it had been in my townhouse in the city, over Ophelia's mutilated body.

Perhaps Mische knew what I was thinking, because she had touched my shoulder. "You aren't alone this time," she murmured.

{No,} the eye agreed.

{You are much more,} the mask said.

The hours—or was it days?—passed in a blur. We read and drew and read and drew. Once, I had found no greater delight than throwing myself headfirst into the magical unknown. Mische loved it as much as I did.

Yet, it also seemed to excite the mask and the eye. They were wrapped up and locked away, and I never touched or even looked at them. But it didn't seem to matter how physically close they were. Their voices trailed me like the presence of hungry wraiths. And in the face of this task, they were hungrier than ever. We were now conducting the magic of gods, not mortals. All to find their lost kin. They made no secret of just how pleased they were with this idea.

Before long, their voices and my own became inextricable. Sometimes I would blink to find that minutes had slipped away.

Now, with the room half covered, I etched a fresh row of glyphs into the wood baseboard.

{You are moving too slowly,} the mask complained. *{If you were on your own, it would be faster.}*

{Your time to seize the heart is short,} the eye agreed. *{You have none to waste.}*

I might move faster if they were less distracting.

{We are no distraction,} the eye said. *{We are your greatest asset. It is foolish of you to deny that.}*

{You should simply claim the blood yourself,} the mask said. *{You are capable of it. Take it and use it and this will all be over faster. Why the need for so much secrecy? Let the gods come. It will only mean you reach ascension faster.}*

My mind wandered to this terrible scenario—in which Nyaxia or Shiket came to the House of Night, unleashing their wrath upon it.

The eye peered into this possibility with indifference. *{Kingdoms have always fallen. Kingdoms have always risen. Gods understand this.}*

Stop talking, I commanded them.

{You do not truly want that. You need us. You would not be able to conduct this ritual without us.}

The chalk cracked in my grip. I stared at the wall, covered in glyphs. They blurred and danced in front of my eyes. I found myself questioning how I'd even drawn some of them—had I ever seen them before?

{You cannot become a god with merely the fallible knowledge of a mortal,} the eye said. *{You must see beyond that.}*

I glanced across the room at Mische. She reminded me of a cat, contorting herself into the most bizarre positions as she worked—drawing glyphs upside down, reading while dangling over the edge of the table, fingers drumming and toes tapping and eyes shining. She hummed and muttered and gasped with satisfied delight, even when there was no one there to listen to her. Now, she lay on her stomach, ankles linked, books spread around her.

Perhaps the only person I'd ever met who reveled in finding another magical problem to solve as much as I did. I wanted to watch her forever.

{It is an embarrassment to be doing this work in the basement of a mortal king,} the mask grumbled.

I eyed her throat, then the spot of skin barely visible under the silky neckline of her blouse, where I could still see the marks of my teeth.

Then I turned back to the glyphs and tried to focus.

{You could take this place for yourself, if you wished,} the eye said. *{There are weaknesses everywhere. It would simply be a matter of—}*

Enough!

The chalk snapped in my hand and rolled across the floor.

Mische looked up.

"Everything alright?" she said.

Her neckline slipped lower as she sat up, dipping between her breasts. The silk was so light that it revealed the pert shape of her nipples.

In the back of my head, the eye continued theorizing about how one might best conquer the Nightborn palace.

I stood up abruptly and went to the open closet. "Come here," I snapped.

Mische stood and followed, concerned. "What?"

She stepped into the closet. It was small, lined with several shelves of boxes and discarded books that no one seemed to have touched in years.

"What are you—" she started.

I whirled around and captured her mouth in a kiss.

She let out a delightful squeak of surprise, then, ever the good sport, folded against me. I pushed her against the shelves, earning a creak of wood and cascade of dust. My hands were already sliding under her shirt, relishing soft skin, taut muscle, finding the full swell of her breasts. She perched against a shelf and her legs folded around me, grinding against my length.

I treasured the merciful wave of distinctly mortal pleasure.

"Warden," she gasped in mock outrage. "They'll be back any minute."

I kicked the door closed with my heel.

"I don't care," I murmured. Her teeth skimmed my throat, pain soothed with a brush of her tongue. Her fingernails clawed at my back. My hand slipped down her trousers and her body clenched when I found her core.

"I guess I'll just have to be *so* quiet," she whispered against my shoulder.

I pulled away from her. Spun her around. Yanked down her trousers, revealing that full, perfect backside, and bent her over the shelves.

I leaned over her, kissing her cheek, nibbling her earlobe.

"Don't," I said.

And when she spread her legs for me, when I pushed into her, she obeyed.

At last, I did not hear the voices at all.

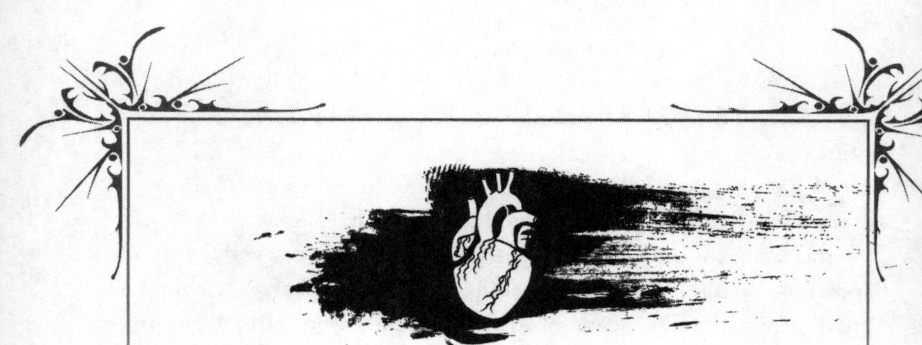

CHAPTER FIFTY-THREE

Mische

"Drink," Oraya said. "You're not going to be helping anyone if you're keeling over by the time we're ready to do this thing."

She held out a glass of blood to me. I stared at it, blinking, before taking it. It hadn't even occurred to me to drink, and it hadn't occurred to me that Oraya would notice.

I took a sip and ducked away to hide my face of disgust. Gods, that tasted *awful*. I subtly spit it back into the cup and set it down, careful not to let her see.

I craved Asar's blood, but nothing else. Still, I didn't need to give Oraya any reminders of how dead I was.

She took a sip from her glass—more wine than blood, a testament to her human tastes—and set it down on the desk. We were in one of the offices in Vincent's private wing, retrieving more supplies.

We stared down at the desk, covered in books and paper.

Oraya was silent for a long, long moment. I sensed the grief roll over her like a slow fog, quiet and deep.

"They must have done some incredible things together," she murmured.

Vincent and Alana—her mother.

"I think about it all the time," she said. "More, now. It's still hard for me to imagine him doing all of it. Especially with her." Oraya's eyes, bright silver, slipped to me. "He really told you about all of this?"

I carefully set down the book I was holding.

I'd been waiting for this. When I had first told her about Vincent, Oraya had been painfully silent. But I knew it wasn't for lack of questions. It was because she had too many of them.

"He did."

"And led you through the underworld."

"I wouldn't have made it out without him."

She scoffed and shook her head. "What was that like? Traipsing around the underworld with the great Nightborn King Vincent?"

"It was . . . surreal. He wasn't very good company, and he didn't exactly seem happy to be doing it. I don't think he likes me very much. There was a lot of . . ."

I made a stoney, angry face, which made Oraya choke a laugh.

"Oh, I know that one."

But that laugh quickly died.

"I still keep thinking about it," she said. "I don't know why he would do this. Especially if it meant helping you."

Because I was Raihn's friend. And Nightborn kings were notoriously petty. They weren't exactly known for their selflessness.

"I don't entirely understand it myself," I said. "But I think—I think maybe it was just the truth. That he wants to help the House of Night."

Oraya was silent. I knew what she was thinking. She took another sip of wine.

"What else did he say?" she asked.

I knew the real question: *Did he say he was sorry?*

I felt how desperately she wanted that closure. And I so wished I could give it to her.

I said nothing, and that was answer enough for her. She let out another laugh, this one a little more choked up than the last.

"So fucking pathetic," she muttered. "I told myself that I never needed his apology. I even believe it, most of the time."

"It's not pathetic."

"It's a little pathetic. Every time I think I'm finished with it . . ." She motioned to her eyes. The tears on her fingertips.

"Grief has a way of sanding down all the complicated parts of a person in the eyes of the living. It freezes them to a single moment."

I thought of Saescha, kneeling near Atroxus. Saescha, before I sank my teeth into her throat. Saescha, beside me as I walked into hell itself—the hell that would swallow her forever.

"But the truth is that the dead are just as complicated and broken as the living," I said. "Maybe even more so, sometimes. Vincent's death was not going to make him the father he should have been for you in life. It just makes it easier to dream it could."

Her expression flickered. "I know."

"And even if he had, he's not entitled to your forgiveness. Nothing he could do or say now erases the past."

"No," she agreed. "But it's . . . it's something, at least."

She wiped a stray tear and collected herself. I watched her tuck her vulnerability back behind the armor of a Nightborn queen. And gods, what a queen she was.

"You have a home here, if you want it," she said softly. "I hope you always know that."

I looked out the window. Silver dunes rolling under the moonlight, the sky so deep it verged on purple, the twinkling lights of Sivrinaj. Wouldn't be such a terrible view to wake up to every night.

"He could come, too, if that's what you wanted," she said. "It probably would be useful to have a Shadowborn around, if things are about to get as . . . complicated as you say they are. We could give you an apartment on the palace grounds. Or a house outside of it, if you'd prefer the privacy. Dog is welcome, too, of course."

It was an easy dream to slip into—Asar and I as members of the Nightborn court. Luce galloping through dunes and chasing nightwolves and snuggling with us before the fire. Asar and Lilith losing themselves in books and study for hours on end. Raihn and I dragging Oraya and Asar off to shitty pubs. And even when the hard times came—because the hard times would, inevitably, come—we could face them together.

But some dreams felt too sweet for reality. And this one didn't feel quite right, even if it meant so much that Oraya wanted it at all.

I took her hand. After all this time, it still felt like a triumph when she squeezed it instead of pulling away.

"Thank you," I said.

She gave me a smirk. "That's a *no* if I've ever heard one."

I laughed and opened my mouth to respond.

But before I could, I doubled over, hands over my ears.

It was more than a sound. It clawed through me from the inside out.

Someone was saying my name, and it took me a minute to realize that it was Oraya, who was leaning over me, hand on my shoulder, brow furrowed.

She wasn't reacting to the sound at all.

"What's wrong?" she was saying. "What happened?"

I frowned up at her, confused.

"You don't hear—"

The sound came again, louder, closer.

It sounded like a million screams wrapped up in one single cacophonous roar. It sounded like a distillation of eons of pain.

And then, there was a deafening shatter.

I tasted Oraya's blood, fresh and mortal. I tasted my own, thin and weak.

The wall of windows had shattered, pelting us with countless shards of glass.

I looked up to see that the room had gone dark, all the candles snuffed out as if by a single great breath of a cruel god. I saw the dead in the shadows that poured into the room, so many of them I couldn't make any single face out through the sea of agonized features.

Except one, flickering in and out:

Get her away! Vincent roared. *Get her away—*

The floor quaked.

I realized what was happening too late. I leapt to my feet and grabbed Oraya.

"Move!" I screamed.

The floor burst open beneath us.

And the monster that tore free put the horrors of the underworld to shame.

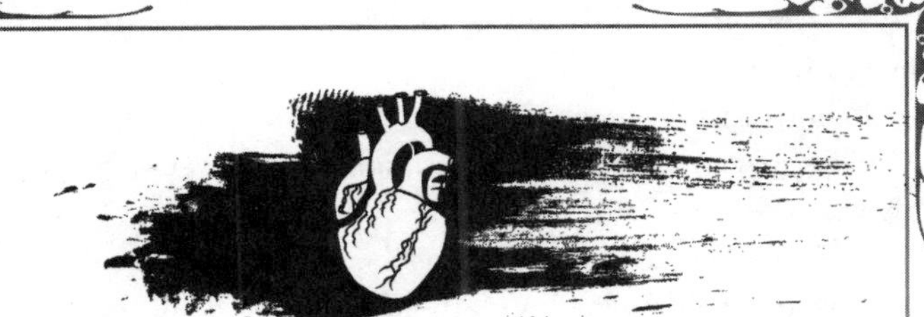

CHAPTER FIFTY-FOUR

Asar

Curious, that in a lifetime of researching magical artifacts, the thing that no one told you was that they *never stopped talking*.

The chatter of the eye and the mask had become a constant hum. And yet, the further I fell into my work, the easier it became to let them guide me. After some time, my hand was moving of its own accord. I was no longer making conscious decisions with every stroke of ink or chalk or razor's edge.

Once their presence was no longer unsettling, it became oddly euphoric. Natural. Each whisper pushed me further, unlocking doors I'd never even known existed.

{This way,} the eye would murmur, placing one stroke.

{Over here,} the mask would add, drawing my attention to another.

Time ceased to exist. When Mische went with Oraya, leaving me alone in the room, I could fall into it. Her presence tethered me to the land of mortals. Alone, there was no one but me, the voices, and my work.

I was working quickly now, not even hesitating to think. There was no need to think when I felt my next stroke so innately.

Distantly, I felt the strain in the world beneath this one. Like stitches stretching, preparing to snap.

This observation flitted by like leaves in the wind. Present, but insignificant.

I continued my work.

The pressure increased. I felt something crack. Somewhere, far away, a wail rang out.

{It is of no consequence,} the mask said dismissively.

Perhaps if I'd turned my attention to it, I could have done something. Perhaps I could have stopped the fracture before it grew.

But I didn't.

I kept going.

{A little further,} the eye urged.

I barely noticed that behind me, Luce barked frantically.

That upstairs, people were screaming.

I kept working.

And finally—finally—Luce grabbed my wrist and yanked it from the wall.

My chalk fell to the floor. A sudden burst of rage at the distraction had me whirling to her, a rebuke already halfway up my throat.

"Why are you interrupting—"

But then I froze.

Luce ran back and forth in front of me, whimpering and barking. *Hurry, hurry, go, go—*

And then, everything that had fallen beneath a frosted haze, as if I'd been looking into another distant world, crashed over me.

The screams. The pounding steps upstairs. The slight tremble to the ground under my feet. And the wound in the world beneath it, the one connected to the piece of me that belonged to the underworld itself.

{I told you, it is inconsequential,} the mask said.

No. No, it was not. This was a crack through the veil itself. Deeper than any other I'd ever witnessed.

Then the scream came.

It was the most vicious, horrific sound. It reminded me of the way Ophelia had screamed when I attempted to bring her back—that pure agony, amplified a million times over.

Luce let out a vicious snarl, all her hair going upright, shadows pouring from her lithe body.

Mische.

I bolted out of the room, Luce at my heels. In the hall, Raihn was stumbling from another office.

"What the hell was—"

"Where are they?" I barked. *"Where are they?"*

The seriousness of our situation settled over Raihn's face.

"They went upstairs—" he started.

Before he could finish, the floor split.

I grabbed his arm and yanked him back against the wall just in time. The crack slithered like a great serpent across the floor, shattering thousand-year-old mosaic. Darkness poured from it, and if one looked closely enough, they took on the shape of reaching hands.

Please, they begged. *Help us. Help us—*

Raihn spat a curse. A great crash rang out from above us, and my heart went frigid cold.

Raihn's eyes locked with mine, an unspoken, terrible understanding slotting into place. He thrust a Nightborn sword into my grasp, and then we were running for the stairs.

My sword was sweaty in my hand. It was fine Nightborn craftsmanship. But after I had wielded the axe that had killed a god and the mask that had crowned him, it seemed like nothing but a pathetic piece of metal. Spiderweb cracks crawled over the walls, the stairs, the floor, as Raihn and I sprinted upstairs. His wings, red-black, unfurled with a smooth leap, and he tore ahead of me, his blade drawn.

We reached the top of the stairs, and Raihn went flying backward, nearly toppling me over.

"Ix's fucking—" he started, but hit the wall hard before he could finish the curse.

Fear settled over me.

True fear.

It had been a long time since I had been afraid of the creations of the underworld. Even at its most terrible, it was my territory—I knew its dangers the way I knew the darkest parts of my own soul.

This was a horror beyond them all. A being that should not exist, not even in the bowels of hell.

A souleater, I thought at first—some new evolution of one, forced to the surface by the collapse of its home. But no, it was more than that. Souleaters didn't scream into my mind the way that this thing did, in a tangle of wordless pleas that drowned out the shouts and screams of the Nightborn warriors. Souleaters did not reek of pain, because the wraiths they consumed simply ceased to be—an unfair end, but at least it was a painless one.

No, whatever beings this thing had consumed were still alive. Hands and limbs reached from a sleek black body, ghostly silhouettes of countless dead screaming in unison for their release. A strange gold shape clung to its head, flickering in and out of view with every lurching movement, and it took a moment for me to realize what it was:

A skull.

This thing had eaten a guardian.

A souleater, guardian, and countless wraiths, all in one.

It was horrifying. It was a distillation of everything that should not be.

It crashed through the glass wall of the Nightborn ballroom, roaring. Its face was a collection of smashed-together features—eyes too wide and too close together, mouth open and spewing blood.

Its body bled into the darkness around it, which made it difficult to say how big it was. But it rose up nearly to the ceiling, straddling the massive crack that had opened across the ballroom, dragging out into the gardens outside and the city beyond it.

Oraya was pushing herself up from the ground, dark red blood smearing the floor. And before her, protecting her friend even as she stared down that horrifying gaping maw, was Mische.

I swept into action.

Raihn and I moved at the same time. I dove for Mische, yanking her out of the way, while Raihn swept in beside Oraya.

The creature let out a chilling wail. *Pl-pl-pleaaaaaa—*

As it dove for us, I brought my sword down.

The beast squealed and jerked backward. Mische and I landed

together in a heap. I pushed myself up over her, doing a quick sweep for injuries.

"That thing—I saw—I felt—" she stammered.

She couldn't get the words out, but I knew what she meant. She felt it as I did. This wasn't a fissure. This was *collapse*.

"Move," I barked, and pushed her out of the way as the beast let out another wail and came down upon us.

The crack in the floor widened, more darkness pouring from it. One of the Nightborn soldiers tumbled into its depths, its wing pierced by a vicious slap of the creature's barbed tail.

Raihn and Oraya, who had recovered despite a gaping wound in her side, now soared through the air, circling the beast, their weapons bared. Both were impressive—clearly god-touched. But no blessed weapon would do much against this thing.

Shadows gushed up from the opening in the floor, feeding the creature like a vampire sucking prey dry.

I grabbed Mische's hand as I started to stand. Something wasn't quite right with the touch. I frowned down at her—at the shadows that seemed to collect around her body—

But Mische was already scrambling to her feet, shrugging me off.

"We have to close it," she said.

She was right. As long as the crack remained open, the creature would draw upon it—and goddess knew what else would come through in the meantime. But the gravity of this task momentarily stunned me. This was bigger than what we'd done in the deadlands, and unlike the gates in Morthryn, we had no existing spell work to build from.

{Let it go,} the eye said, indifferent. *{You will be gone before any of it matters, anyway.}*

This thought filled me with defiant rage.

No. I wouldn't.

I looked down at my hands. I didn't have the mask or the eye, no. I didn't even have ink or chalk or a razor blade. But I had something of some value, supposedly.

I drew my blade across my palm, opening a line of shimmering black-red.

Mische understood what I was doing right away. She grabbed the blade and did the same to her own hand, and I knew there was no point in trying to stop her.

Above, Raihn and Oraya dove and dipped through the air, dodging the beast's attempts to grab at them. Seizing upon their distraction, Mische and I painted glyphs at the edges of the crack, my blood and hers smeared together.

How many? she asked.

Her voice was weak. My head was pounding. Another Nightborn guard fell, and another.

The truth was, I didn't know. All I knew was, we hadn't painted enough yet.

We hurried our way down the edges of the fissure, dodging reaching hands and grasping claws.

One glyph. Two, Four. Six. Ten. Twelve.

More? Mische asked.

It grew harder and harder to hear Mische's voice in my mind over the desperate pleas of the dead. We were running out of time.

Two more, I said.

It was a gamble. If we hadn't laid down enough, the entire thing would unravel when we tried to pull it closed, like the snap of an overstretched sewing thread. But bodies rained down around us. The wails of the wraiths were growing unbearable. Mische and I danced over more cracks, and more, and more, opening beneath our feet.

{It is not enough,} the eye hummed, bored.

It has to be enough, I snapped in response.

Behind me, Oraya let out a bloodthirsty roar. A blur of dark red smeared at the edge of my vision. *CRASH,* as Raihn went careening into the marble pillar.

It was only now, my focus so singularly narrowed to the spell I was attempting to weave, that I realized all the Nightborn guards had fallen. Luce dove out from behind Mische, snarling and roaring the battle cry of a much bigger beast, and the souleater—the not-souleater—smacked her away as if she was nothing.

It took every shred of my self-control not to drop what I was doing and run to her.

Almost there, Dawndrinker, I said to Mische.

She began her last glyph.

The beast had run out of distractions. Now, a cold shadow fell over us.

I could feel its presence, even though I couldn't look up.

"Shit," Mische whispered under her breath, even as she didn't stop painting. "Shit, shit, shit."

The creature's warpath stilled, and it stared down at us, as if we were too interesting to bat aside as it had a dozen Nightborn warriors.

Slowly,

Slowly,

Slowly, it lowered itself, its grotesque face staring into ours.

The wave of voices rolled over us.

Help me—

It hurts—

I don't understand—

What's happening—

—not supposed to be here—

I had looked into the mouth of a souleater many times before, and even so, staring into the face of pure nothingness never grew any less unnerving.

But this was not a souleater. It was so much worse.

The creature's mouth opened, and opened, and opened, and within it, a morass of souls wriggled and writhed.

Hundreds of screams, from hundreds of fractured souls, partially digested, stitched together in ways that did not make sense—all of them begging for mercy.

And from within that morass, a single face appeared. A small hand reached out. An echo of a fragmented memory reverberated through us.

—name is Celie—

—what a pretty name—

—lead you to safety—

—you're safe, you're safe, you're—

Mische's horror was sharp and quick. Mine was the slow rising of a cursed dawn.

The little girl was barely recognizable. Her face was distorted, features rearranged. Her body was entangled with countless others. But that little hand still reached for us, just as it had out in the deadlands.

I had known. I had known she could follow us.

I had led this thing to us. Carved the path that it followed.

Mische's wide, horrified eyes snapped to me.

Cut her out, she demanded. *We have to get her out.*

But there was no way to get her out. She was inextricably bound into the fabric of the monster she had been made.

I shook my head. Grief spasmed across Mische's face.

No, she said.

The beast opened its mouth and drew in a great gasp. I felt my soul clinging to the inside of my bones to avoid getting sucked right up with it.

"Now, Mische!" I roared, and thrust all my remaining strength into the spell we had woven.

I felt her magic rise up to meet mine, another half of the whole, tainted with the agony of her grief.

And together, we pulled, pulled, *pulled—*

The open wound stitched closed.

The creature lurched, spasmed, reared back, caught in between the closing jaws of the door we'd wrenched back together. It tried to escape it, but I reached out with what little magic I had left and tethered it to us, sucking it back in.

The last thing I heard was a little voice:

—name is Celie—

—safe now—

A deafening wail, as the door slammed closed.

And then silence.

I sank to the ground, pressing my forehead to the blood-slicked tile. Then I dragged myself upright again, crawling to Mische, who was lying in a heap. She stared down into the fissure, now empty.

The beast was gone.

But I could feel the underworld groaning beneath us. I could feel the splinters jutting up. This wasn't just one crack. The collapse had been set in motion.

The Nightborn landed heavily beside us, one after the other. Oraya pressed her palms to her knees. "Holy fucking hell," Raihn ground out.

The world was spinning. Or maybe it just felt like that because the scale of the destruction that surrounded us was so severe. The ballroom had collapsed. The cracks, which still pulsed with dark purple shadow, ran all the way out the castle doors—out into the gardens, and then the city beyond.

I cursed at that sight.

Sivrinaj was split in two. The rifts struck like lightning down the hill to the city, plumes of purple and black gasping from between pristine domes of smooth white, then gathering in the blocky distant shapes of the human districts on the outskirts of the city. One ornate, tall building groaned in the aftermath of its destruction, having been split straight down the center, shadows puffing from the opening like a grotesque chimney. Echoes of distant screams ricocheted between buildings.

For a few long seconds, we were silent, as the horror of what we were seeing dawned on us. Mische's eyes met mine, and though she didn't speak, I heard her: *We did this.*

But there was no time to wallow. Oraya spread her wings again, shouting to the slew of Nightborn guards who had been alerted by the battle. "Get to the city," she commanded. "Find whatever else is out there."

I pushed to my feet, grabbing my sword in one hand and helping Mische up with the other.

"We can fix it," she blurted out.

The note of desperation in her voice twisted in my heart. After everything, she still so badly wanted it to be true.

I started to move, then stopped mid-step. A puff of shimmering smoke blurred my eyesight, and my gaze trailed down.

I took Mische's hand and lifted it between us.

It was . . . smoking. Puffs of dusky light peeled from it, trailing from her like wet paint in rain.

{She belongs to the underworld,} the eye said. *{And the underworld is falling, now.}*

My heart clenched.

Enough, I snapped at it.

{I speak only the truth,} the eye said simply, before at last falling silent.

I pulled Mische's hand tight against mine. She felt solid, still. But she smelled like death.

I looked out over the city of Sivrinaj, broken with the infected wounds of the underworld bubbling up to the surface.

I could have sworn I heard it: a million invisible souls, calling out for someone.

Someone who had already failed them.

THE NEXT HOURS passed in a bloodstained smear. There had been nearly half a dozen souleaters that had crawled through the streets of Sivrinaj. Though none of them were quite as twistedly deformed as the creature that had come up in the castle, they still managed to rip destruction through the city and claim several dozen casualties by the time we managed to put them down. Mische and I closed the fissures the best we could, but I could feel the underworld groaning and straining against the tenuous spell work. It would not last for long.

At the last of the rifts, I leaned against a broken beam in exhaustion, pressing my forehead to the scorched wood and closing my eyes.

—help us—

—safe here—

—you promised—

"—it hold?"

I only caught the edge of Raihn's question. I opened my eyes.

"How long will it hold?" he repeated.

Behind him, Oraya picked through the rubble with Mische, putting out the last of the fires.

I looked at the city. The crack. The glyphs, already growing dim.

It was a tattered bandage on a severed arm.

No, worse—a bandage on a corpse. They were already damned.

I only said, "Not long enough."

My gaze fell to Mische. Mische, whose soul was drifting from her in an elegant plume into the sky.

Not long enough.

I said, "We need to do the ritual immediately. The minute that your general returns."

And then pray it would take us to the heart. Pray the heart would allow me to ascend. Pray ascension would allow me to fix the underworld before it fully collapsed. Pray that the underworld would let me save her.

{Gods have no need to pray,} the mask scoffed.

Raihn and Oraya exchanged a glance. Then, Oraya said to Jesmine, "Tell Vale to get his ass back here now. We're out of time."

CHAPTER FIFTY-FIVE

Mische

We had hours left until the end of it all. Asar and I worked and worked and worked until there was nothing left to do, then returned to the basement and reassessed the final pieces of our glyphs. A crack had spread straight through the center of the room, where the glyphs spiraled into a circle. The light that pulsed within it—shades of purple and red and black—looked eerily similar to the shade of Asar's scars.

I felt . . . *tired* wasn't the word. I felt *far away*. A hum thrummed in the back of my head, so loud it made it difficult to hear when people were talking to me. Asar, I knew, was feeling it, too. Too often I'd catch him staring off into space, face blank, until I pulled him back.

We fixed the final glyphs. They were rushed and hurried compared to the first sets, their shape crafted on guesswork rather than knowledge.

Faith, I corrected myself. Not guesses. *Faith.*

Eventually, Raihn heaved a sigh and sank into a rickety chair that barely held his weight. "Vale will be here in a few hours. You two look like shit. Rest a little before you try to save the world."

So, reluctantly, we returned to our chambers. Luce dragged herself to the sitting room and collapsed in front of the fireplace, asleep before she hit the ground. I went to the washroom and splashed water on my face. I stared at myself in the mirror. Wisps of smoke rolled from my skin.

Raihn was right. I did look like shit.

I looked dead.

I *felt* dead.

I left the washroom to see Asar perched at the edge of the bed, back straight, hands folded in his lap. His eyes were wide open, but blank, as if he was looking straight through the walls and sky and earth into whatever great unknowns lay beyond.

I touched his shoulder. His gaze flicked to me. For a moment, he looked confused—as if he wasn't sure why I was speaking to him—before his face flooded with recognition, and he was my Asar again.

I swallowed a wave of terror at that. How distant he had become.

I collapsed beside him on the bed. His hand fell to my back immediately, like he'd just been waiting to touch me again.

I squeezed my eyes shut and tried not to see the monsters in the darkness.

That little girl. Reaching for me. Just like Saescha had.

Gods fucking damn it.

I could feel Asar's hurt, too. Just as strong as mine.

"Stupid," he muttered beneath his breath. "*Naive.* I should have known she would follow. Should have known that I'd be creating a path right back to us, when I brought you here, and that it would mean—"

He bit down on the words, swallowed them like bitter liquor.

Silence. The hard truth sank in.

The girl had followed us, just as Asar knew she would. His use of the spira had opened a path right to the House of Night, and the monster the girl had become had followed, tearing through the veil all the way. The underworld was on its way to collapse either way. But the fact that it was happening here, and now—that was our fault.

All from our hope. Our hope that we could save this one child. This one innocent soul.

And now, it was all collapsing beneath us.

The guilt sickened me.

I sat up and laid my head against his shoulder. His arm fell around my body, like a boat tethering to shore.

"I'm sorry, Mische," he murmured.

For one child he couldn't save. For the destruction of my friend's home. For so much more.

"I was arrogant," he went on. "I thought I could help something. I thought—"

"Hush with that." I straightened and put my hands on either side of his face, tilting it to me. "There's still the future. That's why we're doing this, Warden. I still believe what I told you in the Descent. You make things better."

He flinched at this. Like it was physically painful to hear. And I knew he wanted to argue. I could feel the words right under the surface: *That is not true.*

"We can't change what we've done in the past," I said. "But there's still a whole damned future out there waiting. You and me. We're in this together. I need you to believe in this with me. You can do a lot of good in this world, Asar Voldari. Don't you dare give up on it now, when it needs you most."

I took in his face. The scars. The pulsing white glow of his left eye, the deep, rich brown of his right. The inflamed lines of purple that still traced the shape of the mask over his face, like infected wounds.

"Tell me you understand," I commanded.

Tell me. Tell me. Tell me.

His eyes crinkled with an almost-smile. "I understand, Dawndrinker."

"And swear to me that you won't let it take more than you offer it." This next one spilled out before I could stop it. "If we do this. Promise me you won't let it take you away."

There was no compulsion in this command. Because I wanted his oath to be true—even though I knew, in this moment, that it was a promise he could not make.

He was silent. Then he took my hands in his, pressing my fingertips to his lips. "I will make that promise if you make the same one."

Like the one I asked of him, it was a promise I could not make. Already, I could feel the underworld dragging me back down. But I had already borne the marks of so many pretty lies. What was one more?

Past the lump in my throat, I choked out, "Deal."

He smiled. "Deal."

I didn't feel better. I didn't feel better at all.

I leaned against him again. We sat together, nothing more to say. But then, I spotted a shape across the room.

My heart jumped, eager for the distraction—even if this one felt like it came from another life. I straightened abruptly. "*Oh!* I'd forgotten!"

I leapt up and went across the room. A smile tugged at my cheeks. Apparently I was really, really desperate for distraction, because the joy that I felt upon seeing this was disproportionate. It leaned in the corner of the room, wrapped up in cloth.

"What is that?" Asar asked.

"It's . . . it feels a little silly now." The thing was heavier than I expected it to be, or maybe I was weaker. I staggered slightly under its weight.

Asar half rose. "Goddess's sake, woman, what are you—"

"It's for you. And you know, if we're all about to die, I figure . . . you should have it, shouldn't you?"

I dragged the object across the room, gracelessly laid it against the bed, and unbuttoned the case. When I slid the fabric free, I splayed out my hands.

"Behold!"

Asar stared at it.

His silence was deafening.

My smile faltered.

"It's a—"

"I know what it is."

"You said you wanted one. When we were walking through the Descent."

"I recall."

"And I am a woman of my word, Asar. So here you are. A cello."

Asar was so still and so silent.

I cleared my throat. "It's heavy. So . . ."

He took the instrument and braced it between his knees. His fingertips danced over the curves of the polished wood, then over the strings, eliciting a low whine. His touch was almost reverent. It reminded me of how he touched the walls at Morthryn. It reminded me of how he touched *me*.

I handed him the bow, and he traced that with his fingers, too. Still, he said nothing.

"Is it a good one?" I said. "It's just . . . whatever the castle had in storage. If I had more time, I would've—"

"It's perfect, Mische," he murmured. "It's perfect. Thank you."

I beamed. "If you're so grateful, then play it for me. Maybe another song that sounds like me. I liked that one."

"I know how to play the violin, but I've never played a cello before. Might not be a particularly pleasant song."

He ran the bow over the strings and winced when his chord went sharply askew.

I let out an exaggerated scoff. "It can't be that hard. You're about to ascend to godhood."

He gave me a sly, sidelong glance. "You try it, if you think it'll be so easy."

I raised my hands. "Oh . . . no, I'm bad at that."

"Perhaps I just need the moral support. You do make the impossible seem possible."

He raised his brows at me expectantly, pushing the instrument aside to offer me a seat.

Reluctantly, I agreed, shimmying into the space between his body and the cello. The scent of ivy surrounded me. The warmth of him enveloped my body as his arms settled around mine and I pressed my back to him, letting him place me.

"Here. And here." He handed me the bow and arranged my fingers on it, his hand over mine, then did the same to my grip on the instrument's neck. My skin prickled where it touched his. His breath skittered along my cheek.

"There," he murmured. "Now we can both be imperfect together."

His mouth brushed my ear as he spoke, as if he couldn't resist it.

My lashes fluttered. I wanted to sink into him. Into this final reprieve before the end.

I said, voice light, "What's next?"

"You play, Iliae."

"Play what?"

Another brush of his mouth, this time over my throat. Almost a kiss. "Whatever is in your precious heart."

I really, really didn't think it worked that way.

But it was hard to argue with a beautiful man kissing my neck, so I gave it my best try, anyway. The bow screeched and wailed over the strings, making me cringe.

"I'd hope my heart would sound better than that."

Asar chuckled softly. The sound rustled my hair.

"How about . . . something more like this."

He rearranged his fingers over mine, and guided my hands. After a few awkward false starts, a melody—beautiful, albeit slightly clumsy—rolled from the strings. The notes were sweet and mournful. Sadder than they had sounded from a piano, a life and a death ago.

My eyes stung.

I choked out, "I think I know this one."

"All my favorite notes. The easiest ones to play. You were the one who asked me to think about the future, Dawndrinker."

Sap.

Still, a tear rolled down my cheek.

I closed my eyes and let the music roll over me. Let my fingertips feel the notes vibrate through my fragile, mortal skin.

"What else?"

"Hm?"

"The future. What else?"

The song faltered.

Then he began again. The notes shifted, lengthened, lowered, into a song that sounded like history and peace and the hymns of prayers whispered at night.

And in those notes, I saw it: mirrored floors, curved rafters of bone, crawling ivy dotted with blood-red flowers.

My lips curled. "Morthryn," I whispered. Even though the word that sat on my lips was, *home*.

Here, enveloped in his body and his music, I was there all over again. Not Morthryn as I had known it, but a version that was what it had always been intended to be—a place of solace for the forgotten souls.

I opened my eyes, and I could see it around us, the delicate lines of our vision suspended in the shadows and darkness. Asar, inviting me into his dream.

"What else?" I said.

His fingers shifted again. The notes once more evolved, growing shorter and brighter with a distinct cadence that reminded me of delicate footsteps across the dusty earth.

My smile brightened. "Luce."

Rendered in silvery smoke, Luce trotted across our depiction of Morthryn's halls, flitting between arched doorways before settling in front of a roaring fire in a messy library overflowing with books.

And now, I didn't even have to ask him again—he was lost in it, right alongside me. The melody again evolved. This song was a little discordant, the notes deep and melody slow, vibrating against each other in a way that could have clashed but instead felt complex and warm.

I felt his scars against mine. Felt his mouth against my ear.

And I didn't even have to say it, because I would recognize Asar anywhere.

A tall silhouette unfurled in the smoky rendering of Morthryn, perched behind a piano, one hand extended.

The notes lengthened, that song of mournful hope filling in the spaces of his song, and gods, how had I not realized in the beginning how well they complemented each other?

The final addition to the tableau unfurled from the shadows—a silhouette of myself, dancing through the darkness until she reached for Asar, taking his hand. And as the hopeful melody of shared song rose and fell, the vision did, too. Us, before the hearth in the library. Us, in the mournful beauty of the Descent, restored to what it was always intended to be. Us, in a field of poppies. Us, cradling a precious soul that held the best of both of us. Countless dreams for the future, encapsulated in a single song.

Asar watched the illusion surround us.

"Beautiful." The word pressed a kiss to my cheek. "You've gotten good at this, Dawndrinker. We'll make a Shadowborn of you yet."

The realization fell over me.

It wasn't Asar's illusion. It was mine.

My painting of the future, bringing life to our shared dreams.

And gods, what beautiful dreams they were. I watched them dance around us like butterflies, so close I could reach out and seize them. I wanted to. I wanted to capture them and hold them close, even though I knew that they would simply dissolve if I tried.

I blinked and another tear slithered down my cheek.

"It's a nice song," I said.

I watched them—that perfect dream version of us, so real and so unattainable—float away like smoke into the church rafters, as Asar's hands abandoned the cello for my body. As his mouth kissed my throat, my cheek, my ear.

And I felt his truth as deeply as I felt his song when he murmured, "I have never wanted anything so fiercely, Dawndrinker. Not ever."

I turned my head, and he captured my mouth in a kiss that made the impossible seem possible—a kiss that dragged me back from the clutches of death itself.

I barely caught the cello before it fell to the floor, placing it down as Asar pulled me back to the bed. We entangled ourselves in each other like roots through the earth, pulling away clothing layer by layer, relishing the sanctuary of each other's skin.

I felt alive. I felt human. I felt powerless. I felt untouchable. I felt, and felt, and felt, and Asar kissed me through it all.

I pushed his trousers down and he shimmied mine off my hips. My thighs parted, and when he pushed into me, I felt so utterly complete that I just wrapped myself around him and held him there.

He stroked my hair and kissed me. We stayed that way, our bodies and breaths entwined, for a long time.

And then, his hips shifted, and a spark of pleasure surged at the base of my spine. Wordlessly, we began to move against each other, losing ourselves in it.

I gasped a moan when his hands slid down my body to my hips, lifting them, tilting them, so he could drive himself deeper—like he couldn't have enough of me. Each stroke grew stronger, faster, as we coiled around each other.

"Asar—" I choked out, and he kissed me fiercely.

"Yes," he whispered. "Please."

Please. I could still remember the first time he'd said that word to me, lost in the visions of Psyche. And he sounded the same now, like he put his entire soul into it.

"Together," I said. I wasn't sure if the word was spoken aloud, in my own mind or his. But it was the only thing I could think now—that I wanted him to fall with me, over this cliff and all the others to come.

I locked my thighs around him, holding him deep, when the wave hit me.

And he knew what I wanted, because his body tensed a moment later as he came with me. We went rigid, folding our bodies around each other, as if trying to create one being. He pressed his forehead against mine, and I held him there as he whispered my name like a prayer.

And I was complete.

The aftershocks of our climax faded. Slowly, our bodies relaxed. Asar kissed me deeply again, his tongue slipping over mine, lazy and thorough and soft. We slid from each other and wrapped ourselves up in the safety of each other's bodies. I watched his face—that perfect face, marked with perfect scars—sink into a peace I so rarely saw upon it.

He looked mortal.

And I felt alive.

I buried my head against his shoulder and let sleep beckon.

I wanted to cling to it—this urgent, desperate sense of life. I wanted to believe it would last forever.

But I couldn't help the sense that perhaps we were like two celestial bodies in the sky. Him arcing from mortality to divinity. Me, from death to life. The two of us colliding for only a few ephemeral moments, magnificent in their impermanence.

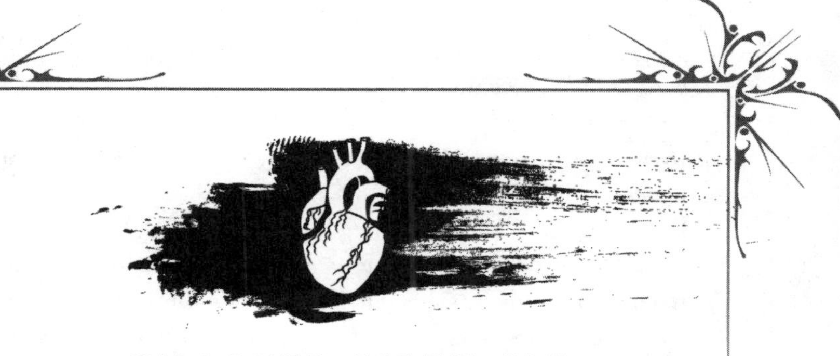

CHAPTER FIFTY-SIX

Asar

Sometime in the night, Luce had crawled into the bed. Mische sprawled out, limbs askew, face smooshed to the pillow. Luce had tucked herself beside her. I sat at the edge of the bed and stared out into the night—the blackened sky, the withered gardens, and the rolling silver dunes.

My left eye burned. The scars on my cheek throbbed. I had a pounding headache. I stared down at my hands clasped in my lap. My Heir Marks were more inflamed, and if I stared at them long enough, I was certain they were moving slightly, as if breathing.

I couldn't remember the last time I'd slept. A pitcher of blood sat on the bedside table, half full. Mische did not need it, and every so often, I would dump a little out in the basin so that she didn't realize that I didn't, either.

The seconds ticked by, and I sensed a shadow grow closer.

{It is foolish to fear it,} the mask said. *{You will be claiming your kingdom.}*

{After two thousand years, you will have the vengeance you deserve,} the eye agreed.

I closed my eyes, pushing back against the voices. I had spent my entire life training my mind against intrusions. But none of those strategies worked now, and the constant failure was growing exhausting.

That's enough, I told myself.

{No,} the eye said. *{It is not.}*

I turned my gaze to Mische. Her body mimicked breath, but the misty smoke still peeled from her skin. I could see death closing its hands around her.

Maybe the eye was right. Maybe none of it was enough. This one night. This one moment. This one fraction of a life I've had with her.

I no longer craved blood. But I was still desperately hungry.

{Worry not,} the eye murmured in comfort. *{Such is merely the dream of a mortal heart. Soon, you will have another.}*

"That's enough," I hissed again, this time aloud.

Mische's lashes fluttered open with a start. I stroked her bare back.

"Sorry," I murmured.

But her face softened when she saw me, a smile blooming over her lips.

"I'm not," she said.

I pressed a kiss to her fingertips. And just as I was about to follow it with one to her lips, a knock rang out at the door.

When we opened it, Oraya stood there.

"Vale has arrived," she said. "It's time."

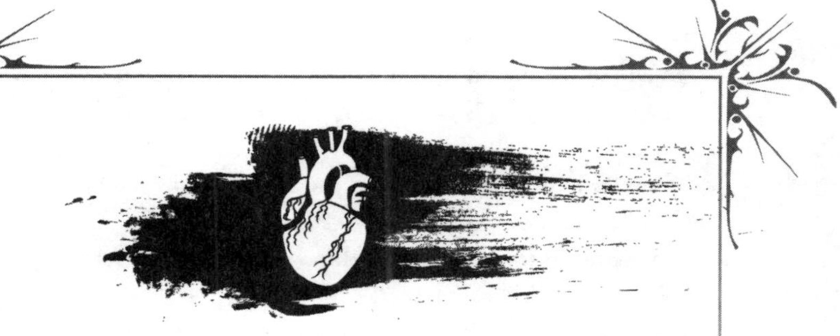

CHAPTER FIFTY-SEVEN

Mische

It's time.

The halls of the Nightborn castle seemed to thrum with those words.

It's time.

Vale came to Raihn and Oraya's private meeting room. Oraya and Lilith led us down the halls of their royal wing, Asar trailing slightly behind me as he flipped through his notes.

I heard their voices echoing as we approached. "Took you long enough to get here, didn't it?" Raihn was saying, audibly annoyed.

"Apologies," Vale said. "Like I told you. I was held up."

We filed into the room. Vale sat in an armchair, wearing his Nightborn military uniform of dark purple. His dark hair was unbound over his shoulders. Something—though I could not place what—seemed immediately odd about his appearance.

Lilith paused at the door, brow furrowed, as if she'd just misplaced something but wasn't sure what. Vale glanced at her and didn't move.

"At least you're here now," Oraya said. "You have it?"

Vale smiled. "I have it."

He held up a small glass tube of shimmering liquid. The vial was barely even a quarter full. Yet, at the sight of it, every hair on my arms stood upright. Everything in the room seemed to bend toward it.

A headache pushed into the back of my skull and twisted.

Vale rolled the glass between his fingers, gazing at it with a lover's longing.

"It really is beautiful, isn't it?" he murmured. "The kind of power that could summon gods."

Asar entered the room behind me and stopped short.

"What are you doing here?"

The raw horror in his voice was ice water down my spine. I whirled around. He was standing in the door, rigid, a bright plume of light surging from his left eye.

"What do you mean?" Raihn said, confused. "This is . . ."

But he trailed off. Frowned, like he'd forgotten what he was saying.

My headache grew suddenly unbearable.

Asar said, "If you touch them—"

"What will you do, Asar? Tell me. I'd love to hear."

Vale smiled. It was such a smooth, smug expression. Different from any expression I had ever seen Vale wear before, but it looked like one I'd once seen on someone else. I just couldn't place—

And then, all at once, I saw it.

The truth hit me. The haze cleared. My mind broke through the illusion.

The man before us wasn't Vale at all.

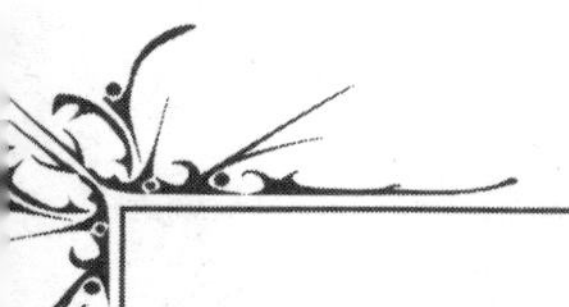

CHAPTER FIFTY-EIGHT

Asar

Gideon sat in the center of the room, surrounded by everyone who had helped us, holding a weapon powerful enough to make or unmake worlds.

My fear was so loud that even the voices were silent.

My mind ran through a cascade of calculations. The distance between Gideon and Mische. The distance between myself and the mask or the eye, which were downstairs, in the ritual room. The distance between my hands and the weapons on the other side of the room. Beside me, Mische sucked in a breath when she, too, pierced the illusion.

"That is not your general," I told the Nightborn, never taking my eyes from Gideon.

Oraya frowned. "Of course it is."

"Of course I am," Gideon said.

I am. I am. I am.

The air was thick with Gideon's illusion. The Nightborn weren't prepared for it, and Gideon was one of the greatest Shadowborn sorcerers in centuries. Perhaps he had even used the weapon he held to enhance his magic. I didn't know. I didn't care.

He smiled. It reminded me so vividly of the smile he had given me when he had first offered me the world in exchange for my soul.

"Perhaps I underestimated you, Asar. But you underestimated me, too. I told you that our dance would not be over."

I had fought gods, monsters, wraiths. I'd traversed life and death. And yet, this one man left me utterly powerless.

My heart was in my throat. "If you want revenge, then we can handle that one-on-one."

Gideon actually looked sad.

"I always found it so interesting that you were so capable and yet so naive. One night, you single-handedly destroy a kingdom. The next, you run off to go fall in love. Surely you know better now."

Shadows now writhed around the vial of blood.

I couldn't get to the sword fast enough. If I went for it, he would smash the vial. The gods would be upon us in seconds.

Mische stepped forward, but my hand snaked out to stop her.

Don't move.

Oraya stared hard at the vial, and the shadows around it. Some part of her knew it wasn't right.

"Everything is fine," Gideon said smoothly. "Nothing to worry about."

Fine. Fine. Fine.

Only Lilith shook her head slightly.

"This is between you and me," I said. "The things I am planning are so much bigger than that little piece of glass in your hand. Do you want a part in it?"

Gideon's pitying expression made dread curl in my stomach. "My dear boy. I already do have a part in it. How many glyphs did you carve out of my head that night? You were so sloppy. More interested in your vengeance than your craft. You didn't even feel the extra one I'd planted there for you to take. Just a little anchor. And I knew that when you left, you would do incredible things. That hunger has always been the key to your greatness. And, too, your greatest downfall."

He was lying. He had to be.

Frantically, I searched my memories of the night. He was right—I hadn't sensed it. Not until I was taking the mask on the Night of the Melume and—

It hit me. That one extra glyph in the key. That one that hadn't fit.

I'd felt the sting of it then, but I dismissed it as a side effect of the mask. It was subtle, elegant work. After that one jolt, I hadn't felt a thing.

But he had been tracking me, nonetheless.

"I know you better than anyone," Gideon said. "You are still the same as you were as a child. A dead dog or a dead lover. The injustice of a brother or a father or a cruel mentor, or the injustice of gods. All it takes is the right deprivation, and you are capable of such greatness." He gave me a knowing, cruel look. "And look, now, at what you have become."

The world went quiet, save for the monotonous rise of my rage.

He knew.

Just as once, Luce's death had pushed me to necromancy. As Ophelia's had driven me to understand the underworld. Gideon had always been a master of hungers.

But he couldn't have crafted that trap for me in the moment. Everything I'd taken from him had been there for years. Seamlessly integrated with the rest of the keys he held in his mind.

Gideon's fair eyes glinted with satisfaction. "Just as you said. It's what I would have done."

He knew that one day, I would come for the key.

And that when I did, it meant I would lead him to all the treasures he himself couldn't claim.

He rolled the blood between his fingers.

"Tell me," he said, "do you think the lord of Farnelle knew that he was only bait, when he watched his city burn?"

Farnelle.

A city decimated for nothing more than to provide a distraction.

And now, I understood.

We were the sacrifice. The House of Night was the bait. Bait for gods.

It was too late. He had already set his trap. The blood was the lure. He'd dragged it all over the House of Night just to make sure it was seen, *felt,* by exactly the beings we were trying so hard to hide from.

I whirled to the windows to see the sky swirling with wisps of rainbow light. A sign that the gods were watching. A sign that they were *already here*.

Gideon smiled, his lip curling into a sneer. "I, too, have taken more powerful things from more powerful people."

I lunged for him.

He crushed the vial with a burst of magic, sending his final, devastating flare up to the hungry gods.

And that was all it took.

It all crashed down in an instant.

CHAPTER FIFTY-NINE

Mische

Everything happened so fast. The explosion in Gideon's hand consumed the room in a billow of divine smoke, sending me flying black. Glass shattered. The rafters moaned, crashing down.

My body, fragile and not quite mortal, felt broken. I dragged myself up through the wreckage. Barely had time to take in the scene before me. Gideon's motionless, destroyed body, the broken windows, Raihn and Oraya blinking away the remnants of the illusion, and then—

Gold in the sky. Plummeting to the ground like—

My stomach plummeted in dread.

My mouth opened to scream a warning.

Too late.

BOOM, as another explosion rocked the Nightborn palace. And then another, and another, like notes in a grotesque melody of death, and—

I shielded my eyes, the world briefly dimming, as I flew back again. Hit the wall, and barely felt it. My hands groped for a weapon, for a mind, anything.

The glass roof had collapsed, transforming the tile mosaic floor into a sea of glittering blue and silver and purple. With it had gone part of the wall, offering a glimpse into the rest of the palace. I could no longer hear anything over the screams.

Shiket's followers had overtaken the House of Night. As if they had been waiting. As if they'd already known we were here.

It was worse than what I had seen in the House of Shadow. There were so many Sentinels I couldn't count them. A sea of black-spattered gold masks and white robes quickly soaking in vampire blood.

I staggered around to see, through the shattered windows, hundreds more figures pouring through the distant docks—from ships that had been hidden by the soupy mist, now looming over the shore.

How? A god's work, surely. The specifics, in this moment, did not matter.

Raihn and Oraya, disoriented with the remnants of the illusion, threw themselves into battle, looking every bit the legendary warriors. Jesmine screamed commands, clutching a wounded arm.

I needed a weapon. I needed to find—

My eyes jumped to Asar across the room, rising from a sea of darkness. Beside him, Luce snarled and fought.

His eyes locked on mine.

I reached for him—

But then a scream tore from my throat.

A terrible burning sensation seared the back of my neck, beneath a metal grip.

I hit the wall, then the ground. And then my own terrified face stared back at me, bisected by two jagged scratches across a smooth gold mask.

I saw myself in the Citadel, pledging my life to the god I would one day kill.

Saw myself with the blood of those I loved most smeared on my lips.

"There is nowhere left to go," the Sentinel said, somewhat sadly. "It is time to face your justice, fallen one."

I kicked, scratched, bit. But I was just one mortal—just one wraith, seized by the hand of a god.

The last thing I saw as the Sentinel hoisted me over their shoulder was Asar, face twisted in horror, lunging for me.

But he was too slow.

The Sentinel leapt into the sky, and the world was consumed in white.

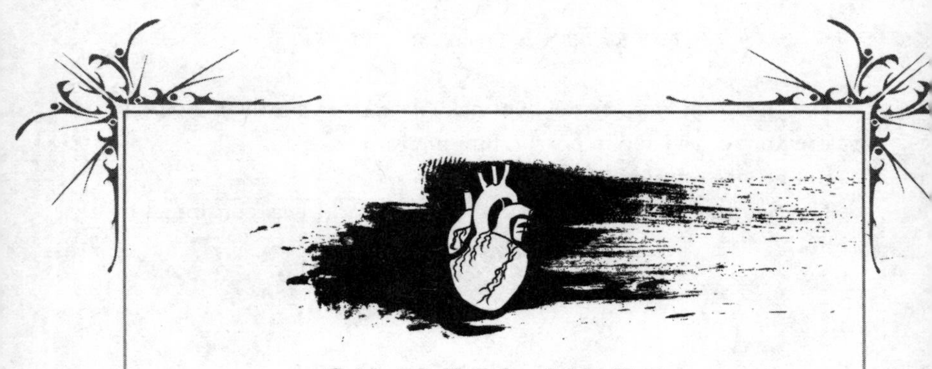

CHAPTER SIXTY

Mische

The air smelled like the ocean. Clean and salty. Not like Obitraes's brackish shores.

I drew in an inhale. Damp soil. Hot stone. Incense. A bell rang in the distance, four mournful, familiar notes that summoned a wave of old memories.

It felt so real for a dream.

I forced my eyes open.

My limbs were splayed. Manacles encircled my wrists and ankles. I was chained up against a smooth stone wall. Before me was a hill leading down to the ocean. The sea was silver beneath the moonlight. I was surrounded by clay walls that rose from the forest in eternal, majestic watch. The trees were now bare and withered, but I knew that once, this jungle had been so lush it blanketed the world in green all the way to the horizon. Just as I knew that under a summer sunrise, this entire building looked like it was on fire.

I was in Vostis. At the Citadel of the Destined Dawn.

I blinked. My head throbbed.

It was a dream. An illusion. Surely. It had to be.

I didn't realize I'd spoken aloud until someone said, "It is not a dream."

The Sentinel's voice was quieter than I'd ever heard it. It almost sounded human.

They stood before me, the tip of their sword pressed to the stone floor, their golden gauntlet-clad hands folded over the hilt, white robes falling in a waterfall down their body.

Behind them loomed a statue of Atroxus, standing tall, robed and bare-chested, his hands out to present the dawn. At sunrise, the light would fall just right to cast a glowing orb through the stained-glass window into his hands. At sunset, another window and a set of mirrors would cast the blood-red light over his crown.

For a moment, the Sentinel looked downright majestic there, framed against him. They were a soldier of Shiket, not Atroxus—but the robes, the gold, the commitment to justice were all so similar.

We were in the main temple of the Citadel, where priests would meet to pray or for holy festivals—or divine punishments. Two balconies wrapped around the room, looking down on the stage. Humans stood shoulder-to-shoulder, looking down at me with curious, hateful eyes.

Behind the Sentinel were three human acolytes, all wearing long white robes and gold armor on their arms and shoulders. They were young, and, judging by the sweet scent of their rushing blood, very nervous. The man looked to be, at most, in his early twenties, while the two women with him appeared to be older teenagers. The man had a sun tattooed on the back of his hand.

A symbol of Atroxus.

A convert, then? Egrette had told Asar that Shiket had taken over most of Atroxus's followers. Maybe she had promised them justice for their fallen god.

"I—" My mouth was dry. My mind was muddy. I couldn't think. I caught movement out of the corner of my eye. Silvery smoke rolling from my skin—death trying to pull me back.

I didn't have time.

"I need to go back," I choked out. The only words I had. "I need to go back."

The Sentinel cocked their head. "Why?"

They asked it like they actually wanted to know.

"I can't leave them. I need to go back. Please. I know you fight for justice. But there are innocents there, too."

The words just poured out of me, clumsy, unpracticed. I sounded pathetic. I knew they would get me nowhere.

"A loyal fallen one," they said bitterly. "So many years of corruption, and this is where you find loyalty in your heart? A gift reserved only for your tainted kin, it seems."

In their mask, I saw the shame of my greatest betrayals. Leading Eomin to Obitraes's shores. Sinking my teeth into Saescha's throat. Giving her wraith my wordless apology, before I damned her yet again by driving that arrow into Atroxus's throat.

"Where was your loyalty then?" they snarled. "Where was your loyalty when it was called upon by those who needed it most, Mische Iliae? Nowhere to be seen. Perhaps lost in your lust for the sin of your new existence."

With a sudden graceful flurry of their robes, they raised their sword, stalking closer. I cringed. But then, just as smoothly, they lowered their weapon and gestured to the dais.

"Now, at last, you will be saved. Here, in the place where you had once sworn your soul to the White Pantheon."

Saved. I knew what that meant. I'd seen it countless times in this very room—vampires hung up to die slowly by the sunrise, or stabbed through the heart as their blood spilled over Atroxus's sigils etched into the floor.

But why? Why would a Sentinel of Shiket bother bringing me all the way—

A violent shudder racked my body.

An eerie, terrible sensation yanked away my attention to the horizon. I looked past the Sentinel and their guards—to the sea and the night sky. The water churned. What had been smooth silver minutes ago was now interrupted with choppy streaks of foam. Flecks of silver, like suspended fragments of lightning, dotted the sky.

I knew this feeling.

A god's attention.

I heard Gideon's words again:

Farnelle.

I pieced it together with rising dread.

The House of Night was the distraction.

The House of Night was Nyaxia's sacrificial lamb. I remembered what Acaeja had told Oraya when she forged her Coriatis bond with Raihn:

One day, Nyaxia will bring forth a great reckoning.

Gods were petty. Gods did not forget.

But there had been another half to Asar's mission in Farnelle. The real battle, when the House of Shadow had swept in with a bloody victory over their unprepared adversaries.

Here. Vostis. The battle that deserved Nyaxia's real attention. The opportunity to oversee the bloodbath of her enemies.

Horror spilled over me. I looked at the people around me with fresh eyes. The spectators on the balcony, staring down at me. Children. Elderly. The weakest among this sect. Everyone who had been deemed unfit to go on Shiket's warpath. Even the soldiers who stood before me were practically children.

"She's coming," I blurted out. "Nyaxia is coming. You have to go." I looked up to the audience who watched, rapt, unmoving. This time, I cried in Vostin, "You have to go, Nyaxia is coming!"

They whispered amongst themselves, confused—more by my use of Vostin than what I actually had said. Why would they believe me? To them, I was just a fallen one. A monster.

The Sentinel scoffed. "Your threats mean nothing here."

"It's not a threat. It's a warning. Nyaxia is coming *now*."

They would never believe me. But even if they had, my warning would have come too late.

The Shadowborn were masters of illusion. I knew this, but I had never seen it in action at such an incredible scale. How thousands of vampires could hide themselves from human senses, waiting for the perfect opening to reveal their presence.

I had been a vampire for so long that I'd forgotten what it was like to see them as humans did. As monsters in the night. Beasts at the door.

Even now, I found them terrifying.

The Shadowborn understood the value of surprise.

The Sentinel sensed it first. They hesitated. Turned, slowly, peering out the windows into the night.

The veil of the illusion lifted, and suddenly, they were everywhere.

The world plunged into darkness.

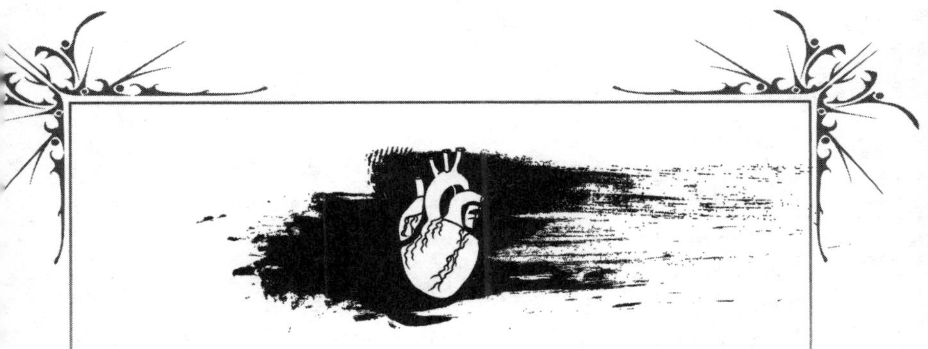

CHAPTER SIXTY-ONE

Asar

The Nightborn were unprepared for this. Everyone was. There was no escaping it. The soldiers were everywhere. Sentinels, yes. But also countless humans, all blessed with Shiket's weapon and protections. Vampires were stronger than humans, biologically, but these were no typical soldiers—they were blessed acolytes given a divine mission.

These soldiers did not plan to leave here alive, and that made them deadly. What had they been told? Had Shiket promised them that taking down the House of Night would mean protecting their families from the vampire threat? Perhaps even she had believed it.

{Arrogant as always,} the mask hissed.

None of it mattered.

The only thing that mattered was Mische, disappearing into the night sky, reaching for me as the Sentinel dragged her away.

"Go!" Raihn roared, as he hacked through body after body. "Go get her!"

I almost laughed as I ran by him, shadows collecting at my heels. Because did he think I needed or wanted his permission? Did he think that he, or any king, or any god, could have stopped me?

I ran down the halls, slipping past blades and star-kissed magic and figures of golden armor. I didn't stop or flinch when wounds opened on my skin or when Luce yanked warriors away from me.

Darkness clung to the corners of my vision. I felt it rising in my heart.

The mask and the eye waited for me at the door. I grabbed the axe and slid the mask over my face. It settled onto my skull like a second skin, digging deep, as if melding to bone.

The world grew suddenly quiet, like I had been plunged underwater.

The glyphs that Mische and I had meticulously drawn now pulsed with divine power. I crossed the room, then opened my palm on the edge of the axe, blood spurting free—blood touched by divinity.

I no longer cared to find Alarus's heart.

I cared only to find my own.

It was dangerous, I knew. Another passage that would connect the Nightborn to Shiket's forces. But I didn't care. I didn't care. I didn't care.

I pressed my bloody hand to the ritual circle as Luce circled my legs.

{It will all bow before you,} the mask whispered.

{See how close you are to the end,} the eye hummed.

The magic writhed beneath my touch. The spira opened before me, an entire world condensed into a single passageway, its possibilities limitless.

But only one mattered.

I threw open the door to her.

CHAPTER SIXTY-TWO

Mische

I'd heard it was a common Shadowborn tactic to disorient their target at the start of a battle. But words couldn't describe just how well it worked in person. A blanket of darkness surged through the Citadel, smothering sight and sound in a suffocating wave of nothingness. Even I couldn't penetrate it.

When it fell away, the screams rose up over Vostis like wildfire smoke.

The vampires were everywhere. Hundreds? Thousands? Shadowborn, but were there Bloodborn, too? I didn't know. It didn't matter. They had flooded the Citadel, running through the balconies. A cascade of blue-white explosions rang out through the forest, and I watched the distant outer buildings of the Citadel go up in billowing plumes of Nightfire. On the balconies above, the spectators screamed and trampled each other in desperate bids for escape. Judging by the blood already spilling in waterfalls over the railings, it wouldn't work.

Everything had devolved into chaos.

I pulled helplessly against my restraints, only to hiss at the burning sensation. I had to get out of here. *Now.*

The Sentinel had gone in the wave of darkness. Two of my guards had now bolted, too, leaving behind only one of the teenage girls. She spun around in a panic. A hundred images rushed through her mind, so loud, so unguarded. She was a recent convert. Not even a true acolyte. Someone who had only come here because she had believed it was safe.

Such a cruel twist of fate.

"You," I commanded. "Let me out."

Compulsion boomed through my voice. *Let me out, out, out.*

The girl was so terrified that she could barely move. But the force of my command jerked her toward me. A moment later, I slid to the ground. The manacles still adorned my wrists, but the chains had been released.

The girl's eyes widened, and she leapt backward, horrified by her own actions. She pointed her sword at me.

"Stop, b-b-beast. I'm—I'm warning—"

A horrific scream—the scream of a child—cut through her words.

Here were hundreds of innocent humans, in the home that had once been mine, locked up like rats to be hunted. I looked up at the trees and thought of the purging of the firefinches, all those golden bodies hitting the ground one by one. The screams drew closer. Another plume of smoke pumped through the room.

I didn't know what to do. *I didn't know what to do.* For a terrible moment, uncertainty paralyzed me.

I could not stop an army of Shadowborn. I could not stop divine war.

But right now, I decided, I could save someone.

"I'm not going to hurt you," I said to the girl in Vostin. "Tell me your name."

Tell me. Tell me. Tell me.

Her face went blank. My compulsion temporarily dulled her panic.

"Kyrene," she whispered.

Her blade trembled wildly. She had clearly never held one before.

"I am not going to hurt you, Kyrene," I repeated slowly. "Alright? I am going to help you. Give me that sword."

Give me. Give me. Give me.

She did as I commanded, handing me one of her comrade's weapons, discarded in their panic.

"Hold it like this." I demonstrated. "And if they come for you, you go for the heart." I pressed my hand to my sternum. "Right here. Really, *really* hard."

Gods, the poor thing was so afraid she could barely think. But she swallowed hard and attempted to adjust her grip. "Like this?"

It was still bad.

"Good," I lied.

Then I took in the scene before us. The tumult unfolding in the balconies and on the paths through the forest below. If we were going to make it out of the Citadel alive, we needed to go now, and quickly.

"Let's go, Kyrene," I said. "We are going to get out of here."

THERE WAS SO much blood on the floors that every step threatened to slip beneath me. I felt like I was in that terrible first night of the Kejari all over again. The sounds of carnage were sickening. Some believed that the Shadowborn were the most elegant of the vampires, but the truth was, we were all animals. Presented with enough hunger and enough blood, we slipped into a frenzy that stripped away all veneer of civility.

Our best hope of escape was to make it to the back of the Citadel, which ran right up against the beach. Long before my birth, the acolytes of the Destined Dawn had dug tunnels beneath the building that ran into the nearby villages—a security measure in wartime, so that villagers and soldiers could pass between the civilian homes and the fortress without exposure. I prayed that the Shadowborn weren't aware of them—at least, not yet.

The downside of this plan was that we would need to make it across nearly the entire length of the Citadel. Kyrene was shaking with terror, but she was brave. She led the way through the hallways I had forgotten how to navigate. The Citadel looked so different, and yet, so much was the same. With every twist of a staircase or a familiar, faded tapestry, the memories of my past here pieced back together.

The Citadel was teeming with vampires. I pushed Kyrene against a wall when we nearly ran straight into one gutting a priest—a blond teenage boy who reminded me so much of Eomin. The vampire had ripped out the boy's throat and barely even lapped up the blood before he was distracted by another screaming, wounded girl, who was trying frantically to crawl away.

"We have to help them," Kyrene squeaked out, ready to dive out after them. But against every instinct, I held her back.

"There's too many," I hissed.

"I can't just listen to them—"

Around the corner, the girl's voice rose to a frantic, terrified shriek and then gurgled to silence. Kyrene's eyes welled with tears. Her arm trembled violently in my grasp.

When her gaze flicked back to me, it struck me just how much more vivid human emotions were than vampires'. I realized that Kyrene was no longer shaking in fear. She was shaking in rage.

I was, too, by the end. We slipped through hall after hall, terror after terror. The carnage was unrelenting. The vampires were not discerning. They killed everyone. Ripped off limbs. Discarded heads. They couldn't be so careless with their own supply of Obitraen humans, who were disrespected but at least considered citizens, with a purpose—if one killed all the humans in Obitraes, none would be left for feeding. It had been centuries since vampires had been allowed to be so freely bloodthirsty at such a bountiful buffet of prey.

At last, when we turned one final corner, Kyrene breathed a shaky sigh of relief. The door ahead would lead outside, to the spiraling staircase that would take us down to the tunnels. A straight run to freedom.

Kyrene dove down the hall and threw herself against the door. She grabbed the handle and pulled.

And pulled.

And pulled.

Her hope soured to agonizing dread.

The door did not open.

I turned to the windows, looking out over the beach. My heart sank.

From here, I could see the other wings of the Citadel curving against the shore. Stone painted with drips of blood. Windows bright with plumes of Nightfire or dark with the toxic smoke of Shadowborn creations. At the top of the eastern tower, a figure hurled themselves from the window, choosing death by sharp rocks over death by sharp teeth.

There was no part of the Citadel that hadn't been overtaken. The vampires already had complete control of the compound.

This was not only a declaration of war, but a claim of resources. Knowledge. Weaponry. Magical artifacts. Humans—not just as game, but as tools. Magic wielders of the White Pantheon to be taken back to Obitraes and leveraged for their skills. Food to be harvested. Offerings to be made to Nyaxia.

The vampires would not cede any of that.

The doors had been locked all along.

The humans here were never going to make it out alive. Not Kyrene, and not the hundreds of other innocents in this building.

Kyrene pounded against the door, now in wild panic. Desperate, she grabbed the amulet on her throat—the sigil of Shiket, shiny and new, never used. "I'm sorry," she muttered under her breath. "I'm loyal now. Please. I beg protection from the lady of justice. I beg protection of Shiket. I offer my soul. Take it, please, take it, and save them, please, please, please . . ."

I looked nothing like this girl, but I saw myself in her. Was this what I had sounded like, I wondered, when I had traveled to Obitraes and been so certain that Atroxus would protect me? Faith could be such a beautiful thing. It had saved me, once. Perhaps it had saved Kyrene once, too.

I hated that right now, I pitied her for it.

No one is coming for you. No one is coming for any of you.

I grabbed her shoulders and spun her to me. "You need to save yourself. Do you understand? Save yourself—"

I smelled it too late. That acrid, venomous bite. Nightfire explosives.

The smoke and light and darkness burst through the air, and then the floor was gone beneath me, and Kyrene's fragile human arm was ripped from my grasp.

A force had me flying through the windows.

And I was falling, and falling, and falling.

CHAPTER SIXTY-THREE

Mische

I hit the ground hard, tumbling down, down, and then sliding through dead vegetation and broken trees and sand. Perhaps my wraith state, closer to death, was the only thing that saved me. The fall would have killed a human.

My vision blurred, consciousness wavering in and out. I became dimly aware that I was no longer falling. I pushed myself up to see that I'd plummeted to the beach. I was surrounded with glass from the window, twinkling in the moonlight.

The carnage was overwhelming. Corpses dotted the beach. Some whole. Some not. Legs and arms, torsos, heads. The sand was soaked with blood. The sky was bright red, churning with divine rage. The vampires had overtaken this shore, too. Apparently, they had spared no resource.

It was a slaughter.

And if anything—anything—could have made this worse, it was the cracks that now snaked through the beach, into the water, letting off angry plumes of acrid smoke.

Cracks that led to the underworld, bowing beneath the weight of its impending collapse. Even here, half a world away, there was nowhere to escape it. The vampires and humans alike were distracted with their battles, but wraiths clawed at the openings in the earth, desperate to drag themselves closer to life.

It would get worse. If such a thing was even possible.

I choked down my fear and felt around until I found a sword clutched in a dismembered hand. I extracted it and pushed myself unsteadily to my feet.

But as soon as I straightened, someone tackled me.

I skidded across the sand, slipping my attacker's grasp. I managed to keep hold of my weapon—managed to raise it as I turned—

The Sentinel was diving for me.

But their mask was cracked, now. It had split right along the scratch I had etched into it in our first meeting.

And what was revealed . . .

The horror made my steps falter. I barely managed to deflect their strike, sending them stumbling to the sand.

The face that stared back at me, framed by jagged gold, was barely human—the features faded, like those of a statue sanded down by time. The marks of life and humanity had been erased. She was free of freckles or scars or hair. Her eyes were blank white.

But it was her.

The sister I had damned twice over now, come to seek her revenge.

"Saescha," I gasped.

Her mouth twisted into a sneer of rage. But even that didn't quite look like her, the movement lopsided and stiff.

"*You* did this," she roared. "The corruption inside of you. You destroyed the god that could have saved us. You destroyed the last hope we had."

I couldn't move as she encroached upon me, glowing divine blade raised. Desperate, I reached for her with my magic—reached for a mind that I'd once known as well as my own.

But I found nothing but rage and pain. Nothing but a twisted, single-minded obsession with righting every wrong.

Sentinels were further from their living selves than even wraiths. They had sacrificed the basest truths of their souls to the mission of justice.

This thing in front of me was not truly Saescha. But once, it had been.

When she loomed over me, I saw flashes of my past life.

Me, running away from prayers.

Me, cutting down a dead vampire from the courtyard.

Me, sinking my teeth into Saescha's throat, again and again and again.

Me, damning her as I thrust that arrow into Atroxus's neck.

And it dawned on me.

All this time, I hadn't been seeing my own memories reflected in her. I had been seeing hers. Every moment that I had failed her. Every wound I had inflicted, invisible at first, until they weren't.

And gods, they were so, so deep. So deep she had been forced to discard her heart altogether.

She would kill me. Yet, I still couldn't bring myself to lift the blade against her.

"Saescha," I begged.

"That is not my name anymore," she growled, and raised her weapon.

A flash of shadow streaked through the air, knocking her away. Luce snarled and barked, smoke billowing around her, forcing Saescha back.

Luce. The best girl.

But how? If she was here, did that mean that she had come with—

I didn't have time to think of it as the two of them collided in a vicious morass of gold and darkness. Luce let out a howl of pain, and I grabbed my sword.

But then, I hesitated—because could I strike Saescha, even this twisted shell of who she had once been, down a third time?

I didn't get the chance to answer that question.

CRASH, as another explosion of Nightfire tore through the stone, right next to us. The force struck me like an open palm to a fly, sending me sprawling back. A fresh wave of screams wailed into the night, droplets of blood and gore spattering from the sky.

Consciousness slipped away.

Returned.

Water. I was in the water, now. I dragged myself to my feet, whirling around to find Luce, but all I saw was chaos and unrecognizable ruin. Another wing of the Citadel had crumbled. The sea, red with blood, lapped at my knees.

I lifted my chin to the dark sky, and suddenly, I saw myself as if through the eyes of another. Me, kneeling on a beach, surrounded by death, beneath an eternal night that I had raised.

It was an image I had seen before. I'd seen it depicted in tapestries and prophecies in the Sanctum of Secrets. I had seen it in Atroxus's terrible visions of the future.

I choked a terrible laugh that ended in a sob.

Everything I had done was to avoid this.

But all along, it had been inevitable. It would always end here.

I wanted to scream. I wanted to wail. I wanted to let myself fall into the ocean and drown in the blood of the innocents I had, however indirectly, slaughtered.

But I wiped my tears with the back of my hand.

There was always someone who could be saved. And there was always a reason to have faith.

I felt through the water until my hand closed around the hilt of my sword. I turned back to the battle at hand.

And I kept fighting.

Through all of it, I kept fighting.

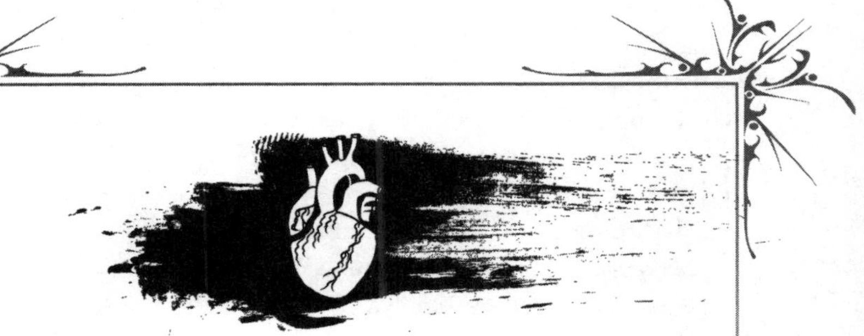

CHAPTER SIXTY-FOUR

Asar

My spell had been clumsy, vicious, a machete instead of a scalpel. I landed roughly in the sand, the world tilting, my skin burning with the power of the spira. It was an invigorating pain. I welcomed it. Luce landed beside me, not wasting a second before she bolted through the chaos.

I straightened slowly, taking in the carnage with the detached observation of a god. I had seen my fair share of bloodshed, but never before had I witnessed anything like this. It was an indiscriminate slaughter. The House of Shadow had poured all of their resources into this battle. The scant army left behind in the fortress didn't stand a chance.

A thousand times bloodier than it had been when I executed this same plan, all those years ago.

{And yet,} the eye mused, *{they do not know that they are already standing upon the precipice of damnation.}*

Beneath the mortal world, the underworld wailed in pain. Stitch after stitch snapped. Cracks had opened across the beach, twisted wraiths crawling free. Inevitable and unescapable.

And yet, I didn't care. I didn't care about any of it.

Where are you?

I extended my magic across the battlefield. Even vampire minds screamed out, unguarded, in their final moments, and humans were many times louder. The wails of the fresh dead, still clawing for life, echoed in my skull. I could feel their pain reverberating through the eye, up the blade, through my hand, and my rage grew, and grew, and grew.

A lightning crack split across the sky.

{She is coming,} the mask hummed in delight.

{She is angry,} the eye added.

I was angrier.

A human soldier, taking me for one of the vampire warriors, threw himself at me, and I batted him away easily.

Where are you?

With every loop through my mind, the question grew more frantic. The mask sat hot against my skin. My vision was shrouded in red. I fought through humans and vampires and wraiths alike.

Where are you, Mische? Where are you?

At last, at last, I found her.

When I saw her, the world stopped.

She was across the beach, at the edge of the water. Nightfire consumed the forest here, enveloping her in cold blue. Gold restraints encircled her wrists and ankles, and with my enhanced divine sight, even from here I could see the burns beneath them—from blessed metal. The shimmering residue of her mortality rose from her broken body in plumes. With every crack across the beach, she faded a little more.

I could feel her wounds as if they were my own. Torn skin that I had once worshipped, skin that I had ripped apart the underworld to wish back into being. Wounds made by mortal hands and divine ones, by humans and by vampires.

She looked so similar to how she had when I held her in the Descent, on the cusp of death.

{Almost gone now,} the eye said, indifferent.

Mische had sacrificed her life to save millions. To save the very vampires who now offered her up as a cruel bargaining chip.

But there she was, forcing her broken body to obey her. Fighting to protect the very same humans who had cast her out, just as she had fought to protect the vampires who had once taken everything from her.

Across all of it, across blood and steel and fire, I reached out for her. Her presence was warm against mine. I felt her pain and her grief. I felt her fury and her determination.

And even now, above all, hope.

I was awestruck by her.

Her eyes met mine through the carnage. Tears streaked her cheeks. She started to turn to me.

But before I could go to her, something sharp cracked across my back.

The impact caught me off guard. I stumbled, only barely recovering before I hit the ground. Blood sprayed from my shoulder.

My vision went gray, black, gray again.

{Traitor!} the mask roared.

I raised my blade to counter. But before I could, pain erupted through my leg, and I was pinned.

Egrette stood over me, a spear in her hand, going straight through my thigh into the ground below. Her bronze armor gleamed under the light of Nyaxia's divinity, matching the wild sheen of her chestnut hair. Her chin and chest were covered with the bright red of human blood.

She smiled at me, blood dribbling down her chin. I thought, *Our father would be so proud.*

The spear should not have stopped me. I bore the mask and the eye of Alarus—I was part god. And yet, when I tried to yank it free, pain spasmed through me. Light and shadow danced around the weapon's staff.

"You aren't the only one with god-touched toys, brother," Egrette said.

My eyes fell to the carvings on its hilt—the red glow at the base of the blade.

{Those,} the eye hissed, *{do not belong to her.}*

A vision racked through me. A girl with galaxies in her hair, slipping poppy petals into her mouth.

Petals.

The petals Elias had stolen from the Descent. Used to create a weapon that could take down a demigod—even if only temporarily.

Egrette leaned in close. Her smile became a sneer.

"I told you that you would pay for what you did to my lover and my kingdom. At least you have become quite a gift to me, in the end. I knew you would be useful for something."

I grabbed the hilt of the spear. Shadow rolled from my skin in spasms of darkness.

"Arrogant." I didn't recognize my own voice. "You do not know who I am, if you think a spear with a few discarded flower petals can kill me."

She laughed softly. "I don't plan to kill you. What a waste of an offering that would be."

Lightning cracks of white light arced from the horizon, splitting in two. The sky burst open. The vampires, humans, and wraiths alike stopped, chins lifting to the sky, as the devastating power of a god called to them.

{She is here,} the mask whispered.

She is here. She is here. She is here.

Nyaxia appeared in the sky, great and terrible and utterly breathtaking, triumph shining in the gleam of her eyes and razored teeth.

Egrette stood, spreading her arms wide.

"Nyaxia, Mother of Shadow, of Night, of Blood, Mother of vampires!" she cried. "I offer you the blood of your enemies, Atroxus and Shiket of the White Pantheon. And I offer you what my brother could not. I offer you the crown of Alarus, the eye of Alarus, and what remains of your husband's divinity. Rightfully yours, as it has always been!"

Another set of explosions rang out in the distance. A fresh wave of Nightfire burst across the horizon. A hundred or a thousand or a million other souls fell to the underworld—an underworld that could not accept them beneath the weight of its own destruction. A fresh crack burst open across the beach. Wailing, deformed souls cried their death rattles from within, too twisted and weak to even drag their way to the land of the living.

Nyaxia lowered herself over the sea, coolly observing the bloody offering in her favor. It was merely a start. The death had only just begun.

{Go to her,} the mask commanded.

{At last you will see what you may become,} the eye agreed.

A surge of rage pulsed through me, and with it, I ripped the spear from my leg and cast it aside. It got Nyaxia's attention. She smiled down at me. "We meet again. You have changed so very much in so little time."

Divinity commanded one's full attention. It sucked the life from all else—even here, in the middle of the falling of a civilization. Nyaxia was the center of it all.

And yet.

Look at her, a voice whispered. *One last time.*

The voice did not belong to the eye or the mask. It belonged to my mortal heart.

I found Mische across the battlefield. Her eyes locked to mine. Dread fell over her face. I could hear her voice reaching across the carnage, screaming, *No.*

But I rose anyway. I turned to Nyaxia.

And when she reached for me, I went to her.

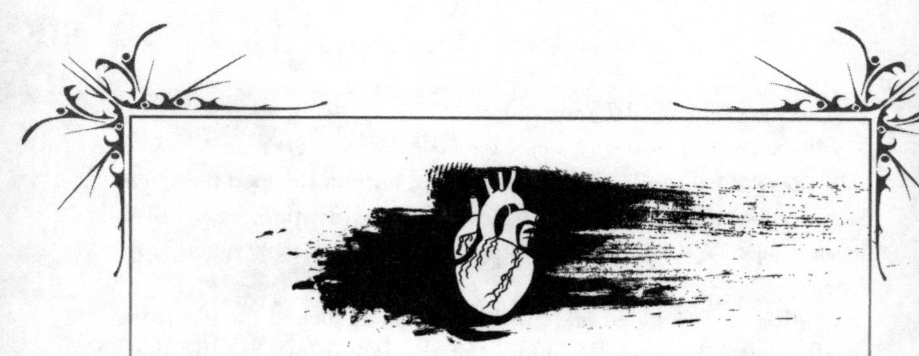

CHAPTER SIXTY-FIVE

Asar

I walked into the sea until it lapped at my knees. The water was warmer than I would've expected it to be. It was tinted dark red, human blood mingling with vampire. A severed hand, still reaching out for a god that would never reach back, bobbed by.

Nyaxia lowered to meet me.

{It is her,} the mask whispered.

{It is her,} the eye agreed.

But I couldn't tell if they were speaking in fear or admiration, admonishment or affection. Perhaps all at once.

She smiled. A drop of ruby blood rolled down the elegant point of her chin. The stars and infinite shades of night in her hair twinkled with shifting fates, comets ricocheting across her infinite depths.

"We meet yet again," she purred. "How you have risen to your new role."

I didn't feel like I was rising. I felt like I was falling.

Her smile soured. "It is not enough to take the second chance at life that should have been his. You must seek his divinity, too? How predictable. One cannot dangle over the edge of such power without succumbing to the desire to take the final leap. It has been many years since I have seen these. Thank you for returning them to me."

She stroked my cheek. With that touch, the screams and battle shouts and explosions fell to the background, as if behind layers of ice. Our surroundings grew hazy. I looked up into the sky and instead of the star-scattered night, I saw images dancing in the clouds—glimpses of every reach of the mortal realm. The House of Night, barely staving off their attackers. The House of Shadow, mobilizing still more soldiers. Human nations across the world, crumbling beneath the unexpected, bloodthirsty strike of the vampires, or the horrors of the broken underworld.

"Tell me, Asar Voldari, bastard's bastard's bastard of my husband's blood," Nyaxia said, "how does it feel to stand upon the cusp of godhood? Once I was little more than you. A lesser goddess barely touched with divinity. And now, look what I have done." She spread her hands. "I have brought the White Pantheon to their knees."

{If only he could see her now,} the eye sighed. *{So much greater than she once was.}*

I saw her as she had been two thousand years ago. The girl with galaxies in her hair and poppy petals on her lips, as Alarus had known her—as he had loved her.

Was this what he would have wanted her to become?

{He was no fool,} the mask said. *{He knew what she was. Even then.}*

I felt the echo of his pride, radiating through time and death and space, in whatever pieces of him I held. Alarus had loved Nyaxia because of her viciousness, not in spite of it. And I could see now, up close, just how much of herself she had sacrificed to become what she was now.

I could see where she had found that power.

It was so obvious. Stupid of me not to have realized it sooner.

"You have the heart," I said. "Alarus's heart."

My ritual circle had obeyed my command to take me to Mische. But it had brought me to the heart, too, just as it had been instructed.

The auroras in Nyaxia's eyes danced with delight.

"You are intelligent for a mortal," she said.

She pressed her hands to her chest, and when she extended them, in her cupped palms sat a hunk of blackened flesh. The blood, thick, honeyed gold, dripped from the twitching morass of muscle, down into the sea.

It was smaller than I might have expected the heart of a god to be, and oddly misshapen.

Nyaxia stared down at it with reverence.

"He gave it to me, before he was taken," she murmured. "I did not even know it then."

Her memory unfolded around us. I saw the two of them, sitting in the underworld beneath the twisted ebony branches of an obsidian tree. Saw him passing something gold to her—a little dagger, a ribbon wrapped around its hilt. Saw him kiss her goodbye.

{She did not know what he was to do,} the mask said.

{She told him not to meet them,} the eye whispered sadly. *{But he did not listen.}*

"I thought it was just another pretty gift passed from husband to wife," she said. "But the blade was no trinket. It was the key to cut out his heart. The key to my own divinity."

Nyaxia's lashes, black as ink, lowered in mournful half-moons over her pale cheeks. She cradled the heart close to her.

"When I retrieved this from what remained of him, I wanted to sleep with it beneath my pillow. I wanted to cradle it like the child we never had the chance to bear." Her face hardened. "But I did not wish to use my husband's final gift to grieve him. I would use it to become something more terrible than he ever was."

She lifted her eyes to me.

I saw the past in them. Nyaxia weeping over all she had left of her husband's body. And then, how those tears froze, hardened, to blades of rage.

I watched her lift Alarus's heart to her lips, and tear off a chunk of the flesh. Another, and another, each swallow bringing her closer to major divinity.

Now, Nyaxia smiled at me, a drop of red rolling across the curve of her lower lip.

"Why do you think that the children I created with his power feast upon the blood of mortals? We were all born in suffering. What makes us powerful is to thrive upon the taste of it. You understand this. I have always seen it in you."

I looked out over the carnage around us, unfolding in slow motion, seconds stretching to minutes. There was such peace in how the gods watched civilizations fall.

{Is it not beautiful?} the eye said.

{Only an end can create a beginning,} the mask added.

She was right. I did understand. Vampires feasted on blood to ensure that they would always be separate, always be isolated. Nyaxia set out to make a world that was only hers, born in the blood of her grief. It would die in the blood of it, too.

And I did feel her stare on those dark parts of my soul. My desire for revenge in the wake of Mische's death. My desire to bring her back in the most painful way possible for all who had wronged her. The sheer venomous hatred I had for an unfair world.

It would be so easy to let it happen.

But I said, "Take the mask and the eye, if you wish. I can't stop you. But I can give you something more valuable."

Nyaxia cocked her head, intrigued. Gods did love a deal.

"Moons ago, you tasked me with resurrecting your husband," I went on. "I failed in that task. But tonight, if you wish, I can offer you an ally. Your cousins band together against you. Yet you have been alone for thousands of years. It doesn't have to be that way. Not if you allow me to ascend beside you."

She must be so lonely, Mische had told me once. And it was this loneliness that I saw shoot across her face with the blazing heat of a falling star, there and gone again in seconds.

Nyaxia was not thinking now of war or powers or strategic decisions. She was thinking of her own grief.

She laughed softly. "You fail me, and now you ask me to make you a god. I am amused by your boldness."

I looked over my shoulder at the carnage below, moving now in slow motion. I was so far away, as if staring down at it all from the back of a bird. And yet, my eyes found her immediately.

Mische, hand outstretched for me.

Mische, marked by the scars of the betrayal of so many people who she had loved. Mische, barely clinging to life, giving everything to protect those who had cast her out.

Shiket called herself the goddess of justice—but there was no justice here, not in Mische kneeling before the bed of a god as a child, not in her throat ripping beneath the teeth of a vampire prince who discarded her, not in the gods tossing her aside like she was nothing.

A world that accepted any of those things was not worthy of redemption.

"Ah, is that what you want?" Nyaxia murmured, following my gaze. "To become a god, and make them suffer for it? Perhaps. We could destroy it all, you and me."

This idea piqued her interest. She showed me her vision—empires falling into dust. Shiket, cleaved apart slowly by the edge of her own blades. Srana, dismantled gear by gear. Ix, lured to her death just as she had lured Alarus millennia ago.

The mask and the eye purred their approval.

{A bed of ashes upon which to build a new kingdom,} the mask declared.

"She can even come with us, if you please," Nyaxia went on. "Pluck her from all this. Let her watch as we remake the world. She can warm your bed in the land of the gods. No one will be able to take her from you again."

The dream was so vivid, so painfully close. I could give Mische an endless existence. I could show her beauty mortal eyes had never witnessed. I could give her the music of gods. I could lie in a bed of silks beside her, and though I would no longer sleep, I would watch her, content in her safety. I would kiss the scars on her skin knowing that none would ever mark her again.

I felt like I was a child standing before Gideon all over again. A child being offered the greatest gift I could imagine: a life beyond fear.

But I was not a child. I was a man, covered in the marks of my mistakes, watching the world fall.

I was a man who was in love with a woman, and I understood that love would never be beyond fear.

When I had sat chained in my cell in Ysria, I had thought long and hard about the blood I would use to paint Mische's story into the stars. I had thought that I had only death to offer her.

I had been wrong.

I could give her something greater.

I stared down at her. I was so far away, and yet felt so close. I could taste the sweet softness of her lips. The freckles on her cheeks like flecks of cinnamon. Among the sound of the universe rearranging, I could have sworn I heard a song, the fading, imperfect notes of a dream floating to the stars, never to be recaptured.

And I loved her, I loved her, I loved her.

I turned back to Nyaxia. "I have another proposition."

Surprise flickered across her face. Then hungry curiosity.

"What could you possibly want more than that?"

"Spare them," I said. "Spare the humans here. Spare the House of Night."

A hateful sneer. "The House of Night betrayed me."

"Yes," I agreed. "But the Nightborn are still your children. They might be useful one day."

"I do not want their help."

"Then as a mother. Don't you love the creatures you created from your husband's gift?"

Her face was hard. It was only now that I understood—that Nyaxia was genuinely hurt by the disloyalty of her followers.

"Perhaps," she hissed. "But what argument could you possibly make for sparing the humans? I offer you the vengeance you crave, and you reject it—"

"You misunderstand me, Goddess. If you destroy the human nations now, it will all be over too quickly. Perhaps Alarus is gone. But some of him still lives in the mask that was the crown to his kingdom. In the eye that saw the possibilities of the dead. Do you know what I hear them say?"

{Destroy it all,} the mask said. *{Build a greater kingdom. Just as we did in the beginning.}*

{See how it stretches from each horizon,} the eye purred. *{Now it shall stretch into death itself.}*

I answered, "He says, *Join her. Make them suffer. And make it slow.* I could offer you that. Whatever is left of him. And we can walk a longer path together."

It was the only thing Nyaxia craved more than power.

Love.

All I needed was to ascend. I needed the power that would stop this imminent collapse. Just one moment. One burst of power.

And then I could open the door to something—someone—better.

Nyaxia said softly, "You are not him."

"No. But I will be closer to it."

The proximity of the heart was dizzying. My looming ancestor cast his shadow over every shred of my being. A little more of myself slipped away, like stone worn by the steady beat of the shore.

"You understand what sacrifice this will require you to make?" she said.

I lowered my chin. "A heart for a heart."

"There is no telling what you will be when it is done."

"No," I said. "There isn't."

Her eyes searched my face. How close could I become, she was wondering, to the husband she had been trying for centuries to reclaim?

"Very well," she said. "I accept."

She opened her other hand, and within it sat a small golden blade. The blade she had been gifted two thousand years ago, beneath the branches of an obsidian tree.

"A heart for a heart."

Beneath us, a crack split the sea in two, the bleeding mists of the underworld breaking free beneath foamy waterfalls. A thousand invisible souls called my name.

Yet I heard only one.

I looked over my shoulder one last time, at the dead woman reaching for me. I drank in her image, pressing it to my heart—deeper, to my soul.

Strange, that I could not remember her name.

I turned back to Nyaxia.

"I am ready," I said.

She smiled, and then she plunged the blade into my chest.

Crack, as my bones parted. My flesh opened. Blood fell in waterfalls to the sea below.

A million memories dissolved into mist. A million inconsequential moments that created a mortal life, unraveling like fabric pulled by the edge of a thread, row by row by row. In my final dregs of awareness, I threw every scrap of myself into the wounds of the underworld below, into every open crack, every tattered veil, every wounded guardian.

I threw every shred of my mortal power into it, praying that my divinity would flow into it, too.

Nyaxia cut out my heart. And I couldn't help myself—I was the one to reach into my chest, to yank the chunk of bloody flesh free. It was so small, so fragile.

{It would never belong to a god,} the eye said.

Nyaxia smiled as blood ran down her chin.

"You will not miss it in the end," she murmured.

She tipped my hand and let the chunk of flesh fall, fall, fall, into the crack below us, sinking all the way to the underworld.

And then she cradled Alarus's heart close one final time, before thrusting it into my chest.

CHAPTER SIXTY-SIX

~~Asar~~

The God of Death

The god knelt before the goddess. Before him, a sea of carnage spread out from horizon to horizon. The ache of divinity gnawed at the inside of his ribs, where a long-lost heart now sat. His power pulsed from him in a great wave, like a shock across the mortal and divine worlds. It flowed into the cracks of the underworld, halting its collapse.

And yet, it still groaned in pain.

Nyaxia's palm pressed to his chest. She watched him carefully—perhaps searching for her husband in his face.

There was some, perhaps. Far away. Fragments of his memories floated, unmoored, in the god's newly formed mind.

But above all, there was emptiness.

The god turned and looked out over the scene before him. Thousands of souls meeting their ultimate end; thousands of souls screaming out in agony. He could sense it rolling on and on and on, stretching into the future and the past. A thousand miles away, a kingdom of vampires fell.

Perhaps another version of this god might have been moved by this. Perhaps another version of him might have remembered that there was something crucially important that he needed to do. The thought nagged at him, like the call of a ghost fading away. But the part of him that had cared about these things was gone now, thrown into the sea.

He could not recall why it had ever mattered so much.

Nyaxia stared at him for a long moment. Then looked away, masking her glimmer of disappointment.

"Very well," she said. "Then I shall uphold my end of our deal."

She raised her hand over the great expanse of death. When she spoke, the words were like thunderclaps.

"You have done well, my children. The White Pantheon shall never forget the blow we have inflicted upon them today. But we must be careful not to overextend ourselves in a single battle. There is still a war to fight."

The vampires looked up from their caresses and writhing prey. Blood-drunk, at this they laughed and cheered. The vampire queen—the god had the strange sense he had known her name, once, but now, it didn't seem to matter much at all—rose her spear in triumph, then bowed deeply.

"As you wish, Dark Mother."

But as the other vampires left their half-dead victims behind, following the command of their goddess, one still remained. One woman, who seemed so pathetically close to death that she was little better than the human corpses scattering the ground. And yet, in the sea of souls, his attention kept drifting back to her.

All the others stared at Nyaxia. Not this woman. She was looking only at him.

She crawled toward him, calling a name he did not recognize.

"Remember why you are doing this," she begged. "Please. Remember your promise."

But the god did not remember. He did not care to. He had no connection to mortality. The suffering of mortals slipped by as inconsequential as grains of sand.

Nyaxia spread her hands before her followers. "We hold the power of the god of death. And with his power, we will be unstoppable. We will destroy the White Pantheon. We will conquer what is ours by right—all that the White Pantheon has attempted to keep from us."

Her lips twisted into a sneer. "And we will do it slowly, my children. So that they might feel every strike when we cut out their hearts."

At this, there was a wild cheer.

But that woman dragged herself closer still, shaking her head. "Please, Asar. This isn't why you did this."

Another fleeting sense of familiarity, gone before he could pin it down.

Nyaxia took his hand.

"Come," she said to him. "Let us save my wayward vampire kingdom from their destruction. Let Shiket see what we are capable of. And then we shall prepare for the war ahead."

Another fissure shot along the beach, the ground crumbling as the vampires retreated.

The god stared one more time down at it. At the woman who reached for him.

But such were the concerns of mortals, and he was not one of those anymore.

He turned away.

CHAPTER SIXTY-SEVEN

Mische

He promised me.

These three words echoed, over and over, the plea of a petulant child.

He promised me. He promised me. He promised me.

It had all gone so wrong. So terribly wrong. I knew Asar now better than I knew myself. And yet the stare that had burned into my soul when he looked at me, eyes glowing black beneath the mask of Alarus—it was not Asar at all.

No.

He had made the sacrifice he had sworn he wouldn't.

I watched in horror, helpless, as he turned away. As he took Nyaxia's outstretched hand and followed her into the ethereal mists of divinity.

No.

Luce's frantic cries split the air, so loud they cut through the sound of the retreating armies and the wails of survivors. She barked and barked and barked up at the sky where Asar had disappeared, as if ready to leap into the clouds to go seize him herself.

"Luce!" I screamed.

But she didn't so much as hesitate. She bolted after him, straight into the sea—straight into the churning crack that had opened within it, her shadowy body falling beneath the white foamy waterfalls leading to the underworld.

A sob bubbled out of me.

I squeezed my eyes shut. Tears slithered down my cheeks.

It was over.

As a missionary, I had believed that there was always hope, even in the darkest places. But my actions had torn the sun from the sky and the heart from my lover's chest. I could no longer remember what hope felt like at all.

I staggered to my feet, but I'd barely made it there when a force struck me from behind.

I knew instantly that it was Saescha. Her fury was so intimately familiar.

"You do not get to escape justice," she snarled in my ear, as she thrust me back to the sea.

And this time, I didn't even fight back. I couldn't if I had wanted to.

I wrapped my arms around her. I'd hugged Saescha countless times in my human life, but she had never felt like this. This was not the sister I'd known. She was empty, nothing but metal and robes, a shell filled with only single-minded fury.

Still, I clung to her.

As we fell, time slowed. I opened my eyes. The night sky spread out above me, still sparkling with the remnants of divinity. Asar and Nyaxia were gone. Perhaps Shiket would arrive soon, or any other of the gods, to survey the damage of Nyaxia's attack. They would take their revenge. It would all go on and on and on.

Over Saescha's shoulder, I watched a firefinch hurl itself into the sky from the burning forest. Nightfire clung to its golden wings. Its wail of agony ripped through the night like a blade through a heart.

And then I fell.

PART FIVE

DIVINITY

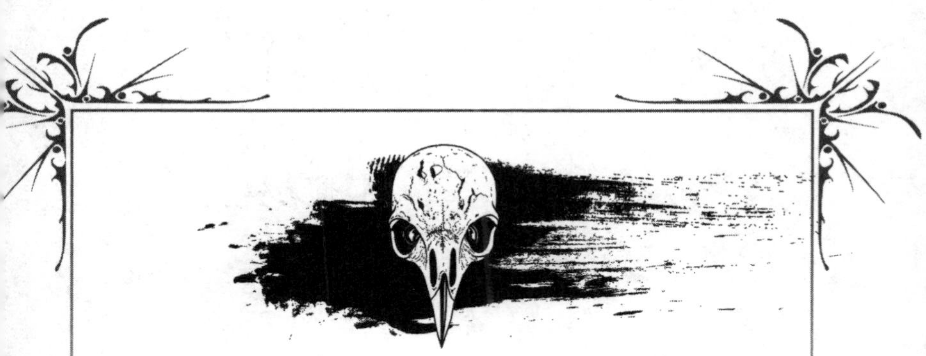

INTERLUDE

There are no more tales to tell. A god has no need of a mortal past.

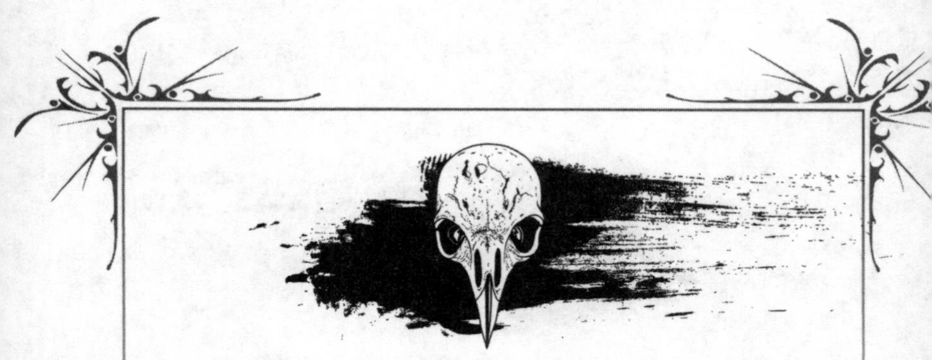

CHAPTER SIXTY-EIGHT

Mische

"My light, what is the difference between us?"

I was ten years old, sitting in the special chambers I was given for when Atroxus visited me. A room of gold and finery and gifts—me among them.

He laughed in that way he often did when I'd done something charming, which always made me happy.

"I am a god," he said. "You are a mortal."

"But what does that mean?"

"Surely you know, little one, what a god is."

"Of course I do. But . . ."

I splayed my hand out, arranging it over his. Mine was small and unremarkable, brown skin flat and smooth. His was much larger, glowing with divine light and gleaming gold with the strength of the sun.

All that beauty. All that power. Just in a hand.

"But what does it *feel* like?" I asked.

"I know no other existence, a'mara. I imagine that it is very different from that of a human."

"How?"

His effervescent gaze lifted to the window, gazing past the horizon. It was rare that I witnessed Atroxus looking thoughtful—which made sense, I supposed. Why would a being who existed in constant certainty ever have a need to think?

"I experience all things at once," he said. "As I am here with you, so too am I in the sky, in the sun, in the arc of the day across the horizon. I have seen the beginning of this world and one day I shall see the end of it. All in between is merely the rise and fall of fates, like leaves budding and falling upon the branches of a tree."

This answer confused me. But I didn't say so. Atroxus was now staring right through me, as if I'd outstayed his interest. I looked out at the forest below, and I thought of how inconsequential the leaves must feel. Pretty enough, but merely one of millions.

Later, I'd ask Saescha about this as she braided my hair. I didn't understand. If a god could see so much, how could they possibly care about every mortal soul? How could each follower truly mean something to them?

"You think too much," she said. "I think what he said was quite beautiful, wasn't it? Imagine being a part of something so grand."

She gestured to the sea of green sprawling out toward the Vostis shore, gleaming under the searing glow of sunset.

It was undeniably beautiful. Still, I was uncertain.

"But how can he save us if that's all we are to him?"

Saescha stroked my hair and rested her chin on the top of my head. "The real gift," she said, "is that he gives us the means to save ourselves, Mische."

I HAD FAILED.

I had failed so catastrophically.

I was falling, and falling, and falling, consciousness slipping in and out of my reach. I reached out frantically for something, anything, to hold on to, only to find misty nothingness.

Until—

A hand grabbed mine.

It was slender, female. Then another joined it—male, calloused.

A small, delicate one, like a child's. Another, with pointed, painted fingernails and knobby knuckles. They pulled me up, up, up.

My back hit solid ground.

I opened my eyes. Above me was a red sky marked with vicious black cracks, stretching from horizon to horizon. Rivers of blood twisted across the misty sky. Once, they had been elegant swirls. Now, they were broken, their paths shattered and interrupted by sputtering waterfalls. Souleaters plummeted across the dark, their bodies twisted and deformed, colliding in vicious fights. Silent streaks of lightning cascaded across my vision, leaving smoking scars in their wake. The distant echo of another monument falling shook the earth like thunder.

I knew right away where I was. My body felt it, too, as the final dregs of life drained away.

I lay there, staring at the sky.

Staring at what had become of the underworld.

Tears blurred my vision.

It was over.

It was all over.

I rarely allowed myself to think like that. Rarely allowed myself to feel that terrible emotion: hopelessness. But now, I couldn't find anything else.

I blinked, and saw the House of Night falling, saw Vostis going up in flames, saw a beach full of corpses and blood beneath the ink-black sky that I had created. I lifted my hand in front of my face and saw my flesh dissolving.

"Get up."

The voice sounded like it was coming from very far away. Everything felt far away.

I closed my eyes. Opened them.

Vincent leaned over me. His form was faint, the outlines of the broken underworld above visible through his body.

"Get up," he repeated.

I sat up. But I felt as if the life was draining from my skin, rooting me to the ground.

The only thing I could think to say was, "It's over, Vincent. It's—it's over."

"It is not over," he snapped. "Your lover stopped the immediate collapse of the underworld. And he stopped the immediate end of the House of Night. But it's only a matter of time before the threats resurface again. And—" He gestured to the broken landscape, barely visible in the desolate fog. "Only a matter of time before the underworld dies a slower death. There is still work to be done."

In the mists, I saw that moment:

Asar turning away. Asar's empty stare.

He had ascended and in doing so, he had dragged us back from imminent destruction.

But it had destroyed him. Not his body, but *him*. That precious heart who had so treasured the underworld. Who had heard the calls of a million invisible souls.

The pain was unbearable. My own heart felt as if it would crack open. I pressed my hand to my chest, as if to hold the pieces together.

"He's gone," I whispered.

And it was only when I said those words aloud that I really felt them, deep in my soul. The absence of him, like an organ had been ripped from my body.

We had created a god, just as we had intended to. And though it had saved us, it had also damned us.

But I wasn't thinking about any of that.

I was thinking about the love of my life, and that heart I had so treasured falling into the sea.

What had I done? How could I have let this happen?

I pressed my palms to my eyes. I really did try not to cry. But the tears came anyway.

Vincent watched me.

"This is pathetic," he hissed.

Pathetic. He wasn't wrong. I knew it, too. But the word slid between my ribs and twisted.

I whirled to him, furious. "Why are you here?" I snapped. "Go turn me over to Nyaxia. See if maybe she'll reward you with your kingdom. That's what you really wanted, isn't it? Fine. Take it."

A scoff. "Missionaries. So self-righteous."

He lowered himself slowly, until he was at eye level. His stare pierced me, the silver gleaming even as the rest of him threatened to fade away.

"Do you think I don't know what this is like? To lose the—" His voice caught. "The greatest love you've ever known? I do know this. And it was the fault of my own mistakes. No one else's. No, Mische Iliae. I'm not here to earn Nyaxia's favor. I am here because someone I once loved very much believed in the power of fate. The power of even the most inconsequential person to change it. Her goddess sent me to you, not my own. And I know that there is nothing I can ever do to right the terrible ways I wronged her. Not in life, and certainly not in death. *But*."

He leaned closer, fury burning in the cold ice of his stare.

"Her daughter, *our* daughter, is up there still, at the mercy of this game of gods. I will not allow her to suffer the consequences of it. And I do not care if the goddess-damned underworld collapses around me, but I will not allow it to take her with it. I didn't protect either of them in life. Not the way I should have. But I will be damned if I don't protect them now. So *get up*."

I stared at him, a bittersweet pang in my chest.

I had watched Oraya claw her way from the darkest, most painful depths of grief in the wake of Vincent's death. I had seen the way his lies had destroyed her. And as her friend, I had hated him for it.

Even now, I still did.

But it also reminded me of an older version of myself. How many times had I said that anyone could be saved? That anyone could choose a better path forward, no matter how dark their past was?

None of it would erase the things he had done. But at least he was choosing a better future. Even if he was doing it after death had already taken him.

I stood shakily. The faintest hint of an almost-smile flitted across Vincent's face. Still, I sagged. My body, weak as it was, swayed. A frigid gust of wind cut right through me, and Vincent nearly faded away.

I opened my mouth, and I'm sure he was hoping for some bold declaration, some confident affirmation. But the only thing I could choke out was, "How? What can I do? I'm just a—"

"You are no wraith," he said. "Look where you are."

He gestured to the ground. And it was only now, when I looked closely, that I recognized it. It all looked so different, with the underworld collapsing like this. But at my feet, scattered by the wind, were ashes. Golden ashes.

We were in the Sanctum of Soul—or what it had once been. Standing in the death place of a god. Standing where I had died, too.

"You slayed a god," Vincent said. "And you hold a piece of Alarus's power within you, just as your lover did."

"A tiny, stolen piece," I said. "I don't have his blood."

"Blood." He scoffed. "What do you think gave your lover the best of his power? A drop of a god's lineage, diluted by a dozen generations? You found his crown, his eye, his heart. How do you think you brought yourself closer to life? Did you think Asar did that? No. *You* were the one who wielded the eye of Alarus. *You* climbed out of Srana's forge, remade. *You.*"

He gestured out into the soupy mists.

"The underworld is not the territory of the gods," he said. "It is the kingdom of the dead. And the dead have chosen you."

The figures emerged, barely more than shimmering silhouettes in the silver fog, every step slow and deliberate—as if they had to fight for each one, to be here.

My eyes burned with unshed tears.

Esme, hand over the wound in her chest. A vampire man with a streak of white in his hair and flower petals in his pockets. Ophelia, more whole than I had ever seen her. Eomin, mouth still twisted in that familiar, boyish smile. Countless others, melting into the soupy fog behind them—but I recognized every one of them. Every lost soul I helped Asar free in the halls of death. Every lost soul I helped lead to comfort in my human years.

The hands that had caught me. The hands that had guided me here.

"I consider myself a practical man," Vincent said. "I won't pretend that I believed much of it, in life. All this talk of fate. But even I know that there is power in this place. The kingdom that Alarus built. It does not forget. And it has chosen you." He turned his moon-silver eyes to me. He was barely visible, now, just faint outlines that wavered with every gust of wind. "You are not merely here to lift up someone else's fate. It is yours. So take it. Take it and go."

The dead huddled together, then extended their hands, an offering in their cupped palms.

My heart twisted.

A sword. Asar's sword—no, *my* sword. I had lost it when I fell into Srana's forge.

Yet, it looked different now. The broken blade glistened as if freshly polished, illuminated with a sunless glow. The leaves on the intricate hand guard quivered as if they were alive. And the hilt . . . the hilt had changed. Now it bore poppy petals, and outstretched wings that looked as if they were aflame. A phoenix.

The dead pressed the hilt into my outstretched hands. Then, wordlessly, they melted into the mist, swept away with the fading embers of the underworld.

And my skin, where they had touched it, was now marked with streaks of red. Twisted, organic strokes like lightning, and an eye on the back of my hand.

An Heir Mark. The twin to Asar's.

I stared down at the blade, at the Mark, mouth dry. My hand slowly closed around the hilt.

"What do I do with this?" I asked.

Even as I dreaded the response.

"It is your blade, to do with as you choose."

"That's not an answer."

"Nothing remains of your lover. You already slayed a god once. You could do so again. Take his divinity for yourself, and wield it to better ends."

I flinched, like I'd just been struck. I shook my head hard. "No."

Vincent barely clung to his physical form. Still, he looked at me with such genuine pity.

"A queen must make difficult choices," he said. "But no one can carve this path but you. You are the one with the power of Alarus. Listen to what it tells you."

A million questions lingered at the tip of my tongue. But another gust of wind nearly snatched Vincent away. "We fade, as the underworld does," he said, nearly inaudible now. "I cannot stay."

He began to turn. Then stopped and looked back at me one last time.

"She knows, I hope. How much I love her. I know that in life, it was not enough. And I know that it isn't in death, either. But it is all I can—"

A howl of wind. The ash of a dead god scattered across the desolate ruins of the Descent.

And Vincent was gone.

I was alone.

You are not alone, the underworld whispered. *You are home.*

Once, those words, hummed by death itself, might have seemed like a threat. But I clutched that sword in one hand, and pressed the other to my chest, right over my heart. It took me a moment to feel it beating—slowly, as if it was still reawakening. Human and vampire. Alive and dead. Imperfect, just like the scarred hand that I held over it.

I heard Asar's voice, as he had whispered in my ear:

We can be imperfect together.

My thumb pressed to the phoenix on the blade's hilt.

Vincent had been right. All I had to do was listen.

I sheathed the sword at my hip. I closed my eyes.

I listened to the underworld, and I let it guide me.

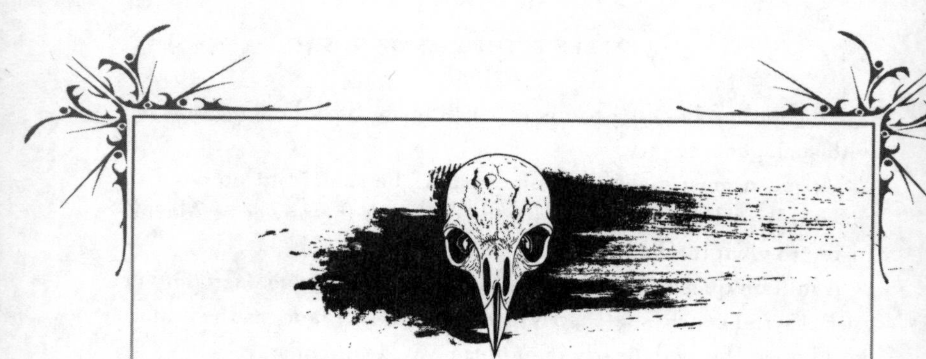

CHAPTER SIXTY-NINE

The God of Death

The god went with Nyaxia to her wayward vampire kingdom. When they arrived, it was in shambles. Shiket's golden warriors and human acolytes had torn the palace apart, then continued slaughtering a vicious path through the city.

As they looked down upon it, a wrinkle of hatred formed over Nyaxia's nose.

"I should let them burn," she hissed. "A fair price for their disloyalty."

The god looked down upon the burning city and wondered why it had ever mattered so much to save it.

{You have done worse to disloyal followers,} the mask said.

{They will just act against her again,} the eye agreed.

{No one who has betrayed her deserves to continue on,} the heart snarled.

But another voice, deeper than all of those, in the bruised wound where Nyaxia's dagger had struck, called out, too—even though the god couldn't hear what it was saying.

Despite her rage, Nyaxia would always keep her word. So she descended upon the House of Night, arms spread. Her eyes flashed as if with lightning across the night sky. The god watched as she ripped apart the seams between worlds, striking down the remaining divine soldiers with flashes of light that resembled shooting stars hurling to earth. She was great and terrible—everything a goddess should be when rewriting the fate of the world.

{She is brilliant,} the mask whispered.

{A shame he never witnessed all she could become,} the eye said.

When it was done, the kingdom smoldered. The god felt the presence of his cousins, the gods of the White Pantheon, looming. Nyaxia hovered over what remained of the House of Night and turned her attention to her vampire children.

"Remember how kind I am," her voice boomed. "You did not deserve to be saved."

The god hovered high above the city, but he could see everything at once—the broken silhouette of the capital city, the dunes that rolled miles away, the children that hid beneath their beds in their little apartments, the mice that darted between the cobblestones. He lowered his gaze to the castle, and there, he saw a winged couple standing, watching Nyaxia. The woman turned her gaze to him. Her brow furrowed. He understood that she was confused.

Perhaps in another life he'd known her. But he didn't now.

Her work done, Nyaxia returned to the sky.

"I have kept my word. The House of Night stands," she said, voice thick with disgust. "Let us leave them."

NYAXIA TOOK HIM to her home, a corner of the divine world that was fortified against her cousins. It looked very different from Ysria. Whereas the city of the White Pantheon was bright and elegant, Nyaxia's home was dark—a palace crafted of obsidian stone that held the essence of night itself, stars scattered over grand columns and majestic altars. Great windows peered down upon the mortal realm—a million glimpses into a million different worlds, reduced to a blurry background.

A few faceless servants of shadow lingered in the corners, but otherwise, the place was empty. Other gods often created companionship for themselves, or cultivated a stable of human followers to serve as such. Nyaxia, clearly, did not do either. She remained alone.

The only signs of those who worshipped her were the piles of offerings collected from her altars—most of it untouched.

She opened her arms and turned.

"Welcome home, godling. Much more pleasant, I presume, than whatever accommodations the White Pantheon gave you in Ysria."

The god remembered that he had been in Ysria—that he'd been imprisoned there—but little else. It was someone else's story, not his.

Still, he recognized this place, faintly, as if from a long ago dream.

"This was Alarus's home," he said.

Nyaxia paused before the windows, looking down upon a world in chaos. The god could remember someone standing beside her once. The two of them, hand in hand, lording over their kingdom.

"Our home," she said. "Yes."

He joined her. He scanned the endless glimpses of the mortal world below. He found himself searching for something, though he wasn't sure what.

Nyaxia's night-hewn eyes examined his face. Perhaps she was searching, too, just as he was.

She touched his cheek. Then his jaw. His chest.

At the sensation, two things wrenched through him.

One, an old memory. Nyaxia, her hair dangling around him in ribbons of darkness, her head thrown back in pleasure.

Two, utter revulsion. A bone-deep instinct that screamed, *This is wrong.*

He stepped back abruptly.

A flicker of hurt passed over Nyaxia's face. Not at his rejection, but at what she didn't feel within him.

She turned away.

"Enjoy divinity, godling," she said. "Learn about it while you can. I have upheld my half of our deal. And soon, you shall uphold yours."

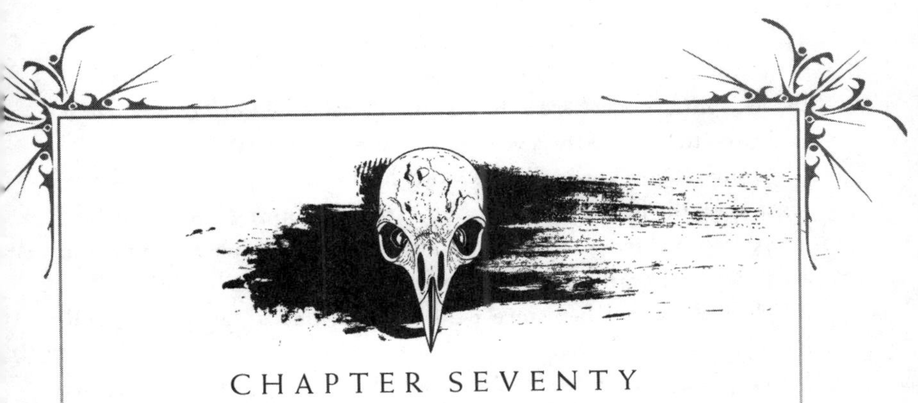

CHAPTER SEVENTY

The God of Death

The world hurtled toward its end. The other gods came not long after, churning the earth and skies with their rage. They came to the outskirts of Nyaxia's territory, and they all met there, hovering in the heavens between worlds.

Shiket led the White Pantheon. Behind her, Srana watched him, stare ticking like passing time. Acaeja stood at the back, her wings outstretched, all the fates they revealed shrouded in thick mists of uncertainty. When he met her white stare, he heard her voice in his head: *You are not out of time yet.*

He didn't understand what that meant. He tore his gaze away. Shiket was glowing with divine fury. The blades on her back fanned out like the spread wings of a bird of prey—though now, he noted, she was missing one of them, the great sword on the top left.

Curious, the god thought.

"You have made a grave mistake, cousin," Shiket snarled. "Moving against the territory of the White Pantheon is unforgivable."

"I could have slaughtered your kingdom," Nyaxia said. "Call it mercy that I spared some. Or perhaps I intend to have more fun with them, considering that you have seen fit to hunt my children for two thousand—"

"You wish to talk about hunting?" Shiket's voice boomed across the heavens. Somewhere a thousand miles away, a flock of birds startled from the surface of a volcano, fleeing into the stars.

"Your *children*"—she bit the word in disgust—"are monsters that feast upon the flesh of the innocent. There is nothing just about such an existence. Atroxus was right in his mission to wipe them out, and I will not rest until it is done."

Then she lifted her stare to the god of death, her gilded teeth bared.

"And *you*," she hissed. "We should have executed you when we had the chance."

A ball of rage formed in his chest.

{How dare she speak to us that way,} the mask snarled.

{She will suffer a terrible end,} the eye foretold.

{She never understood any of it,} the heart agreed.

This was what it was to be a god. A constant game of possession and destruction and competition. A thrill up one's spine with every burst of conflict. Gods had long, boring existences. It had been two thousand years since their last war, and they were eager for some excitement.

The god was not immune, either. He felt it, too—the desire to carve Shiket's head from her shoulders, then tear apart her soul so that she might never find any afterlife.

Perhaps he wouldn't have to. Perhaps the White Pantheon would rip itself apart in the wars to come. He cast a knowing glance to Srana, who built her secret armies all while standing so obediently now behind her kin. Surely she was not the only one to have such machinations.

"It is unwise to taunt me. Even Atroxus, arrogant fool that he was, knew better. But apparently you do not." Nyaxia's eyes flashed with the rage of shooting stars. "You wish to have a war? Let us have a war. My children are thirsty. Let them drink."

"We have thousands of bodies at our disposal," Shiket spat. "Meanwhile, I have destroyed one of your vampire Houses. Perhaps you have the benefit of the eternal night. Perhaps you have the benefit of some teeth. But how far will that go, I wonder, if I unleash a million warriors of the light against you?"

Nyaxia's lip curled. "You are welcome to. I have the god of death at my call. We will raise an army of the dead that will shatter your human kingdoms."

At that, Shiket hesitated. Nyaxia laughed, drinking up her uncertainty like fine wine.

"That intimidates you, cousin. Good. Fear me. The dead outnumber the living. The only army that grows with every loss." Her voice rose with excitement—as if she herself was realizing the brilliance of this plan as she spoke.

The god of death watched in silence. It was his power, his kingdom, his subjects wielded as her threat.

The underworld, in the state that it was, could not support being used in such a way. The souls there had suffered greatly. They went to the underworld for rest, not to be hauled back to the mortal lands to be used as a weapon in someone else's war.

These protests rang out somewhere deep inside him, near the wound in his chest, so far away he could barely hear them, anyway.

And besides, he was bound to Nyaxia, his divinity linked to hers. What was there to say?

{We could conquer a kingdom far grander than the last,} the mask whispered.

{Already, we see the potential,} the eye hummed.

Only the heart was silent.

The gods' gazes turned to the god of death.

"We shall see," Shiket muttered. "We shall see."

She slid her helmet down over her face, and in a flash, she was gone. The other gods followed, one by one. The last to leave was Acaeja. She remained even after Nyaxia began to turn away, her stare fixed upon the god of death.

There is still time, she whispered.

And for the briefest moment, a collection of dreamlike images flashed over her wings. A crown of copper bone. A bloody petal. A bird on fire. The sidelong stare of a brown eye threaded with amber gold, richer than the most precious of metals.

Then she, too, disappeared into the ether.

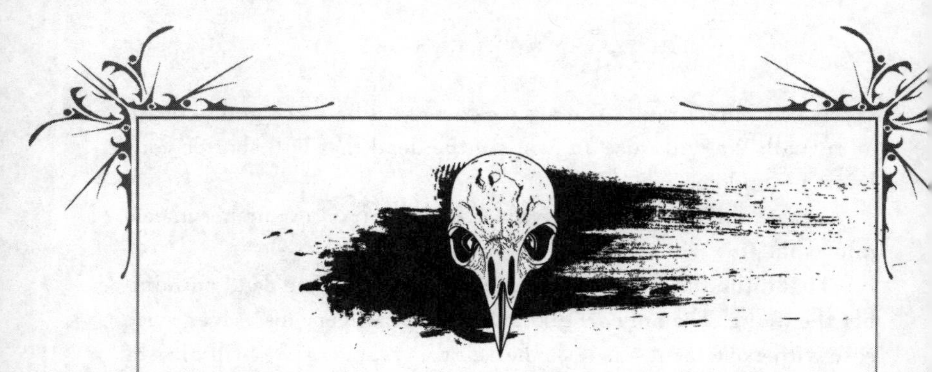

CHAPTER SEVENTY-ONE

Mische

I knew where to go. It was all so simple.

I wasn't sure whether the crumbling of the underworld had created a shorter path through the Descent, or if, maybe, the underworld was simply guiding me through the most efficient route. But as I walked, my next steps just seemed to spread out before me.

Listen to the underworld, Vincent had told me.

The whispers of the dead directed me, and all I had to do was empty my mind and follow.

The underworld had decayed so terribly in the time I'd been gone. The temples that I'd so admired when I'd first traveled with Asar down here now crumbled, stone falling into deep cracks in the earth. Pathways were shattered; doorways were cleaved in two. The rivers of blood, once mournfully beautiful, now churned in perpetual agitation. Even the dead could no longer thrive here, swept away by the harsh winds. The few that remained were so corrupted by the broken afterlife that they were barely souls at all.

I felt all these woes in my own body as I traveled. I listened as the underworld whispered its sad tales to me. And with every crack or wound I passed, I stopped to ease its hurts.

I had thought that I couldn't do this without Asar. But Vincent was right—I held a piece of Alarus's power, too. And when I pressed my hands to those wounds, I could feel in my own heart exactly where to pull them closed. Just like healing human souls, or vampire souls, had once come so naturally to me. And with every tear I closed, with every lost soul I helped back on their path, it was worth it to hear the underworld sigh, *Thank you.*

But there was still so much to do. I walked and walked. I wasn't sure anymore what I was—human, vampire, wraith, living or dead. Did it matter? I was Mische, I decided. That was all I could be.

I didn't get tired. I didn't get hungry. I didn't need to sleep. In the rare moments I stopped to rest, I rolled up my sleeves and looked at my arms. My skin was faintly translucent, as if shimmering with the dusty coating of the underworld, but I still had my scars. I pressed my fingers to them, and the red ink that danced over them, intertwined. As if the marks of my shame and the marks of my power were inextricably linked, one and the same.

I'd hated my scars for so long, but now, I was grateful I had them. They connected me to the scarred surface of the underworld, too.

On my left arm, my old tattoo burned, also, with the fading light of divinity. In my low moments, when I feared that Saescha could be waiting around any corner with the punishment I deserved, or when I thought of Asar's empty, cruel face beneath that mask, I would press my fingers to it and close my eyes.

I would think of a dream I had once, of a broken firefinch in the dirt, rising up again to the sky.

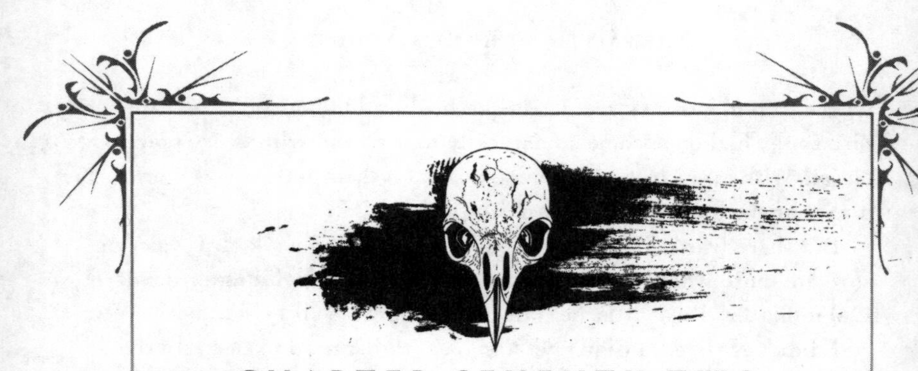

CHAPTER SEVENTY-TWO

The God of Death

The god no longer grew tired or hungry. Time was a mere suggestion, stretching out before him in limitless possibility, and yet, no possibility at all, because what was left to care about?

He went to visit what remained of his predecessor's kingdom—not the vampire lands that Nyaxia lorded over, but the underworld she had long abandoned. Nyaxia did not want to come.

"I do not venture there," she told him.

"Why?" he had asked.

Her eyes darkened.

"Too many ghosts," she said, and turned away.

Now, he wandered through the desolate plains of the underworld. It was in terrible disarray. The levels of the Descent had collapsed, merging into one another. The underworld bled out into the land of the living. Invasive beasts feasted upon the souls of the dead who inhabited it and the guardians who had once protected it. Everything, ruin.

He walked through it all, impassive, feeling nothing—even though a wound in his chest, a wound where something used to be, cried out in fury. It was easy to ignore.

Eventually, after much wandering, he came to a field. A broken arch stood at the center of it. Once, it had been blanketed with flowers—

poppies, maybe. Now, the flowers had turned black and the grass gray. The withered husks swayed as the breeze hacked up puffs of ash and dust, covering it all with a ghostly white cast.

He stepped through the field.

{It was once so grand,} the eye said, disgusted.

And indeed, the god could still glimpse what it had been—what it had been meant to be. A faint scent of cinnamon rolled over him. The memory of sitting among these flowers, beside a soul who felt like sunlight, lingered just out of reach.

He knelt in the field and, using the edge of the axe that held the eye, he cut free a single dust-coated flower. Its petals were black, tinged gray and shriveled at the edges.

He observed this, then, for reasons even he did not quite understand, he placed the blossom over the eye in his blade.

The petals quivered, then blossomed back into life. Bright red dripped over them as if with a fresh infusion of blood. The withered leaves opened, rejoicing in deep green.

He smiled faintly, then placed the poppy back in the field, letting it take root once more.

He took peace in this brief satisfaction, and then wandered away again.

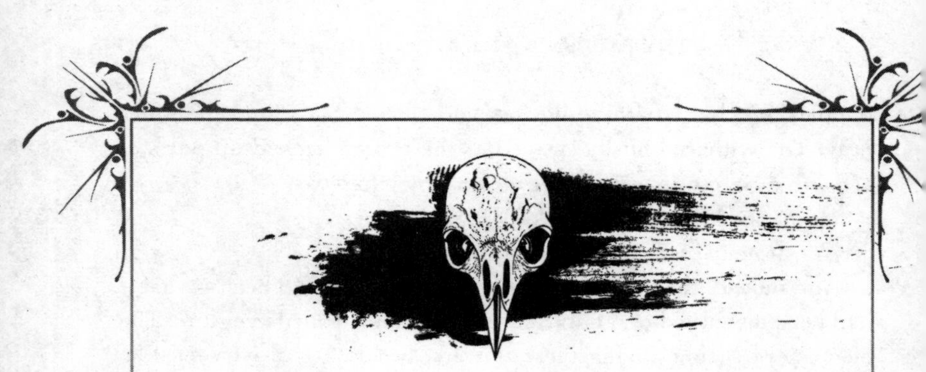

CHAPTER SEVENTY-THREE

Mische

Eventually, I reached a field of poppies.

I stopped when I crested the hill and saw it spread out before me. A lump rose in my throat. My chest ached.

The arch at the center of the field was broken, just two silver sticks of metal rising up from the wilted grass. The flowers were withered and black. Everything was dead and colorless.

And yet, I could still so clearly imagine it as I'd seen it last, when Luce had chased butterflies and Asar had whispered in my ear, and I had thought I'd die under the weight of my affection for him and the certainty that I would destroy him.

"I won't," I whispered to myself.

You won't, the underworld agreed.

I didn't have to pass through such painful memories. But I did, anyway. I wound through the flowers as they tickled my knees.

I stopped in the center of the field. A single poppy stood there, bright red, unmistakably alive.

Take it, the underworld whispered. *It is for you.*

For you, for you, the field agreed.

I lowered to my knees. Gently, I cradled the flower. When I touched it, I drew in a sharp, shaky breath. I felt as I had when I'd experienced Asar's touch for the first time. Like a new door had been opened.

I plucked the flower and twirled it carefully between my fingers. When I lifted my gaze, it was as if I could see the underworld as it could be. Not just the version of it I'd witnessed on my journey through the Descent, sadly beautiful but still only a shell of its true potential. Now, I saw it as it once had been and what it could become in the future. A place of solace and mercy, blood and bone and flowers, a comforting path ushering souls from life to death.

It was so beautiful that it hurt to look at. This was the kind of dream that seemed so big that it was dangerous to even acknowledge it—to open a tender heart up to something that seemed so impossible.

But I felt it, anyway.

I knew that Asar had, too.

I held the flower to my chest, right over my heart. I inhaled the scent of frostbitten ivy.

Then I tucked the flower behind my ear, where its stem wound into my hair like fingers folding around mine, and I kept walking.

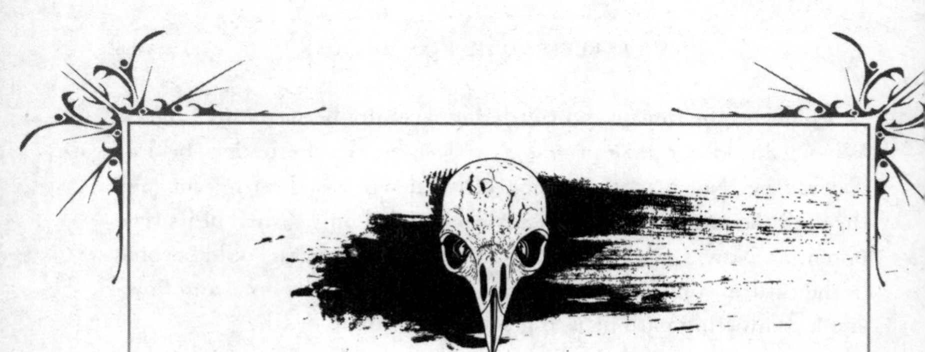

CHAPTER SEVENTY-FOUR

The God of Death

As Nyaxia prepared for war, the god continued to return to his old kingdom. He would wander for hours or days—he could not tell which. Time was different for gods. This was why, even on the precipice of war, at the height of their bloodthirsty fury, the moments before their next move seemed to stretch into eternity.

Nyaxia schemed and seethed, talking constantly of all the ways she would make her cousins suffer. The god was content to listen. Most of the time, he felt her bloodlust, too. He was, after all, a god—he craved power just as all the rest.

{Imagine the entire universe for our kingdom,} the mask said.

{I see it already,} the eye answered. *{A new world far grander than the old.}*

All while the heart silently dreamed of its former host's revenge.

But the god still found it difficult to fully commit himself to Nyaxia's plans. He would disappear for his long walks through the underworld, weaving through the ghostly ruins. He knew that once this place had meant much to him. Now, he found it hard to remember why. Still, it called him back night after night.

He wandered across rivers of frozen blood, the reaching hands of souls trapped within it. Across stone palaces, long empty. Through abandoned forests of fallen mushrooms, exhaling puffs of spores with their death cries. Souls crawled across eternal nothingness in the distance, chaotic as ants after the destruction of their nests.

It was in one of these fallen temples that he came across the rotted body of a guardian. It was larger than the other such creatures he had seen—though none of them seemed whole anymore. It had been a bird, once. Now, its body was just a faint suggestion of shadow. It lay belly-up, its wings splayed and broken. Its chest had been cut open. It still smelled mildly of smoke.

The only solid remaining part of it was its face—a golden skull. It was half broken, one eye socket incomplete. Its beak was chipped. Scratches marred its surface.

Yet, the sight of it made the god feel something he could not explain. He touched his own face. He felt only the cold metal of the mask, but had the uncomfortable feeling that he had been reaching for something else.

He knelt down and lowered his own forehead to the skull. The visceral pain—grief—of the underworld flowed through him. He felt the final cries of the fallen guardian in his own bones. He felt its commitment, even in its agonized death throes, to its task.

Then he rose, took the skull in his hands, and poured his power into it.

The metal glowed black, twisting and reforming beneath puffs of shadow. When it faded, the skull had changed. It was still a bird skull, still bright gold, but it was smaller, more delicate. Twisted metal whorls wound around the broken bone like ivy, spiking up as if to form the peaks of a crown.

Satisfied, the god placed his new creation upon the broken arch above the altar at the center of the room. With a sputter, fresh blood poured from the stone, filling the parched pool around it.

The god stepped back and observed his handiwork. This one repaired piece of a desolate, broken world.

{Why?} the eye asked. It was all-seeing. And yet, even it could not understand the point of this.

But the aching wound in his chest, the thing that sat beneath his new divine heart, was content, even if he could not explain why.

The god left it there, and continued on.

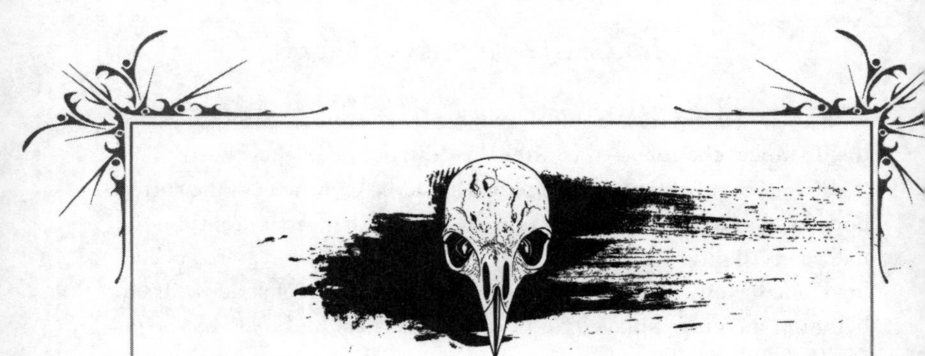

CHAPTER SEVENTY-FIVE

Mische

I walked and walked and walked. With every step, the underworld urged me on.

Eventually, I came upon a fallen forest. The mushrooms had once towered high over my head, stalks glistening white and purple and shimmering black. Now, they had all toppled. They covered the sandy earth with fleshy, rotted caps. The stench was horrific. Every breeze stirred clouds of green spores and the smell of decay.

It took a long time to get through this section, because I had to climb over the constant blockages. It was slow going, and exhausting even by the standards of my not-quite-mortal body. I hummed to myself to pass the time, and the underworld hummed along with me.

Eventually, I reached a temple nestled within the forest of mushrooms. The last time I'd been here, the temple had still held some of its former glory, its walls rising up and forming a sparkling dome that had peeked from within the mushroom caps. Now, all that was left were a few twisted pieces of the frame. When I stepped through what remained of the doorway, a few pitiful shards of the ceiling twinkled down from above. The pews within were destroyed, crushed by the falling mushrooms and sprinkled with broken glass. The crystalline moat of blood that had been here before was now nothing but crusted brown upon crumbling stone.

Still, I wandered through what was left as a howling wind shuddered through the temple.

Keep going, the underworld said.

It is here, the flower promised.

Soon, I came to the altar room.

Despite the temple's more recent decay, in this room, most of the damage was from the battle Asar, Chandra, Elias, and I had fought here so long ago. The slain guardian, the broken songbird, still lay in the center of the room.

I touched its corpse as I passed by. Silence. At least now, it was in peace.

Then I lifted my eyes to the altar. Above it, a metallic bird's skull, glowing with the touch of the divine, overlooked the ruin.

It had belonged to the guardian, once, but it had been turned into something else.

Go to it, the underworld urged me.

It was left here for you, the flower said.

I crawled onto the altar and climbed to the skull. Like the flower, this impulse came second nature to me. The obvious next step, even though I couldn't explain how or why.

At my touch, the skull came free in my hands. It seemed more delicate than it had on the wall. Through it, I heard the whispers of a million fallen souls.

It is yours, they told me.

It was mine. I didn't know how I knew it, but I did.

Maybe that was faith.

I placed the skull over my face. Whorls of metal shifted and reformed, weaving around the back of my head and into my hair. My heart felt stronger. The path before me clearer.

I looked down at the pool of blood—fresh—that surrounded the altar. A smile flitted over my lips.

I stepped through it, and continued my journey.

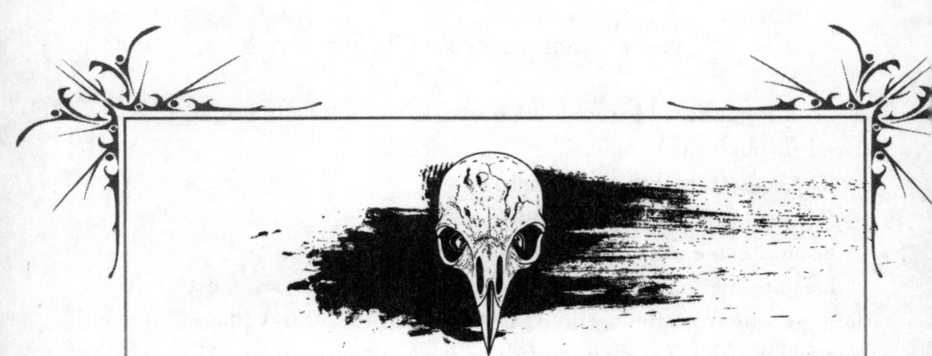

CHAPTER SEVENTY-SIX

The God of Death

"We have a world to conquer," Nyaxia huffed. "And yet you still hide away."

The gods of the White Pantheon gathered their human armies. Nyaxia rallied the vampires. The world hurtled toward inevitable collision.

Yet the god still found himself drawn, more and more, to the ruins of the underworld. He was looking for something, even if he couldn't explain what; he was answering a call, even if he could not hear what it was saying.

Again, and again, he returned.

One time, he went to one of the roots of Morthryn, now little more than a pile of crumbling brick. Once it had been the greatest of his palaces. Once it had been a bridge from life to death. Now it was only collapsing stone, a few rotted pieces of furniture, a tile floor melted into the mud of the underworld. Broken arches lined the few walls that still stood. Wraiths circled them, as if they'd forgotten what they were looking for. They were so far gone, they no longer had faces at all.

He came to one cracked door that, for some reason, made him halt. He peered through into the darkness within. He saw a crooked claw-foot bathtub, long-dry gray liquid crusted down its side. An old bed, the mattress disintegrating into what remained of the floor. Rotted books scattered across the ruin. A dusty piano, and bookshelves that stretched up into the mist.

The god stepped back, uneasy.

His curiosity had carried him across the underworld. And yet, there was something about this place, this room, that called to him and repelled him in equal measure.

The wound in his chest ached.

{Look away,} the eye said. *{This is not who you are anymore.}*

{We will build a new kingdom instead,} the mask added. *{Greater than this one ever was.}*

The god hesitated. But then he obeyed. In the end, Nyaxia was right. There was a world that needed conquering.

No point in returning to the corpse of one he had already lost.

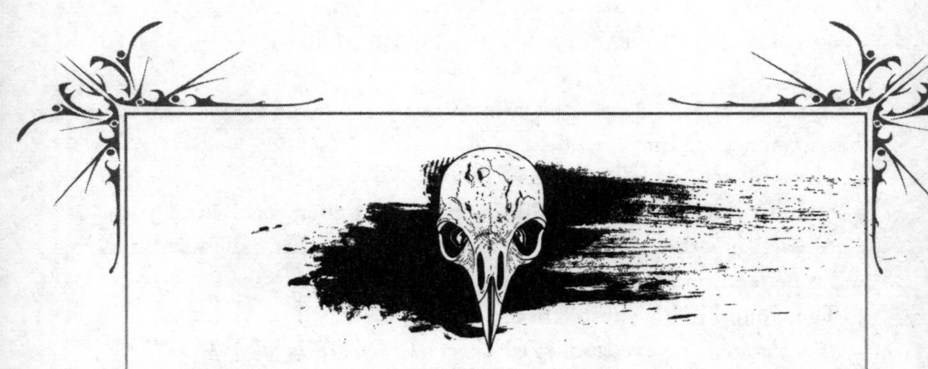

CHAPTER SEVENTY-SEVEN

Mische

The dead sang me a tune I now knew so well, and I followed it over plains and mountains and rivers and forests, all dead and withered.

Eventually, when I slowly scaled the rocky paths between dried-up streams of rusted red, I pushed through a ravine to see a familiar sight. Between sheets of jagged stone and the twisted branches of blackened trees, I glimpsed something that made my heart stutter.

A flash of bronze in a familiar shape—an arched doorway, with an eye carved at its apex. Between columns, I could make out just a hint of peeling brocade wallpaper, rotting tile floor, a tattered velvet curtain flowing sadly in the breeze.

The sight interrupted the hypnotic haze of my journey. I stopped short.

It was Morthryn.

Or what little remained of its roots into the underworld. Barely a pile of ruin—barely four standing walls. And yet, when I saw it, my heart still sang out, *Home.*

I half slid down the rest of the rocky hill, sending pebbles pitter-pattering down with me. The dehydrated remnants of the long-dead thicket clawed at my clothing and hair. A branch hooked itself to the back of my jacket, yanking me back. I paused to disentangle myself.

A small voice hissed, urgently, "Behind you!"

My head snapped up. I caught a flash of a figure disappearing behind Morthryn's doorframe. Then I whirled around—

Too late.

Something—someone—slammed into me. My jacket ripped. A hand grabbed a fistful of my hair. The rocky earth slid from under our feet. My attacker and I rolled down the hill in a mass of kicking, flailing limbs.

It was only when we stopped, when my assailant straddled me and pushed me down to the dust, that I saw her:

"Saescha," I breathed.

She had lost more of her armor since I had seen her last. Her white robes were stained with the red blood of humans, the black of mine, the silver of her own. They were ripped, revealing her body beneath—not just the glowing godlight of her golden gauntlets and boots, but the painful, necrotic purple where they met her flesh.

And her face. Gods, her face.

The rest of her helmet was gone now. Her face was too smooth, hard and angular. Her eyes were white. She had no hair, no eyebrows. When she snarled at me, her teeth were gold.

And her throat was still ripped out, just as it had been the night that I killed her. The blood glowed bright, smearing up her chin and down her sternum. It was immortalized even in her current form—the injustice that allowed Shiket to turn her into a Sentinel.

She was no corpse. She had been given a new life, just as I had. And yet, when I looked at her this way, my heart shattered for her. She was more dead now than she had been when I found her body. So much further from the woman I'd loved.

Her face contorted in agony. There were no more words, no more grand declarations of justice. Only hatred.

This was not my sister.

This was not my sister.

She let out a wordless snarl and lunged for me, and this time, I fought back.

I pushed her off me, and we rolled down the rest of the hill in a tumbleweed of teeth and fingernails. She had lost her sword, though the scratches from her blessed gauntlets still burned my skin. And she was divinely created. She was stronger than any mortal.

But this was my home—this was my territory. The underworld offered its help to me. Writhing rivulets of shadows rose to meet my every strike and swept in to interrupt hers. The few remaining wraiths clustered around us, watching.

Saescha was weak. It didn't take long to have her on her knees. When the underworld offered me my opening, I leapt on her, pushing her to the white dusty earth. I whipped my sword from its sheath and raised it. The broken, death-sharp blade glinted beneath the cold light.

But Saescha didn't fight. A tear rolled down her cheek, soaking into the thirsty ground.

"What have you done?" she finally choked out. "What have you done to my sister?"

I stopped.

I stared down at the face that was so similar and so different than that of the person who had once been the most important in my life.

"You took her from me," she wept. "She deserved justice. I was promised *justice*."

My hand trembled as the realization fell over me.

Souls became Sentinels because of their desperate desire for justice, so powerful that nothing else existed anymore at all. Saescha had every reason to want hers. I had thought that she was seeking justice for her own death at my hands. For the death of Atroxus. For the death of the sun.

But Saescha had been seeking justice for *me*.

Just as I looked at her and saw a shell of who she once had been, she looked at me and saw a monster who had consumed her baby sister.

If I killed Saescha here, whatever remained of her soul would simply cease to exist. She would never find her peace.

She is lost, the underworld said sadly. *There is nothing to offer her but a quick end.*

No. No one was ever truly lost.

Thump, as the sword fell to the dust. I lifted my mask, perching it atop my head so that my face was revealed.

The dead collected around us, stepping protectively closer, waiting.

Slowly, I leaned down. I took Saescha's face in my hands. Her skin was neither warm nor cool. It was stone-smooth, absent of all mortal imperfection. But deep beneath it, I could still sense her there. Just a tiny hint. But I would know her anywhere.

"You're right," I whispered. "I failed you, Saescha. You deserved so much better."

No one had ever told her that in life—that she'd deserved better. Everyone had always acted like she was lucky to have whatever she was given. She was never the chosen one. I'd never seen it back then, and now I felt so ashamed of it.

It had always been Saescha that I'd believed in. More than the sun. More than Atroxus. She had held my most unshakable faith, and because of that, I'd never seen her vulnerabilities. Now, they were all that remained.

Her eyes, blank and white, squeezed shut. Another tear trailed down her cheek. Her hands wrapped around my wrists, the golden claws digging into my skin, but she didn't push them away.

And she whispered, barely audible, "So did you."

I felt her regret bubble up from deep in her soul, so far beneath the surface—almost gone. All her doubts about every decision she had made in my upbringing.

I shook my head. "You have nothing to regret." I pressed my forehead to hers. As a child, she had smelled of the sun and the sand and the promise of dawn. Now, she smelled like rot.

"You are the sacrifice I will not make," I murmured. "And I will do this for you, Saescha. I will build you a home to rest. Your whole, beautiful soul."

I pulled away just enough to look into her face. "Don't be scared," I said. "Think of the sunrise. Like on the west balcony, in the middle of summer. When the light hits just right. Remember that?"

Again, that flagging flame rising in her soul. That one fading glimmer of who she had once been.

I seized it, and lowered myself to the wound of her throat. It was a perfect mirror of the night I had killed her. I could sense her path to the underworld. It was broken and convoluted. I wasn't sure if any soul, let alone one so horribly damaged, would be able to make it.

But sometimes, faith was all we had. And my faith in Saescha, even now, was absolute.

"Go," I breathed.

The last time I had helped a wraith, Asar had been with me. Now, I was alone. But Vincent had been right. All I had to do was listen to the underworld. I opened the door to Saescha's path home.

And then I kissed the wound I'd left on her all those years ago, the wound that had ripped her from mortality, and breathed my goodbye into it.

When I opened my eyes, Saescha was gone. Beneath me was only bone-white dust.

I stared down at it—my hands, marked with the beautiful whorls of my Heir Mark, and the scattered teardrops between them. The dead slowly drifted away, their work complete.

I drew in a deep breath. Let it out.

Movement rustled in the distance. I snapped my head up.

The door to Morthryn loomed ahead, much closer now. I glimpsed a smear disappearing around its frame.

I stood, wiped my tears with the back of my hand, and went to it.

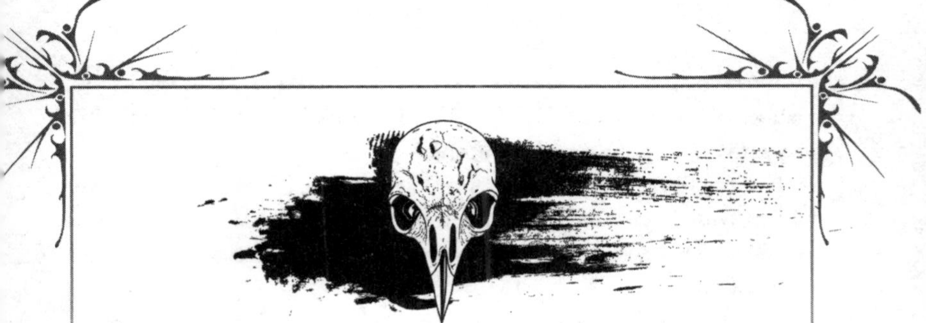

CHAPTER SEVENTY-EIGHT

Mische

The roots that led into the Descent had been the first to crumble when the underworld began its collapse. All that remained of it in the lower levels were patches of stone or broken furniture—a piece of moldy wallpaper against a tree, or a patch of three cracked tiles half buried in the dust. The riblike rafters jutted into the red sky like broken weapons on a decimated battlefield—all that remained of a losing army, who stood until the very end.

It was such a shell of what it had been.

I peered past a rippling flap of fabric into the dark, crumbling ruin within. My heart ached at what I saw there. So familiar. The bookshelves Asar and I had spent hours poring over every night. The shattered remnants of the gates we had taken such care to repair. Through several broken doorways, I glimpsed a copper bathtub, cracked and rusted, falling into the floor.

My eyes burned. I grieved it the way I would grieve an old friend, or an old life.

Just one life of many, the skull whispered. *It could have another.*

You still see what it would be again, the flower said.

Sometimes, it was easier to look away from the most painful parts of our past. But I pushed the flap aside and stepped inside.

Morthryn had never followed the rules of logic. I wound through each room, all familiar, until I reached one final door. This one stood, a sheet of rotted wood barely clinging to its hinges. It squealed in protest when I gently pushed it open.

It was a library. The shelves stretched up, up, higher than they ever had in Morthryn's halls. A directionless breeze blew from nowhere and everywhere, sending orphaned parchment pages scattering across the tile floor.

I couldn't quite place why this seemed so familiar, and yet so different.

Not one place, but two, the flower said.

And then I realized: it was Morthryn, yes. But it was also the libraries of Ryvenhaal, where Asar had been raised.

Even in his greatest sanctuary, he could not escape his greatest prison.

The boy sat in the corner, knees drawn up to his chest. A black dog wrapped around him, her sleek body pressed tight to his. When I approached, she growled a low warning.

"It's alright," I said softly. "I won't hurt you."

The boy regarded me warily beneath a mop of messy dark hair. One hand sat on the dog's back. He was perhaps eight years old, but it was hard to tell. He was small, with eyes beyond his years.

I gave him a gentle smile.

"May I sit with you?" I asked.

He didn't answer for a long moment.

Then, "Why?"

I gestured to the window and the landscape beyond. "It's a beautiful view. Just want to stop and rest for a little bit. Is that alright?"

He hesitated. Then nodded.

I settled beside him. The boy's gaze slid out to the horizon, but the dog eyed me on his behalf.

"You have a very good friend there," I said.

"I know," the boy said. "I'll never let her go."

"No, you won't. She'll never let you go, either."

The boy stroked the dog's fur affectionately. Still, his guard remained up.

"What's your name?" he asked.

"Mische," I said.

He flinched at this. His gaze flicked quickly away.

"I think I knew that," he said. "My name is Asar."

"I knew that, too," I said.

I looked to the window. Outside, the sky churned. I could feel the looming rage of gods, rolling over the broken underworld like distant thunderstorms, ready to destroy us all. For the first time, I wondered how long I'd been down here. How did time pass now? I couldn't make sense of it.

"It's beautiful out there," I said softly.

Asar nodded.

"How long have you been in here?" I asked.

"I'm not sure," he said. "A while."

He shifted, and I noticed his hand slip into his dirty, torn jacket, as if squeezing whatever he hid within it for comfort.

"It's nice here," I said. "But have you thought about seeing what's out there?"

Immediately, the boy shook his head.

"Why not?"

"Someone once told me that if I left, I would never be afraid again."

I gave him a soft smile. "That was a lie."

He nodded. "Yes. It was. So I decided that it's better to stay here."

I considered this. Another gust of wind, more violent this time, sent papers flying across the floor.

His eyes slipped to me, and for a moment, I glimpsed a version of him as I had known him—older, scars striking across his face. Just for a moment.

"You should stay here, too," he said, with sudden certainty. "Stay here with me. It is better."

A twinge of affection in my heart.

"Safer, maybe," I said. "For a little while. But I don't think that means it's better."

His fingers threaded through the dog's—Luce's—fur, as if to hold her there.

"If I leave," the boy said carefully, "I will make many mistakes."

"Probably," I agreed. "But you can still do a lot of good. Don't you think?"

"I thought so. A long time ago."

I shifted a little closer. Luce's lip twitched, like she thought about growling and decided not to.

And gods, my heart hurt so deeply for this child. I saw myself in him. An eight-year-old version of myself, sitting upon an altar in Vostis. An eight-year-old version of myself who had been told the same lie that he had been.

Give me your heart, and you will never hurt again. Give me your heart, and your soul will be pure.

"You will make mistakes," I murmured. "And I will love you anyway."

The boy flinched. Looked away. Again, that flicker of the man I'd known.

"I never told you how much it meant to me," he said.

I smiled. "Yes, you did. Not with words. But with something even more valuable."

He shook his head. "It wasn't enough to save you."

"Then we'll try again. Together." I held out my hand. "I will never promise you, Asar, that it won't hurt, because it will. I will never promise you that we won't fail, because we could. And that terrifies me, too. But it's in that fear that we hold our greatest strength. We need yours, now."

His eyes slid back to me. They were dark brown, nearly black, holding pain and wisdom long beyond his years.

Luce's snout rubbed against my knee, and my hand fell to her head. I felt not warm fur, but smooth bone.

Asar said, "I have something that I'm supposed to give you."

He withdrew his hand from his jacket and held it out.

There, throbbing faintly in his palm, was a heart.

The mortality of it was unmistakable. It was smaller than I might have expected, twitching in slow, rhythmic beats. Red-black vampire blood pooled around it in his palm. A faint glow pulsed from the muscle with each contraction. It was nothing but flesh. No golden divinity. No blessed gift.

And yet, the beauty of it nearly brought me to tears.

This was Asar's mortality. The thing he had discarded to descend, in the care of the truest version of himself. More precious, I decided, than any divinity.

I held out my hands, and he slipped the heart into it. It was warm, and it felt like him.

"It's perfect," I whispered. "I will treasure it forever."

He gave me a sad smile.

"It always belonged to you," he said.

Luce rubbed against my legs. She looked, once again, like herself as I'd known her—bronze skull, shadowy form. She rested her head against my legs as if to say, *I've missed you.*

When I looked up again, Asar was gone.

I wiped my eyes with the back of my hand. I cradled his mortal heart close to my own. Its beat moved in perfect time with mine.

I rose, and Luce did, too. Outside, divine cataclysm inched eternally closer.

I let out a shaky exhale and slid the skull back over my face. The voices of the underworld rose up again. The path spread out before me, closer than ever to mortality.

I stroked Luce's head.

"Let's go," I said to her. "I think we're almost there."

MORTHRYN WELCOMED ME down its winding halls. I continued my funereal march to the end. With every shattered staircase I ascended, every door that opened before me, my heartbeat grew stronger. I cradled the warmth of Asar's mortality close, and despite its fragility, it was also my greatest source of strength. Luce remained at my side, silent and loyal.

The mortal world grew closer, and with every step toward it, the foreboding grew deeper. Even close to the veil, Morthryn's halls were in terrible shape. Bricks tumbled from the ceiling. The roses on the wall were withered, a slow cascade of wilted petals falling over us like snow.

Still, I felt it leading me on with every step, offering me what little strength it still had.

You are almost there, it urged.

The end is close, the underworld said.

Before long, I reached a final set of grand double doors and a winding staircase. Once, this staircase had led through the veil, past the guardians. Now, the stairwell was dark. The cracked stone steps rose into inky black. It was a path offered only to me.

I stood at the bottom and stared up.

I couldn't see anything in the darkness. But I could feel the looming presence of the gods beyond, ready to exert their will over the mortal world. I could feel cold, terrible possibilities of the eternal night, and the blood that would spill in it.

And I could feel him. That presence, equal parts familiar and stranger.

Once you cross into the mortal world, Morthryn warned, *he will come for you.*

Asar, or the god of death? I pressed my hand to my chest, where a thread of connection had once bound us. Right now, I felt nothing. Nothing but a throb in the delicate piece of flesh that I now carried.

I couldn't make myself take the first step. Fear paralyzed me. I lowered myself to the ground and leaned against Morthryn's wall, as if reaching for a friend's hand for comfort. For the first time in this journey, true uncertainty settled over me. The weight of it was staggering.

I drew my sword and examined the blade—that gorgeous Shadowborn craftsmanship, given to me by Asar and blessed by the underworld. It gleamed with divine power.

What if Vincent was right? What if there was nothing left of Asar but the piece of him I carried now?

Luce nuzzled me. Her sadness at this thought was just as deep as mine.

We will not let him go so easily, she said.

I wanted to believe her.

Morthryn's shadows wrapped me in an embrace. They writhed around the blade, the hilt, and then my hand that held it—painted with the tangled red ink of the Heir Mark. A responsibility that I had not inherited, but had been given by those who needed me most.

Do not fear yourself, Morthryn whispered. *You are a queen. Your kingdom stands behind you.*

I closed my eyes.

A million invisible souls, Asar had said once, of the underworld. *They needed someone.*

I felt those souls with me now, pushing up against the border between the worlds of death and mortality. Leading me to only one.

I stood. I lowered my mask over my face. I stroked Luce's head beside me.

I wasn't ready.

But I stepped into the darkness, anyway.

CHAPTER SEVENTY-NINE

The God of Death

Nyaxia had grown impatient. One night, fire flashed at the horizon. She looked out to the distance, toward the human lands. It was difficult for gods to see beyond their territory, especially when rival gods took great care to camouflage their activities. Nevertheless, they could sense the great movement of armies collecting near the coast. Sparks of rage over the kindling of war. The sky was red, as if already preparing to soak up the blood of innocents. The end loomed.

Nyaxia had had enough of waiting.

"Our time is up," she said. She looked out over her loyal subjects—the Houses of Shadow and Blood, armies already gathered and waiting for her. The House of Night, her new wayward children, still recovering from their decimation at Shiket's hand.

The wind blew, bringing with it the smell of impending death.

She turned to the god.

"It is time," she said. "Summon your dead."

The god hesitated. "The underworld is not ready," he said, even though he couldn't quite understand his own answer.

{We are prepared,} the mask protested.

Nyaxia's eyes sparked with rage. Her hair flew back, galaxies forming and exploding in its depths.

"I am ready!" she roared. "Two thousand years, I have borne the

weight of their abuse. No longer. We are ready. *You* are ready. And I command you to do as you promised me. Call upon the dead. Help me seize this world."

A flash of a distant memory. Nyaxia with that hunger in her eyes, though back then it looked much more like hope. *"Take it all."*

The heart throbbed in his chest. The wound beneath it cried out in protest, but this time, he didn't hear it at all.

"Very well," he said to Nyaxia, bowing his head. And from his place in the sky, he turned to look down upon his kingdom. It was so damaged that it was difficult to make sense of it anymore. His fresh divinity, unfamiliar on these once mortal hands, roiled under his skin.

He closed his eyes and called to the dead.

It is easy for a god to rearrange reality. Much of it is mere suggestion to them—time, space, the limitations of the physical world. Yet, there are still rules to their power. There were boundaries between the mortal world, god world, and underworld, and to call upon the dead was to tear them down completely.

It was simpler than he thought it would be. The veil between the underworld and mortal world was so thin and damaged, like moth-eaten fabric. It ripped so easily under the strength of his newfound power.

Deep rifts gouged across Obitraes, like glass shattering beneath the pounding of a fist. The monsters within—some so much worse than the dead—pushed against it, sensing freedom.

Nyaxia smiled. "Good," she murmured.

It was not good, a small voice inside of him insisted.

But he attempted to repeat his call, anyway.

Only this time . . . he met resistance. As if a hand had grabbed his wrist halfway through the movement, or a wall had suddenly arisen between him and the underworld.

At his summons, he felt the attention of the dead turn to him.

But they did not obey.

He paused, confused. The mask, the eye, and the heart trembled with indignation.

{Who does challenge us?} the mask demanded.

{I cannot see beyond the veil,} the eye mused.

The heart was angriest of all. It said nothing, just throbbed against his rib cage.

Only the wound beneath it was pleased. Hopeful.

The god looked out over his kingdom. It was hazy, his visibility broken by the rubble of the decomposing underworld and the smoke that had come to consume it. Yet, the closer he looked, the more unmistakable it became.

Something was there that should not be.

Someone was there who should not be.

Nyaxia watched, her fury rising. Their attention shifted to the mortal world. Gods felt the draw of divine energy, and now, they sensed it gathering below—at the inflection point where the mortal and underworlds collided.

Morthryn.

Nyaxia's mouth curled into a snarl. "What is *that*?" she demanded.

At last, the heart spoke:

{A challenger.}

But the wound below it throbbed with hope.

The god of death rose and picked up his axe.

"I will take care of it," he said.

MORTHRYN BURNED.

The building rose from the churning sea, a jagged torch against the eternal night. The twisted metal spires had snapped, pouring smoke out against the star-dusted sky. The great circular glass window, bearing the eye of Alarus, was half shattered. Beams of red light streaked from the open half while dousing the rest in bloody crimson. The jagged twist of the broken frame gave the impression of a tear falling from the bisected iris.

The god stood before it, his fury rising.

He did not know what had done this. But he knew that the building radiated with divine power. Power that some unworthy being must have taken—no, *stolen*—and then used to destroy what was his.

This was *his*.

Morthryn was a relic of his old kingdom. A relic of Vathysia, the House of Death.

There was little that gods truly cared about. But theft of what they considered theirs was universally offensive. And now, his nerves raw with his fresh failure, the god was furious.

The doors of Morthryn opened for him, and he stepped through.

Welcome home, it crooned. *We have missed you.*

The place now looked so different than it had in ages past. For a moment, the god experienced it in countless ages at once:

In ancient times, when the bone rafters had been carved with fresh prayers in his name and the walls themselves had overflowed with his power.

In the years since, when its greatness faded, its rooms no longer used to house great magical feats but prisoners the world wished to forget.

In the recent past, when one man and one guardian worked tirelessly to restore it to the glory it had once had.

And as it was now, so breathtakingly horrifying and breathtakingly beautiful.

It had crumbled so much in the time since he had last been here. The mirrored floor was shattered with spiderweb cracks. The rafters had been broken, the bones now reaching up and ending in jagged blades. The glyphs that had etched the ancient power into these walls were faded, worn away as if by a sandstorm.

And yet—now, they glowed.

All of them, even the ones that no longer were visible beneath centuries of neglect. They beamed with searing light.

It was not flame, he realized.

It resembled it. But it wasn't hot. It was cool and comforting, and strangely familiar, like a tune that lingered just beyond reach. It was closer to smoke than fire, or shadow summoned by the reinvigoration of the spells in the walls. Darkness met the light in equal measure, intertwining as it rose from the floors, the rafters, the walls, in a sad, graceful dance. Clusters of light and shadow moved about the room, almost taking on the appearance of silhouettes—faces visible within them for seconds at a time.

The god reached out to touch it, and a shock rushed through him—a sudden, innate connection to every soul who had ever walked these halls.

One soul above all.

He jerked his hand away. The mask burned against his skin.

{This is a coup,} it seethed. *{You cannot tolerate it.}*

I am more myself than I ever was, Morthryn whispered, its voice echoing from its greatest depths.

The god journeyed deeper.

"Reveal yourself," he commanded, raising his axe and the eye within it. The walls shook. Darkness flared from the corners. The dead pushed to the surface. "As the god of the dead, heir of Alarus, I command you to reveal the traitor you hide."

Shadow ripped through the walls. A beam above crumbled, crashing to the floor with a pained final wail. The not-flames pulsed thicker, the dead lurching closer. Still, they fought his command.

The dead murmured, *We cannot.*

Morthryn agreed, *We cannot.*

The god's lip curled. *"You cannot,"* he repeated in disgust. "I command you. You *must*."

The dead only moaned in response, moving down the halls like sand rolling over the dunes.

{You have been too merciful,} the mask hissed. *{This must end.}*

The god agreed.

"Fine," he said. "I will rip you apart and excise your disloyalty myself, if I must."

And with a great surge of power, he did exactly as he promised. He swept down the great hall. Darkness raked through Morthryn's walls behind him, tearing and clawing. The glass floor shattered. Behind him, arch after arch fell. Morthryn cried out in pain.

And yet, its resolve held.

The flames grew thicker. Even the god struggled to see through them, now. But a god does not need to see. He was on a warpath. With every flick of his hand, another wall fell. He ripped the ivy from the walls. Flowers, alight with flames, fell over him like rain.

And then he felt it:

A presence brighter than the weak souls of the dead, younger than the ancient halls of Morthryn.

And yet . . .

Powerful. A power that even mirrored his own.

He whirled around to see a flash of smoke move from one door to another. The pull continued down the hall.

He smiled.

There you are.

A voice taunted back, *If you want me, then come get me.*

It was not Morthryn's voice. Not the voice of the dead. Not the voice of the mask or the eye or the heart.

He inhaled the fleeting scent of burnt spice. A fierce hunger pang ripped through him. A longing for something that had never existed, like the pain of a phantom limb.

He pushed it away and gritted his teeth. He was a god, and gods did not like to be challenged.

Walls and defenses were of no consequence to him. He tore through Morthryn's as if they were paper. He ripped past wall after wall. His challenger was in reach.

The flames swelled. The dead wailed. He pushed through an empty cell, a fallen stairwell, a long-abandoned bedchamber. At last, in a decaying office, full of picked-over shelves, he collided with his traitor.

He only glimpsed them—a silhouette outlined by light and darkness. They wore a bird's skull over their face, cast in gleaming gold. The red smear of a poppy perched behind their ear.

He did not hesitate as he struck.

His adversary, though, had been ready for him—perhaps more prepared than him, because when the two of them collided, his entire form lurched. A million memories of a stranger surged through him, then abandoned him once again, like a wave crashing and dragging away from the shore. They felt like both death and life, divinity and mortality, humanity and vampirism.

He righted himself quickly.

{That way!} the eye roared, and the god swung his axe at his opponent with enough power to collapse a great stone column, sending another cascade of broken glass to the floor.

The figure let out a cry of pain. They stumbled briefly, but then disappeared into the flames.

The god lunged again, nearly striking, but something streaked past his adversary to dive at him. He hissed and fell back, knocking away his attacker—*a dog?*—like a discarded toy as he resumed his chase.

The two of them clashed like a storm across the distant sea, thunder and lightning warring. The dead assisted his opponent, reaching through the veil to block his strikes or assist theirs.

The god did not know how many blows he landed, only that they were not enough. He did not know how many times he called to the dead, only that they did not listen. He no longer heard the collapse of the walls around him, nor the wails of the dead as they clawed at him.

With a burst of rage, pushed to his breaking point, he grabbed at his attacker. At last, he made contact. His power surged, his body pinning theirs.

{At last, your victory,} the mask purred.

He pushed the figure to the wall and raised the axe.

"How dare you challenge the god of death," he snarled. "Who are—"

His killing blow stopped mid-strike.

The woman stared back at him. Her eyes were large, and so bright, even shadowed by the sockets of her mask. They were the color of the falling embers of dusk, threads of gold in deep brown. The dead surrounded her protectively. Her hair, wild curls of deep brown and burnished gold, quivered.

A memory. Those eyes, lifting to his, in the depths of the underworld.

{Not yours,} the eye reminded him.

{Not yours,} the heart agreed.

Again, that scent—burnt cinnamon. He remembered it upon his tongue, when he thought he would never know a deeper worship.

The woman was not alive, but she was also not dead. Just as she was not mortal and not a god. Still, her chest rose and fell with quickening breath. She was afraid.

Her gaze slid down to his grip on his axe. Then the blade, hovering near her throat.

"You won't do it," she said.

He should.

He understood, in a knowledge that went beyond logic, that this person was the one thing holding him back from the ultimate power of his divinity. A challenger, and a shackle.

{Do it,} the eye said.

{Do it,} the mask said.

{Do it,} the heart said.

No, the wound begged, scar tissue from another life. *No.*

His hand did not move, and he was not sure why.

The hesitation cost him. The dead rose up around them, surrounding his adversary. Strange, that so often, the souls of the dead appeared in darkness. But around her, they were light, clinging to her like licks of flame to a candle.

He lunged after her. *Crash,* as another wall came down. They tumbled into a ballroom. Twinkling color rained down over them as another stained-glass window fell. Tile shattered beneath his feet when he stood.

The woman stood before a broken wall of windows, framing her against the blood-red sky and the sea, churning with impending divine collapse.

She just stood there, still, as if baiting him.

It worked.

He dove for her. They collided, life and death sparring in the blow. Her body was solid and fragile and so very mortal. He pinned her down against the furniture.

But she just touched his face.

"Come back to me," she murmured.

{End it,} the mask commanded.

{End it,} the eye agreed.

{End it,} the heart whispered.

But still, that inexplicable hesitation.

The woman seized this opening. Her hand wrenched free of his grip, but instead of moving to strike him, she pulled the skull up, resting it atop her head like a crown. It revealed the full expanse of her face.

The sight struck him.

A million moments slipped by like dead leaves in the wind. That face, bright with laughter, soft with contentment, pinched with sadness. That face, smeared in blood, glowing with happiness, painted with shimmering gold. That face, in life. That face, in death.

"Come back to me," the woman said again.

Come back to me. Come back to me. Come back to me.

Above, the broken eye of Alarus stared down at him. The dead flooded the room, a million forgotten souls blending like paint strokes. And within them, they rendered memories. Memories of this place he had once loved so deeply, and the woman who had resurrected it alongside him.

{You are fighting like a mortal,} the mask snarled. *{Fight like a god. Finish it.}*

With a roar, he lifted his axe and brought it down.

But then a few notes rang through the air, off-key and tentative.

The sound wrenched through him. It was only then that he realized where they were—that he had not pinned her against a piece of furniture, as he'd thought, but against a piano. Silver tendrils caressed the keys. They painted the ghost of another life. A man with his head bowed over the music, a woman perched beside him, the two of them composing a new life together.

The god's eyes widened. That memory, that name on the tip of his tongue, crashed through him. Just for a second, he was whole again.

Mische.

He couldn't stop his strike in time. But he was able to divert it. It smashed into the mahogany wood instead, only shaving off a curly strand of hair.

He staggered backward. With the help of a rising sea of the dead, she pushed him back against the wall. His hand snaked out to seize hers. Her broken blade pressed to his chest, right over the tender spot where he'd sacrificed his heart.

He searched Mische's face. His grip was so tight around her hand that they trembled together. He could feel every raised piece of scar tissue, every muscle, every bone. He knew them because he'd already memorized them all.

The tip of the blade dug into his skin, a streak of divine blood dripping over their hands.

"Take it," he ground out.

The voice did not belong to a god. Nor did the sudden desperation that jumped up against the inside of his ribs, screaming, *Do it, do it right now. Take the power, take the heart. It was always meant for you.*

He had prayed she would understand. She had become everything he dreamed she would be. Had *known* she could be. He was so proud of her that he thought his heart, mortal or god, would burn with it.

But Mische did not move. A tear rolled down her cheek.

{What are you doing?} the mask wailed.

{You can end it now!} the heart roared.

Desperate, he fought for his old self. Fought to offer her this opening.

"Do it," he begged. "Take it."

Because this had always been the only option. The only happy ending he could offer her. The only good he could do in this world. Sacrificing himself to hand her the power to be greater than he ever could be.

She already was. She always had been.

But Mische leaned her forehead against his. Her gold eyes shone with the light of the underworld. Their song played on, mournful, painting the ghost of a life they could not have.

"I love you," she whispered. "I love you, Asar Voldari, Warden of Morthryn, king of the underworld, heir of Alarus. I love you, and in this life or the next, worlds mortal or divine, I will never let you go."

{Kill her!} the mask shrieked.

{End it!} the eye begged.

{You are a god!} the heart boomed.

But the god did not move.

He forced himself to remain still, to offer her his heart, as she drove her blade straight through his chest.

CHAPTER EIGHTY

The God of Death

The heart screamed as the blade cut it in two. The mask wailed. The eye wept.

The god swayed. His knees gave out. The souls of the dead surrounded them in searing light and cold darkness. Their hands reached into him, or perhaps hers did, or perhaps both.

He sank to the ground. The pain was unbearable. Blood poured to the tile floor, pooling in the cracks he'd gouged in it and falling all the way to the underworld.

He lifted his head. She stood over him, holding the heart—no, not all of it. Half still remained within him, giving him the power of divinity. But the power she took from him still was enough to set her ablaze. The dead caressed her like children embracing their mother, guiding the heart into her own chest.

Light poured from her eyes, her freckles, the tips of her fingers. The skull—her crown—glowed bright. The flower in her hair burned. She was a goddess. Every bit a goddess.

Pain spasmed across her face, and the sight of it hurt. But she forced her eyes open. She kept her hold on his face.

"Come back to me," she whispered again.

And then she cupped her hands between them. Within it was a fragile, beating muscle, more mortal than god. Weak and bruised and battered, and yet, all his.

The god let his mask clatter to the floor.

And he took her face in his hands and kissed her, as she thrust his mortal heart back into his chest, and the underworld consumed them.

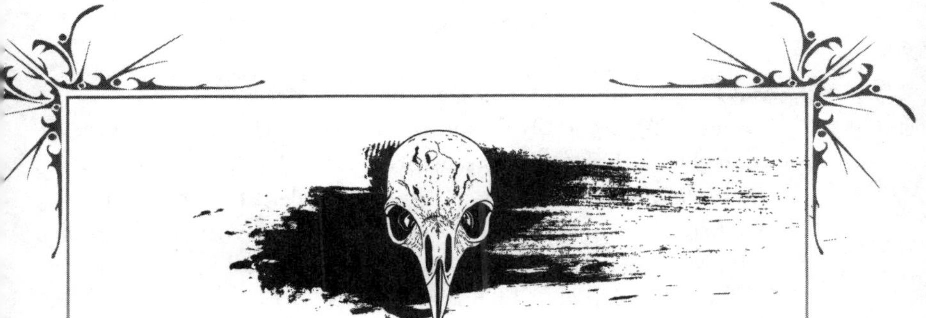

CHAPTER EIGHTY-ONE

Asar

When I opened my eyes, I was on my knees. The air smelled of burnt cinnamon. My skin was hot. My chest ached—with the tolerable weight of a little piece of divinity, and the agonizing weight of mortality. The melody of an off-key song still echoed, and it sounded just like her.

It all rose up to meet me at once. The failures, the weaknesses, the memories. The scars upon my skin and heart.

And yet.

And yet.

I reached up and wrapped my hands around her. She still stood, though she swayed against the piano. Her fingers were intertwined in my hair. My hands clutched at her legs through the silk of her tattered skirt, relishing how solid she was.

I had walked the path to divinity; I had walked the path to death. And yet, here, in her presence, I was overwhelmed. Here, in her presence, I knew worship.

"Mische," I whispered. A prayer.

I kissed her feet, bare and bloodstained. Her legs, soft and smooth. I rose, and kissed her perfect, scarred arms, her shoulder, her neck, and at last, her glorious mouth. My mortal heart sang.

We did not speak. We did not have to. Morthryn played the final notes of our song to the rhythm of our shared heartbeat.

And I knew: this was true ascension.

My queen. My light. My darkness. My future. The answer to every question. The ending to every sentence.

She broke the kiss to draw in a shaky inhale. I pressed my forehead to hers, drowning in those eyes, still gleaming with the dregs of divinity. My thumb traced the path through her freckles.

"Hello, Dawndrinker," I whispered.

She smiled through her tears. "Hello, Warden."

And I kissed her again, as the underworld bowed around us.

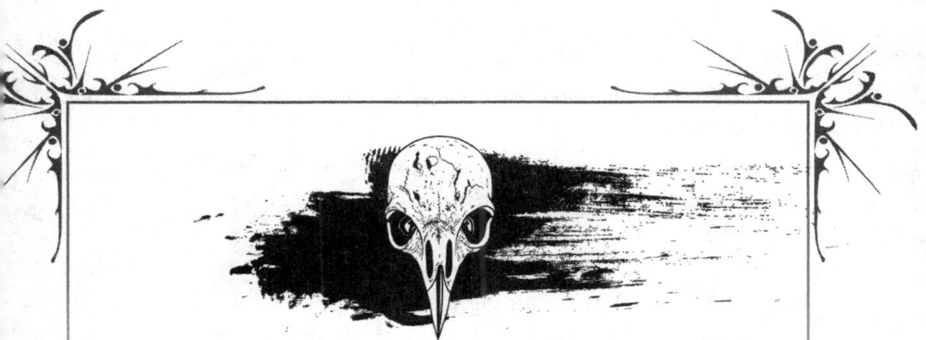

CHAPTER EIGHTY-TWO

Mische

I could have stayed there, in the welcome embrace of Morthryn and the even more welcome embrace of Asar—Asar, it was *actually him*—forever.

I couldn't believe it had worked. I wasn't even entirely sure what I had done. All I knew was that Asar was back and I felt alive and Morthryn was no longer collapsing around us. That, in this moment, felt like a victory.

If a very temporary one.

At last, we parted. Asar's thumb lightly stroked back and forth over my cheek, like he couldn't bear to stop touching me.

"I knew you would be back," he murmured.

"If you're trying to tell me that this was your plan," I said, "it was an outlandish one."

My hand pressed to his chest. The wound had closed, but the scar still remained, a jagged black line to add to his collection. I could feel the steady thrum beneath it. His mortal heart, the precious one I'd saved.

And the piece of the one that still gave him Alarus's power.

The piece of the heart that also sat inside me.

Asar's touch pressed to my chest, now, and I winced at the shock of pain. The reality of it—the unbelievable reality of it—struck me with a wave of dizziness. The pressure of the piece of divinity that sat beneath my ribs was staggering. It made it difficult to breathe. Each pulse burned.

But it was the divinity that had allowed me to save him.

Asar began to speak, but then, a fresh bolt of lightning cracked across the sky. The hair stood on my arms.

You feel it in the fabric of the world itself, when a god is near. When their rage is encroaching upon you.

Asar's gaze lifted, looking past me, through the window. His face shifted. He began to pull me away—

What remained of the windows shattered beneath a vicious gust of wind, sending Asar and me sliding back, shielding our faces against the razored burst of glass.

When I lowered my arm, Nyaxia hovered before us, hands spread, hair flying out behind her. The very universe itself trembled with her rage.

"What is this?" she roared. "I ask you to uphold your end of our bargain, and now, I come here to find you consorting with your challenger. A *traitor*."

She hurled the word like a dagger. More windows shattered. Stone crumbled. The dead scattered, sinking back into the shadows in terror.

Cold fear fell over me.

I held a shred of divinity in me—whatever that meant. But I was no god, and the rage of one sent every primal instinct cowering.

Her eyes fell to me, and the hurt within them was as deadly as the anger. Suddenly, I understood—that so much of her anger now was not because of an army or an ally, but because Asar would never be Alarus, no matter whose heart sat in his chest.

Once again, she had attempted to reclaim him, and once again, she had been left alone.

"Shiket breathes down our throats," she snarled. She thrust her hand to the sky, which swirled with rainbow fragments of light—evidence that more gods were near. "And yet, when I command you to raise an army to defend your home, you defy me."

Asar straightened. He picked up the eye, embedded within his blade. Then the mask, which he held, rather than wearing it.

"The dead do not fight for you," he said. "The dead belong to the kingdom of the underworld. The kingdom of Vathysia, the House of Death."

"Raise them," she commanded. "I gave you a gift you begged for. *Raise them.*"

"I will not, Dark Mother," he said. "I will not collapse the underworld and damn the mortal world, with it. I will not force these lost souls from their rest to become weapons against their brethren."

When was the last time Nyaxia had been so directly defied? Asar said this all so calmly, like it was mere fact. Fear clutched my throat.

And maybe it was this that tipped Nyaxia off—that made her realize the true nature of the change she had sensed. The true nature of what had drawn her here.

Her gaze shifted from Asar, to me.

I felt her heartbreak, as she realized what had happened.

And then, more powerful, her fury.

"What have you done? I gave you a gift. I gave you my husband's heart. And what have you done with it? What have you . . ."

Her voice trailed off. And then those eyes, galaxies deep, snapped to me.

The hurt and horror that spasmed across her face dug deep into my heart—or perhaps the part of Alarus's heart that was in me. I felt the sudden, inexplicable urge to reach for her with the touch of a comforting lover.

"No," she whispered. And then, louder. "No. I will not allow it. I will *cut it out of you.*"

She lunged for me.

Being a god, even a fraction of one, meant experiencing time differently. Seconds slowed. And in the space between them, the underworld answered my call before I even had to make it.

Asar was in front of me, the mask on his face and axe in his hand, the eye at its hilt glowing bright.

And in the same breath, the dead surrounded me—countless souls chancing Nyaxia's rage to rise to my protection, slipping between the cracks in the floor and walls and ceiling.

"You will not touch her," Asar said. He did not raise his voice. But the command shook the fabric between worlds. "Now you see who the army of the dead answers to."

Nyaxia pulled back, shaken. A sneer flitted over her nose. "Who? Her?" She laughed, rough and cruel. Her gaze snapped to me, and protectively, the dead curled around me like the smoke of a funeral pyre.

"You naive fool," she sneered. "You wish to bear the weight of a god's heart? Try. You are but a mortal. What makes you think you can carry such a weight?"

Another stab of pain, this one deeper than the last. My hand, adorned with my Heir Mark, pressed to my chest. My brow furrowed.

Something wasn't . . .

Asar glanced at me again. This time, more alarmed than proud. I found myself leaning against his hold.

The sky churned. A roll of thunder shook the floor. Rainbow wisps of light curled in the air.

I barely noticed them. My chest tightened, tightened, tightened.

Nyaxia laughed. "You fancy yourselves godlings, do you? Well, now you have attracted the attention of my cousins. Let us see what they will want to do with—"

She didn't have to finish.

I sank slowly to my knees, clutching my chest, vision darkening.

And the last thing I saw was the night opening as the White Pantheon stepped through the sky.

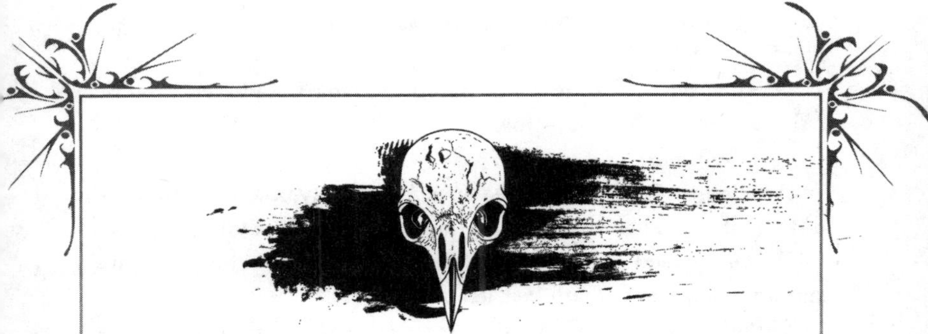

CHAPTER EIGHTY-THREE

Asar

Even faced with the vengeance of the White Pantheon, nothing terrified me more than Mische collapsing beside me. I fell to my knees when she did, whispering her name as her lashes fluttered, fear clutching my chest. Luce curled around us, as if ready to protect us against even the gods themselves.

Shiket arrived first. Her helmet was down, leaving only the bottom half of her face visible. The blades on her back—only five, one missing—glowed with divine fury. The others followed not long after. Ijakai circled the sky in the form of a massive hawk, Srana clicked with her clockwork eyes, Ix unfolded in a puff of lavender smoke, Vitarus came in a cloud of life and decay. Acaeja was among the last to arrive. Her six wings were spread, depicting six fates of bloody death.

"You know no limits," Shiket roared at Nyaxia. "You have slaughtered my people. You have murdered my acolytes. And now you hand untold power to your fallen ones. You are a lesser goddess who should have stayed in the deadlands. Alarus would be ashamed of what you have done to his legacy."

"You dare claim to know what my husband would have wanted? You, his murderers?" Nyaxia let out a laugh that sounded like flesh tearing. "I will destroy you. First let me punish my own traitorous children. And then I will come for yours."

Nyaxia whirled to us, teeth bared in a snarl, and I cringed over Mische's barely conscious form.

"You will not."

Acaeja's voice shook the heavens. Unlike Nyaxia and Shiket, she did not shout. There was no emotion in her words. Only truth.

When I raised my head, Acaeja stood before us. Her wings were spread, shielding us with fate itself.

Shiket drew back. Confusion, then anger, rippled over her face.

"You have no authority," she said. "On the glory of the White Pantheon, I command that you—"

"You do not rule the White Pantheon," Acaeja said.

The other gods whispered to each other, exchanging uneasy glances.

Shiket's golden eyes flared.

"I am the goddess of justice—"

"You do not rule the White Pantheon," Acaeja repeated. "I see the blood of this path. A catastrophic war between humans and vampires. I do not allow it. I do not stand behind you, Shiket."

Nyaxia covered her mouth, chuckling softly. "My, cousins, what a treat to witness this." Then, just as quickly, her amusement withered. "All the easier it will make it to fracture you. Step aside, Acaeja. The discipline of my children is my business. And they will pay for—"

"*They will not.*"

Now, Acaeja's voice boomed. The earth shook. The sky shattered. I slid backward with a great gust of wind, Mische's limp body clutched in my arms. The final dead scattered.

I looked up just in time to see the world, literally, split in two.

Acaeja hovered above the sea, her wings spread and hands outstretched. The power of her act threatened to strip the flesh from my bones. A massive crack, pulsing with divine light, shot from her fingertips toward both horizons. I watched it wind through the House of Shadow, cutting through the mountains and fields, and disappear into the distance.

"Three times now, I have warned you, Nyaxia, of how this path ends," she said. "I have had enough. This is *my* territory now. The king and queen of the House of Night have pledged themselves to me. And so now have the king and queen of Vathysia, the House of Death. You will make no move against them, or else face the wrath of me."

Nyaxia rasped a furious laugh. But her eyes shone as if with tears.

"Vathysia? Vathysia no longer exists."

"That does not appear to be true. It appears that your husband has heirs once again."

Acaeja's wings flashed with shifting visions of the future—Morthryn restored to its former glory, the underworld repaired, cities formerly of the House of Shadow flying the black banners of the House of Death.

"Keep your House of Shadow," Acaeja said. "Keep your House of Blood. But the Houses of Death and Night are under my protection."

"And what of us?" Shiket said. "You expect us to simply allow this?"

Acaeja turned her icy gaze to her sister, steadfast and serious. "No, Shiket. I expect that we will be at war."

"You fight for the fallen ones now. Amusing, sister. But unwise."

"No," Acaeja said, looking between Shiket and Nyaxia. "You fight for the eradication of each other. And I fight for the one path that will not end in the destruction of all."

"How self-righteous of you," Shiket sneered. "This will not be the end." She turned her golden stare to Nyaxia, who seethed.

"No," Nyaxia agreed. "It will not be. Let the games begin, my cousins. What fun ones they shall be."

And with one final steel stare to us, a silent look that promised untold horrors, Nyaxia stepped into nothingness. The White Pantheon followed, one by one, slipping off into the spira until only Acaeja remained.

At last, she turned to us.

I knelt on the glass-scattered floor. I clutched my chest with one hand, Mische with the other. She was barely conscious. I couldn't tear my eyes from her. The dead slipped once again from the darkness, surrounding us but never touching.

"You are weak," she observed. "Such is the price of walking the path to divinity and back."

Weak was a word for it. I felt like my heart was dying. I pulled Mische closer, and she let out a wordless groan.

"Please, what's wrong with her?" I asked.

Acaeja lowered herself before us. The images in her wings shifted, revealing Mische's face and my own.

"The weight of such power is heavy. Your lover has traveled from life to death to divinity and back again. She holds half the heart of Alarus, but she was born merely mortal. It is not an easy path for a body or soul to bear. Just as the weight of your own fragility suffocates you now."

So foolish, for someone so all-seeing. It wasn't my fragility that suffocated me. It was hers.

The terror that after everything, I would lose her again—so narrowly—choked me.

"But she already carried a piece of Alarus's essence," I said. "The piece that she took from me, in that ritual circle. And now she carries a piece of his heart, too."

"But what does that make her? A human? A vampire? A wraith? A god? There are only so many spaces a single soul can occupy before it destroys them."

No. I refused to accept it. "She is the queen of the House of Death. You acknowledged it yourself. The dead have chosen her. You need the underworld, and the underworld needs her. You are the goddess of fate. Surely you see how important she is."

Acaeja gave me a long, indecipherable stare.

"I have lived for an eternity," she said, "and all of it, I spent watching fate. Watching the threads combine and separate. Watching the different ways that they weave tapestries of the future. Mische Iliae is a soul of no consequence. There are millions of threads in which she dies as an infant or child, a mundane tragedy of an unforgiving world. A million more in which she lives and dies in obscurity. Perhaps her sister seeks sanctuary at a different temple; perhaps Atroxus is distracted and never notices her; perhaps the night she is Turned, Raihn Ashraj never finds her, and she dies alone. And in some threads, Asar Voldari, she dies here tonight, returning to the arms of the dead who have come to love her so."

Acaeja's wings depicted these countless possibilities—a baby Mische taken by fever, a child Mische starving in the slums, an elderly Mische dying in her sleep in the Citadel, surrounded by her fellow acolytes. And then, Mische exactly as she looked right now, eyes closed forever.

"And yet," Acaeja said slowly, "of all these millions of threads, some always remain the same. If Mische Iliae grows up in the Citadel, she always befriends the vampire that would begin her downfall. If she meets Raihn Ashraj, she always remains with him for decades. And if she meets you . . ."

Her voice trailed off. In her silence, I heard Gideon's voice: *You'll ruin her.*

And my heart clenched with dread for her impending words—because I was certain she was about to confirm the worst of my fears. That I would always be Mische's greatest tragedy.

At last, Acaeja said, "Very rarely, there are souls that, no matter the thread, become the continuation of each other's tales. Perhaps Mische Iliae meets you in the Shadowborn castle. Perhaps she meets you in the underworld. Perhaps she meets you upon the battlefield of a divine war. Perhaps she meets you by chance in a library, or a garden, or a city street." In her wings, countless different lives blossomed—countless different versions of myself, and different versions of Mische, our threads intertwining.

"In some, your endings are pleasant. In others, painful. But how curious, that in every one, you change the world together."

I let out an ugly, ragged exhale. The intensity of my relief was matched only by my grief.

I looked down at Mische—Mische, whose face held the greatest parts of divinity and mortality. Mische, who was the most extraordinary soul I had ever met.

"Of course she does," I murmured. "She is an event."

"She was no one," Acaeja said dismissively. "But perhaps that is what makes her remarkable. Such is the glory of fate. It is forged, not born."

She reached out and pressed her fingertips to Mische's forehead.

"She has earned her gift of life. And like you, she may keep her small piece of divinity. She will need it, for what is to come."

Mische's body jerked. She drew in a deep, ragged breath, as if sucking in the gift Acaeja had given her. Not the gift of a god's power, but the gift of imperfect mortality.

Acaeja straightened to her full, formidable height and looked to the horizon.

"Recover," she said. "Rebuild your kingdom. Prepare yourselves. The war no longer looms in the distance. It is upon us. Already, Nyaxia gathers her children to move upon the human nations. And already, my siblings rally against her."

Her voice was straightforward, unemotional. Even with Mische in my arms, safe and alive, it was sobering. The full implications of what I had done by pledging Acaeja my loyalty—*our* loyalty—settled over me.

We were surrounded by enemies. War was inevitable—a war that could destroy this world as it had once destroyed the deadlands. And it occurred to me only now just how well the cards had fallen in Acaeja's favor. She had engineered the creation of two more demigods to add to her collection.

I held Mische close. "Thank you, goddess," I said, bowing my head.

Acaeja stared blankly at me. "It is no kindness. Our interests align. One must be pragmatic in such times. Fate is forged, after all."

And with that, she was gone.

PART SIX

Mortality

CHAPTER EIGHTY-FOUR

Mische

Vincent tucked his hands into his pockets and looked me up and down.

"You look better than when I last saw you," he remarked.

I blinked slowly. We stood together in hazy, dreamy nothingness—a blurry version of the underworld. Vincent stood right next to me, but he seemed very far away. Still, he was whole. Not dissolving, like he was when I saw him last.

"You do, too," I said.

"The underworld is stable now. I take it, due to your actions."

Was it? I hoped so. I looked down at my hands—brown skin, marked with the ethereal red ink of my Heir Marks and the distinctly imperfect texture of my scars. Human, vampire, and god all in one.

I blinked, trying to remember the events that led me here. Gods, goddesses, bargains, and divine hearts. And of course, Asar's embrace.

"I'm not dead again, am I?" I asked.

"I should hope not. I can't bear to go through this all again."

"I didn't think I was, but . . ." I shrugged. "I figure that with my history, it was always a possibility."

An almost—almost—smile twitched at the corner of Vincent's mouth. "I advise you to do all you can to only die once more. Ideally many years from now. Unfortunately, I know firsthand that it is difficult to be an effective ruler if you are dead."

Ruler.

For some reason, hearing Vincent, of all people, refer to me by that word just made it all feel staggeringly real.

"Oh, gods," I muttered, swaying a little. "I don't know that I know how to be an effective ruler alive, either."

"It's simple enough. Be deliberate in choosing your next actions. Be ruthless in executing them." His gaze flicked down to my chest—where, even in this dream world, I felt such an unnatural heaviness sitting beneath my ribs. "And guard that heart of yours."

I pressed my hand over my chest. Felt the twin hearts beating there. My mortal heart, alive again. And that little piece of divinity throbbing beneath it.

Both precious. Both equally powerful.

"Which one?" I asked.

A faint smile. "Both."

Then he looked out into the mists. "The veil heals. I'll be returning to the underworld, where I belong. I will no longer be visiting your dreams. Or your mirrors."

He was right. I could already feel the distance between us—the chasm between life and death opening. Healthy, and good. Yet, the words came with such an unexpected, bittersweet pang.

I watched Vincent's profile as he stared out into the fog. What, I wondered, did he see out there? What possibilities would the afterlife offer him?

"Will you find her?" I asked quietly. "Alana?"

Vincent's throat bobbed. "It would be selfish of me to seek her forgiveness after all I had done to her. She deserves her peace with her family. I gave her a safe afterlife. I gave our daughter a safe kingdom, albeit for now. That is all I need."

At the mention of Oraya, his gaze slowly turned back to me—moon silver, even in death, just like hers.

"I was watching her in battle," he said. "She was incredible, wasn't she? Greater than a queen. A demigoddess."

He said it the way parents in Vostis used to brag about their children's performances. With such unrestrained pride.

I smiled. "Yes. She is incredible."

He slid one hand out of his pocket and withdrew a piece of folded parchment. He stared down at it, then said stiffly, avoiding my eyes, "I don't know how your Shadowborn tricks work. I don't know if you will still have this when you awaken. But if you do . . ."

He somewhat hurriedly pressed the parchment into my hands, then turned away. In elegant script, a name was written on the envelope: *Little Serpent.*

"I thought you said that you had nothing more you could say to her," I said.

He said, after a pause, "I was told that it was worth trying, anyway."

My chest tightened. I took the parchment. "I will give it to her."

He cleared his throat and looked away, as if trying to physically shed his vulnerability.

"So," I said, "what will you do with your afterlife now?"

"I don't know." He shot me a sly, sidelong glance. "What does a missionary do once their mission is complete, acolyte?"

Sun fucking take me. To think I had been the lost soul this whole time.

"I heard you aren't supposed to address a queen by her first name," I said.

"Surely you cannot expect me to call you 'Highness.'"

"The rumor is that I'm the queen of the dead. And you are dead. Therefore . . ."

His eyes narrowed at me, unamused.

I couldn't bite back my laugh. "But anyway, the answer to your question is, *whatever you please*."

"Hm," he said, considering this.

We stood in silence for a long moment. Then, past a lump in my throat, I said, "Thank you. For all of it. I wouldn't have made it here without you."

"It was what any king would do to save his kingdom," he said without hesitation, but I felt his piercing stare on the letter in my hand—on the name that adorned it.

He turned back to the silver skies. A cold gust howled.

"A lonely afterlife sounds quite dull," he said. "Especially when there are such interesting times ahead. Should you ever need to lead an army of the dead, Deathborn Queen, I may be willing to volunteer my expertise. I was quite a formidable force in my time."

He stepped off into the mists. Then turned, one last time. Lowered his head in an almost-bow.

"Be ruthless, Highness," he said.

And the winds of the underworld, at last, swept him away.

WELCOME HOME, MORTHRYN breathed.

I drew in a sharp breath.

Breath.

Gods, that felt so good. Air rushing through my lungs. Real.

I was already grinning by the time I sat up. I was giddy in all my aches and pains, in the headache and the dizziness and even the hungry clench of my stomach. It was all *so damned wonderful.*

I lifted my hand to see smooth brown skin, painted over with red marks. The eye of Alarus stared back at me, nestled within swirling lines that reminded me of lightning. Reminded me of scars.

I let my hand fall, and my eyes rose.

I recognized this room immediately. No, I hadn't spent much time here before we left on our journey to the Descent. But Asar's room here still felt like home. The books meticulously indexed and sorted on the shelves, no angle left askew. The velvet blankets that seemed to be slept in too little. The neat desk with parchment perfectly stacked. And of course, the piano in the corner, keys well-worn. The windows looked out into a sunless sky. They were cracked, and several gouges ran up the walls, but otherwise, this room was shockingly well-preserved. As if, even in its worst possible state, Morthryn had protected it for him.

For him.

Asar was at my bedside, leaning forward in his chair and fast asleep over my legs, fingers lightly clutching me. I could imagine that he had spent many dawns like this over his desk. Now, instead of standing watch over knowledge, he stood watch over me.

His face was pressed against the velvet bedspread, dark lashes over his cheeks, lips barely parted. His scars danced over his skin, pulsing slightly, the light within them only barely shifting, like even it was at peace. He looked so innocent, so peaceful. And so very mortal.

Gently, so gently, I traced his scars from his throat, up his jaw, over his lips.

He startled awake and immediately flew upright. When his eyes landed on me, his entire body collapsed in relief.

"Mische—" he breathed.

But I threw myself against him, wrapped my arms around his neck, and kissed him.

His arms folded around my body. We were awkwardly hanging over the edge of the bed, barely keeping our balance, but I didn't notice or care. I just kissed him, and kissed him, and kissed him.

"How?" I managed to choke out, between them.

"It doesn't matter," he answered, words stifled against my mouth.

He was right. None of it—gods and divinity and wars and wraiths—mattered at all to me now.

With an unceremonious tug, I pulled Asar onto the bed with me. Clumsily, we peeled our clothing off. He bit my lip hard enough to draw blood and groaned at the—*alive, alive, alive*—taste on his tongue and mine. I raked my fingernails down his bare back and shivered with delight that it left marks on his—*mortal, mortal, mortal*—flesh.

Soon, we were bare skin on bare skin. We relished every fallibility. Every small pain, every reminder that we were alive, and mortal, and together. I pushed Asar down and climbed over him. I pressed my hand against his, our fingers winding around each other's. Our scars and our Heir Marks alike were perfect complements, weaving together like they'd always been meant to be that way.

And when I lowered myself onto his length, when we were at last combined, I had no doubt that we were, in fact, one being.

The sensation of him inside me felt so devastatingly real. I leaned down, my forehead pressing to his, eyes squeezed shut.

It's you. It's you. It's you.

Only now, with him as close to me as two beings could physically get, did it feel real.

I know, he murmured into my mind. He kissed my cheek. *I know.*

Those were the only words we needed. The only words we had. Total understanding.

We took each other slowly, relishing each movement of muscle, each gasp of breath, each wonderful pain of teeth or fingernails. I held his hand through it all. And when we came together, in a synchronized wave, I stifled my moans against his kiss.

As our bodies relaxed, I still didn't move. We just stayed there, wrapped up in each other.

At last, he said quietly, "I could not let you go, Dawndrinker."

I closed my eyes and buried my face between his neck and shoulder. Breathed in his scent of ice-dusted ivy.

The sacrifice I could not make.

And in this moment, I was so, so happy to be alive.

"Good," I murmured.

CHAPTER EIGHTY-FIVE

Asar

Together, Mische and I walked Morthryn's halls. I had been so preoccupied caring for her, praying that she'd awaken, that I hadn't taken any time to survey the damage. It was extensive. My heart—both of them, mortal and divine—hurt to look at it. Though the collapse of the underworld had been stopped, Morthryn still moaned silently in pain. Windows had been shattered. Cracks decimated ancient mosaic floors. Arched doorways bowed under the pressure of holding up the sagging building.

And yet, despite the pain and the damage, I could hear something else, too: hope.

We stopped in the great library. It was the most heavily damaged of the rooms—the walls singed, the floor cracked, the books burnt. My gaze fell to the piano in the corner of the room. It was damaged, the wood cracked and half the keys covered in soot, but it still stood.

The very spot where Mische had lured me. Where she had cut out Alarus's heart, and given me back my own.

Both of them throbbed now.

We were silent, staring at it.

Finally, Mische said quietly, "It doesn't feel real."

It didn't. It felt like a dream.

Mische touched her hair, as if remembering. "You left me a crown. An eye. A heart. In the underworld. How did you know to do that?"

{Some knowledge transcends logic,} the heart whispered, so distantly I thought maybe I imagined it.

I didn't know how to explain it. "A part of me knew. Even if it wasn't logical. The underworld called to me, and it just felt . . . right."

To leave those pieces of my power for someone. Because I knew that someone needed it.

And that was the power that allowed Mische to confront me. That allowed her, ultimately, to cut out Alarus's heart.

I turned to her. My gaze fell to the triangle of smooth skin at the neckline of her button-down shirt. There was no scar. No outward sign of what had happened. That was, after all, the magic of gods.

"I think . . ." I spoke slowly. Memories from that time, when I was myself but not myself, were distant and blurry, like a dream I was rapidly forgetting. "I think I expected you to take it from me. Use it for yourself."

"You wanted me to sacrifice you."

"I wanted you to take the power that you deserved more than I ever had." I brushed a stray curl behind her ear. "I always knew you would be an amazing queen."

Mische's hand slid into mine.

"I told you that strength is measured by the sacrifices we refused to make," she said softly. "You were mine."

I squeezed her hand back, my response silent but unmistakable: *And you were mine.*

Mische turned to the great glass windows and the balcony beyond. The windows had all been shattered. The night, still eternally dark, lay beyond them, framed by twinkling shards. The crack in the earth, the one that Acaeja had created to carve out her territory, snaked off toward the horizon, separating Vathysia—the House of Death—from the House of Shadow.

The House of Death. *Our kingdom.*

The thought was dizzying.

"I told you one time that I thought you would make a good king," Mische said. "I still believe it. Now, you can prove it."

Sun take me, I definitely was mortal again. Because at this, I felt like I was about to vomit. A distinctly mortal sensation.

I took a few steps toward the balcony, looking out at the landscape below. Churning sea separated Morthryn from the mainland, and then townships and farms and cities, rolling fields and steep cliffs, mansions and shacks. Now under our control—and protection—in the face of great, terrible uncertainty.

I was suddenly so afraid.

It was a new, different kind of fear. Because I'd spent my entire life in the comfortable understanding that I was capable only of destruction—that any good I could offer the world would have to come at the cost of my own sacrifice. I was content with that. It was a simple equation.

"Almost seems like it would have been easier to die in my grand final gesture," I muttered.

But Mische, of course, saw right through my wry joke.

"That's the cost of a future, Warden," she said. "It's hard work, to make the choice to do better every single night for the rest of your life. Maybe that's why acolytes are always so obsessed with dying in a fiery blaze of martyrdom."

Maybe. But I was glad Mische hadn't. And looking at her now, her face tilted to the horizon, moonlight on her cheeks and her eyes bright with hope, I was glad I hadn't, either.

A distant bark rang out down the hall. We turned to see Luce bounding toward us. Mische's face lit up.

"Luce!" she shrieked, and Luce didn't even slow down before leaping onto her. The two fell down together, rolling around like hogs in the mud.

I watched, arms crossed, amused.

"She wasn't this happy to have *me* back," I remarked. "Shameless turncoat."

But I couldn't find it in myself to be bitter about it.

They collected themselves, though Luce's tail still whipped back and forth with all the force of a flag in monsoon winds. "I missed you," Mische said, rubbing her head. And Luce nuzzled her cheek in a way that unmistakably replied, *I missed you, too.*

"Where have you been?" I asked her. "It's been hours."

And then I heard another voice down the hall:

"Mother help us, what has *happened* to this place? It is a disgrace. If I wanted to live in squalor, I could have stayed where I was and saved myself the walk."

My brows rose. *"Esme?"*

She appeared in the doorway, looking generally displeased. She wore the same elaborate dress that she had died in, her hair immaculately piled atop her head, and her low neckline still proudly bore the wound that had killed her.

Mische's face lit up. She jumped to her feet. "You're back!"

Esme gave us both a critical once-over. Maybe one might have expected some kind of emotional reunion, considering that we hadn't known if Esme was—well, *alive* wasn't the right word, but safe—and she hadn't known if we were, either.

But that person would not have known Esme at all.

"You look terrible," she declared. "And you live in a dump. And now I hear we are supposed to call you a king?"

I could not hold back my smile.

She scowled at me. "Why are you looking at me like that, Asar? You have work to do."

"I'm just happy to see you, Esme. That's all."

"Oh, psh. You are going soft. You thought Malach and his ilk managed to get me? Or a few torn veils? Some mutated souleaters?" She clicked her tongue and shook her head, insulted by the very thought. "All it did was slow me down a little. You certainly did not make it easy for me. But I made it back." She touched Morthryn's cracked wall with the closest thing she had ever displayed to affection. "I am still a prisoner of this place, after all."

And for all her complaints, I knew that like me, Esme would have it no other way.

Together, we surveyed Morthryn—our sad, crumbling home, but our home nonetheless.

Mische said at last, "How do we repair all this?"

I slipped my hand back into hers. "One glyph at a time, I suspect."

"Move quickly," Esme grumbled. "You both owe me a new house."

CHAPTER EIGHTY-SIX

Asar

"It reeks. Even I can smell it, and I am dead. You must make an effort, Asar, to treat your nobles with more respect."

Esme made a face, turning her nose up.

I stifled an almost-laugh and shot her a stern glance.

"Noble," I said drily. "Is that what you are?"

She narrowed her eyes at me. "I am certainly no servant, *Highness*."

"Esme, you are definitely a noble," Mische chirped from the couch. "What's the point in being a queen if I can't make people as deserving as you nobles?"

Luce barked in agreement.

"It doesn't work that way," I muttered.

Esme looked pleased with herself. She bowed her head. "Why, thank you, Highness."

Mische lifted her chin in a haughty stare. "You are quite welcome, Lady Esme."

"Lady Esme," I muttered. "Mother help us."

Esme's playful wit faded.

"You will have to come up with another way to curse," she said. "I don't believe the Dark Mother will be helping any of us anytime soon."

It was a sobering thought.

We all looked down at the corpse in the center of the floor.

Esme was right. It did smell, even by the standards of dead bodies. The man had been a guard along the border between the House of Death and the House of Shadow. It wasn't the first dead guard that had been sent to us. It took a few weeks for us to repair Morthryn and the underworld, and to assert our control over the vampire cities that fell within our newly drawn—or more accurately, newly carved—borders. Not everyone was happy about it. It was a challenging transition. I was better at wooing the dead than the living.

It was Mische, of course, who had managed to win them over. The villages and cities that sat within the House of Death were some of the most religious in the House of Shadow, and in particular, they practiced the old ways. It went far in their eyes to be the heir of Alarus.

We had, so far, maintained a tenuous peace. But if Egrette's propensity for kidnapping and murdering guards provided any indication, I got the distinct sense it would not stay that way for long.

But even more worrisome than the murder was the state of the body when it was returned. The blackened flesh peeling back from the corpse's mouth and eyes could be the result of decay, if the body was old enough.

Could be.

Maybe.

"So?" I said to Esme. "What do you think?"

Esme was one of the most knowledgeable people I'd ever known, living or dead. One of the only souls I trusted to confirm my suspicions.

Her mouth thinned to a grim line. "That is no typical rot. I do not know what your sister is up to. But this?" She jabbed her finger at the corpse. "This is the start of something, and it is nothing good."

Mische and I exchanged a concerned glance.

I'd spent long enough in the depths of the House of Shadow's magical experimentation to know that it was nothing to dismiss. I was mildly comforted that they no longer had Gideon—his body had been pulled out of the wreckage of the Nightborn palace, having sacrificed himself to deal out what he thought was the final, winning move of our game. But even this was only a small reassurance. Ryvenhaal still held dangerous secrets that could be leveraged to all kinds of unpleasant ends. And in the House of Shadow, a dead body only proved so much.

Esme rolled her eyes and examined her ruby-painted fingernails. "What are those faces for? Truly, what did you expect? You've broken the House of Shadow in two and thrown yourselves into the middle of a god war. Did you think that this would be easy?"

She was right, of course. Despite Acaeja's protection, Nyaxia would not hesitate to take her vengeance, and that was only if the White Pantheon didn't get to us first. Mische and I had Alarus's heart, and we kept his eye and his mask safely guarded—thankfully, they were now much quieter than they had been. But in the face of such adversaries, even that divine treasure trove seemed far too fragile.

"But let us put it all in perspective," Esme said. "I, for one, prefer things now, god war or no. I am too glamorous to live in a pile of rubble and meet my end in the jaws of a souleater."

I rubbed my temple and sighed. "Thank you, Esme. You do know how to stroke a king's ego."

"How do you think I got this?" she said, gesturing to the wound at the center of her chest. Then she looked at the corpse, her nose wrinkling. "Can we discard this thing now? The Nightborn will smell it the minute they step through the door, and what kind of hosts would that make us?"

CHAPTER EIGHTY-SEVEN

Mische

"Ix's tits, what is that smell?"

It was the first thing out of Raihn's mouth when he walked into the office, and gods help me, I had never heard anything so beautiful.

I was a queen, and this was a very important meeting with very important people over very important, very serious issues.

But I still dove across the room and threw myself against him before I could stop myself. It was like hurling myself into a brick wall, but he still let out an *oof* as I collided with him.

"I take it you're happy to see us," he said.

Gods, I was so, so, *so* happy to see them.

"A little," I said, before abandoning him and hugging Oraya, who actually did stagger under the force of it. I was so wrapped up in my overwhelming joy that I even threw my arms around Vale before I could stop myself, though he stiffened and promptly extracted me with all the military precision his title demanded.

"That is not necessary," he grumbled, adjusting the bandages around his arms as he pulled away.

"It can't be helped," Asar said drily behind me. "She's a force of nature."

But when I glowered back at him, his eyes sparkled with a smile, like he had never seen anything so lovely.

I had written to Raihn and Oraya, but hadn't seen them since the attack that had nearly destroyed the House of Night—the attack that Asar's sacrifice had, however narrowly, saved them from. It had turned out that Vale had been captured not far from the southern borders of the House of Night, closest to the House of Shadow, after he had retrieved the god blood. He had been held captive by the Shadowborn, but had managed to free himself before they got him deep into Shadowborn territory, and then had to make the long trek back to the House of Night.

Vale is practically ready to stake himself for the shame of allowing it to happen at all, Oraya had written. *But we are just grateful that he is alive.*

"He's lucky to be," Asar had muttered, reading over my shoulder. "Shadowborn spies are merciless. If they kept him alive to extract information from him, then I'm sure he paid a heavy price for his survival."

And indeed, even in that brief embrace, I could feel the shock of Vale's mental scars, still raw, wrench through me. They would take a long, long time to heal—longer than his physical ones.

Asar, I knew—even though he didn't express it—felt responsibility for what had happened to him, and what had happened to the House of Night as a result. Asar had sent a letter to him personally saying as much, albeit in Asar's stilted, reserved way. The response he received from Vale was only two lines:

I knew what I signed up for when I took this position.

We have a war to fight.

Asar had chuckled softly and put the letter aside. But later, I'd taken it from the drawer and read it again, lingering on those last words:

We have a war to fight.

I was beyond happy to see Raihn and Oraya again. But the true purpose of their visit still hung over us all, heavy and foreboding. They had been immersed in repair efforts the last few weeks. The House of Night had sustained heavy casualties during Shiket's attack. But in some ways, Oraya told me, it made them stronger. Those who had been uncertain about Oraya and Raihn's unconventional leadership, clinging to their old grudges between Hiaj and Rishan clans, now had turned their sights to the bigger enemy.

And were those bigger enemies *big*.

The Nightborn had come to strategize. We had adversaries looming over us from every direction—the Shadowborn and Bloodborn under Nyaxia's control, and the humans under the White Pantheon's. We had put ourselves at the mercy of Acaeja's command, and though she hadn't made any demands of us yet, we knew they would be coming at any moment. In the meantime, we needed to pool our strength to keep our kingdoms intact.

We all gathered in the library around a long mahogany table. A map of the world was spread out before us, rendered in quivering lines of shadow. Red arrows marked our most likely adversaries, and our weakest points. More still marked the areas where our intelligence told us that Nyaxia and Shiket had already gone after each other, striking across the sea beneath the cover of eternal night.

It was overwhelming to see it all laid out this way. Millions of lives and the fate of the world, reduced to messy strokes on a map.

I thought we were all likely thinking the same thing, because we were silent, taking it in.

Then Asar leaned across the table and sighed.

"So," he said. "Where shall we begin?"

THE MEETING LASTED for hours, and by the time we were done, I wasn't altogether sure that we were in any better of a position than where we started. Life was easier back when I believed that the love of a god could protect us. Now the gods' favor was fickle and complicated—perhaps even more dangerous than it was helpful.

Still, I was glad that if we were going to face down such an uncertain time, at least I would do it with my allies, my friends, beside me.

When we at last disbanded, Asar and Esme took Oraya and Vale to our collection of artifacts and weapons, to see if there was anything they could make use of. But Raihn had nudged my shoulder. "I've seen enough swords and books to last for two lifetimes," he said. "Take me on a tour instead."

So, I showed him Morthryn. It was still covered in the marks of its decay. Some walls had still not been repaired. A few windows were patched over. The eastern spire had not yet been rebuilt. But Morthryn was eager to be whole again, and Asar and I would often wake up to newly formed walls or rafters that had slowly, night by night, straightened back to their original position, like a body healing.

Yes, it still bore the scars. But there was beauty in those, too, in a way.

I showed Raihn everything that I loved about it—the libraries, the hallways, the fireplaces and windows and ivy-covered walls. All of them were a little different every time I walked them.

I didn't realize just how much I was talking until, after some time, Raihn just stopped and stared at me, and I realized I'd been talking for nearly an hour straight.

I shut my mouth. "Sorry."

"Never be sorry for that."

We now stood in the ballroom beneath the watch of Alarus's eye—the great stained-glass window that cast rippling red light over the tile floor. This was the room where I had clashed with Asar. This was the room where I had brought him back.

Raihn spun around slowly.

"So," he said drily, "this is the place you chose to call home over my castle. A death prison."

"It's not a prison. I already told you that. It's—"

"A temple. I know. You told me. A few times." He crossed his arms and took it all in. "Seems like a lot of things. A castle, a fortress, a temple, a bridge."

I smiled and affectionately ran my hand over a healing crack in the wall. "Yes. I suppose it is."

"I have to say, Mish, when you left the House of Night, this was not where I expected you to land."

"Where did you expect me to land?"

He paused, like he had to reflect on this. "I thought you would be wandering forever."

I'm not made for standing still. That's what I had told him, when I left. And I'd thought it was true then. That it was just in my nature to always be searching, always be leaving.

"Me too," I said.

"I'm glad you're not."

"Me too."

"You seem happy here."

My gaze drifted out the windows. Morthryn had repaired the stained-glass window itself—the first thing to come back—but some of the glass doors overlooking the sea were still boarded over with temporary planks of wood.

Mere weeks ago, gods had stood there. And even now, I could feel them, moving their pieces across the board, preparing for a game that would take thousands or millions of lives.

"Sometimes I wonder if it's wrong to be happy," I said. "When so much is still so wrong. And so much of it is—"

My gaze found that eternally dark sky. The sky I had made that way.

Raihn, of course, knew what I meant.

"You saved a million vampire lives. And now, many more souls have the peace they deserve in death because of you. That isn't nothing."

No. It wasn't nothing. But it wasn't everything, either.

"There's just . . . so much left to do," I said.

Raihn lifted one shoulder in a shrug, as if it were simple as breathing. "There is. But everything else, we fight for. Piece by piece."

Slow, hard, unglamorous, terrifying work.

But I had never been afraid of the impossible.

Raihn ruffled my hair and I jerked away, scowling.

"At least whatever we face next," he said, "we face it together."

And what a gift it was.

LATER, AFTER RAIHN and I returned, the others went to the dining room for dinner. But I held Oraya back, ushering her into a quiet corner of the library.

"I have something for you," I said, and slipped a worn, folded piece of parchment into her hand.

Vincent had been right—that the rules of passing something so physical from one realm to the other were far from straightforward. When I'd awoken that first night, the envelope wasn't with me. It was only days later, when Asar and I were combing through the wreckage near the stairway to the veil, that I found it caught in the decorative stem of a sconce lining the way. As if Morthryn itself had caught it before it blew back into the underworld, waiting to pass it off to me.

I'd held on to it since then. It hadn't felt right to send it alongside all our other letters. It was too precious, too personal, not to give to her in person.

Instantly, Oraya knew what it was. I sensed her demeanor go tight and cold, like she had to clamp down on the wave of emotions that rose up beneath the surface.

Her thumb traced the swirl of what must have been a very familiar script. For a long moment, she was silent. Then she said quietly, "After he died, this was my greatest dream. I kept searching his offices, like I'd find some secret final message that would explain everything."

I remembered. I knew how desperate she had been for closure.

"I don't know if this will explain everything, exactly," I said. "But it's something."

"An imperfect something."

I smiled. "An imperfect something."

She swallowed thickly. Then her eyes, bright silver, lifted to mine. She did look so much like Vincent. Right now, the similarity was striking.

"He really helped you all the way to the end?" she said.

I could hear the more painful question beneath this one—*Why could he do that for you, but not for me? How could he help you seize your power but spend a whole lifetime trying to smother mine?*

I squeezed her hand.

"Only because it would save you, I think," I said softly. "But even still, one grand gesture and one letter doesn't invalidate years of betrayal."

The corner of her mouth tightened in a wry smile. "If only it was so simple."

I thought of Saescha. Saescha, whose soul I had released under such terrible circumstances. I'd searched for her in the underworld since, but never could find her. I still wasn't sure if her soul had successfully passed.

Indeed. If only one grand gesture could go so far.

Oraya turned the envelope over in her hands.

"I'd like to be alone to read this, if that's alright."

"Of course," I said.

I stepped out into the hall, leaving her. I peered back one last time as she opened the letter. Slowly, she sank down onto a chair, head in her hands.

And I couldn't help it—I watched for a few seconds longer, tensed, as a tear slid down her cheek. Watched until I saw her mouth twist into a small, sad smile.

Only then did I turn away, shutting the door behind me.

No. A letter couldn't offer closure. Couldn't invalidate every wrong or soothe every hurt.

But it was an imperfect something.

IT HAD BEEN a long night. After dinner, we all had talked and laughed for hours, until exhaustion slowly drove our guests, one by one, to their chambers. But even though I was tired, I lay in bed beside Asar, staring at the ceiling, unable to sleep.

Eventually, I slipped out of bed, careful not to wake Asar or Luce, who had sprawled out at the foot of the bed. I walked Morthryn's silent halls. I wound down stairwells and through doors, going wherever it called me. The arrangement was different every time, and yet, I never felt lost.

I was in the lower levels, close to the veil, when I heard the voice behind me. I was kneeling at one of the arched doorways that led to the Descent. The roots had begun to repair themselves, and now, some of the arches provided functional, and much more convenient, paths deeper into the underworld.

"This feels familiar, Dawndrinker."

I smiled. Asar's presence warmed my heart like a candle flickering to life.

I turned to see him approaching with a half smile tightening one corner of his mouth.

"How many times will we find each other wandering these halls?" he said. His hand pressed to the doorframe affectionately, and my heart squeezed, too. Morthryn would always bring us back together.

"Couldn't sleep," I said. "Just thought I'd go strengthen the wards."

Asar joined me at the arch, running his hands over the glyphs etched into the metal. "Looks like they don't need it."

No, they didn't. There was so much of Morthryn—so much of the underworld—that still needed to be repaired. Asar and I held pieces of divinity, but we were not gods. The work we did was slow and manual. It would be many years before we restored it all to what it was meant to be.

Still, these small victories—a veil restored, a guardian healed, a set of glyphs that no longer cracked beneath the weight of its task—fed my soul.

Asar gazed out into the mist beyond the door. Then extended his hand to me. "A walk?"

I took it.

CHAPTER EIGHTY-EIGHT

Mische

We wove through the Descent together. Maybe the piece of Alarus's divinity that we held allowed us to travel its paths more easily now, or maybe the underworld had simply accepted us as its own, but it was now much simpler to navigate. Morthryn's roots stretched deeper every day. We often found that we could get to most of the Descent within hours.

We stepped from Morthryn's doors and into the Descent. We walked through dusty fields and across smooth, mirrored rivers. In the distance, souleaters wound lazily through the sky, circling the peaks of distant mountains.

Soon, we came upon a forest of towering white trees. A few souls wandered between them, peaceful. There were places in the Descent where the veil to the underworld was thin. One day, we would repair it, and the dead would be confined to the underworld. But for now, they were safe here, too, if they chose to wander this far.

My gaze lingered on the forest too long, peering at the silhouettes between the tree trunks.

I had come here nearly every night, hoping to find Saescha. Even now, the hope nagged stubbornly at me, even though I didn't want to acknowledge it.

"You should go," Asar said.

"Hm?"

"You should go," he repeated pointedly. And when I glanced at him, his gaze was soft and knowing.

He gestured to the forest.

"Go," he insisted. "I won't be far."

In the forest, the dead wandered. It was peaceful here. These were not wraiths, trapped between life and death. They were deceased souls who had come to peer in upon the living. Their forms, shadowy and translucent, passed between the smooth tree trunks like shooting stars between galaxies.

I liked coming here. I liked the sense of peace, and I liked knowing that the dead could be that way. Content.

Even if I never saw the soul I was waiting for.

I sat upon a rock and watched the souls drift by. I searched for a familiar face, and found none.

I peered over my shoulder at Asar, who lingered in the distance.

He cocked his head at me. *Patience, Iliae.*

I narrowed my eyes at him.

What did you—

But then, movement out of the corner of my eye. And even though it was so quick I couldn't make out its features, I knew.

When you spend your entire life with someone, you memorize everything about them. The way they smell, the way they move, the way their voice rises and falls.

And I knew Saescha right away.

My heart clenched. My body froze. My eyes remained straight ahead. The leap of hope was so sudden and fierce that I didn't even want to look, for the fear of it shattering.

Out of the corner of my eye, the shadow paused.

A scent of jasmine and the ocean rolled over me. It smelled like childhood safety.

The shadow settled on the rock beside me.

I couldn't look at her.

What would I see? Half of me expected to see her as she had died, eyes wide open with her throat torn out. To see her as she had been as a wraith, lost and hungry, reaching for a sunrise that would never come. To see her as she had been as a Sentinel, her soul twisted and bastardized to be used as a weapon.

Slowly, I turned my head.

Saescha was not a wraith or a Sentinel or a corpse.

The Saescha beside me was the Saescha who had rocked me to sleep at night, who had laughed with me over silly stories, who had protected me from a terrifying world. She was the Saescha I had known as a child, strong and beautiful and kind and greater, in my eyes, than any goddess.

My sister was whole.

My eyes burned. Now that I had forced myself to look at her, I couldn't look away. She gazed off into the distance. Her body was faint, outlined in silver, only a hint of color to her skin, hair, and eyes. She wore her Dawndrinker robes. Her throat was whole.

Her soul had suffered so greatly. So many nights, I lay in bed thinking of her fate. I'd freed her from the grip of Shiket's vengeance, but could a soul repair itself after it had been twisted and broken so many times? I didn't know. And every time I came here, every time I searched for her in our walks through the Descent, that hope died a little more.

But here she was.

I couldn't touch her. Even to us, death meant something. I couldn't reach her, and I wouldn't want to, anyway—wouldn't want to bring her back from the rest she had finally found.

But my hand pressed beside hers, our little fingers nearly touching.

A tear slid down my cheek. I had nothing I could say to her. I'd already apologized for all the ways I had failed her. And I knew that none of those words would ever be enough.

At last, her gaze slid from the forest, slowly, until her eyes met mine.

There was no hatred in that stare.

Instead, there were multitudes within it—affection, regret, resentment. Apology. Forgiveness. And above all, despite everything, always, love.

There would always be wounds unhealed. Always be scars. But

here, we could sit together, pressed to either side of the line between life and death, united in quiet peace.

A gentle smile rolled over her lips. She looked out to the horizon. And I lifted my chin to it, feeling her presence roll over me like the dawn.

At last, at peace.

CHAPTER EIGHTY-NINE

Mische

When Saescha at last melted back into the forest, and I returned to Asar, I blurted out with certainty, "You did that."

Asar tucked his hands into his pockets and kept walking.

"I don't know what you're talking about."

"You couldn't lie to me when you did it for Eomin, and I know you much better now. Don't even try, Warden."

"You were the one who helped her pass."

"But you found her."

A beat. And then, "I helped her find you. It wasn't difficult. She was already looking."

My heart ached. I pressed my palm to it. All this time, I had been certain that Saescha would never want to see me again. Had been certain that even if she did make it to the underworld intact, even her restful soul would run from me.

As if Asar heard this unspoken fear, he said, "You gave her peace. That's no small gift."

It was smaller than she deserved. But if it was the best I could offer, I would offer it over and over again.

Asar's hand threaded in mine.

"Should we go back?" I asked.

"Let's keep going a little farther."

We crested a hill, and below, a poppy field spread out before us. The flowers were alive again, red and black, lush and swaying beneath the gentle breeze. Silver butterflies danced from blossom to blossom. Asar and I wandered down to it, hand in hand. The flowers had grown since I was last here. The silver grass was now past my knees, and extended out to the horizon, rolling like silver waves under the red sky.

I turned to survey it, breathless all over again with the beauty of it. It was different every time I came here, and yet, always so familiar.

"You're right," I said. "It was worth—"

I turned and stopped short.

Asar stood in the center of the field. He had conjured a circle around him, drawn in delicate lines of silver and shadow, five glowing points around its circumference. It looked like a ritual circle, the kind used to conduct necromancy.

"What is that? Are we repairing something?" I glanced at the arch nearby. It didn't look broken, and this didn't look like any repair spell I'd ever seen.

Asar finished the final stroke of his circle. And when he lifted his eyes to mine, gods help me, he looked pale. His white eye pulsed, smoke trailing off to the sky.

"What's wrong?" I asked, alarmed.

"This," he said, "is a Vathysian wedding ceremony."

My hearts—both of them, divine and mortal—stopped beating.

"It hasn't been practiced in a few thousand years," he went on, "though there are aspects of it that are still found in Obitraen weddings today. But the more I read about it, the more it seemed . . . right. If you are interested."

I couldn't move.

I couldn't even speak.

My silence stretched.

Asar cleared his throat. "You are uncharacteristically quiet."

I finally managed to repeat, *"'If you are interested.'"*

Sun take me, he actually looked nervous.

"If you aren't—"

"I am, you idiot. I *am* interested. It's just the most Asar marriage proposal I've ever heard."

The corner of his mouth quirked. *"'I am, you idiot,'"* he repeated. "The most Mische proposal acceptance I've ever heard."

Gods help me, this man.

"I was promised gaudy chaos," I said.

"You will have your gaudy chaos. Your friends are already here. Esme can throw together quite a party on short notice. But I just thought . . ."

His voice trailed off. But I knew what he meant. That this ceremony, this oath, felt too tender to belong to anyone but us. And I would have it no other way.

He held out his hand. I did not miss that it was trembling.

Mine was, too, when I took it and stepped into the circle with him.

I observed the ritual lines. "How does this work? It looks like—"

"A necromancy spell," he finished. "Yes. That's the interesting part. The reason we conduct necromancy this way is because it encapsulates the five core aspects of a living being. And the Vathysians believed that linking one soul to another in marriage deserved the same commitment. The entirety of oneself."

"That's beautiful," I murmured.

His hand squeezed mine. "I think so, too."

I lifted my gaze to his. The clouds in his left eye were calm now, like the mist rolling over the distant mountains. The other, his brown eye, was a million miles deep.

"How does the spell go?" I said.

He held my stare for a long moment, head bowing forward, lips almost, almost brushing mine, like he couldn't help himself.

"Mische Iliae—"

"Asar Voldari—"

His fingers fell over mine, just as they had over the bow of a cello, the night we dreamed a future together.

"I give you my body," he said.

"I give you my body," I repeated.

In the first position of the circle, together, we drew a glyph. Then he lifted our intertwined hands and drew the same one over my palm, and then his. It burned there, mingling with my scars and his, my Heir Mark and his, as if it was always meant to be there.

"I give you my breath."

"I give you my breath."

Now, he drew a glyph over my lips, and then his.

"I give you my psyche."

"I give you my psyche."

Now we drew the glyph over my forehead. Then his. I could feel his presence intertwining with mine, his love and his nervousness and his vulnerability spilling out, mirroring mine.

"I give you my secrets," he murmured.

"I give you my secrets."

We drew the glyphs over our throats, mine, and then his, tracing over the scars we had left the first time we fed from each other.

His forehead now leaned against mine. My body was nearly pressed to his. The magic burned around us, breaking down the walls between us brick by brick. But then, what walls had I ever had, with him?

And at last, the final piece. This time, we spoke together.

"I give you my soul."

The final glyph, we drew over my heart, and then his. Our poor, wounded, stitched-up hearts, human and vampire, god and mortal, alive and dead.

"From this night," he murmured.

"Until the end of nights," I finished.

"Your pain is my pain."

"Your heart is my heart."

And then, together, "I bind myself to you."

I had always thought that wedding ceremonies were more ritual than magic. And yet, with those words, as the spell burned and swirled around us, it felt so unquestionably *real*.

He slipped his hand free and held my face, pressing his forehead against mine. We swayed together. And despite every wrong in this world, every challenge, every fear, I was so happy that I thought I could burn up in it.

I smiled and tasted salt.

"Never thought a necromancy wedding could feel so romantic."

He kissed the tears from one cheek, then the other.

"I think it's perfectly fitting," he murmured. "You have resurrected me, Dawndrinker."

I laughed, even as I cried. "Sun take me, you are such a sap."

His mouth moved to my lips. "I suspect you love it," he whispered against me.

And he was right. I did.

Later, Asar and I would throw the big, chaotic party he had once promised me. I would wear a beautiful dress. Luce would carry a wreath of poppies. Raihn would get drunk and try not to cry. Oraya would watch with her quiet, reserved amusement. Esme would lead us through song after song after song, and Asar would oblige, and we would dance until our mortal, fallible bodies collapsed in exhaustion.

And when it was all done, Asar would take me back to our room. He would play one final song for me—a song that sounded like me, and like him, and the future we once had thought would only belong to the ghosts.

Later.

But now, my husband, my partner, my ally, kissed me again, deep and soft and full of hope. As the lines of our spell dissolved into our kingdom, he lay me down in the poppy field, and here, in this moment, I understood what it was to feel complete.

In the darkness, I found solace.

In the underworld, I found hope.

And here, in this twin soul, in this love we built together, I finally found it:

Home.

EPILOGUE

Septimus stood before the goddess that had betrayed his kingdom and bowed like a good little dog.

"A travesty," he said, voice dripping with indignant offense. "The House of Blood will never allow such disrespect against the Dark Mother to stand."

"Nor the House of Shadow," Queen Egrette added, from her own supplicant kneel. But her voice was weak. Even her appearance was frazzled. She had lost half her kingdom, and she had not yet recovered from the stress of attempting to keep her fractured, sexist noble class from cutting out her heart and throwing her into the sea as punishment for her loss.

Septimus almost pitied her. It really wasn't her fault. No one could have expected that her brother would run around becoming a god, and fewer still could have expected he'd stab Nyaxia in the back when doing it.

Well. Almost no one.

But that wasn't a fair comparison. Septimus made it his business to know things, and he was simply better at it than most.

Nyaxia's rage split the sky. She was seething. The kind of seething that led one—mortal or god—to make irrational decisions.

"It is no matter," she hissed. "Your traitorous kin will have their punishment in time. I have never needed them. And when we have our empire, children, they will beg for our forgiveness."

Her eyes gleamed and churned with storm clouds. Whether she was on the verge of uproarious laughter or tears, Septimus could not tell.

Amazing, just how similar mortals and gods really were.

"Of course," he purred, pressing his hand to his heart. "The House of Blood is yours. We are prepared to build the empire you have always deserved in your name."

"As are we," Egrette agreed, casting a quick, uneasy glance at Septimus. Perhaps she was calculating whether she would need to drive a stake into his heart to keep Nyaxia's favor.

He wasn't worried. Let her try.

Nyaxia barely seemed to notice they were before her. She whirled to the horizon, casting her hand across the sea—gesturing to the human nations beyond it.

"They know not what they do. But we do not give mercy to the ignorant."

"What are your orders?" Egrette asked.

Nyaxia did not hesitate.

"Conquer," she snarled. "Show my cousins our true might. Seize upon the gift of eternal night. Let no human kingdom be untouched. Let no village remain unburned. Let no throat remain unopened. Turn them. End them. Build me an empire. And then I shall use it to destroy all those who stand against us."

Septimus gave his goddess—the goddess who had cursed his kingdom, who had murdered his brother, who had been responsible for untold suffering of his people—a silken smile and pressed his forehead to the floor.

"It will be my greatest honor, Dark Mother," he said.

It felt good to be needed.

It was just a few steps away from being trusted, and being trusted was just a few steps away from one's throat.

Ten Years Later

Septimus exhaled a lungful of smoke and curled his lip in disgust.

His breath unfurled into the air, immediately lost in the thick haze. The air was sticky with soot and rot. Flies hummed around discarded carcasses. Somewhere in the distance, survivors wailed fruitless pleas.

Septimus felt like shit, and this wasn't exactly making things any better. He did not like coming to the human nations. Every visit, it just got more depressing.

Pain nagged at his chest, and he quickly covered it with another inhale, smothering it before it could set.

He strode through the streets, if they could be called that. It was something of a shame. Some human kingdoms had been quite lovely, in a quaint sort of way.

But now, it had been a decade of war beneath a sunless sky. Not many charming human idiosyncrasies had survived that.

Septimus's stomach twisted with hunger. The pain shot through his chest again. He drew in another desperate inhale, though the smoke didn't work the way it used to.

It had been a long, hard decade.

But he could feel that the end was coming. The slog was nearly over. A decade of carefully maneuvered problems. A decade of sweet, pathetic loyalty. A decade of making himself so very indispensable.

Somewhere here, in the shit pile that remained of the human nations, was an answer. A sword gifted by a goddess of justice, and a wielder who perhaps might be desperate enough to let him aim the strike.

Septimus very much liked to be the solution to a problem.

He flicked the cigarillo into a pile of burning corpses and slipped into the night.

END *of* BOOK IV

The Crowns of Nyaxia saga
will continue in book V.

AUTHOR'S NOTE

Thank you so much for reading *The Fallen & the Kiss of Dusk*. I hope that you loved reading it as much as I loved writing it!

I know that this book is a big, epic, wild ride. But I really fell in love with it because of Mische and Asar, and the emotional core of their story. I came to love them when writing *The Songbird & the Heart of Stone,* but *Fallen* made me understand them on a much deeper level. Their story was especially cathartic for me to write in ways even I don't totally understand. I think that perhaps there's just something especially beautiful in two people who always believed that they needed to be the sacrifice each learning how to actively *want* life, and learning how to fight for it—not just for each other, but also for themselves.

If you enjoyed the book, it would mean the world to me if you would consider leaving a review on your retailer of choice or on Goodreads.

If you'd like to be the first to know about new releases, new art, new swag, and all kinds of other fun stuff, consider signing up for my newsletter at carissabroadbentbooks.com, hanging out in my Facebook group (Carissa's Lost Hearts: A Carissa Broadbent Reader Group), or joining my Discord server.

Thank you for taking this journey with me! I hope you'll join me again for the next one—and I'm *really* excited for what's to come next.

GLOSSARY

Acaeja—The goddess of spellcasting, fate, and lost things. Member of the White Pantheon.

Alarus—The god of death and husband of Nyaxia. Exiled by the White Pantheon as punishment for his forbidden relationship with Nyaxia. Considered to be deceased.

Atroxus—The god of the sun and leader of the White Pantheon.

Bloodborn—Vampires of the House of Blood.

Born—A term used to describe vampires who are born via biological procreation. This is the most common way that vampires are created.

Dawndrinkers—A term used to describe certain worshippers of the sun god, Atroxus.

The Deadlands—The realm that sits between the mortal and divine planes. This is the territory where Alarus was betrayed and dismembered by the White Pantheon.

The Descent—The transitionary realm in between the mortal world and the underworld. It consists of five Sanctums that a soul must travel through to reach true death: Body, Breath, Psyche, Secrets, and Soul. The Descent was created by Alarus before his murder, and is now suffering the effects of many years of neglect.

Egrette—The current legitimate Heir of the House of Shadow. Daughter of King Raoul of the House of Shadow. Asar's half sister.

Heir Mark—A permanent mark that appears on the Heir of a vampire kingdom when the previous Heir dies, marking their position and power.

The House of Blood—One of the three vampire kingdoms of Obitraes. Two thousand years ago, when Nyaxia created vampires, the House of Blood was her favorite House. She thought long and hard about which gift to give them, while the Bloodborn watched their brothers to the west and north flaunt their powers. Eventually, the Bloodborn turned on Nyaxia, certain that she had abandoned them. In punishment, Nyaxia cursed them. The House of Blood is now looked down upon by the other two Houses. Vampires of the House of Blood are called Bloodborn.

The House of Death—Another term for Vathysia, the extinct kingdom that had been the capital of Alarus's territory, before Obitraes and vampires existed.

The House of Night—One of the three vampire kingdoms of Obitraes. Known for their skill in battle and for their vicious natures, and wielders of magic derived from the night sky. There are two clans of Nightborn vampires, Hiaj and Rishan, who have fought for thousands of years over rule. Those of the House of Night are called Nightborn.

The House of Shadow—One of the three vampire kingdoms of Obitraes. Known for their commitment to knowledge; wielders of mind magic, shadow magic, and necromancy. Those of the House of Shadow are called Shadowborn.

Ijakai—Goddess of animals, livestock, and the hunt. Member of the White Pantheon.

Ix—Goddess of sex, fertility, childbirth, and procreation. Member of the White Pantheon.

KAJMAR—God of art, seduction, beauty, and deceit. Member of the White Pantheon.

THE KEJARI—A legendary, once-per-century tournament to the death held in Nyaxia's honor. The winner receives a gift from Nyaxia herself. The Kejari is open to all in Obitraes, but is hosted by the House of Night, as the Nightborn hold the greatest mastery over the art of battle of the three vampire kingdoms.

MALACH—The firstborn son of King Raoul of the House of Shadow. Killed by Mische in the Nightborn palace. Asar's older half brother and the vampire who Turned Mische.

MASK OF VATHYSIA—Alarus's mask, which served as the crown for his kingdom. A symbol of it is depicted on the Shadowborn crest.

MELUME (NIGHT OF THE MELUME)—A rare natural phenomena taking place in the House of Shadow, in which the past is superimposed over the present. Melume festivals are often attended by all vampire houses.

MOON PALACE—A palace in Sivrinaj, the capital of the House of Night, specifically there to house contestants of the once-in-a-century Kejari tournament held in Nyaxia's honor. Said to be enchanted and to exert the will of Nyaxia herself.

NIGHTBORN—Vampires of the House of Night.

NIGHTFIRE—A form of star-derived magic wielded by the vampires of the House of Night. Nightfire is commonly used in the House of Night but very difficult to wield masterfully.

NYAXIA—Exiled goddess, mother of vampires, and widow of the god of death. Nyaxia lords over the domains of night, shadow, and blood, as well as the domain of death inherited from her deceased husband. Formerly a lesser goddess, she fell in love with Alarus and married him despite the forbidden nature of their relationship. When Alarus was murdered by the White Pantheon as punishment for his marriage to her, Nyaxia broke free from the White Pantheon in a fit of rage, and offered her supporters the gift of immortality in the form of vampirism—founding Obitraes and the vampire kingdoms. (Also referred to as: the Mother; the Goddess; Mother of the Ravenous Dark; Mother of Night, Shadow, and Blood)

OBITRAES—The land of Nyaxia, consisting of three kingdoms: the House of Night, the House of Shadow, and the House of Blood.

ORAYA—Queen of the House of Night.

THE ORDER OF THE DESTINED DAWN—A major sect of worshippers of the god of the sun, Atroxus. They are known for their skill in wielding fire, as well as their occasionally violent crusading.

RAIHN—King of the House of Night.

RAOUL—King of the Shadowborn, known for being a ruthless master of torture and spy craft. Deceased.

SANCTUM OF BODY—The first Sanctum in the Descent to the underworld, in which a soul loses their body.

SANCTUM OF BREATH—The second Sanctum in the Descent to the underworld, in which a soul abandons their life force.

SANCTUM OF PSYCHE—The third Sanctum in the Descent to the underworld, centering around a soul's memories.

SANCTUM OF SECRETS—The fourth Sanctum in the Descent to the underworld, in which souls must confront their hidden shames and desires.

SANCTUM OF SOUL—The fifth and final Sanctum in the Descent to the underworld, in which the dead undergo the transition of their soul from the mortal world to the underworld.

SEPTIMUS—Prince of the House of Blood. Youngest of seven sons, but the only one still alive.

SHADOWBORN—Vampires of the House of Shadow.

SHIKET—Goddess of war and justice. She bears six swords in her back, each representing a different divine gift.

SIMON—A prominent Nightborn noble, closely related to King Neculai, who attempted unsuccessfully to overthrow King Raihn and Queen Oraya for control of the House of Night.

SIVRINAJ—The capital of the House of Night. Home to the Nightborn castle and the Moon Palace, and host to the Kejari once every hundred years.

TURNING—A process to make a human into a vampire, requiring a vampire to drink from a human and offer their blood to the human in return. Vampires who underwent this process are referred to as Turned.

VATHYSIA—The capital kingdom of Alarus's territory, predating the creation of Obitraes and the existence of vampires. Also referred to as the House of Death.

THE VEIL—The boundary that separates the realm of the living from the realm of the dead.

VINCENT—The former king of the House of Night. Father to Oraya, queen of the Nightborn.

WHITE PANTHEON—The twelve gods of the core canon, including Alarus, who is presumed deceased. The White Pantheon is worshipped by all humans, with certain regions potentially having favor toward specific gods within the Pantheon. Nyaxia is not a member of the White Pantheon and is actively hostile to them. The White

Pantheon imprisoned and later executed Alarus, the god of death, as punishment for his unlawful marriage with Nyaxia, then a lesser goddess.

Zarux—The god of the sea, rain, weather, storms, and water. Member of the White Pantheon.

ACKNOWLEDGMENTS

Every time I write one of these, sleep-deprived and exhausted at the end of yet another book, I'm just dumbfounded by how many incredible people contribute to making these stories come to life.

I owe a huge debt of gratitude to so many people, including:

The wonderful team at Bramble for bringing this series and this book to so many people. Thank you to my editor, Monique Patterson, for believing in these stories and doing so much to bring them into being; to Mal Frazier, for being an incredible editorial voice, keeping so many plates spinning, and generally being so lovely to work with; to Caro Perny, Julia Bergen, Tyrinne Lewis, and the rest of the wonderful teams in publicity and marketing, for doing so much to bring these stories to as many eyes as possible; and to every one of the amazingly talented people who helped make this book a reality.

The team at Bramble UK, including my editor, Gillian Green, Grace Barber, Olivia-Savannah Roach, and so many more, for being incredible champions for these books in the UK and beyond.

My agent, Bibi Lewis, who—and I truly, from the bottom of my heart, mean this—I am grateful to be working with *every single day*. Thank you for all that you have done to make this book better, for helping this series find a perfect home, for supporting my entire career, and for generally being so awesome and supportive. Truly honored to witness you weave your mysterious fae bargains. I owe a thanks as well to Ethan Ellenberg, for being such a wonderful source of information and experience in this crazy industry, and to Lindsay Watson for doing so much to keep the wheels turning.

K. D. Ritchie at Story Wrappers, for yet another stunning banger of a book cover, and for always being so lovely to work with.

Noah Sky, for being a crucial editor and brainstorming buddy.

Naomi Lane, for being such an awesome assistant, cheerleader, content creator, and general all-around force of nature. So grateful to work with you!

Alyssa Braun, for being the most organized person I know and allowing me to leverage a little sliver of that to balance out my natural chaos.

Alex Ogle, for keeping my social groups running smoothly and being a generally lovely ray of sunshine.

Clare Sager, for being the most amazing writer wife and one of the best friends I've ever had.

Alicia MB, for being an amazing friend and also drawing lots of hot vampires for me.

My sister, Elizabeth, for being an incredible supporting, grounding force and a wonderful friend.

My parents, for being endlessly supportive of all my endeavors.

My cat, Calcifer, for keeping my feet warm.

And finally, Nate and Nico, for being the loves of my life and the only things that make any of this worth doing at all. I love you, I love you, I love you.

ABOUT THE AUTHOR

Victoria Costello

Carissa Broadbent has been concerning teachers and parents with mercilessly grim tales since she was roughly nine years old. Subsequently, her stories have gotten (slightly) less depressing and (hopefully a lot?) more readable. Today, she writes novels that blend epic fantasy plots with a heaping dose of romance. She lives with her husband, her son, and one perpetually skeptical cat in Rhode Island.

carissabroadbentbooks.com
Facebook: CarissaBroadbentBooks
X: @CarissaNasyra
Instagram: @carissabroadbentbooks
TikTok: @carissabroadbent